Ice in the Heart

Books by M. C. Topham

Shadows of Light series:

The Captor's Shadow

The Power of Silence *(Coming summer 2025)*

FBI suspense series:

Ice in the Heart

Ashes in the Soul *(Coming Fall-Winter of 2025)*

Ice in the Heart

M. C. Topham

To my husband,

who encouraged my dreams and goals from day one.

Acknowledgements

I'm grateful to everyone who has helped me in any form with getting this book out, which is probably more than I will put down here.

My editor Abby McLauglin did an amazing job with her edits and helping me with plot consistency and development. I appreciate her efficiency and dependability. I am also thankful for my brother's friend who helped me with some edits.

I'm thankful to Brinlee Mendenhall for her efforts in making my book cover. I know it was out of your usual style, but you did an amazing job!

Thanks to Megan Beckstrand who helped, through the company Books and Blades Publishing, with my formatting for this book.

Thanks to my writing group. It's been great to get together to write and chat and hold each other accountable on our projects.

And of course, I will be forever blessed to have such supportive family members and friends! My husband, who has encouraged me from day one and steps in to help with any tech or design help I need. My parents, who have always been huge fans of me and my work, and my siblings and best friend, some of whom have heard countless rants about my books and the woes of publishing.

Thanks to everyone else who has been a part of my project.

Part One

≈]≈

Maeve didn't feel all too confident as the taxi dropped her off and she was faced with the house in front of her. In fact, her hands were shaking, and she hesitated to take a step.

The house was seemingly unimposing, standing tall yet somehow welcoming and warm. The landscape was immaculate but not in the rich, standoffish way. It made her feel calm, yet the idea of such drastic change still sent a thrill of panic through her, paralyzing her feet.

Rip it off like a Band-Aid. Shaking her head, she finally forced her feet to move, and within a couple seconds, she was at the door. She had to keep her mind focused on what she was doing, not where she came from. It was hard, and where she was going wasn't all her favorite either. She had no idea where her future would lead, and it terrified her.

She knocked firmly before she could let herself think it through. After a few seconds, she heard movement from inside, and before she could flee, the door swung open and an exuberant, old—but lithe—lady stood in its place. She had a huge smile on her kind face. She was a skinny lady, and Maeve was confused as to what age she was. She looked to be in good health, but her hair was a light gray, and her skin had wrinkles.

"You must be Maeve." The lady took her hand and shook it enthusiastically. "I'm so glad to see you! I'm Elisa Conten. Did you make it okay? Come in, come in."

Before Maeve could decide to move, she was pulled inside—probably a good thing because otherwise, she may have run the other direction. Or passed out. Either option was possible.

Elisa pulled her to the living room and practically sat her down on the couch. "You stay right here! I'm going to get us some tea and a snack, and you can tell me about yourself." She left. Maeve swallowed heavily, dreading the questions Elisa may ask. She wanted to make a run for it, again, but she doubted her trembling legs would let her get very far. So, she folded her hands and continued to sit for a couple minutes while she waited for her host to make it back.

She studied the magnificent room around her. Maeve sat on the white couch. Colorful blue and red pillows sat on either side of her. Across from the couch sat two white chairs and an end table. A ceramic leaping dolphin sat on the table. In between the chairs and the couch sat a glass coffee table.

Behind her, sunlight filtered in from the window, and on either side of that window, she found beautiful, boxy mirrors. The room was just about spotless. Suddenly Maeve found herself frowning. It looked as though this house already got cleaned every second of the day; why would Elisa think about hiring Maeve?

Under Maeve's feet, she felt the soft strands of a rug. She pulled her right foot out of her sandal and let her toes gingerly rest on the carpet as she looked to the side of the rug to the dark wood flooring.

She felt out of place even though she wore better clothes than she had in a while. A red blouse with a little ruffling and some black pants. She didn't belong in this elegant house. She swallowed nervously again, then looked over to the door as Elisa came back in. She was carrying a tray.

Immediately Maeve jumped to her feet. "Let me help you with that." She grabbed the tray from the lady, who smiled at her.

"Thank you, dear," Elisa said as Maeve put the tray on the table between them. Elisa sat in the chair on Maeve's right with a sigh. "Dear me, I'm getting far too old."

Maeve let a reluctant smile slip on her face. "You don't seem it, Mrs. Conten."

Elisa laughed. "Oh, you're too sweet." She gave a dismissive wave. "And you can just call me Elisa, dear."

Maeve nodded, then Elisa continued. "Okay, Maeve. I know you're looking for a job. House cleaning, correct? That would be quite exquisite, as I am in need of help since I have this thing called 'getting old.' This is a big house to care for all on my own. Ever since my Edward died last year, and all my kids are now married or have their own life…" She looked sad, though proud, as she thought on it for a moment but pulled herself together and looked at Maeve with another smile. "Oh, but enough about that. You wanted to earn some room and board. Well, we can definitely do that. I would just love having another person around, a young lady at that."

Then she jerked, as if realizing something. "Oh, dear, I haven't even poured you any tea. Do you like peppermint? Take some food."

"Oh, um, sure." Maeve leaned forward, looking at the options. Little cucumber sandwiches and cookies. Maeve grabbed a small plate and gently placed two sandwiches and one cookie on it, then nodded when Elisa asked if she wanted some honey. Elisa poured herself some tea, then looked back up at Maeve.

"Kay, dear. I want to know about you. Tell me about yourself."

Maeve took a slow sip of tea to postpone the answer for a moment. "Well, I suppose there's not too much to know. I am just looking to turn my life around a bit. I've been having a hard time, and I really want to be able to get two feet underneath me and become something in the world."

Elisa gave her a worried look. "Of course, dear. And how is your commitment and dedication?"

Maeve hesitated, then decided on truthfulness. "Depends, I suppose. I'm working hard to keep it, but if I lose reason behind doing it, then I will stop easily."

"I think that's true for everyone dear," she said with a chuckle, then slowly nodded, her eyes narrowing as she took a sip. "Well, I'd love for you to stay with me. What do you think?"

Maeve looked around carefully. "I'd like to. I'm just…"

"Just what?"

"I've just noticed, your house is really clean. It doesn't look like you need me."

Elisa laughed. "Oh, you're sweet. No dear, I keep this room cleaner than the rest of my house. Also, it's not just cleaning that I would want. I really need company. I miss having someone living with me in this huge house." Elisa drank down some more of her tea, then looked imploringly at Maeve. "I know this is fast, and you don't have to decide yet, but the job is yours if you want it."

Maeve paused before answering, thinking about it. She did need a place, and she liked to earn her keep. This lady was sweet, and it was a relief not to have any men living in proximity.

Maeve decided to take the chance while it was open. "Yes, ma'am. I would really like to be here."

Elisa smiled happily and said, "I'm glad."

Maeve didn't know what to say, so she grabbed one of the sandwiches and started to eat it. She still couldn't believe that this was where life was taking her. As a young girl, she'd been so excited about life, she had made plans of how she wanted everything to go. Now all those plans and dreams have faded as the world taught her what kind of hardships life really brought. Who was she to become? And why should she really put her heart into anything new in life and trust that it would be something good? Where would she go now? Life had gone wrong for her for years, she couldn't believe that suddenly everything would change for better.

Well, first step…here, apparently. One day at a time.

¤ ¤ ¤

Ethan stepped into the restaurant with clenched fists. The eyes of the young woman haunted him even still, weeks later. He couldn't get her out of his mind. Even worse, he couldn't digress from the guilt that was eating a hole in his stomach. Seeing what happened and not doing a thing. Sure, he couldn't blow his cover when they were this close to a bust, but he also couldn't watch all those terrible crimes happen and not step in to stop it. He'd been able to help a lot of people while being undercover, but any failure or inability to save someone tore at him. He'd been able to call the police or FBI with tips, and he was glad for those times.

Ethan knew tomorrow there would be a bigger crime, but his only way to stop it from happening was to betray the men he'd been forced to befriend and risk his life. Strangely, the "risking his life" part didn't bother him much anymore. He just hoped he could save as many as possible if he was going down.

The goal had been to infiltrate and earn trust. But he'd gotten too close. Being with someone so often made it near impossible not to enjoy the companionship, even if he knew the dark side of the man as well.

He took a deep breath, knowing he needed to appear in control for this meeting. Slowly, he unclenched his fingers, straightened his tie, and moved to the hostess of the restaurant.

She smiled at him, her hair up in a bun, lips red with lipstick. Seemed perfect, but Ethan could still see the line where her foundation on her face mixed with her neck.

"Hello, sir. What's the name?"

"Derek," he lied, smiling to appear relaxed. His real name had not been uttered in months.

She consulted her board, then stepped out from behind the desk. "Excellent. This way." She led Ethan to one of several empty tables. Only one other was taken, in fact. Ethan eyed the couple but determined he didn't know them. It was always risky to meet with his handler; people could recognize him and blow his whole cover. But there was a lot of risk in this job.

He took the seat and muttered a thanks to the host, eyes already scanning the building before declaring himself safe.

He ordered himself water when Andrew the Waiter came, but when it took longer than necessary for his handler to get there, he decided to order wine. He wanted to drink it, just to take the edge off, but mostly he got it to keep up looks. Most people come to these restaurants and buy some fancy wine and dinner. He stared down at the dark color as he twirled the glass slowly.

"Hope you're not planning on drinking that," a voice said. Ethan looked up and noticed his handler taking the seat next to him. She wore a purple dress that came halfway down her thighs, which looked super uncomfortable and restrictive, but Ethan knew the dress had to be formidable if Patricia Welles would wear it.

Ethan looked up at her, then let go of the glass with a sigh. "I was thinking about it; it wasn't a part of any plan." He stood before Patricia could sit and went to pull out her chair for her, adding, "Nice to see you here, Welles."

"Nice to see you not dead," Patricia responded as he kissed her knuckles on her right hand. He then walked back around and took his own seat. Patricia was rather beautiful, so the fact that they could play this off as a date made his cover safer. Dangerous, still, but definitely more safe When Ethan betrayed them and something went wrong, Patty could easily become the next target if she was ever seen with him by someone he knew. That was hard to think about, but they both knew the risks.

This time, it wasn't likely they'd be seen. Ethan had been sent to Kansas to help prepare some details about an upcoming shipment, and he'd taken the chance to touch base with Patty in an easier way.

"Hmm…" Ethan looked at the wine in front of him, realizing he still hadn't responded to Patricia's statement about him being alive. She liked to joke, but currently he was in no joking mood. He was tired. "I suppose, for now."

"Something wrong?" She leaned toward him and grabbed the wine, moving it away from his immediate grasp. "You seem off, Derek."

Ethan shrugged. "Nah, fine."

"Yeah, that was entirely convincing." The sarcasm was strongly laced in her voice.

Ethan met her eyes, then forced his mind away from the torturous thoughts and gave a quick look around. "Santorini is planning something for tomorrow, Welles."

Patty perked. "What's that?"

Ethan had a hard time keeping her eyes. He knew that he was merely an undercover agent but being Santorini's—or as the mafia family knew him, Bullet Oscar's—practical right-hand-man for the last seven months, had Ethan feeling guilty for the betrayal. He hated betraying trust, even if it was fake. Feelings aside, this deal needed to be intercepted. This man needed to be stopped.

"Bullet Oscar is meeting with Nova tomorrow night—Nova smuggled in a group of Pakistanis." He spoke softly but quickly. "Apparently, Nova went to do business there, came across some wealthy landowners. Little gambling happened, that kind a thing.

Landowners lost the gamble, and to repay Nova, he sold some of his farmers."

Ethan knew the "farmers" were likely indentured servants who became such because they took out a loan they weren't able to repay other than by working on the landowner's farm. Being servants until a debt is paid off made sense in Ethan's mind, however selling those servants to human traffickers is against the law, because that is essentially making them slaves.

He never would agree to slavery, and definitely not human trafficking, even if he did agree that they should work their loan off. They should be home with their families, not on some foreign ground, trafficked into a worse system than they had already been in.

Patty looked sickened at the thought. Ethan hesitated a moment, then continued. "At seven, they flew into Killarney, Ontario, then took a boat. They're docking at Northshore, after closing times because of their connections. It'll be Bullet Oscar and Nova, then they'll drive to meet Rossi, the Street Boss in Angling. Not sure exactly where yet. That's where it would be best to set up a bust if you decide to do anything. You'd have to follow from Northshore, probably."

Ethan's hands shook. He eyed the wine, wishing she would give it back. She didn't seem to notice his gaze; if she did, she didn't care.

"I doubt I can get a better set-up than that. Santorini is starting to get suspicious that someone is talking with the cops, busting up his groove. Sooner or later, he'll look into it, and we may never get a chance."

Ethan shut up as the waiter approached again, this time with a pad of paper and pen.

"Do you two know what you'd like to eat, yet?"

Ethan hadn't even looked at the menu. Neither had Patricia. But that wasn't a problem. Ethan knew what he liked; he ate there all the time before he was "Derek," and it had been a meeting spot with Patty a few times when he'd had the chance to come during this assignment. Bullet Oscar had sent him a few times to Kansas to deal with the branch there. He'd actually sent him to quite a few places, which was beneficial to slowly unraveling his grip in the mafia as Ethan had been able to use quite a bit of the information to help put a stop to some of the illegal activities.

"I'd like to have the Chicken Iridescence." Ethan told him.

"Yes, sir. And you, miss?" Andrew the Waiter looked at Patty. Ethan didn't miss his appreciative gaze as he looked at her.

"Ora King Salmon, please." She focused on the man with a smile.

Andrew the Waiter beamed at her attention. "Yes, and any other wine?"

"No, thank you."

"Of course." The waiter took their order away, smiling.

Ethan waited several moments after he had left. Patty kept quiet, her eyes unfocused on the world. Probably imagining how they would bring down Bullet Oscar.

Finally, Patty came back to the world. Ethan still felt tempted to grab the wine, but he knew he needed a clear head. And one small part of him couldn't justify drinking. But that small part was alarmingly weak right now. He'd been raised not to fall into that addiction, and this would be the worst time to start.

"What's wrong with you, Derek?"

Ethan didn't even try to meet her gaze, just tapped on the table. He knew he shouldn't ask, but he had to.

"Do you know anything about the cops' actions in Chicago these last couple weeks, uh…month?"

Patricia's gaze closed off, which gave Ethan an answer. "What about them?"

"I wanted to know how the girl was doing, the one Santorini had—"

Patty shook her head. "No, Derek. No. You cannot distract yourself with that. I know you brought her out, but that was dangerous on its own. You could've blown your cover by bringing her out. We're so close to bringing these guys down."

Ethan narrowed his eyes at the words. *And what?* he asked himself. *She mattered more than the case. I had to get her out of there.*

"No, it wasn't too risky," he said. "You guys knew something was going on. The cops heard her scream once they arrived outside the alley—they would have found Bullet, would have seen…that. I offered Bullet a way to get out of trouble. He agreed because he knew he'd be otherwise trapped."

"Yes," Patricia agreed. "However, you got away so easily after we confirmed your authenticity. It could have brought suspicions."

"No, it just would have made them think that my lawyer, my story, or my prestige was legit. Besides cameras from the store across the street proved me getting to the alley after everyone else, helping aid my story that I just heard something down the alley and chased the men off." Ethan found his tone getting sharp. He just wanted to know what happened to the woman. If Ethan could, he'd help all the girls stuck with Bullet Oscar and his crew. He doubted he'd make that big of a difference on his own, but by passing along any information he could, he might be able to help the poor people coming tomorrow. And after they got Bullet Oscar, they would be able to get all the people stuck with him too. Depending on Patty, Mygyer, and the other federal agents above his role.

Patty frowned at him. Ethan took a deep breath and looked away, toward the door.

Patricia softened. "Derek…I know this is hard…to be among these people like this. They're not good, and you see a lot of terrible things that happen to others—"

Ethan snorted. "Yeah, terrible things I have to see. I can't help any of the people in trouble as much as I would like, merely allowed to pass the information to you guys so that you can help them instead. But even worse, I…" He cut himself off, afraid to say it.

"What?" Patty leaned forward, inviting him to speak. Ethan swallowed heavily, shaking slightly now.

"I am starting to care about the prick," he admitted, not looking. It took a lot of effort to keep his voice steady. He couldn't believe he was telling Patty, and he rushed to continue when he saw her confusion and start of concern. "Not necessarily of their welfare. I want them all to get what they deserve. They need to be in jail, I know it. I just…I see some little moments of good, of humor, and of connection. It's easy to talk to Bullet. We've gotten close, which was the point. I need him to trust me, but I hate that I must betray that trust in the end. I hate what he's doing, but I care about him like an idiot brother who keeps choosing to do the wrong stupid things. And I know the consequences will catch up to him, and I know that it will be me to do it. There is a lot of bad in him, yes, but there is still *some* good too. At least a little."

Patricia was silent. Ethan couldn't look at her. He wanted to be finished with the meeting, but their appetizers hadn't even arrived yet, so there was no way he could get out of there. Why did he ever think he could do this undercover role?

You wanted to make a difference; this is how you can. You can do it.

However, those small encouragements have had to come nearly nonstop lately, forcefully inserted between his belittlements and negative thoughts. What he was doing was *good*. It was just *hard* as well.

They stayed silent so long, the bread appetizer got there before Patricia finally spoke. But it wasn't on what Ethan had just said.

"You going to have some?" she asked as she grabbed some bread. Ethan looked at the food, nauseous with the idea, but took one and put it on his plate anyway. He picked at it a moment, then ate about half. He looked down at his watch, wishing the time would tick faster. He had a flight at eight; it was five-thirty. He had to be at the airport by six-thirty. This restaurant was right next door.

Felt like forever.

Neither one of them seemed to know what to say anymore. They both kept mostly quiet as they finished the bread. Ethan tried hard to meet Patty's gaze but couldn't quite bring himself to. That was definitely unlike him. He was an outgoing, confident type of man. He usually flirted with Patty. Now he could barely rise to his feet when she left to go to the bathroom right before the food came out. He'd been taught to be a gentleman by his mother and father—no need to disappoint them even though they weren't there.

Father always treated Mom kind; rose when she left the table, treated her like an equal, but worthy of being a princess. Ethan tried to follow in his footsteps.

That made Ethan wonder what his dad would say about this undercover work. Would he be angry that Ethan made a living of lies and surrounded himself with crime? Probably not. His father never seemed to be angry about anything like that. He knew the world needed people in law enforcement and that they should always respect those willing to step up and take the role despite the threat.

Ethan suddenly felt vulnerable. He missed his parents. He wanted to get *home*, away from this treachery, doubt, and tension.

He clenched his hands and took a deep breath, then heard Patty approach the table again. He relaxed his grip and stood as he sought control over himself again. Slowly he regained his hold. He looked up and met her gaze at last. Before either could speak, Andrew the Waiter came to set the meal out.

"How's it going with your work?" Ethan asked when he left again.

Patty shrugged. "Oh, it's going alright. You're the highlight of most of my work lately. A lot of paperwork."

"I see. Keeping you busy though?"

"Yes. There's been a lot of new tension in Kansas. We think a new crime boss is trying to gain land and people. No deaths or huge things yet, but…" Patty shrugged. "Not anything we can't take care of."

Ethan nodded, then made small talk as they finished up the dinner. He was interested to know more, since Kansas was his home, but Patty didn't know that. By the time dinner ended, he was feeling better…mostly. Nervousness rose back in him when he realized he had to get back to the action, constantly watching for a threat. He forced himself not to focus on anything upcoming. He was going to have a good flight back to Illinois and get a good night's sleep. Tomorrow, he would be back to the task, and hopefully Ethan didn't find himself exposed again by the time the deal was over.

Patty called Ethan back as he turned to leave. "Hey, uh…Derek?"

He turned back. "Yes?"

"That woman you saved…She is alive. She's getting her life back together. And I'm glad you saved her. You did the right thing. You did good."

Ethan's heart calmed suddenly, the ache dissipating, mostly. He remembered the feel of the woman in his arms, looking into her eyes the moment before they closed, body shutting down due to shock and fear and pain as he carried her to the police and ambulance. His whole body reacted to the news as his hands unclenched and shoulders relaxed. He sighed. *Thank God.*

¤ ¤ ¤

Patricia made sure the door was shut behind her. The room was empty, which relieved her. She wanted a couple minutes to compose herself before the meeting. To think through the news.

What Derek said troubled her—about the smuggling, yes, but even more so the way he acted. Sure, she'd noticed a change in him as the time went on and he stayed undercover, but this was something else entirely. He hadn't stopped shaking the entire time she'd sat with him. He seemed unsure of himself. And he had hated betraying this capo, even though the crime boss had done so much through illegal and unethical means. She knew his position was getting shaky and he would end up with his cover blown one way or another since he couldn't seem to pull himself together. They needed to pull him out.

Patricia couldn't fight down the feeling of dread. She felt Derek was right; this would be the best chance they had, especially because she firmly believed that if they didn't take this chance, Derek might not make it to the next opportunity alive.

One day was such a small amount of time for preparation. If they decided to act, they would have to alert the local police. Then Patricia knew her director would want her and a couple of others to fly out to help. At most, they would only have a few hours to set up the dock.

She slipped out her phone, looking up the hours for the dock Ethan said they'd be landing on. They closed early, at five, because it was Independence Day the next day.

So, yeah, that would only give them two hours after the dock closed to get situated. It didn't give them a lot of time, but it would have to be enough.

She thought back to Derek again. He was a handsome fellow, but he had changed almost completely since she first saw him. He'd picked up the accent that the mob in Chicago used—made it seem like half the words weren't being pronounced all the way, more of a mumble. She didn't know how to explain it exactly, but she noticed it.

Patricia sighed and tilted her head on the back of the chair as she closed her eyes. It'd been a long day, but she knew she had it easy. At least she didn't have to be constantly on guard like Derek did.

The door opened behind her. She opened her eyes and looked over.

"Patricia." Patricia saw the FBI Director, Adam Mygyer, behind her. She straightened her back under his intense gaze. "How's our boy doing? Any news?"

Patricia sighed, wondering how to respond first.

Mygyer sat in a seat, eyes turning immediately concerned. "That sounds bad."

Patricia hesitantly nodded. "Well, he's got news, for sure." She relayed all the information to him. Mygyer ran his hand along his chin, his eyes concerned but thoughtful.

"He doesn't believe he'll get a better chance than this," Patricia told him. "I happen to believe him; he was shaken when I saw him. I doubt he could keep the façade up much longer. Seeing that woman raped really rattled him. Which, I mean…" She gestured as if to say *"yeah, who wouldn't be rattled by that?"*

"And he's starting to get *too* close to Santorini," she continued. "He hates betraying the man." Patty didn't understand that. The man was evil. She knew it, and Derek knew it.

Mygyer sighed and pulled his hand away from his face. "That's fairly typical. It happens a lot more than you'd think. We'll have to get him out of there at this bust then, for sure. Probably have to keep him out of field work for a couple months so he can recuperate…get his mind back on track."

Patricia nodded, then Mygyer continued. "Alright then, Patricia. We need to set up surveillance at the dock as soon as possible. Shall we call intelligence and the Chicago branch in? See if we can agree on a plan before our boy gets himself killed?"

≈2≈

Ethan kept his pace fast as he moved along with Bullet Oscar down the hall. "We contacted all the people. The line is set up for today. Last minute, I know," Bullet told him.

Ethan nodded, then paused in confusion. "You mean for meeting Nova?" They had already got that all set up days ago. It wasn't that last minute, not for how Bullet typically worked. Was there some new guy added to their mix that could potentially throw the possible bust?

"Yeah."

"Is there someone new?"

"Nah, Ice." Bullet looked at him weird. He also used only a part of Ethan's street name, the full name being Alley Ice. "Did you not hear? Last night? Change of plans."

Ethan swallowed nervously. "Um…No, I had go in late from Kansas last night remember? had a possible client while I was there. Missed out."

"I dig, Ice. How'd the meetin' go?"

Ethan shrugged, uncomfortable. "She didn't want a thing past dinner, couldn't bring her in."

Bullet laughed. "Still got that small bone we gotta break with ya, eh, Ice? You always been bad at bringing in the girls. One day, I'll have to teach you that you don't ask *nicely*. You tell 'em you'll walk them home, then bring them in. You didn't pick up on that the other night?"

Oh yeah, Bullet taught him something that night. Ethan felt disgust rise in his gut. May have been the worst night of his life. He just felt glad he'd gotten there, even if he had walked in late, so he could get her to the police after he called them to cut it short.

"About the meeting today, Bullet?" Ethan steered the conversation back on point, carefully not reacting to the statement outwardly.

"We're meeting our client early. He got an earlier boat and will be there at four instead." Bullet went right on walking as he ambled down and got to the cubicles. No one spoke to them as they passed, most completely averted their eyes. Santorini, aka, Bullet Oscar, was a deadly, vicious man if pushed, so no one dared get on his bad side. Alley Ice, Ethan's own mob nickname, was rumored to be precise and ruthless if things don't go as planned.

Hard to portray such a ruthless man when, in reality, Ethan couldn't break any major laws.

At this moment, Ethan felt his gut sink with dread. The bust would happen three hours earlier than what Ethan had told Patty. Ethan knew that the FBI would likely be set up as early as they possibly could, but with so little notice, he wondered if they'd be able to get things set up in time. What if they completely finish up before any agents even got in place?

"I thought the place didn't even close until five?"

"Technically not, but I pulled some strings. I convinced our guy to close it for safety reasons tonight." Bullet adjusted his suit. "You'll be ready by then, Ice?"

Ethan nodded, outwardly cool, inwardly cursing

"Oh yeah, I'll be ready."

"Good deal." Bullet ambled away from Ethan into his office. Ethan stared after him, wondering if he should risk calling Patty to tell her the new situation.

"Derek, come on!" Someone yelled behind him. Ethan jerked and turned to the voice to find Thomas. "Gotta get to work."

Well, Ethan wouldn't be able to yet. He'd have to find a time to sneak away.

¤ ¤ ¤

Maeve had spent the week learning the ropes to Elisa's beautiful home, where everything was, and how Elisa liked everything done. She felt so inadequate staying in this grand home that Elisa had clearly put a lot of love and thought into; she wondered if she looked as awkward as she felt. She felt like God had plopped her from a Mary Higgins Clark book right into a dull—but luckily safe—Jane Austen novel. Her life before felt so surreal, looking back now, she could scarcely believe anything bad had happened because of how drastically things have changed for the better now. And it'd only been a little over a week! That's how wonderful a home and how gracious a host she had in Elisa. The only thing that made her realize it was true was her nightmares and memories. Her memories were hard, but at least during the day she could distract herself so they didn't keep her trapped too long.

Maeve just wanted those terrible images to leave her. She refused to let herself dwell on them, even if it was hard.

Yesterday, Elisa had taken her to church. Maeve had always believed in God, mostly in the back corner of her mind because she was too scared to ask Him anything and didn't know His will for her. She never prayed to Him, but somehow, He had answered her unspoken prayer anyway—to save her.

The church Elisa had taken her to wasn't any like Maeve had been to before, but it was still a beautiful service. And now that Maeve was trying to get her life back on track, she felt she could actually approach God with questions.

"Maeve?" Elisa's gentle voice cut into her thoughts, and she looked over to the vibrant lady. "Dear, I'm about to go shopping. I'd love it if you came with me." Elisa was wearing a beautiful sheen green dress and some dangle bracelets. She always looked so put together.

Maeve hesitated, holding the broom she was using to sweep the kitchen. The kitchen was stunning. All the appliances were stainless steel, but always clean, and a lot of the detail work was made out of granite and a dark wood.

In the end, Maeve nodded. "Alright, let me just finish up in here, Elisa, and then I'll be ready."

"Perfect." Elisa smiled warmly at her, then fled the room as she started to hum.

Part of Maeve thought she should try harder with her wardrobe and figure, especially when she was going out with Elisa, but she didn't have that many—or rather, *any*—nice clothes; Elisa never seemed to mind how she looked though.

Maeve swept the small pile into the larger one on the floor. Now that she'd been here for a week, she was starting to notice other little things that were messy, things she hadn't noticed before.

She finished sweeping the ground, focusing intently on every pile she brought over to make sure she got everything she could see. She wanted to do good, but more than that, focusing like that helped her thoughts stay in line with present and not past.

Maeve finished up the floor and dumped it into the trash that slid out from the cabinets. She thought that was cool but confusing for the first couple of days since she had tried to pull the wrong handle and found herself staring into some utensils instead.

She put the broom into the utility closet, then went into her room to scout for her shoes.

After slipping them on, Maeve found her host reading in the sitting room, but as soon as Maeve entered, she put the book down and beamed at her. "You ready?"

"Uh, yeah." Maeve brushed her hands on her pants and looked down at her blouse. It was a light turquoise color. "Is this okay?"

"Of course, dear!" Elisa looped her arm through Maeve's. "Actually, I was thinking it would be nice to go shopping for *you* this time. You know what I like, but last time you didn't pick out a single thing you were interested in. I want to get you something you'd like."

She started pulling Maeve as she found words to protest. "Oh, no, Elisa. I don't want to…"

"Yes, Maeve! It's one of the ways I get to know people. See what outfits they pick out. Let me do this for you." They entered the garage and Elisa patted her arm in a motherly way but didn't wait for a response before letting Maeve go and moving to the driver's seat of the car.

Maeve hesitated but didn't know how she could possibly say no to Elisa, so she got in and decided against saying anything.

Elisa chatted as they drove together, mostly about her family. Her husband—"bless him"—had been an amazing support all her days. Elisa had been left with a good inheritance when she was about seventeen. Her parents had been in a terrible accident, and they left her with pretty much all their money and house and all. Elisa couldn't stand being alone in the huge house, and during that time, she had been dating Edward. Granted, she hadn't been dating him seriously at the time, but after the funeral, Edward was a great comfort to her. He had never asked about money; in fact, he never cared about it at all.

Elisa fell hard for her husband during that time. She believed that Edward loved her as well, yet she had been worried because he had been careful to take it slow with her. She had been warned by her parents that there were a lot of leeches out there, people who hung onto others only for the money. She didn't want to get involved with someone who just wanted the money, so she decided to test him in a way.

After they had been dating for nearly six months, Elisa finally told Edward that she couldn't stand being in this house anymore, among all the people and things that had been there when her parents had still been alive. She was leaving.

That was the first time Edward mentioned anything about her inheritance. "Elisa, you know that you have enough money to buy a mansion in Hawaii if you wanted. What do you want to do?"

Elisa had decided she wanted to sell the house and donate most of the money, only keeping enough to buy a small place for her to live in far away from here.

"Edward had smiled at that," Elisa told her. "He said that sounded like a beautiful thing to spend the money on." She had a dreamy look in her eyes. "He told me that he would help in whatever way I needed. So, I had him help me sell my house. We sold it for a fortune, I swear."

Then it came time for Elisa to leave. "I really hadn't wanted to go alone," Elisa told her. "But I couldn't coerce Edward into leaving with me." Elisa had been prepared to break off the relationship when he came over, but before she could, he had proposed. "I opened the door and he immediately fell to his knee, begging me to marry him. That he would go with me to wherever I decided I wanted to go."

She sighed at this point, her dreamy look more pronounced. "I asked him question after question, to make sure that's what he really wanted; warning him that I didn't have much money anymore, after donating it. He told me he didn't care about money, that he would take care of me. We could start from scratch. We started some small businesses, and they grew substantially—if you couldn't tell."

Then Elisa started talking about her kids. "We had five kids. It was nice to have this big house by the time we had all of them, even though sometimes it felt a little too large. Most of the time, it was enough to satisfy the kids at least when they were younger. Now, the house seems empty with just me. But sometimes my youngest comes home, in between jobs. And the others visit with their children. It's nice then, and now that you are here, it's bearable."

Then she talked about some of the challenges of raising her kids. "We had five kids within eight years. It was a handful to have that many so close! It was really nice to have had money for nannies and such for occasions."

Two of her boys were big troublemakers, along with their younger sister. The youngest boy stayed sick a lot when he was young, so he got into less trouble and received a lot more attention. The older sister—second oldest in the family—had taken on the responsibility she felt she owed, taking care of the family whenever she could. "Oh, I adore all my babies, but they're not so much babies anymore. They all have their own kids now, except my youngest. And Riley, my youngest daughter. She recently got married, and they're trying for kids too."

By that time, they had made it to the mall, which Maeve felt sure was the only reason Elisa stopped talking. Maeve didn't mind at all; she liked the stories Elisa told. They distracted her well.

When they got in, Elisa continued her chatter, except for exclamations of adorations and criticism as they passed many windows, went into other stores, and when Maeve tried on clothes that Elisa tossed her way. All in all, it was a very fun day; her mind stayed away from any unwanted thoughts, and Elisa's attention made Maeve feel very loved and special. She went home with two separate bags of clothes, happiness wanting to burst like a bubble, and feet dead-tired from walking.

But the day wasn't over yet. Elisa came in just minutes after Maeve collapsed. "Oh, dear Maeve, please tell me—a dear friend of mine invited me to dinner, and I'd love for you to come!"

"Oh, Elisa, I couldn't impose—"

"Nonsense! It's no problem. My friend has a daughter in town. Her name is Kelly. Oh, she's a dear—she's coming with her mom as well. It will be fun! Please say you'll come?"

Maeve took a deep breath and looked at the bags next to her. "Alright, Elisa, I'll come. Can I get more put-together first?"

"Of course, dear. Come find me if you need help—I can get your hair and makeup done if you need it." She fluttered out of the room with a wave and a little laugh. Maeve couldn't help but smile. That lady cracked her up. She was so darling!

What did Maeve do to deserve such a friendly host?

Maybe it was her reward for getting through such a terrible past.

She stood up sharply and started pulling clothes out of her bag, suddenly frustrated with herself. She'd been doing so well.

She pulled out the dress she had bought. Mostly white fabric with patterns of red roses on the bottom foot or so. It had a lot of movement when she swayed and walked, and the fabric looked thick. It fit great, and she felt amazing in it.

Maeve did a little twirl as she got it all on, then moved back to the bag to pull out the white lace heels she got with the dress. She put them on quickly but moved carefully after. She hadn't had much practice in heels yet, and she didn't want to make a fool of herself.

She brushed her hair, then left the room. She didn't know how to do her hair or makeup well at all. She wondered if Elisa's friend would care that much.

But again, Maeve didn't have to worry about it. Elisa pulled her into the bathroom the moment she got down the stairs. "You already look so beautiful, Maeve, so I'll just help you highlight the beauty you already have."

Maeve blushed. She didn't feel that beautiful most of the time, but today, she felt more so than ever. "You're sweet, Elisa," Maeve murmured, looking down.

Elisa pulled her face up. "I'm serious, dear. You are stunning." Then she went about adding some curl to Maeve's hair, and a little mascara and blush before declaring Maeve done and beautiful. "The boys won't be able to stop staring."

Maeve didn't respond. That made her uncomfortable and nervous, but she didn't want to give Elisa any clues as to what happened to her in the past.

Elisa smiled at her in the mirror, then pulled Maeve. "I think you'll like Kelly. She really is a sweet girl—much like you, but a bit more talkative."

Maeve followed her host into the car again, and this time she found herself parked outside a restaurant within minutes as Elisa chatted on, this time about how her house was built.

They entered the restaurant, which was a crazy fancy restaurant. Stunning and grand, of course. They were met nearly immediately by this beautiful lady about the same age as Elisa, but slightly less lean than Maeve's new host. Behind her followed a gorgeous young woman.

Elisa greeted her friend, then introduced the two ladies. "Maeve, this is Janice and her daughter, Kelly."

Janice shook her hand, smiling kindly, but didn't say much before she turned back to Elisa.

Kelly held out a hand. "Nice to meet you, Maeve."

"You as well." Maeve took it, smiling politely.

Despite Kelly's beauty, Maeve somehow didn't feel inadequate. Kelly's gaze was completely kind and almost approving.

"You look beautiful," Kelly told her.

"Oh, thank you," Maeve said. "You as well."

"Thank you," Kelly said sincerely. They both fell silent a moment, and Maeve heard Elisa and Janice talking rapidly to each other.

Maeve shared a smile of amusement with Kelly, and suddenly felt as though Elisa was right. Kelly may indeed grow on Maeve.

Ethan frowned at the car windshield, frustrated. He had tried Patty's cell, but she hadn't answered. She was probably on a flight to get here, or just busy or something, but Ethan felt terrified. This whole situation was nerve-racking anyway, but what if something had happened to Patricia? What if they couldn't do the bust tonight?

Not that it matters, Ethan thought sourly. *They have the wrong time anyhow.*

He had thought about calling the cops, but didn't know if he could trust everyone there, and he hadn't had the time to do so, having barely managed to squeeze in a call to his handler that wasn't even answered.

"Ice, what's up?"

Ethan tried not to show his apprehension as he looked over where Bullet sat driving. "Nothin' man. Just this deal. I haven't worked with the guy yet; I hate working with people I don't know."

Bullet laughed. "Yeah, you're on the other end this time. Usually you hook me up with people and run these deals. This time, I get to lead, and you get to be in the dark with whether you can trust the dude."

Ethan smiled. "That's true. I suppose I can sit back and let you take the reins this time."

"Ha! No. You'll have to help me transport the new merch. I'm sure they won't like this."

Ethan knew Bullet was right about that at least. Who *would* like something like this happening?

Noticing his foot was tapping, Ethan forced it to stop. His gut was telling him that something tonight was going to go completely wrong. Well, technically it already did go wrong; the FBI wouldn't get to the meeting at the right time. Ethan just had to hope that the police would be able to get there early…and not be stupid when they got there.

After a couple minutes of silent driving, they finally pulled into the dock. It was quiet, which was expected.

It was also darker than Ethan had been expecting; it wasn't late enough for the sun to have disappeared, but it looked like it was going to rain in mere moments. That would make it easier to load the new people up without anyone noticing, so they would likely be done way faster.

Ethan stepped out of the car and immediately felt a raindrop hit his arm. He grimaced and wiped the rain from his arm, hating that he had to be right.

"Should be fast." Bullet seemed to have the same thought. Ethan didn't bother to reply but did look over at Bullet. The man moved toward the end of the dock, eyes set toward the sea. Ethan followed his gaze and saw a boat. Nova was right on time.

Ethan sighed softly, resigning himself to the fact that this night, one way or another, was not going to go as planned—or hoped.

Ethan stared at Bullet's back, wondering why a part of him was glad that the man he was meant to befriend then betray wasn't going to know Ethan had deceived him. This was what he trained to do, and yes, he would go through with the plan, but he couldn't help but wonder if he should have stayed away from this assignment.

Then he wondered if he would have been allowed to say no to this assignment and still stay in the agency. Maybe not.

And Ethan knew he couldn't have resisted—he had wanted to do something worthwhile to help.

By the time they got to the end of the dock, the boat had pulled up. It was small since it had to sneak in easily, but big enough to hold the ten "farmers." Ethan's family had a boat, but it was smaller than this one here, just meant for a themselves. Or one person, as it usually held when Ethan used the boat. He usually liked to go out alone. Sometimes his family would go, especially his oldest brother. The two of them were insanely close, even though Mason was married with a couple kids by now. Mason always knew exactly where Ethan would be and how to find him. Even with Ethan's job, Mason knew most everything. With this mission, since it was more dangerous, Ethan decided against telling Mason exactly where he'd be. Just told him that he'd be out of town and that he'd try to call about once a week.

Ethan had told his mother and other siblings far less. He didn't want them to worry. Mason could handle knowing a little, but his mother would stress out and get no sleep, so Ethan only told her that he was going on a mission and not to panic if he didn't call her much. And yes, of course he'd be safe.

Ethan shook away his thoughts, focusing on the deal in front of him. It was funny to Ethan; Bullet and his crew had a surprising streak of love for their family. They understood family issues and such. Oddly, Ethan never thought that they would care about family; he thought that they were just monsters to be able to do so many terrible crimes, but they had family that they cared about and who cared about them. Family was one thing nobody in the crew could even make jokes about—and if the family got a threat, you know you messed up bad.

"Bullet Oscar!" A voice interrupted Ethan, and he realized that even though he had tried to stay on task, his mind had drifted. What was wrong with him?

He straightened his shoulders, forcing himself to stay on task. Looking past the darkness, Ethan squinted to see the face of the new man. He sounded slightly familiar.

"Hello, Nova. You have them all?"

"Yes indeed." Nova did a casual tie with the ropes that told Ethan he wouldn't be staying for long.

That voice…

Too late. Nova noticed Ethan right as Ethan realized that he did in fact know this man.

"Ethan?" Nova asked, aghast. "Man, what a surprise seeing you here! I swear it's been forever! What are you doing in Illinois? Last I heard you had started out training to become a cop in Kansas—" Nova cut off immediately, realizing his mistake. Ethan felt a tremor in the air as Nova swore. Bullet went tense beside Ethan.

"*Ethan*?" Bullet said, voice hard. The chipper mood Nova had five seconds ago vanished. Ethan scrambled for something, anything.

"I think you've confused me with someone else," Ethan forced himself to say, noticing Nova's panic. Nova was really named Lance, and he was in the same high school graduating class, as well as an old sort-of friend. Ethan doubted Lance wanted trouble for Ethan, nor would he have wanted to get caught red-handed. "You can call me Alley Ice."

Bullet threw a punch at Ethan. Ethan saw the movement out the corner of his eye and reacted instantly. He blocked the punch, and twisted around Bullet, pulling his arm up behind him. That usually would have worked well, but not with Bullet; he knew the move and knew how to get out of it.

"You're the mole, Ice?" Bullet hissed.

Ethan didn't dare respond. He didn't want to say yes, but the answer was obvious. Besides, Ethan was just trying frantically to think of some sort of plan. If he could take Bullet down, or even make a run for it—

But he hadn't been planning on how Lance—his old peer—may have acted.

Lightning pain flashed through his skull, and Ethan fell to his hands and knees. He wondered if this feeling of deception was what Bullet felt as well. How could Lance turn on him like this?

But Ethan couldn't let that blow keep him down, not if he was to live. He started to stand despite pain and darkness in his eyes, turning as he did so to attack or defend again, but he heard the sound of a gun go off.

Ethan saw the gun Bullet aimed at him before he felt the pain, and he fell before the pain fully registered. A shot to the thigh. Not deadly, luckily. But man…the pain.

Bullet Oscar stepped closer to Ethan. "What do the police know? Do they know about this deal today?"

Ethan put his hands on his leg, keeping his hands as steady as possible, and stared evenly at Bullet. He ordered his brain to put the pain into a separate box in his mind so that it didn't distract his other thoughts. *Oh, God. Help me.*

"Maybe we should go," Nova's voice said. He was still behind Ethan.

"We need to know what he's told the police. And we need to finish this deal." Bullet Oscar lowered the gun and stepped closer. "Have you told anyone else?"

Ethan didn't answer right away. He could see the anger and hurt from the treachery in Bullet's eyes. He wondered briefly if he could use it.

Bullet Oscar glared over Ethan, then at Nova, and Nova sighed as he stepped closer, the boards creaking and shifting. "Sorry Ethan, man. Shouldn't have got mixed up in this."

¤ ¤ ¤

Liz stepped into the surveillance room, ready to take her shift, then frowned when she saw Cameron. The other man had his head on the desk in front of him, clearly sleeping. Liz scanned the screens quickly as she sighed and moved to Cameron. She poked him.

"Cameron?"

Cameron jerked upright, rubbing his face. "Liz…" He swore. "I didn't mean to fall asleep. I'm so sorry."

Liz gave a little smile. She knew that Cameron took his job seriously and would never allow himself to fall asleep if he could help it.

"How's Kammy doing?" Liz asked, knowing that would be the only reason he'd be exhausted to work properly.

Cameron sighed and rubbed his face. "She's adorable, but she has an ear infection and cried all night. I stayed up with her so Missy could get some sleep for once."

"Well, it's okay. We aren't expecting anything to happen for another couple hours, anyway." Liz scanned the screens again. It was raining in Chicago, the screen that they needed to keep watch on in a couple hours. A couple of other screens showed other threats, but they didn't expect anything with them either.

The rain fell hard, nearly blocking all the view. Hopefully it cleared up by the time the deal would go down.

"Did you get the ear infection checked out?" Liz asked him, turning her attention to him.

Cameron shrugged. "Yeah, that's how I know what it is. She had been crying and running a fever the last couple of days, so we took her in. Nothing has helped her yet."

"Dang, I'm sorry, man."

Cameron smiled toward her, but turned his view back to the computers, studying them. He was still on duty for another half an hour, but he looked so tired that Liz put a hand on his shoulder. "Cameron, you head home. Go get some sleep. I'm here now; you can leave."

Cameron put a hand up to shush her, then leaned closer to the screen for the Illinois dock. They had local trusted FBI agents to install the cameras early this morning so that they could get any proceedings on tape. They had warned the owner of the dock of doing so and warned him not to say anything to anyone, and since he was alarmed that one of his employees had obviously been using his dock for his own nefarious purposes after hours, he had immediately agreed.

Liz leaned closer as well, wondering what had caught Cameron's attention. She couldn't see anything but rain and darkness, but then she saw a glimpse of movement, like a mere shadow. She put a hand on the back of Cameron's seat as he started to zoom in frantically to the shadows. She saw a light briefly flash, then it was dark. But Liz knew what she was seeing.

Cameron swore in front of her as Liz pulled out a phone, calling Mygyer.

¤ ¤ ¤

Patricia watched Mygyer, wondering what he was thinking. His eyebrows were furrowed as he drove. Patricia was exhausted—she hadn't slept the night before. She got a little rest on the flight over, but she had a hard time settling when in the air.

Then, as if she wasn't stressed out enough, she realized she had missed a call from Derek. He knew not to call her except in case of emergency, and he hadn't left a voicemail. Something had to be wrong.

What if something changed? or his cover had been blown, and he was now lying in a ditch somewhere?

Mygyer drove into a gas station and pulled up to the first pump. It was raining hard outside, and it made it a challenge to see much.

Mygyer looked outside skeptically. "Hope it clears up."

"Yeah, me too," Patricia said, looking at the gas station store. "I think I'm going to run in and get something to eat."

"If you want to wait while I get gas pumping, I'll come in with you." Mygyer told her. "I'm looking forward to some coffee or something."

"Good deal." Patricia nodded, then grabbed the umbrella from the back and stepped out of the car with Mygyer. He went to pay and start filling up, then came over to Patricia and grabbed the umbrella. He held it over them both, and they walked in.

The rain pounded on the top of the umbrella in no steady rhythm. Patricia loved the rain, especially summer rain like this, but she didn't like it when she had a mission to complete; it made it way harder to get the job done.

Mygyer held the door open for her, and they entered the store. Patricia felt her nose scrunch up—it smelled like cigarette smoke in there. She knew Mygyer smoked, but he always stayed away from it when he was working, so he didn't smell too strongly. This felt like she walked right into a cloud of the smoke. The idiot worker was the culprit.

She coughed lightly, then continued to breathe carefully through her mouth, trying not to smell and wishing at that moment she didn't have to breathe. Mygyer smiled sympathetically at her and went over to the drinks. Patricia followed him part of the way, then stopped to check out what chips they had.

She pulled out a bag of chips then walked quickly back to Mygyer, wishing to hurry out of this store. Mygyer saw her look, smiled, and grabbed a cup for coffee. "How's life at home going?" he asked her.

Patricia groaned a little, knowing where Mygyer was going with this. Patricia had broken up with her last boyfriend a month ago after going out for a couple weeks. Patricia just sucked at keeping a guy. She also knew it was her fault; she kept finding faults in all the people she dated, and those faults weren't outweighed by any love she may have had with the guys. So, she broke up with them.

The last man had taken it worse than most of the others. He had continued to try and contact her, so she blocked his caller ID. Then he started coming to her house uninvited, so she threatened to arrest him if she saw him anywhere near her place again. He'd tried to guilt trip her before, but now, finally, he'd left her alone.

Mygyer laughed. "Sounds interesting. Let's hear it."

"Just this idiot I dated wouldn't leave me alone after I broke up with him. That was about a month ago, and I haven't dated anyone since. And no, I don't need your matchmaker games right now. I'm far too worried about Derek."

Mygyer went silent a moment, enclosing the coffee cup with a lid. "Derek is a good guy," Mygyer told her. "He might be interested in a date when we get him out of here." Strangely, he frowned. That was odd.

"What is it?" Patricia asked.

Mygyer sighed. "I have a bad feeling about this. This whole bust thing. Nothing substantial or anything, but my gut is telling me something is off."

Patricia felt her chest tighten in alarm. She may not have mentioned it to anyone, and Mygyer may have guessed it, but Patricia had started to care for Derek—a lot. "What should we do?" Patricia asked him, trusting his gut feelings. Especially when they echoed hers.

"I don't know," Mygyer said. "I'm thinking I'll just go to the dock and wait it out, then we can watch it as it unfolds."

Patricia nodded slowly. She wanted to do more. She wanted to know why Derek had called her earlier today. And mostly, she wanted to know why they were both thinking something was wrong.

Mygyer finished getting his coffee, then moved to the cashier. The clerk wouldn't put down his cigarette butt, so Patricia got a new blow in the face a couple times before he even picked up the few items to ring them up.

Mygyer grabbed the butt from the man's lips. "Hey Richie," he said firmly, reading the name from the nametag, "how about you get us loaded up and stop blowing smoke into the girl's face here? It's not appreciated. When you get a customer, you put the cigarette down and take care of them."

Richie glared at him but seemed to realize that he wouldn't win any fight—Mygyer was a very threatening figure—so he just grabbed the chips and rung the coffee, then gave them their total so Mygyer could pay. As soon as he did so, Mygyer thanked him and gave the butt back, and they left.

Mygyer sighed as he got the umbrella over them. Patricia smiled in amusement at her director.

"Well, he was just friendly, wasn't he?" Patricia said sarcastically.

He smiled at her. "Oh definitely. I think I'll even call the manager to tell him what a great employee he has in Richie."

Patricia laughed, but her laugh cut off as his phone started to ring. Anxious, they hurried to the car and Mygyer put his coffee on the top before pulling out his phone.

"Mygyer."

He was silent a moment, then his countenance seemed to darken. "Liz, slow down and start over. I'm putting the phone on speaker so Patricia can hear." He turned to Patricia. "You drive, Patty. And hurry." He handed her the keys.

Patricia darted to the other side of the car and put the gas pump back before pulling the driver's door open and sliding in.

"Kay, start Liz," Mygyer said into the phone, then put it on speaker. Patricia pulled out of the station quickly, toward the dock.

"They already started the deal. They started early! They're already at the dock, and the smuggler is there, transporting the slaves, and Santorini is beating up Derek. I don't know what happened!" Liz was hysterical. Patricia understood why. Her hands tightened on the wheel, and she picked up speed.

"How long ago? How did nobody catch this earlier?" Mygyer asked.

Liz sobbed. "It's raining so hard we can barely see! I only can see when the smuggler comes out with one person at a time. He's holding a flashlight. It looks like they've been there for a while. Derek isn't doing well, as far as I can see."

Another voice came in. "Liz, you've got to relax." Cameron.

"Cameron, call the FBI down here and tell them the deal is happening sooner than expected," Mygyer said calmly. Patricia looked over at Mygyer, noting the lines on his face. He was just as stressed as they were. He just knew how to keep rational.

"Yes, sir," Cameron said, tense.

Suddenly Liz gasped and everyone was quiet on the other end.

"What is it?" Mygyer asked sharply.

It was Cameron who answered. Liz just sobbed. "They just shot Derek. They're leaving him there."

Mygyer was silent a moment, then his orders came out quickly. "Liz, connect Patricia's phone to the call as well. Cameron, you keep an eye on that car at whatever cost and call the cops already—we need officers with us. Patricia, drive to the dock. I'm going to get out and care for Derek, and you'll have to follow Santorini."

"But I want to know how Derek is!" Patricia protested.

"You'll be on the line. I'll let you know. I need you to follow Bullet."

Patricia didn't like the idea, but she couldn't protest to Mygyer again; he was probably thinking most logically anyway.

"Is Derek moving at all?" he asked Liz.

"Can't see for sure. From this distance and the rain, I can't be sure. But the others are gone now. They just left him to die!"

Mygyer jumped out of the car as he got to the dock, ignoring the rain that drenched him immediately. He clicked on the flashlight. "Keep going, Patricia. I'll make sure Derek is okay." Mygyer shut the door without a response and ran down to the end of the dock.

It was hard to see with the rain falling in his eyes, so he slowed slightly, not wanting to slip or run into something.

The concern for Ethan had been escalating ever since Patty told him about the meeting with him the day before, and the fact he had ordered and had been about to drink some wine. Patricia didn't know how big a deal that was for Ethan; since the man had always been stalwart in his beliefs, and not drinking alcohol was a part of that.

Finally spotting Ethan, Mygyer picked up his pace until he could crouch beside his agent on the ground. He rolled Ethan over and checked for a pulse as his eyes and flashlight scanned down his body to assess the damage. He was a little surprised that Ethan hadn't been dumped over the dock before they left.

Mygyer saw Ethan's chest rise unsteadily right as he picked up the faint pulse. He sighed and finally caught sight of the blood surrounding Ethan. It was getting washed off from the rain; he worried the water would make his blood run faster or something. It also made it hard to tell how much blood he was losing, though it was obviously a lot.

"Come on, Ethan. Hold on." Ethan's jaw looked bruised already, and his nose and many open wounds on his face were trickling blood, but Mygyer was far more concerned about the damage he found to Ethan's abdomen.

"Ethan?" a voice from Mygyer's earpiece said. Patricia. "That's his real name?"

He didn't bother to respond; he was too concerned about Ethan. Patricia decided on another question. "Mygyer, how is he?"

"He looks real bad, Patricia." Mygyer checked Ethan's pupils but didn't receive much response.

"The ambulance is on the way," Liz told him, as if trying to reassure all of them. Then Cameron continued with guiding Patricia after Santorini.

Mygyer didn't know what else to do, so he took off his jacket and used it on Ethan's abdomen to staunch the bleeding.

Still scanning Ethan, he found another wound on Ethan's leg, mid-thigh. He hesitated a moment, then put the flashlight down next to him and held his other hand on Ethan's leg. With the light on the ground and pointing to Ethan, it made it a lot darker out there and cast shadows on Ethan that made him look even more gaunt.

"Come on, Ethan," Mygyer whispered. "Come on, you can make it. Just stay strong for me."

Over the sound of the rain, he heard sirens. He looked up in anticipation and sighed in relief when he saw flashing lights. He continued to press against Ethan as he watched for breath from the agent.

Minutes later, footsteps rushed down the dock. An officer ran up, along with a paramedic. Both wore headlamps. The paramedic nodded quickly at Mygyer, then turned his attention to Ethan. He checked pupils and heart rate nearly simultaneously. Then he opened Ethan's mouth—that surprised Mygyer. Why would that be one of the first things to check?

"Sir, how well do you know this man?" The paramedic asked, not turning his attention away from checking Ethan.

"Fairly well. I'm his boss," Mygyer told him.

"Does he have allergies or take any medications? What can you tell me about what happened?"

"No allergies or medication. He was shot in the abdomen and thigh, and definitely had a beat down."

The paramedic nodded and cut Ethan's shirt off. "More are coming down, just preparing the gurney and bringing more equipment. I need you to remove your hands now and step back for me."

He wanted to protest, not wanting to leave Ethan's side until he was doing better, but he knew that he needed to be out of the way, so he did as the paramedic asked and stepped back with the cop.

"Do you have the numbers to any of his family? Someone you can call?" The paramedic asked above the sound of the rain. "We can get him stable, but until we get permission, we can't do anything more than that."

"Yes," Mygyer said. "He gave me his brother's number. I can get his number and call him." Ethan had always had his brother as his emergency number, not wanting to worry anyone else.

"Do so." The man nodded. "But better wait until we get to the hospital." A couple other paramedics joined the last one. Mygyer hadn't noticed before because of the rain, but he realized they had been communicating through their radios connected to their shirts.

It took longer than Mygyer wanted. They needed to be sure Ethan could travel and be stable enough to even get to the hospital.

Mygyer closed his eyes and rubbed his face, exhausted and worried. *Come on, Patricia, catch these guys. Let's at least get this bust.* Even more than that, Mygyer prayed Ethan would pull through.

¤ ¤ ¤

Mason watched his wife dance to the music, her hands on the broom, hair up in a headband and clip, her dress loose around her stomach that held their unborn child. She might only be a few weeks along, but he could just imagine the baby growing inside her. Mason leaned against the doorway, amused to find his wife in such a trance.

Tyra continued to sweep her pile, then turned and saw Mason watching her. She paused, smiling. "What?"

Mason just smiled and pulled away from the door. "I was just admiring the view." He pulled her into his arms, hands on the low of her back. "Have I told you today that you look lovely?" Even after all these years, he still couldn't fathom how he had received such a treasure.

She laughed, throwing her head back and showing her dimples, then quickly sobered and pressed closer to him, standing on her toes. "Hmm…I don't believe you have yet."

Mason grinned. "Well, you are stunning." He kissed her. "And where did our little rascals get to?"

"Little rascal number one went over to Daniel's house. Little rascal number two is making a beautiful picture in the family room." She smiled at him, then shoved him away playfully and adjusted the broom. "And if you mess up my pile, I'm going to be very upset with you."

"I wouldn't dare," Mason told her, looking down so he could spot the pile, realizing he had nearly walked right through it.

"What are you doing home?" Tyra asked as she continued to sweep. Mason watched her another moment, then went to the fridge and grabbed the other broom from between the fridge and the wall and started on the opposite end of the kitchen from Tyra.

"The job canceled." Mason worked as a construction worker building decks and things like that. Today, they had been going to build one in a beautiful house about half an hour away. "They decided they weren't ready for the change yet, and we don't have another job yet, so we went home." Mason wasn't worried; they paid him well. He didn't have to work all the time.

Tyra smiled as he began to help her. "I'm glad you're here! I was missing you."

Mason laughed. "You saw me yesterday."

"Yes, but you left without waking me up this morning."

"You were sleeping so peacefully. I didn't want to disturb you."

Tyra gave him the look. "Mason, I don't like it when you leave without waking me up. I don't care if I'm sleeping peacefully. I can go back to sleeping peacefully right after you leave."

Mason ceded, knowing he wouldn't win the argument. He may not wake her up every time even still—probably wouldn't, knowing from past experiences.

Mason instead just smiled and finished his side of the kitchen, then realized he smelled something heavenly. "Mmm…are you making lunch?" Usually he got home later.

Tyra chuckled. "Indeed. Nothing special, just chips and cheese with beans."

"Sounds amazing." Mason hadn't realized how hungry he was until then.

They swept the piles together, then Mason crouched to hold the dustpan while Tyra swept it into it.

"Shouldn't you be resting?" Mason asked her, standing and putting a hand on her stomach as he reached around to dump the dustpan into the trash.

"What do you think I've been doing?" she asked, humor in her voice. "This house would be way cleaner if I haven't been, besides, it's not like I'm fat yet."

Mason looked around. To him it looked clean, but also knew that she was right. It would be way cleaner if she had been trying.

Right then, Lila—their four-year-old—ran into the room, shouting at the top of her lungs and holding a coloring book above her head. "Daddy! Daddy! Daddy!" She held her hands up and he smiled as he lifted her into his arms.

"Hey, my sweet Lila."

"Look what I drew." Lila held her coloring book. Mason tried not to chuckle as he saw the scribbles all over the page. She could draw in the lines perfectly fine if she wanted to, but much preferred "expressing herself" as Tyra had told him countless times.

"Oh, it's beautiful, sweetie." He kissed her forehead. "Good job."

Lila laughed. "Missed you, Daddy."

"I love you." Mason told her as she squirmed out of his hands and ran to show Mommy her drawing.

Mason chuckled and turned to the oven as the timer beeped. He pulled out the chips and put them on the stove.

The home phone rang. Mason tilted his head, confused. Very few people called his home phone anymore—Mason had been planning on getting rid of it for a while, but his brother had asked him to keep it in case he needed to call.

Expecting an ad or recording, he answered, "Hello?"

"Hello." The voice that answered seemed strained, not the voice of a recording. "Is Mason Conten there?"

"This is him." Mason covered his open ear, trying to block out the sounds of greeting as Mason's oldest son came in.

"Oh, okay. Mason, it's about your brother, Ethan. You were listed as his emergency contact."

"What?" Mason asked, voice breathless, nausea sweeping over him. He grabbed onto the counter and his hand tightened over the phone. "Emergency? What happened?"

"Hon, what's going on?" Tyra asked behind him. Mason looked at her but couldn't find an answer.

"Can you talk now, Mason?"

"Um…yes. Of course," Mason murmured, turning away from Tyra as his wife ordered Owen to take his sister upstairs to wash up.

"First off, I need to know if I can get permission for doctors to operate on your brother," the voice said.

"Of course," Mason said again. "What's going on? What surgery?" He felt a hand on his back, and Tyra rubbed slowly.

"Has he told you much about what he was doing and where he was?"

"Not that much," Mason admitted. "He didn't like us in danger or to worry too much about him. He only told me he was going to be on assignment for a bit. But is he going to be okay?" Seeming to sense how shaky Mason felt, Tyra pulled up a chair from the counter and guided Mason to a sitting position.

"Mason, I'm sorry. I can't answer that truthfully yet. He had gone on an assignment for us, and it has ended bad." The voice cracked. "He's been shot twice, and nobody is sure yet. They're doing tests now."

Heat washed over Mason, and he felt glad for Tyra's foresight of a chair as his vision darkened.

"Where is he? What hospital?"

"U-Chicago Emergency, in Illinois."

"I need to be there."

The man was silent for a couple long moments.

"Mason, you are listed as the only emergency contact. He never wanted to worry anyone, but I'll let you decide if you want to tell anyone else. You do what you think is best. As for coming down here, I can arrange everything and send you the information."

"Who am I speaking to?" Mason forced the words through numb lips. How could he ever explain to his family what had happened to Ethan?

"Adam Mygyer. I'm the director of this branch of the FBI." His voice held sympathy.

"Mr. Mygyer, I'd appreciate that. Thanks."

The voice paused again. "I'm sorry, I can't tell you more yet. I'll keep in contact with you whenever you're not on a flight. Will you be coming alone?"

Mason looked at Tyra. He couldn't pull Tyra and his family away from everything. Tyra had doctor appointments and was pregnant, and their kids had school. "Yes, sir. I'll be coming alone."

"Okay. I'll keep in contact. Just call me Mygyer," he said, then ended the call.

Mason took a shuddery breath and put the phone down.

Tyra leaned in front of him, holding his face between her hands. "What happened?" she asked tenderly. The softness in her voice made tears slip out of his eyes, and he couldn't bring himself to wipe them. Tyra did so instead.

"It's Ethan. He's in the hospital. His assignment went wrong, and he'd been shot…twice. Mygyer is sending me down so I can be with him."

Tyra gasped. "Is he okay?"

Mason shrugged miserably. "I don't know, they haven't told me anything. Sounds like they don't even know yet."

"Have they told your mom yet?"

Mason looked down, shaking his head. "No. Ethan had me as the emergency contact. He didn't want to worry the others…" Mason closed his eyes. "I think I'll go see how he is first, then figure out a way to tell them."

"Okay, well, you know I support whatever you do." Tyra lifted his face. "You just promise me you'll be safe. When do you leave?"

"He's going to send me the information." Mason swallowed heavily, looking at the clock. How would he make it these next couple hours without knowing how Ethan was?

Prayer. Lots of it.

As if Tyra heard his thought—or had inspiration of her own—she folded her hands in his. "Let's pray, shall we? God has Ethan in his hands."

¤ ¤ ¤

Mygyer was sitting in the waiting room when Patricia finally made it to the hospital. Her feet dragged on the floor, her eyes weighed heavily, but she made her way quickly over to her director. "How is he?"

Mygyer met her gaze and stood. He looked as beat as she felt. "Haven't heard much yet. I talked to his brother; he's coming down." Mygyer rubbed his face. "They got the permission they needed from Mason, then disappeared since then." Mygyer looked down at his watch. "In fact, his brother should be here within minutes."

Patricia hesitated. She wanted to be here for Derek—*Ethan*—but also would hate to just wait forever.

"Want me to do anything?"

Mygyer smiled grimly. "No, Patty. You've done enough today. I need you to go find a hotel and get some rest. I bought out three rooms at the Marriott across the street under my name. Go to the room and get some sleep."

Patricia shook her head. "No. I need to stay here. I wouldn't be able to sleep anyhow."

Mygyer put a hand on her shoulder. "There's nothing you can do here. I will call you as soon as there is any news about Derek. At least go and try to sleep before you collapse."

Patty looked at him. "You need to take your own advice."

He laughed. "Oh, I will. Don't worry about me."

Patricia sighed and looked down. Her nerves were run-down, she was stressed about Ethan, and Santorini hadn't been her favorite person to bring in. Mainly because he kept gloating about killing the mole…and he may end up being right. Ethan might die.

"There's got to be a chance," Patricia said desperately. "They wouldn't be trying still if not. He's still alive, still fighting."

Mygyer pulled her into a hug. "Yes. He's fighting. Now go, Patty. Or I'll make it an order."

Patty forced a little smile. "It already sounded like one."

"And you better not disobey," he teased.

Reluctantly, Patricia nodded and turned out of Mygyer's embrace. "I'll go, right after I meet Ethan's brother."

He sighed. "His name is Mason."

Patricia nodded, and Mygyer moved to go sit.

"So." he sat and looked at her. "How did the bust go, anyway?"

Patricia shrugged. "Fine. They were angry, of course, but we have enough proof to run the investigation and probably win in court. Mainly hard because Santorini kept trying to get us on edge by boasting about how he caught the mole. He had tried to play innocent, but I told him we had a recording of the proceedings, and now he was held for attempt at murder as well." Patricia thought about the slaves. "The smuggled were relieved though. Some of them decided they wanted to go back to family, others want to work to bring family here. I turned them over to immigration and everything to figure out that mess."

Mygyer nodded. "That's good then." His voice sounded flat, as if he didn't care about the bust.

His attention sharply diverted to behind Patricia. She turned as she heard the rush of footsteps. A man nearly ran up to them.

He stood. "Mason?"

"Yes." Mason shook Mygyer's hand. "And you must be Mygyer. Have you heard anything new on my brother yet?"

"Not yet. I'm sorry. And if it's all the same to you, I need to refer to your brother as Derek for safety reasons for now." He turned his attention to Patty. "This is Patricia. She's been Derek's handler this last assignment."

Mason shook her hand. "I'm sorry, I'm not familiar with what you mean by that," he admitted.

"That's alright," Patricia assured him. "It merely means I was the person who met with, uh, Derek." She looked at Mygyer. "Derek got the info, I took the info and decided what was important, then brought it to Mygyer's awareness so we could decide what to do with it. I also made sure Derek stayed in optimal mental and physical health throughout the assignment."

"And did…Derek stay in good health? I just want to understand what happened. What was the assignment? Why is he injured?" Mason seemed pale to Patricia. Worn and shaky.

And very confused.

Mygyer ran a hand through his hair as if debating how much to tell him. "We don't know all the details. Derek had some information while undercover about some illegal movement. He told Patty here when he met up with her last night, and we decided we wanted to intercede. The deal was supposed to be at seven, but something must have happened, so they changed it to an earlier time. We had placed cameras early that day so we would have evidence. It was pouring rain, but people on surveillance noticed something off. That's the only reason Derek is even alive right now. Otherwise, the deal would have gone off and Derek would've been left for dead. We're still not sure how his cover was blown."

Patricia took over, noticing that Mygyer only answered one part of the question. "Derek hadn't been doing well when we met last night," she told Mason. He turned his anxious gaze on her. His eyes seemed to pierce deep. "He was shaken from some of the recent things that had happened, and he knew that those above him were starting to get suspicious. That's one of the biggest reasons we decided to do the bust today. We figured we wouldn't get a better shot and we needed to get Derek out of the danger."

Mason frowned. "He was just hours away from getting out of there?"

Mygyer and Patricia both nodded. Then Mygyer turned to Patricia. "Patty, go get some rest now."

Patricia looked at her watch. "It's too early to sleep."

Mygyer shooed her. "Go eat dinner and stuff too, then. Unwind. Relax."

"Doubt I'd be able to," she muttered as she turned away. "Call me when you get news of Derek."

Mygyer's phone rang then. Patricia paused, wanting to know who it was before she left.

"Excuse me," he said to them, answering the phone. "Mygyer…Did he? What has he said?" Something about his tone told her to pause again. "I see. That's why then? Huh, you'd think a smuggler would be smarter. Yeah, you're right. Okay, sounds good. Let me know."

"Short conversation," Patricia said. "Who was it? What did they say?"

"Said Lance—the smuggler, alias name Nova—sang like a canary. Wanted a possible lighter sentence and didn't care if he betrayed anyone. Said Derek's cover had been blown because he recognized Derek from school and had started chatting like best buddies before he realized his mistake. Lance said that he hadn't wanted to get Derek in trouble or anything."

Mason narrowed his eyes. "That name sounds familiar."

The sound of shoes hitting the floor sounded a moment later. They all turned to see a nurse coming toward them.

"Are you three for the gunshot victim?" she asked.

"Yes," they answered simultaneously.

She nodded and focused on Mason, seeming to realize from the frantic step he took toward her that he was the one closest to Ethan.

"Okay, I was just sent to give you an update on, uh…"

"Derek," Mygyer supplied.

"Yes, thanks." She smiled at him. "On Derek. Are you his emergency contact?"

"Yeah." Mason nodded. "And you can speak in front of them too." He gestured to the other two without looking at them.

"We just took him back to surgery for the bowels. The bullet hit him in his extremities, but ricocheted. We're trying to assess all the damage. We gave him a CT scan, and it showed bullet fragments in his stomach and small intestines. Dr. Arnold is now undergoing the surgery to remove the fragments.

"Besides the bullet, the thing we're most worried about is the possibility of infection. Because the bullet tore the stomach, there has been some leakage that heightens the risk. The shot to the leg is minor comparatively, but the exit wound tore some muscle that will make it hard to walk or move at first. If he can get through these next couple hours, he should be fine; then we will have to keep watch for infection and secondary shock."

She paused for breath and eyed them. "He has really deep bruising too, but that should be fine—painful, but survivable. His ribs are bruised, and a couple cracked, and we will get them wrapped."

Mason seemed to have grown stiffer and more tense with every word she pronounced, but he nodded numbly as she finished.

"Thank you," Mygyer told her.

"Of course," she said sympathetically. "Look, it's going to be a long night, and visiting hours will be over soon. Go out for the night, and I'll call you when he's out of surgery and let you know how he does. Go get some food and some rest."

Mason looked as if to protest, but the nurse smiled softly and continued, cutting off any words. "Give me your number. I'll contact you. There's really nothing more you can do here tonight. We'll be open again at five tomorrow morning."

Mason hesitated, then nodded. "Paper?" his voice cracked. She turned the clipboard and let him write down his number, then Mygyer took it to write down his. She took the clipboard back as Mygyer sighed.

"She's right. We really can't do anything else here today. Come on, Mason. I bought out a couple rooms at the hotel across the street."

Mason nodded but hesitated again. "Miss, I know this is strange to ask..." He swallowed heavily. "But is there any way I could try to give my brother a priesthood blessing? It's a church thing..."

The lady seemed surprised, meeting his gaze. Then a small smile spread on her lips. "You know, I think I know exactly who would love to join you on one of those. Let me see what I can do."

~5~

Mason was back at the hospital at the start of visiting hours three days later. He'd been in every day for as long as he could get away with, and yet Ethan had not yet woken; his complexion staying a waxy pale. Mason hated seeing how beat his brother looked. Ethan was relying heavily on machines to keep him from infection and to keep him hydrated and such. He couldn't do anything other than breathe, essentially, so they were doing everything else for him.

They said that the drugs they gave Ethan to help with pain would keep him nearly comatose most of the time. He'd be extremely tired—not that he couldn't wake up, just that he would probably fall asleep quickly and be weak if he did. Mason still couldn't decide whether to call and tell his family, specifically his mom, about Ethan, or wait until they had a better idea whether he'd be okay. He didn't want to worry his mother, but she had a right to know. He kind of wanted to wait and see what Ethan decided.

Almost precisely when he entered the hospital, his phone rang. Mason pulled it out and saw that it was Tyra. He answered quickly, worried because this was early for his wife back at home.

"Hello?"

"Hey, honey. I couldn't sleep well. I knew you'd be awake. You in yet?" Her voice was quiet, probably so as not to wake the kids.

"Just getting there now." Without meaning to, Mason met her level of voice. He hadn't had much sleep the last few nights either. "Just hold on a minute." He moved to the front desk. The desk clerk looked up as he approached and gave him a small smile.

"Still in the same room, Mason. Go ahead and get in there. No change yet. Please get off the phone and switch over."

"Thank you. I will," Mason murmured, walking past her. His hands trembled when he heard the words, he wished his brother would be better. "Hon, let me call you back in a minute."

"Alright, dear."

He hung up the phone and worked his way up to Ethan's room. When he got there, he nodded at the officer standing outside Ethan's room. Mason was glad that they kept someone there to protect his brother.

The officer nodded back at him and let him pass. Mason sighed, then entered the room. As he looked at his brother, he felt that wave of sadness wash through him and grabbed the phone on the side when he realized that he was still not awake.

"Any change yet?" Tyra asked him as she answered. "Do they think he'll make it?"

"I don't know, hon," Mason said quietly, holding the phone to his ear. "He hasn't changed much, according to the doctors. They're still not sure if he can beat any infection or shock…and I don't know about his mental state either. They think it will be hard for Ethan to cope when he wakes up."

"I'm sure he'll be okay," Tyra told him. "I'm praying for him."

"Thanks." Mason paused a moment. Then, trying to distract his wife from worry, he continued. "How're the kids?"

Mason practically heard the smile. "Missing their dad. I told them you were with Uncle Ethan, but I only told Owen why. He could sense something was wrong. I told him Ethan had been injured so you were staying with him while he healed, but that's it."

Mason smiled lightly. "Maybe we can fly you guys down over the weekend or something…I miss you guys already too."

As Mason sat down, he grabbed his brothers' hand, studying his bruised face. Some of the bruises seemed to have burst or something and were now scabbed over. Or maybe he'd been cut while the bruises were also being made.

Frowning, he sighed.

"What is it, my dear?" Tyra asked softly.

"He looks so bad, Tyra. I wish I could help. And I wish I knew what to do. Should I call my mom?"

Tyra didn't answer right away. When she did her tone turned to what she used when she was trying to tell the kids something hard. "As a mother, I would want to know if one of my kids got injured. I can guarantee your mom would want the same, but it isn't my decision."

Mason closed his eyes, knowing she was right. "Okay…Okay, I will."

Sudden movement from Ethan made Mason look up quickly. Ethan's hand twitched in Mason's, then he groaned. "Hon, I'll call you back. Love you," Mason said quickly, then hung up and put his phone on the table beside the bed before leaning closer to Ethan. "Ethan? Bud?" *Oh, God, please tell me he's okay.*

Ethan struggled to get his eyes open, and when he finally did, they were distant. They could barely meet Mason's gaze. Ethan's hand started to shake within Mason's, and he couldn't help but tighten his grip.

"Nurse!" Mason yelled, unable to look away from Ethan. He put one hand gently on Ethan's head, checking for fever while also wanting to calm his brother.

At the touch, Ethan met Mason's gaze more firmly and gasped. "Mason…" His voice sounded different, a little hoarse and tired. "You're here. How…?"

Mason rubbed his thumb on Ethan's forehead, pushing back hair and feeling his tears threaten to spill down his cheeks. "God, Ethan…"

"You're…You're crying." Ethan murmured with a wince. "I'm sorry."

"Ethan, are you—Oh, God, you're alright. You're okay."

Ethan's hand trembled harder, and he squeezed his eyes shut. "I hurt."

"I know," Mason told him softly. "I know. I'm sorry. Let me get a nurse."

"No, stay here, please." Ethan closed his eyes, but his hand tightened on. He didn't say anything for a long moment, but Mason settled in more firmly beside him, not wanting to leave, even though he didn't want his brother to be in pain. "Did you tell Mom I'm hurt?"

Mason looked at his phone. "No, I was just about to, right before you woke up."

"How—when—did you get here? How long have I…" Ethan asked, his eyebrows furrowing as he opened his eyes back up to meet Mason's, stumbling over his words as though he wasn't sure what to ask.

"Three days ago. You've been out since I got here. I was so worried about you."

Ethan shuddered. "I don't want you to tell Mom. She'll panic. I don't want her to see me hurt."

Mason swallowed uncomfortably. He had all the same thoughts as Ethan; however, he agreed with his wife even more. Mom had a right to know. She was going to find out eventually. Better to tell her now.

"Ethan, I'll respect your wishes, but I think you need to think about that. Mom will want to know; you know she will. She'll hate it if we don't call her. Plus, I…I don't know how you will be later; I don't want to lose a chance for Mom to hear from you if something…"

Ethan didn't respond for many minutes, then spoke slowly, in between gasps. "Okay…call her. But don't tell her everything. Just say I was hurt on assignment, then I want to talk to her." Ethan's face was set in clear pain. He looked really weak.

Mason nodded and grabbed the phone. As if it was an afterthought, Ethan spoke again. "Mason…Where are we?" Mason looked up from the phone, right before dialing, and found Ethan staring back at him. Mason frowned as he saw the anguish in Ethan's eyes—such anguish had never shown from Ethan. Ethan had always been a happy kid, and that had followed into his adult life, but this assignment shook up the foundations.

"U-Chicago Emergency Hospital," Mason told him.

Ethan narrowed his eyes. "I don't understand. How did I get here? Why do I hurt so bad? Where's Bullet?"

Bullet? Mason shifted uncomfortably. He wasn't sure what Ethan was talking about.

"Do you not remember?" Mason asked. Ethan shook his head, bewildered, but then he winced.

Then suddenly Ethan's hand tightened, and his gaze darkened. "I remember…But how am I alive? I thought Santorini would kill me. Did he bring me here?"

As Mason thought about how to answer, another voice came in. "No." He looked and saw Mygyer walk into the room. "He didn't. He left you to die. You're only alive because Liz and Cameron caught sight of movement on the dock from the cameras we'd placed. You were there three hours early."

Ethan looked over to his boss but couldn't move much. "I know. They changed the time that morning. I tried to call Patty to tell her…" he licked his lips. "Did you catch them?"

Mygyer pulled up a chair and sat beside Ethan on his other side. "Yes. Patricia managed to pull it off without a hitch."

"That's good then." Suddenly tears rushed down Ethan's face, and Mason wasn't sure if it was from pain, shame, or if he was upset about what happened. Or maybe the meds, they probably have a big part of it as well. "I'm sorry. When Lance started to speak to me, it threw my cover. I was such an idiot. I should have come up with some better cover-up, but I was just so surprised. I didn't know what to say, that—"

"Shh…" Mygyer put a hand on Ethan's shoulder. "No. You did nothing wrong. Nothing at all. I'm only glad you're still alive."

"I'm pretty screwed over," Ethan muttered, glancing down at his body.

Mason put the phone down a minute, moving his hand back to Ethan's head. "You'll be alright, Ethan." Mason saw the look Mygyer flashed him, and knew it was probably because he wanted Mason to use Ethan's undercover name, but he didn't care. He couldn't say it. "We're here to help you."

Ethan nodded and closed his eyes as his breath suddenly came in gasps.

Right then, a nurse came in. She slowed a little as she saw that Ethan was awake. "Hi…Derek, how're you doing?" She came to the side that Mygyer was on, checking the IV in his arm and the packet.

Ethan didn't answer for a moment. "My throat is really dry and painful…Can I please have some water?"

The nurse smiled sadly at him. "Yes, just a little." She grabbed a water bottle from the table. "Mason, would you help me?" Mason adjusted immediately, standing and nodding. "I need you to help him sit up just a little. He's already sitting up mostly, but we want him up just a little more. Be really careful, and grab him here..." She guided his hands, on to his mid back, the other supporting Ethan's neck. "Derek, take a breath for me. This is going to hurt a little."

Ethan nodded, face screwing up into the look that told Mason he was prepping for pain.

The nurse opened the water bottle. "I'm just going to give you a little and see how you handle it." She nodded at Mason, and Mason lifted his brother a little, until the nurse put the bottle to Ethan's lips. Ethan's eyes scrunched up, but he took a couple sips of the water before a sob disrupted him. The nurse pulled back and motioned for Mason to let him lay back.

Mason did so, letting him lay back and grabbing his brother's hand. "Hey, bud…it's okay. Are you hurting?"

Ethan nodded. "Especially when I move…and I feel weird, like I'm going to puke."

The nurse frowned. "I'm sorry, Derek. You're going to feel off a bit. The bullet and bruises in your stomach did a number on you. You had surgery on your intestines; the tube is to help them from clogging up. And your stomach isn't in good shape either. But it'll wear off with time, you'll see." There was a forced chipper attitude about her, all of them could tell. Mason knew it and wished that he didn't see the despair wash over Ethan a moment later.

The nurse seemed to also see the look, as she changed the subject. "Can I do anything for you, dear?"

Ethan hesitated, then shook his head. He looked at Mygyer as the nurse left and spoke as soon as she turned the corner. "Mygyer…Do I have to go by Derek anymore? My cover was blown already. They know who I am, my real name, and…and I don't like to think about Derek."

Mygyer paused, studying Ethan, then he finally shook his head. "No, of course not. Look, I promised Patty that I would call when you woke up. I'll go do so now; you get some rest."

Ethan swallowed, but didn't respond as his boss walked away, then turned to Mason.

"It's not what I trained for, you know?" he said. Mason cocked his head in question. "I mean…I'm supposed to be better at this, stronger…mentally. But I just feel beat."

Mason rubbed his hand with his thumb. "It's okay, Ethan. Right now, you only need to worry about getting better. I don't care how much you have to scream or cry to get there."

That got a little smile out of Ethan, and Ethan gestured with his hand. "You going to call Mom?"

"Oh yeah, of course." Mason grabbed the phone with his free hand but refused to let go of Ethan's hand. He typed in her number and clicked call.

It took a couple rings for her to answer. "Hello?"

"Hey Mom, it's Mason."

"Mason? Hey honey? What's up? All okay?"

Mason smiled a little, but mostly in relief. He swore that's how she always answered the phone these days. "Mom…I need to tell you something. Are you sitting?"

Mom paused a moment. "Yes. Dear, what's wrong? I've had this terrible feeling in my gut these last few days. Is something wrong?"

Mason hesitated, looking to the ground because he was starting to tear up. He tried to swallow back a lump but choked on it instead. He could sense Mom's worry grow even over the phone. "Mason, please tell me what's going on."

Mason managed to force words out. "Mom, it's Ethan…He's been hurt on assignment. It happened a couple days ago. I know you would've wanted me to call you immediately, but I had to see how he was doing first."

Mom's breath caught. "Is he okay? Where are you? Who hurt my baby?"

"Can I talk to her?" Ethan asked. Mason looked at him, then nodded. Ethan's hand shook when he tried to move, and he winced, so Mason shook his head and leaned closer, resting his elbow on the bed and holding the phone to Ethan's ear for him.

"Mommy?" Ethan said, starting to cry again immediately. Mason could hear his mom talking quickly but couldn't make out all the words. He let his head fall toward his chest, blinking back tears. He didn't think he had heard Ethan call their mother "Mommy" since he was sick when he was young. He had been sick a lot, and she had been his source of comfort at those times. Mason wondered if the drugs or the situation itself caused him to resort to the name.

"I'll be alright. I promise...No, Mom. I don't want you to come down here yet. Not yet, please. I really don't want you to see me like this. Just give me a couple days or so to get better...No, I will be fine. I was just working undercover, and my cover got blown. I'm really tired right now, but the nurses are taking care of me, and so is Mason." Ethan smiled at Mason softly, squeezing his hand lightly. "Mason will call you and let you know how I do. I promise I'll tell you where I'm at soon, I just...I can't yet. Please, I'll be okay. Okay, I'll talk to you later. I love you."

Mason lifted his head as Ethan finished and pulled the phone back to his ear. "Mom."

"Mason, how is he doing, really?"

Mason squeezed Ethan's hand. "I'll be right back, Ethan. Okay?" He was grateful that the phones were not connected to any cord.

Ethan nodded weakly, but his eyes were closed.

Mason exited the room, walking past the man on guard. "Mom, he's really bad. The doctors aren't even sure he'd survive any infection if he got it—and chances are high for infection. He's weak and hurting. I'm worried."

Mom cried. "I need to come down and see him. I need to see my baby."

Mason leaned against the wall, putting a hand to his eyes. "He really hates the idea of you coming and seeing him like this. I'll stay here with him. If he gets worse at all, I'll call you and get you down here. I'll call you a couple times a day and tell you his progress, and I'll take good care of him. As soon as he's fit for it, I'll bring him back home."

Mom sobbed. "Mason, I'm worried. I want to be there for him."

Frowning, Mason felt his heart ache. How could he deny his mom? "Momma...I'll see what I can do, alright? I promise. Just...let me call you back."

¤ ¤ ¤

Maeve frowned, staring at herself in the mirror. Something was wrong with her body; she'd passed her monthly—she hadn't even realized that it had stopped happening.

That's so stupid, she thought. It probably had just skipped this month. She was worrying over nothing.

Maeve shook her head, unable to stop the concern anyway. That certainly wasn't helped by the fact that a desk clerk from the hospital had done a follow-up call to Maeve and asked her how she was doing and if she'd had her period. At the time, it had been such an uncomfortable question that Maeve had answered without thinking. *Of course* she'd had her monthly cycle, why?

They had just wanted to check in.

But then, why had they asked?

Maeve thought harder. Come on. She must have had a cycle. Was it when she was in the hospital? No, she'd been fine then.

She bit her lips. "Should I call back and tell them that I hadn't really had it?" Maeve asked herself quietly. Immediately she shook her head, she didn't want to admit that there might be something wrong. "No, I'm sure I just skipped it this month; that's happened before. I'll wait until next month, and we'll see that there's nothing wrong." She snapped her mouth shut, realizing she had been speaking aloud. Nervously she opened the bathroom door and felt relieved that Elisa was not nearby to hear.

Maeve went scouting for her host, knowing that Elisa had an appointment at the eye doctor to get new glasses. She had wanted Maeve to go with her.

She went downstairs and wasn't surprised to find Elisa in the family room. She was surprised, however, to see that she was sobbing in her hands, curled into herself.

"Elisa?" Maeve asked, feeling concern of a different kind fill her body. "What's wrong?"

Elisa looked up, dabbing her eyes with a tissue. "Oh dear, come please," she said, reaching out her hand. Maeve came closer and took her hand, then was surprised as she was pulled onto the couch beside the crying host. Maeve hesitantly put her arms around Elisa into as best a hug as she could manage.

"What is it?" Maeve asked her quietly.

Elisa wiped her eyes again before answering. "My son, my youngest—the FBI agent—he was hurt on assignment."

Maeve closed her eyes, understanding the tears. Elisa was so fond of her family; it would hurt to know that one of them got hurt.

Maeve thought back on the man who had rescued her, wondering why it was so important for her to be moved somewhere she couldn't blow the man's cover. Of course, that thought brought up other, way worse thoughts, so she shut the door on that thinking almost immediately.

"Is he okay?" Maeve asked her.

"Well, I got to talk to him. And my other son, Mason, he's down there. But Mason said he's really injured. He sounded bad. If you know my boy Ethan, he's always happy and positive and strong-minded. But just barely he started crying. Something happened, and they won't even tell me where he is so I can see him."

"Why won't they?" Maeve asked, surprised.

"Ethan doesn't want me to see him hurt. As if that matters to me. I'd rather be there than just sit here and hope he'll be okay." Elisa wiped her nose. "I haven't seen him for months—he's been gone. I just am so worried."

"I'm sorry," Maeve murmured, rubbing her arm. "He must be okay, though, right? Otherwise, they would have sent for you immediately."

Elisa nodded, wiping her tears again and giving a small smile. "I'm so glad you're here. I'd be going crazy with worry without you." She sighed. "Now, I should probably call Ethan's other siblings and let them know Ethan has been injured." She got a sort of dreamy look in her eyes. "I'm sure my husband is taking care of my boy. And so is my God." Relieved to see Elisa calm down a little, Maeve nodded eagerly.

"I'm sure they are," she agreed. Even if she didn't know it for sure herself, she couldn't doubt this woman's—the mother's—faith in those facts.

Elisa patted her hand. "Alrighty, let's get going to my appointment, I guess." She stood. Maeve stood in arm with her, worried because the enthusiastic host that first greeted her was now shaking nonstop.

Maeve squeezed her hand lightly. "It'll be alright, Elisa. If your boys are anything like you, it will take a lot to beat them down. I know it can get hard sometimes, but they'll be okay."

Smiling, Elisa rubbed Maeve's arm. "You're right, of course. I'm just worried about him. But God will take care of him. And they promised to keep in contact with me."

"Good, then." Maeve didn't realize it until then, but with the worry of these men that Maeve had never even met, her own concerns for her health had fled. She knew she'd be okay; now she found herself praying for this Ethan and Mason.

Elisa pulled out her phone. "I'll call my kids on the way over to the office. You drive?"

"Sure can." Maeve nodded, though she was nervous about it. She'd only recently gotten her driver's license.

Elisa nodded in thanks as she got in the passenger side.

Maeve walked around and got in. When she did so, Elisa sighed and dialed on her phone. Even before Maeve pulled out, Elisa started talking. After hearing so much about her family, it made Maeve think of hers. But as soon as she started thinking about her past, she had to stop because all thinking led back to the day they died.

"Hey," Elisa started. Her voice sounded calm for how much she was shaking. "What are you doing?"

Maeve could hear the answer. "Just working, Mom. What's up?"

"Can you talk for a minute?" Elisa's voice shook a little.

"Um…sure. What is it?"

"It's Ethan. He's been injured during his job and is at the hospital."

Maeve heard a gasp and a soft uttering of a prayer, then someone else asked if Isabelle was okay.

The conversation that ensued was full of questions of whether Ethan was okay, where he was, how bad he was hurt. Through it all, they both cried.

Elisa called her son next, but received voicemail, so she just hung up. Then she had a very similar conversation with her youngest daughter. Through it all, Maeve only found herself praying that the family would be alright.

¤ ¤ ¤

Fallon wiped sweat from his brow, staring at his latest project in approval. The last few stones were being laid by Jimmy and Collin. It was maybe one of Fallon's best pieces of work. Of course, the credit couldn't—and wouldn't—go all to him but his entire crew. The driveway looked fantastic; the light stones complemented the dark, and the pattern had been done very well. Smiling, he looked up at the sky. He had also finished early, a day early. It didn't matter too much, except Fallon liked to do his projects with efficiency so that he and his crew of three others would get recommendations.

"Fallon, your mom is calling," the last member of his crew told him. He smiled. The last member also happened to be his wife. She and their daughter, Zee, sat behind him on the back of his truck. Jessica was swinging her legs as she watched her daughter color.

Jessica was a wonderful lunch-maker; the team voted to keep her on the crew even with their daughter tagging along because she was great company and great at knowing exactly what they needed.

"I can call her back in a minute," Fallon told her, coming closer. "Just want to go talk to the owners first."

Jessica shrugged. "That's, like, the fifth time she called today. I doubt she would keep calling when she knows you're at work if it wasn't important."

Fallon kissed his wife. "I know you're right, hon. I just want to finish this first. I'll go right now and call her back as soon as I'm done."

Jessica looked concerned. "Baby, you know your mom is getting old, right? I hate to say it, but what if you miss your chance? Family is always most important."

Fallon hesitated, but ultimately, he knew she was right. Waiting another five minutes to tell them they finished wouldn't hurt, and Fallon would hate himself forever if he missed the call to something important. He grabbed the phone from his wife and answered quickly. "Hey Mom, I'm at work. What's up?"

"Hey Fallon. I knew you'd be at work, I'm sorry. I can call back later if you'd rather." Her voice sounded strained, not chipper. Something was definitely wrong.

"No, what is it? You sound stressed."

Mom took a deep breath. "It's Ethan; he's in the hospital."

Fallon felt winded. "What? What happened? Is he sick again?" Ethan got sick so often when they were younger, it was a wonder sometimes that he'd lasted so long. When Fallon was younger, he used to get jealous of all the attention his brother would get from everyone. With being the middle child, most people ignored him unless he was doing something wrong…which led to him doing a lot of stupid things.

But Ethan hadn't gotten sick for years, not since fourteen. That was when they'd finally figured out the problem and had surgery to remove it. By then, Fallon had grown rather fond of his brother and would kill to protect him.

"No, he was on assignment as an undercover agent. He got injured when his cover got blown. I'm sorry, Fallon, I don't know all the details. Nobody would tell me. I don't even know what hospital he's at!" She sounded immensely frustrated.

"What? Why not! You're his mom! We're his family!"

Mom sighed. "I know. And it's not even that. Ethan is the one choosing not to tell us. They called Mason because that was Ethan's emergency contact apparently. Ethan doesn't want his family to get too worried."

"It's too late for that!" Fallon nearly yelled it, frustrated. "You don't know where he's at? At all? How could he not tell us all?" But Fallon understood in a way. Mason was an obvious choice for Ethan to turn to—he had idolized his oldest brother growing up. Mason had always been there for him and had always invited Ethan along to watch movies and such with his friends. Not wanting to tell anyone—not wanting to make anyone worried—was understandable but frustrating as well. He hadn't told his mom when he'd injured his foot on the job a couple years ago either, but that had been fairly minor.

Fallon could sense his mother's weariness. He lowered his tone of voice as his wife grabbed his hand and his daughter looked up at him. "I'm sorry, Mom. Didn't mean to yell. How bad is he? Will he be okay?"

Mom hesitated. "They're not sure yet. Mason is scared. Ethan is…well, Mason said he isn't doing well physically or emotionally. I spoke to him for a minute, so I know he's alive, and Mason said he'd keep in contact, but…I just don't know enough yet, Fallon. Look, I am about to go into an appointment. If you hear anything, let me know, okay?"

"Yeah, Mom. I will. Promise. You do the same."

"Love you."

"Love you too. Bye." Fallon hung up, putting the phone on the truck as Jessica grabbed his hand.

"What is it? Who's hurt?" Jessica asked.

"Ethan. On assignment. I…" Fallon trailed off, unable to finish. His chin fell to his chest and Jessica stood and pulled him into her embrace, running her hand through his hair.

A moment later, Fallon felt a tug on his hand. He knew it was his daughter, so he wrapped an arm around her too, wanting her close.

It still amazed Fallon how Jessica could make him feel calm and safe without a word, just her touch calmed his frantically beating heart. He paused a moment, then grabbed his phone and pulled away from his wife. "I'm going to call Mason. He knows more about how Ethan is."

"Okay, dear." Jessica put her hand on his cheek. "I'm sure he'll be okay. Trust that God has a plan."

Fallon smiled at his wife but didn't answer. Her faith was stronger than his.

∼6∼

Ethan wished Mason could stay with him through the nights too—or even better, Ethan could just go home. Ethan's nights were harder alone; he'd wake up from his nightmares and no one was there to comfort or ground him.

At least he was on the mend. Yeah, he still hurt, but it had only been two weeks, and he was making progress. The doctors had removed the tube from his gut; they said he had healed inside well enough to eat without it, and they no longer needed it to unblock his intestines. They said today he could start to move. Only a little.

Ethan was most worried about the meds. They were switching from constantly feeding him pain medication through an IV to pills, which in turn meant he wouldn't stay out of pain constantly. He already hurt quite a bit even with the medication. He feared how bad it was going to hurt later.

Ethan looked over at the clock, anxious for the time to change already. Mason had been there nearly the minute visiting hours started almost every day, and Ethan wanted his brother. His dream had left him shaking this time, and he couldn't fall back to sleep.

Still twenty minutes.

As that realization oddly shook him, the door opened, and a nurse walked in. Ethan nearly yelled in relief.

Nurse Mackey smiled at Ethan. "Hey. You're awake." But then she seemed to notice his trembling. "You feeling alright?"

"I'm...I'm okay. I just had a bad dream." Ethan wanted to punch himself as soon as the words passed his lips. Where had all his training gone? He used to be super skilled at separating his panic and pain from his job and survival. Apparently now that his job was over for a while, he didn't care to keep up appearances.

Mackey came closer and put a hand on his forehead. Her lips twisted. "Are you ready to pull out the IVs and get some pills in you instead?"

Ethan gave a half shrug, not wanting to aggravate his wound by moving too much. He did want to be on the mend, but he worried about the idea of more pain. "I…I have a question."

Mackey looked at him as she grabbed out a cotton ball. "What's that?"

"I want to go home…" Realizing he had not asked a question, he continued, "Am I well enough to go yet? I can fly back and stay at my mom's house, maybe? She has room to spare." He didn't look near as bad now, and he'd been making little movements. "I can stay in my bed just as well at home and make a little progress there too."

Mackey hesitated as she slid the needle out. "I'll tell you what. I'll talk to your doctor. I know he'll want to see how you do off your IVs and with taking short walks. When you can walk decently for a good amount of time, then I think we can get you back home."

Ethan nodded, disappointed. He did need to get better; he didn't want his family to see him so bad off, but he also missed them. He hadn't seen any of them but Mason for months. They called every day since he'd woken up from surgery to check in, and Ethan tried to tell them as little as possible about his condition; instead turning their conversations to their lives. He knew they worried about him. They wanted to see him.

Mackey smiled at him sympathetically. "I know it's hard. Why don't you just have them come down here to visit?"

Ethan tapped on his arm with his fingers, suddenly uncomfortable as his mind turned back to his dreams. *I don't want them anywhere near this fake life, these dangerous people.* He realized that he was hoping when he got home, life would just go back to normal. The sudden thought made him realize that wouldn't be the case at all.

"I don't know," Ethan murmured, not wanting to share. Most of the people that would hate Ethan lived here. He wanted as few people he loved as possible here. He had asked Mygyer to keep Mason safe; luckily Mygyer told him he had people watching out for Mason as well as Ethan.

Mackey smiled at him. "Okie dokie. When Mason gets here, we can try to stand. Don't start until I get back with you."

She checked the clipboard on the end of the bed, then walked out of the room. Ethan looked over at the clock again, relieved to find that more time had passed than he thought. Mason should be here within minutes.

He closed his eyes, exhausted. His thoughts immediately flew to the woman that night with Bullet. He remembered the disgust and fear of that moment—how he had to try so hard to keep his role straight.

The swing of a door jerked him, and he knew without looking at the clock that he had fallen asleep. He gasped as he awoke, body trembling, and opened his eyes to see Mason, right as he felt his brother's hand on his head.

Ethan instinctively grabbed Mason's hand that lay by his side and sighed.

"Hey…" Mason sat next to him on the bed. "I didn't mean to startle you. Are you okay?"

Ethan nodded quickly. "I was awake for a bit. Only fell back asleep for a minute."

"Bad night?" Mason asked, brow furrowing.

"Bad dream."

Mason frowned. "I'm sorry."

Ethan closed his eyes and shrugged, relieved to feel Mason's thumb run along his hand.

"I'm sorry I'm taking you away from your family for so long," Ethan said without looking.

"You're not taking me away. I chose to be here."

"I know you must be missing them though. How are they doing?" Ethan wanted to see Mason, but his eyes wouldn't open back up.

"Missing me. Worried about you—at least my wife and Owen are. You know how much he loves you."

Ethan smiled a little. "Did you tell him I love him too?"

"He doesn't need me to; you tell him enough." Mason let go of Ethan's head and relaxed onto the chair next to the bed. "They took out your IVs."

"Yeah, like twenty minutes ago."

"Are you ready to try and move?"

Ethan paused, starting to drift off. "I'm ready to go home, to see the family."

"Why don't you just let them come down?"

Before Ethan could respond, a sudden gunshot sounded outside the door, followed by a thump. Mason jumped to his feet in alarm as Ethan's eyes flew open. He scrambled to the side of his bed. Mygyer had given him a gun when Ethan had asked for one, for emergencies, and he managed to pull it out from the crack between the hospital bed and pad.

As the door swung open, revealing a slightly familiar and very dangerous man that he had seen with Bullet before, Ethan shot twice.

¤ ¤ ¤

Mason hadn't been able to tell who the man had been aiming for before two shots rang out and the man screamed as he fell to the floor. One shot through the hand that had held the gun, the other through the man's leg. Mason couldn't move for a moment; his body seemed paralyzed, but Ethan's voice jerked him out of his funk. "Mason, grab his gun."

Mason looked back at Ethan for a split second as he moved, noting that it was Ethan who had done the shooting, a gun suddenly in his hands as he tried to fully sit up. Mason kept an eye on the man on the ground as he approached the gun, quickly grabbing it and taking a far step back.

The man glared up at Ethan and Mason, swearing between his teeth as he put pressure on his wounds. Mason's hands trembled, but he pointed the gun in the general direction of the man, finger far from the trigger. Outside the door, he saw the officer on the floor, shot. Down the hall, he could see a nurse calling for security and cops.

"You okay?" Ethan asked, voice tight. Mason looked back at him, surprised to find that Ethan was now sitting on the side of his bed and still moving, even though his gun stayed pointed toward the man. Mason moved closer to him.

"Stay there, Ethan."

Ethan looked at him, his eyes hard. "The officer outside?"

Mason looked out the door at the officer. He felt sure the officer was dead, but he couldn't tell Ethan that. "I'm not sure yet. Security is coming." Mason watched as the new officers ran down the hall. Mason was surprised to see Mygyer as well. While some officers went to the new man and secured him, others went to the dead officer outside the door. Mygyer headed straight to Mason and Ethan.

"You two okay?" Mygyer asked, voice even harder than Ethan's had been, but concerned.

Mason held out the gun to Mygyer almost instantly and Mygyer gestured to another officer, who grabbed it with a plastic bag. Mason wiped his hands on his pants and moved close to Ethan, putting his hand on his brother's shoulder.

"Let's lay you back down," Mason said, rubbing his back.

Ethan looked over at him. "That's why I don't want our family here," he said, voice suddenly trembling again. And, yeah, Mason could understand that.

Mygyer looked at him. "We need to get you somewhere safer than this," he decided. "How's your stomach feeling?"

"Fine," Ethan muttered. Mason knew the lie because Ethan's jaw was clenched tight, and he was tilting a little.

Mygyer frowned. "I'm going to set up a flight for later today. I know you don't want to, Ethan, but you need to call down your other brother. You will need help while you're on the plane, and Mason won't be able to do everything on his own."

Ethan hesitated, frowning. "He won't be here for long, yes?"

Mygyer shook his head. "Merely hours."

Ethan nodded. "Alright. Just give me details. I'll call him now and see if he can." Ethan looked toward the door. "How's the officer?"

Mygyer followed his gaze. "I'm sorry," he said simply, eyes soft and worried.

Ethan swore, rubbing a hand down his face, and Mason couldn't help but agree with the sentiment.

"I'm glad you convinced me to leave the gun," Mygyer added, as though trying to distract him.

Ethan shrugged, eyes dull as his shoulders slumped and he leaned his shoulder against Mason's chest. "These men are dangerous, and some are reckless. They had been very loyal to Santorini—probably still are. Santorini really hates me now." He swallowed heavily.

Mason grabbed his brother's side. "Ethan, lay down," Mason said forcefully, pushing him back and guiding him to his back.

Mygyer put a hand on Ethan's arm. "I'll go figure out details. You call your brother."

Ethan nodded, looking suddenly worn out. "Mason, can you call him?"

"Of course," Mason murmured. His heart still beat frantically, but he took a deep breath to calm himself as Mygyer walked out. He avoided looking at the blood on the ground as he pulled out his phone and dialed Fallon's number.

Though Mason knew Fallon might still be asleep this early, the phone was answered on the fourth ring.

"Hello?" Fallon's groggy voice answered. "What's up, Mason? Ethan okay?"

"Yeah, well…actually, I got to talk to you."

"Alright." Fallon's voice turned wary. "What's wrong?"

"Do you think you can get on a plane today? Get work off?"

"Mason, of course I can, but what is wrong? Ethan's not worse, right?"

Mason looked at Ethan as his brother's eyes closed and reached for his hand. Ethan squeezed it softly, but Mason felt sure he was starting to fall asleep again.

"No, he's getting better. Look, I don't want to get into details right now, but we need to get Ethan back home. It's not safe here. I want you down here to help me get Ethan back home."

"Finally," Fallon muttered. "Where are you guys?"

Mygyer came back in, looked at Ethan, and lowered his voice and spoke to Mason. "I'm going to send information for a flight you can send him. It'll be at eleven. Then we'll get Ethan home once your brother is here."

Mason repeated the question to Fallon, but turned his attention to Ethan again, pretty sure his brother had fallen asleep at last.

"Yeah, I can do that," Fallon agreed. "Can't believe you're in Illinois, man…And you haven't told us."

"It wasn't my decision."

"Can I tell the others now, and tell them Ethan'll be coming home?" Fallon's voice begged.

"Yes, just don't let them come down with you; it really is dangerous."

"Mason…What happened?" Fallon asked quietly. "You sound really nervous, and this is really sudden. Something must have happened. What is it?"

"I'll tell you later."

"I'd prefer if you tell me now. I'd rather be prepared for anything that may happen."

Mason hesitated. He too wanted Fallon to know beforehand. "Ethan had gone undercover, you know?"

"Yes."

"Well, he upset a lot of people in the mafia when he betrayed them. One man came into the hospital today, killed the officer guarding Ethan's door, and would have shot both me and Ethan if Ethan hadn't had a gun on him at the time. Mygyer wants Ethan out of Illinois as soon as possible, and we need an extra person to help us, so we called you."

Fallon was quiet for a moment. "No one knows where Ethan is going, right?"

"No."

"But they know his name? And what he looks like? And what about you?"

Mason frowned. "I'm worried too, but I'd rather him be home with us and out of immediate danger. I know there's a risk anywhere, but I don't want Ethan to disappear into Witness Protection or something. If he did, we would never know where Ethan ended up."

"I just want to make sure you guys know what you're doing. And that we'll all be safe." Fallon paused. "How is Ethan, you know…emotionally, with all this happening?"

Mason sighed. "He's changed, bro. A lot. He tries to be happy, but I can see that he's not. He's scared, and always seems so sad now. And when he shot the man, he suddenly became blocked off, like he wasn't allowing himself to feel any emotion at all. I don't know if that is his training, or something that happened in the field, or both, but…I want Ethan back, you know? I want my chipper little brother who was always happy even while sick. I swear, nothing could tear him down. And now…"

Fallon didn't respond right away. "And now it will take some time to heal, but you'll see, Ethan will make it through. You're right. Nothing can tear him down. He'll make it."

He'll make it… Mason stared at Ethan's face. *But will he ever be the same?*

¤ ¤ ¤

The pickup from the airport was awkward. An officer held a piece of paper with 'Isaac' on it. That wasn't anyone's name, but Fallon had been told to use his brothers' names as little as possible, and to not use his last name at all or his own first name. This was one moment Fallon wished he had a different name—one that every other male seemed to be named.

The officer shook his hand, told Fallon that his name was Richard, and said not to be thrown off when he—Richard—followed him *everywhere*. He then explained that with what has been happening, they didn't want to risk Fallon getting injured or killed too.

Then the officer proceeded to the car, where he didn't talk unless Fallon talked to him, and Fallon didn't talk much because he worried more about his brothers than making small talk. He couldn't even think of something to ask outside of how Ethan was. He could only think about his brothers and his own family. Fallon wished his wife could have come with him; she was so much better than he at being friendly, and an amazing support, which he wanted right now. But it wasn't safe for any of them, and he wanted her far away from everything here.

He had texted his wife to tell her he had landed safely; she had messaged back that she was glad and assured him she and their daughter were fine.

Other than that, there had been nothing to distract Fallon.

So, the half hour or so ride to the hospital was quite uncomfortable.

As soon as they pulled into the parking lot of the hospital, Fallon pulled the handle to get out, and the officer finally turned toward him. "Pay attention to your surroundings while you're here. If you see anyone who looks suspicious, let me know. Don't be distracted."

Fallon nodded and opened the door. Why couldn't Richard explain this to him while they were driving, rather than take more time away from his brothers?

Fallon shook his head, but decided to do as Richard had asked, keeping an eye out for any suspicious activity. Of course, now that Richard had said that, everyone looked suspicious to Fallon, so he didn't tell the officer anything.

Another man met him inside the entrance to the hospital. Fallon eyed him, but when he held his hand out and told Fallon he was Director Mygyer, Fallon relaxed. Mygyer looked threatening, even though he was clearly at least fifty. Nice to have this man on their side.

"Nice to meet you," Fallon said, taking his outstretched hand.

Mygyer nodded and turned to walk further into the hospital. "Ethan is on the second floor." Mygyer led him down the hall. Fallon looked back to see that Richard followed just a few feet behind. Oddly, Fallon did feel safer with this officer here.

"When I left the room, Ethan was awake, out of his bed. The nurse is trying to get him moving again a bit. I'm pretty sure he would try to do more if Mackey wasn't there—she really knows her patients and knows how long she should let them be out of bed. She'll probably have him back in bed about now." He talked quietly, and paused a lot, making this trip to the hospital room a lot less awkward than the drive. They took the stairs up to the next floor.

Fallon blanched as he saw blood stains on the ground outside a room on the second floor that a couple people were trying to get cleaned up. Mygyer seemed to sense his mood as he guided him past that room. "Ethan was in that room. They decided to move him to a different one." They stopped about halfway down the hall at an open door. Fallon heard talking and knew immediately it was his brothers. There was a little laughter right as Fallon looked in. Ethan was sitting on the end of the hospital bed, smiling a little, and a nurse—probably Mackey—was laughing. Mason's back was to Fallon where he stood, so Fallon didn't see his face right away.

Ethan looked over as Fallon came in, and his smile spread. "Hey!" He seemed to catch himself before he spoke Fallon's name.

Fallon couldn't help but smile. Sure, Mason had said Ethan was struggling with being happy, but he was still trying, which told Fallon that his baby brother wasn't giving up.

Mason turned toward Fallon and smiled at him. Fallon moved over to them quickly, giving Mason a hug first since he was closer. He was surprised by the firmness in Mason's hug.

Fallon went to Ethan next, sitting on the bed next to him and pulling him into a gentle hug. Ethan hugged him back. "I've missed you, Fallon," he whispered.

"Me too," his brother replied, then pulled back, keeping him at arm's length to look him over. "You look better than I'd been expecting. Where are you hurt?"

"My thigh and my stomach." Ethan met his gaze. "My thigh's not too terrible; I should be able to walk—or at least limp—on that leg in another week or so. For now, it just hurts if I put weight on it or when it stiffens up."

"And your stomach?" Fallon looked at his stomach, as if he could see through the hospital gown to the wound itself.

"Still sensitive. Better now because I don't have to have the tubes and stuff anymore. But I have to be careful, or I can tear the stitches, and it just kind of hurts with movement still. Even with painkillers." His face scrunched up and he looked at the nurse. "When is my next dose of painkillers?" he asked.

"Is it starting to hurt more?" Mackey asked, moving to look at his clipboard.

"Yeah."

"You have another hour until you can take them." She looked at him. "Can you make it?"

"Of course," Ethan said smoothly. Fallon tilted his head at his brother, amazed at how calm he seemed to be. Ethan had always been like that, though. But now there seemed to be a lack of emotion as well. Mason was right about that.

Ethan turned back to Fallon. "How is everyone?" The emotion was back with the question, a worry, a longing, a sadness.

"Good other than they're worried about you. They're happy you'll be coming back home today, and you better expect them all to be there for you when you get back. Speaking of, are you planning on going to a hospital around home, or someone's house?"

Ethan smiled. "No, I want to go back to Mom's house…" He paused, smile falling. "Do you think she'll mind?"

Fallon snorted. "You kidding? When I got off the phone with her, she said she would be putting your bedroom together, getting it all clean and ready for you. She kind of expected you to come back home sooner or later."

Ethan gave a short laugh. "I miss her, a lot. I'm excited to see her and the family."

"She has a woman living with her now," Fallon told him. "Cute thing, she is. Her name is Maeve. She's made Mom really happy."

Ethan narrowed his eyes. "Why?"

Fallon shrugged. "I think she hates being in the big house all alone, plus she's starting to get tired of cleaning her house, so she hired some live-in help. From what I've seen and heard, the woman goes with her shopping and stuff, as if a daughter, rather than much of a house cleaner. However, she does do a good job with cleaning as well." He paused a moment. "I don't know if she could have made it through these last few weeks without her, to be honest. She's been quite a blessing."

Ethan nodded slowly. "Well, if she's helped Mom, I don't care. It won't be weird living in the house with her there?"

Fallon shook his head and shrugged. "It shouldn't be. It's a big house."

"Then yeah, I want to go to Mom's house." Ethan put a hand to his stomach softly.

"What do we need to get ready for Ethan to head home?" Fallon asked, directing the question more to Mygyer than anyone else.

Mygyer sighed. "That's mostly for me. I'm going to get Ethan some clothes and finalize the travel plans. Ethan, you just rest, I'll be back by three to get you all." He nodded to Ethan, then looked at Fallon and Mason a moment before turning away.

Nurse Mackey stood there awkwardly but with a smile on her face. "Alright, Ethan. I think you've earned a rest from moving until three. How about some lunch?"

Ethan shrugged. "Sure. I'm not too hungry yet."

Mackey frowned. "We need to keep your strength up. I'll just bring you something small for now, dear." Then she looked at Ethan's brothers. "And what can I get you boys?" She smiled at them. Fallon felt weird being called a boy by this lady because she looked younger than he. It must just be in a nurse's nature to treat patients like that.

"Same thing you got me before." Mason reached into his pocket for his wallet.

"What did you get?" Fallon asked.

"The turkey sandwich," Mason said, looking through his wallet.

"Oh, yeah, I'll have that too," Fallon said.

The nurse nodded and looked at Mason. "Don't worry about it, Mason. I've got it." She left the room before Mason could argue.

Fallon looked at Ethan, punching his shoulder lightly. "Don't ever do that again."

Ethan rubbed his shoulder absently, wincing, then tried to play innocent. "Don't do what?"

"Well, I'd prefer if you just don't get hurt again. But at the very least, you better not keep it secret so long." He included Mason in his glare and Mason took a quick step back and raised his hands to his ears. "You know if I'd been injured you would've wanted to know where I was so you could visit me. I hated not being able to see you." Fallon put a hand on his shoulder. "We were all worried about you."

"I didn't want you guys around any danger of my job," Ethan said, looking at Mason.

"I understand that, Ethan, but you know the family just wants to see you, to know how you're doing."

Ethan shrugged and began to lay himself back on the bed carefully. Mason jumped forward to finish helping him. Fallon paid attention to how Mason helped, wanting to be able to help if he needed to later.

They spent the next couple of hours catching up on what had been happening in each of their lives. Talking to Ethan for longer made Fallon realize how right Mason was about Ethan. Ethan tried to put up a happy front, but his eyes clouded over in sadness a lot, and his hands shook more often than not.

Mygyer came back at two instead of three but put his finger to his lips for them to be quiet and gestured for them to follow him.

Furrowing his eyebrows, Fallon looked at the other two. Mason looked confused but obeyed, starting to lift Ethan. Ethan, however, didn't look surprised as Fallon moved to help.

Between Fallon and Mason, Ethan managed to move fairly quickly, though Mason took most of the weight off his injured leg. They followed Mygyer to the bathroom down the hall.

"Get dressed quickly." Mygyer handed Mason Ethan's clothes.

As Mygyer went out the door, Fallon turned to Ethan. "What's going on?"

Ethan shrugged as he leaned against the sink so Mason and Fallon could help him. "I don't know. But I'm not surprised. We have to be careful with how we plan things; Mygyer probably has fake routes to cover up real plans, so if anyone is keeping an eye on us, they have less of a chance of figuring out what's really happening."

"Oh." Fallon unbuttoned the gown from Ethan and held him steady while Mason started to pull on underwear and pants. The explanation made sense but told Fallon how much danger they were in.

Ethan bit his lip, and Fallon paused. "Are you hurting?"

Ethan looked at him. "A little, but mostly I'm just really weak."

At that, Fallon adjusted his grip, determined to keep most of the weight.

What followed was the most advanced ride to an airport ever known. They drove as if heading to the airport Fallon had taken, then under a bridge with three car decoys; they swapped cars and came back the way they came. They took an indirect route to a smaller airstrip after pausing for a while at a gas station. By the end of it, Ethan collapsed onto the chair of the private plane, legs trembling.

Fallon only wondered if the crazy course was even necessary, terrified if it was.

¤ ¤ ¤

Santorini sat in the seat, waiting impatiently for the door to open, but refusing to show his annoyance. He knew an officer stood behind him, watching him. His lawyer would not be able to get Santorini out of this one, not when the police and Feds both have proof of him on tape, and Alley Ice—*Ethan*—was still alive as a witness. They might be able to argue it was a violation of privacy, but Santorini doubted they would get far with that.

That left only one more thing for Santorini. The one thing his "lawyer" would help him with.

The door opened. Santorini looked up and met the officer's gaze that came in, with Mr. Dase behind him. He kept his gaze unwavering on the officer until both cops left the room, then turned his attention to Mr. Dase.

"I made sure we're talking alone," Mr. Dase told him as he pulled out some papers from his case before sitting. "Ice played you the fool. Didn't I tell you he was trouble? Even his name tells it all—Alley Ice. You never see it until you slip." He shook his head with a chuckle. Santorini smiled in amusement.

That was something Santorini felt was different about himself from most Capos; he knew how to look at the bright side of things, didn't mind being teased, and laughed at his own mistakes. Fixed the mistakes too, which was what he planned to have Mr. Dase do for him.

"I did give him the perfect name, didn't I?" Santorini said. "Too bad Derek—Ethan—is going to slip on that same ice he made." He leaned forward and lowered his voice, just in case they were indeed listening, then switched his language over to Welsh.

"Have you found out where he is?"

"Yes." Dase switched into that same language. "He's been staying at U-Chicago Emergency. However, he is leaving today, or maybe even has left already. I have a tail on him, and Kude put a microphone in the room Ethan stayed in when he shot that other officer. Not the way I would've done it, but then, Kude never cared if he did get caught." He chuckled. "I don't think he planned on Ice hiding a gun in there, but now we know their plan a bit. Bet they'll make a couple decoys, but it won't be too hard, the brothers had slipped a couple times and used each other's names."

"And we know where he likely lives, or at least lived," Santorini added.

Dase looked at him eagerly. "Where's that?"

"Nova let it slip that Ethan was making a cop out of himself in Kansas last they saw each other," Bullet told him. "If he doesn't go back there, you at least have a trail to start following. Find high school records if necessary. And if you can't find Ethan at first, try to find Nova."

Dase smiled.

"That'll be a good start. Everyone is pissed off that Ice got you in here, played the double game. They want him dead. I'll send out the scouts to find him and his family."

~7~

Maeve stood facing the mirror for maybe the millionth time that day. Something was wrong. She should have had her period by now, but nothing. Instead, she became nauseous. She needed to take a stop at the hospital, she knew, but she didn't *want* anything to be wrong with her. She didn't want any confirmation. Besides she didn't even know where in the hospital to go. Hospitals were massive.

I can't go today anyway. Elisa's son will be home today. She'll need the support and so might her son. Elisa had already asked her to be there and to help serve some tea for her family while she was there. She wanted Ethan and her to become acquainted since they would be living in the same house. It made her nervous, but Maeve had agreed. She did need to know who she'd be living with, after all.

Men just made her nervous. Even when she had been out with Elisa and occasionally Kelly, boys had cat-called her and Kelly, even tried to ask them out, and Maeve just declined.

"Maeve!" Elisa's voice cut into her thoughts. Maeve pulled her hair back into a clip, trying to keep semi-presentable, and opened the bathroom door, rushing out of her room and down the stairs. Elisa met her down the hall, rushing down the steps with Maeve. "They're on their way. Ten minutes away! Will you be a dear and get some pomegranate tea for my son and me, and whatever you want? That's his favorite. And bring out the treats too. My boys may be feeling hungry. All three will be here."

"Of course," Maeve answered calmly, even though she was freaking out inside.

Maeve entered the kitchen while Elisa fluttered to the window to watch for their arrival, even though they'd still be ten minutes away.

About five minutes later, Elisa ended up in the kitchen, pacing away. "Oh dear, I'm so nervous! I want to give him a big hug and all. But what if he's hurt too bad for that? What if he's completely changed?" Her hands fidgeted with her dress.

"It'll be fine." Maeve took hold of her hands, holding them between her to try and calm her frantic host. "Just give him a gentle hug. I'm sure if he's moving, he can take a hug."

Elisa nodded and squeezed Maeve's hands. "I don't know what I'd do without you, my lovely girl," she said, then the sound of a door distracted her. Maeve felt warmed by the words, still surprised by the acceptance in the lady's actions.

"Mom!" a voice called from the other room, and Elisa whisked away, calling out greetings, half crying as she went.

"Oh Mason! Ethan! Ethan, I've missed you so much. Come, sit here my baby, let me take care of you. Thanks, Mason. For bringing him home. But where is Fallon? I thought he was with you."

A gentle rumbling voice answered, too quiet to hear much. Maeve smiled but continued to prepare the tea, grabbing cups and pouring hot water into the tea pots for seeping. One peppermint, one pomegranate. Hopefully she'd picked a good one.

"Maeve? Maeve, dear, would you bring the tea? Come meet my sons!"

"One second!" Maeve took a deep breath, grabbed the cookies, and put them on the tray, then pushed open the door just enough to peek through.

Maeve stifled a gasp and let the swinging door close as she took a step back. Her entire form suddenly flashed cold, and she felt like she would fall. The man that sat in the foyer…no. It couldn't be.

Unbelieving what she had seen but scared to look again, she continued to stand there. The tray seemed to have frozen in her fingertips—at least she hadn't dropped it.

This man was her son? She couldn't fathom the cruel twist life threw her way—she thought she was done with hard parts, and that she could finally move on. How could fate be this cruel?

"Maeve, is everything alright?" she heard Elisa ask from the other room. Maeve realized she was taking a long time standing there, hiding, and she forced herself to take a deep breath and enter the room. She plastered a pleasant smile on her face and carried the tray to the coffee table, avoiding both her host's eyes and her son's. Only her one son was there, the one probably injured, since he was sitting on the couch with exhaustion written clearly on his face.

She could feel a sudden tension in the room as the man stiffened in surprise. That was the only sign he gave that he recognized her. Maeve refused to let herself show any emotion at all.

"Thank you, dear," Elisa said, then gestured her to join them. Maeve wanted to make a run for it, but she couldn't deny her new friend and mentor. "This is my son, Ethan. Ethan, this is Maeve."

Ethan pushed aside his surprise and held out a hand. He leaned forward but didn't stand. Still, Maeve felt surprised he would even move that far in his state. "I'm pleased to meet your acquaintance." His hair was just slightly unruly, slightly spiked. He really was a handsome fellow, but Maeve hated him—more because of what he reminded her of.

When she took his hand—just intending to shake it—he turned it and kissed her knuckle. Maeve's breath caught and she once again felt as though she was thrown right into a Jane Austen novel. Handsome man, nice button-down shirt, nice old lady, tea and pastries, and a pathetic girl who became weak-kneed whenever men came around. What was her life?

Okay, not every girl in Austen's books was as pathetic as she felt currently, but most definitely fell head over heels for a man as nice-looking as this Ethan. One difference: Maeve didn't feel light-headed just because he was handsome. She feared she would collapse from the weight of memories.

No! She would not go there—no thinking. Not now, especially not in front of the Contens. She pulled her hand back as soon as she could without seeming desperate.

"Yes, yours as well, Mr. Conten. Elisa talks fondly of you." Elisa may have introduced him as Ethan, but she kept it formal—distant. She shivered, then felt relieved when Elisa sat on the couch next to her son, gripping his hand, allowing Maeve to sit in a chair across from them before her legs betrayed her. She held the inside of her chair, feeling the fabric, but her mind flashed back to alleys, the men, the darkness. The fear.

Maeve clenched her shaking fist and looked up to Elisa, focusing on her host's face to distract herself from her memories. Elisa was like an anchor to Maeve; whenever she found herself floundering, the lady was steady.

Slowly, her shivers repressed. She could breathe fully. However, she did not dare look Ethan in the eyes, afraid of what she'd see there—afraid it would toss her back to that terrible night.

Maeve forced herself into the conversation. "Where did your brothers go? I thought they were here."

Ethan looked at her, his eyes piercing and studying her. "Mason went to the bathroom. Fallon is just bringing my suitcase in and upstairs to my room."

As he spoke, another man came into the room, smiling. "Mom!"

Elisa stood immediately, exclaiming "Fallon!", and threw her arms around him. Fallon hugged her tightly.

"You okay, mom?"

"Sure am." She dragged him over to the couches. "Fallon, this is Maeve." Maeve stood to meet him.

Fallon took her hand but shook it rather than what his brother had done. "Pleasure to meet you. My mom really likes you here. Thanks for taking care of her." He winked at his mom.

Maeve laughed. "No, she's been taking good care of *me*. Your mother is amazing."

Elisa laughed as well, then another voice came in. "That I don't doubt. Mom is wonderful, and she can't help but take care of everyone who comes her way." Maeve saw one more man, obviously older than the two brothers, but smiling as well—though his smile seemed more strained.

"You're Mason, I suppose?" Maeve asked, shaking his hand.

"Yes, indeed." Mason smiled at her, then seemed to notice that Elisa and Fallon had sat beside Ethan, so he sat in the chair next to Maeve.

Maeve brushed out her dress, still trying her hardest not to look at Ethan, but she couldn't help but find that her gaze went toward him. Man, he really was handsome. Even on that first night of seeing him, while he got her out of danger, she had fallen in love with his eyes, automatically feeling safe in his arms. But why did seeing him have to bring back the bad memories too?

But she liked to see Elisa so happy with having her boys all there together.

"What about our sisters? Weren't they coming over?" Ethan asked suddenly.

"Oh, yes," their mom answered. "But we had been expecting you later, so when you called and said you were almost here, I told the girls. They said they'd be over in twenty-ish minutes." Elisa rubbed Ethan's arm. As she wasn't looking, Mason grabbed one of the cookies from the plate and started eating it. "Oh, honey, you're so pale. Are you doing okay?"

Ethan smiled weakly. "It's been a tough day," he admitted. "My body wasn't quite healed enough to be moving around that much, but I wanted to come home."

"I'm so glad you're here," Elisa told him, looking at all her boys. "Mason Conten! How many times have I told you to keep a plate under the cookies to stop crumbs? You're going to make a mess out of the floor Maeve vacuumed so well for me."

Maeve couldn't help it—despite her nervousness being among these people, she had an uncanny sense of security—she snorted, covered her mouth, and laughed. The statement was just so out of character with their discussion, but something Maeve expected from a loving family.

She immediately felt embarrassed as all their gazes turned to her, and she tried to stop laughing, but she was pretty sure her mind was releasing her tension in the only way she ever allowed herself to. It was either laugh, scream, or cry, and the latter two seemed far more humiliating.

Mason chuckled as he grabbed a plate. Elisa laughed as she patted Ethan's arm. Ethan was studying her with his intense gaze again. It made her uncomfortable and delighted at the same time. Ugh! She really was turning into one of those stupid girls that fell in love with their hero. How could it have happened to her?

Well, it didn't matter. She couldn't drag this poor man into her life. She turned away from Ethan and grabbed a teacup and saucer so she could pour some tea. "Does anybody want some? I have peppermint and pomegranate here, but I could go get some others." She half-stood, ready to pour some.

She noticed Ethan flash an amused look to his mom. He started to sit forward, but winced and relaxed. "Um, yeah." His face suddenly paled even more. "The pomegranate one for me, please, Maeve."

Maeve brought her eyes up to his, seeing the darkness in them that made her nervous. The sweat that started running down his face worried her. His eyes squeezed shut.

Elisa rubbed his arm, her eyes worried, but she seemed at a loss for what to say.

"Here, let me help you." Mason stood and put some of the cups together with saucers. "Who wants peppermint?"

"I'll take some," Fallon said, looking worriedly at Ethan.

"I want pomegranate," Elisa said quietly.

After Maeve and Mason finished pouring everyone tea, Maeve settled with her cookies.

"Dear, could you make one more pot?" Elisa asked her. "The girls will want some when they arrive." Maeve nodded, moved the cookies onto the coffee table, and grabbed the tray.

"I'll help," Fallon murmured, jumping to his feet. He went around the chairs and went to hold the door open for Maeve. She smiled at him in thanks.

Fallon let the door close and grabbed out more teabags before he spoke. "Thank you, Maeve. For helping our mother through this. It's no doubt been hard on her. You've been a blessing to her."

Maeve blushed and ducked her head. "You guys are so kind. She's helped me more than you can imagine."

Fallon put a hand on her arm, turning her. "I know this is a lot to ask you, but…" He sighed and looked to the door. "I won't be able to stay with Ethan all day, and Mason really shouldn't—he's already taken weeks off work. Mom wants Ethan here, for sure, but I think she doesn't understand how much help Ethan is going to need. Yes, she's cared for him before, but she's so much older now, and—"

Maeve put her hand on his arm. "Don't worry," she said before her mind could scream at her. "I promise I'll make sure he has everything he needs. I'm not against helping your brother. Just leave me a list, and I can make sure he's cared for."

Maeve found that the words didn't worry her as much as they should. Yes, she worried about the fact that she had immediately felt a draw to him. She didn't want to be a burden, and she still needed to go to the hospital and figure out what in the world was wrong with her. But despite all that, she cared for Elisa, and she had grown to care about Elisa's family by the way she talks about them. She wanted to help, even if she had to hide any fear or recognition of the youngest brother.

Fallon sighed, worry that had been weighing his shoulders seemed to disappear as his shoulders slumped in relief. "You're a lifesaver, Maeve. I'm not even kidding. I wish we could repay you for all you've done already."

Your family already has, she thought. She looked after Fallon as the brother walked back into the family room with the tray before Maeve could take it. She admired Elisa, the beautiful host and mother of these boys—boys who had taken her in without a second thought— then Ethan, the man who had saved her life. She remembered the conversation she had overheard between him and that man who'd attacked her—Santorini? Ethan had been trying to convince the man to leave her alone, to not kill her. She remembered the fear and cold and emptiness when Santorini had left her naked on the ground.

She remembered the slight hint of alarm in both voices, then she was being scooped up. Over time, after the event, she had managed to piece together what they had been saying. Santorini, wondering how the cops could have possibly found them. Ethan offering to take her out to the cops and pretend he was her rescuer. She'd learned since then that he'd been undercover and had been the one to call the cops, and knew that if he had blown his cover, they both would have been killed. So he'd done the only thing he could think of.

She remembered the pain when Ethan lifted her into his arms. She had tried to protest, to get out of his arms, but her body felt worn. She felt darkness crowd her vision. She saw the light blue of his eyes, meeting hers intensely, and how much she wished her eyes would open back up as Ethan spoke soft, cajoling words to her. She hadn't felt any embarrassment then, but now, when she thought back on that night, shame was one of the biggest feelings that swamped her. Under that, fear of Santorini and fear of what she felt about her rescuer.

And now that rescuer was here, right when she thought she was getting her mind off that night.

¤ ¤ ¤

Ethan could feel his hands shaking every time he brought the tea to his lips. The tea tasted amazing, of course. His mom knew exactly how he liked it. But the effort to move his hand to the cup, then the cup to his lips, made it so he only managed a couple small sips here and there. He closed his eyes as he managed another drink, letting it sit in his mouth for a moment before swallowing. He just wanted to go to bed. He was exhausted, completely worn out from the day. His body seemed to rebel with even the thought of moving to his bed. He wanted to crash, right there, right then.

As he thought, a wave of pain crashed over him so painful, he thought he would scream. He opened his eyes back up, immediately finding Maeve, since she sat across from him.

Maeve stunned him. The fact that the woman he had thought about continuously after Bullet forced himself on her was here, in his home, seemed like some sort of weird twist of fate—and he couldn't decide if that was good or bad.

But not only that, Maeve looked stunning. Beautiful. Breathtaking even. Staring at her seemed to calm the pain, so he continued to do so even if it became awkward. Luckily, she was right in front of him, so there was reason to stare at her.

That didn't stop her from staring at everything aside from him.

That wasn't true; she met his gaze and studied him enough, but Ethan couldn't see any hint of recognition in her eyes when she looked at him. Either she didn't remember him, or she was amazing at hiding emotions. Ethan hoped it was the former. He would hate to be a bad memory of that night.

Maeve laughed at something, though Ethan had been too zoned-out to know what. Her laugh, her joy, made him smile. How amazing that she could do so, so soon after Santorini…

He swallowed heavily, trying his hardest to push away the dark thoughts. Bullet did some terrible things; Ethan had known it but being with him sometimes made it hard to remember that fact. That night had proved Ethan's hopeful wishing that Bullet wasn't so bad wrong. He tried to shake the girl's—Maeve's—screams from his mind. He hadn't known what Santorini what to expect when Santorini had told him to meet him, but walking in on him assaulting a woman wasn't it. He had gone, thinking he would get something else good to tell Patricia, and instead ran into a "lesson" he never could have prepared himself for.

He had practically begged Bullet to stop when he showed up, as much as he could have while also playing a role, but the man wouldn't listen. And what could Ethan do? If Ethan had tried to pull him off her or attack, he'd have gotten himself killed; the two other men who had come with him would have killed him without thought—they both had guns.

Ethan…Ethan hadn't had a gun. He wished he had.

Instead, he'd dialed for the police on his phone while it was in his pocket. The police had gotten there within fifteen minutes, but too late to stop the screams and begging from being ingrained in his mind.

That had been his unraveling. He knew he couldn't keep the act up for long after that.

Fighting down fury, Ethan curled his fist slightly. He realized he was missing everything his family was talking about and tried to focus.

The front door opened, and Ethan craned his neck to see both sisters come in at once.

"Ethan!" Isabelle shouted gleefully. The younger of the two sisters, Riley, beat Isabelle to a hug, however.

Riley crouched beside him and threw her arms around him, sobbing into his shoulder. Riley had always been more of the crier in the family, so it didn't surprise him. He let her cry, rubbing her back and trying his hardest to swallow down pain that rose up. Wasn't it time for his next pills yet?

"Hey, I'm okay…" Ethan murmured.

Riley pulled back, sniffling. "I was so scared."

"I know. I'm sorry," Ethan told her sincerely. Then, feeling amused, he rubbed her arm, where a blotch of paint had gotten her. He smiled. Some things stayed the same. "Did you just come from painting?"

Riley looked at her arm, then laughed and wiped her eyes and leaned back so Isabelle could have a turn hugging him. "Didn't realize it. Just came straight to you."

Isabelle ruffled his hair as she leaned back. "Man, don't do that, Ethan. I don't think you realize how hard it is that you're hurt, and we can't come to see you. I could barely sleep."

Ethan laughed a little. "You barely sleep anyway."

Isabelle punched his shoulder. "No, don't even do that! You know what I mean."

Ethan rubbed his arm, wondering how many times he would get punched there today. He turned somber. "You're right. I'm sorry I didn't tell you guys where I was earlier. I was just worried."

Ethan found his gaze drawn back to Maeve. Riley was distracted, hugging their mom, but Isabelle followed his gaze, arched her eyebrows at Ethan, then hurried over to introduce herself.

Awkwardly, Ethan forced his eyes away from Maeve. Isabelle had always been the best at knowing when he—and anyone else—had a crush on someone. He hoped that Isabelle merely thought Maeve had done good taking care of their mother.

Honestly, Ethan didn't know what to think of Maeve. He thought she was beautiful, knew she got along well with his mom, was very thorough by the looks of the house. She also had recovered well from the rape, and Ethan had the urge to protect her from harm—but that wasn't surprising when remembering what he'd seen.

Ethan let his head fall back on the couch, listening to the murmur of his family talking. He didn't focus on any conversation, but he gathered that Isabelle's business was thriving lately. She was a seamstress, fixing people's clothes, and fitting suits and dresses to people. She also designed her own clothes, but hadn't sold much.

Riley had gotten her paintings into a local shop with pretty good business. Riley's belly had grown since he'd seen her last, telling him she was getting close. Her husband was an author, doing pretty well also.

A hand touched Ethan's shoulder maybe twenty minutes later. Ethan had fallen half-asleep but was too pained to fully drift off.

Ethan opened his eyes to see Mason over him. "Hey, bud. It's time for your meds now. Should we get you up to bed for a rest?"

Ethan looked at his family. He wanted to stay down with them and visit, but he was so tired, he could barely think.

Mom rubbed his arm. "Go get some rest, sweetheart. We'll visit with you later."

Ethan nodded and let Mason get under him to help him up.

Fallon moved quickly under Ethan's other side. Ethan hated being so dependent. He'd been dependent half his childhood, and he had hated it then as well. But after they learned what the problem was and he'd healed from the surgery to fix it, he hadn't been so dependent.

"I should come up too," Mom said, starting as if to stand, but Maeve beat her to it.

"It's okay, Elisa. I'll go with them. You visit with your girls." She smiled pleasantly, looking over all of them.

Elisa returned the smile and reached her hand to Maeve's. "Thank you, dear."

Maeve nodded as Elisa stood and gave Ethan another hug. "I'll see you when you get some rest, bud. Sleep well."

Ethan smiled. "Love you, Mom." Then he waited as his sisters quickly gave him hugs and assured him they'd see him tomorrow after work.

Then Mason and Fallon helped Ethan out of the room and struggled with him up the stairs. Maeve followed close behind and then slipped to the front to open the door to Ethan's room.

The room was much like he had left it. Ethan had always loved nature, so his room had about ten plants, and they had obviously been cared for since they were still alive.

The only plant that wasn't doing the best was his succulent. He looked at it then smiled. "Looks great in here." He got the reward of seeing Maeve blush as she turned away toward the succulent plant.

Maeve shrugged. "No matter how hard I try, I can't get this one to come back," she said, fingering the pot. "I've tried watering it more, and less, and putting it in the sun, and everything, but it won't come back for me. Maybe now that you're here, you can bring it back."

Maybe without knowing it, Maeve had cheered him up. He'd been upset about having to be dependent all over again, and she gave him a reason to be needed, even if it was small.

Ethan smiled. "That one is one of my favorites," Ethan told her. "My dad bought it for me when I graduated high school. It took me a while to figure out how to keep it alive and well, then turned out the be the easiest plants to care for."

Maeve laughed and turned back. "Oddly, that doesn't surprise me. Most problems have a simple answer, I swear."

"Let's get you situated," Mason told Ethan. He had almost forgotten about the fact that he was exhausted and that his brothers were still holding him.

"Yeah." Ethan looked at his brothers as they sat him on the bed. "Thanks, you guys."

Mason smiled at him. His face seemed strained still, worried. Ethan knew that it was time for Mason to get a break from worrying constantly over him. "It's not a problem, Ethan."

Fallon turned and grabbed hold of the pills Ethan had to take. "Could you get a glass and fill it up with water?" Fallon asked Maeve. She nodded, grabbed a cup and pitcher from the dresser that Ethan hadn't noticed until then. She brought the cup over and folded her hands when Fallon took it and handed the pills, then the cup to Ethan. Ethan swallowed it down quickly, hating how badly his hands trembled.

Then, after those two, followed four more pills. Ethan swallowed them down together. He knew he needed two of the painkillers, one to fight infection, and then some specific to helping him keep his nutrition, since his intestines had been shot.

Maeve watched them closely, her arms folded. Ethan found himself uncomfortable by her gaze, but he didn't want to tell her to leave.

"Pajamas?" Fallon pointed toward the dresser. Maeve jumped into action again, opening the correct drawer. *Man, she must have been shown the full rundown of the house*, Ethan thought.

Maeve held up a pair, one with a button down the shirt. "This one okay? I figured button-up might be easier than pull-over."

Ethan raised an eyebrow in surprise. Observant and intelligent. No wonder Mom loved her. "Yeah, wonderful."

Maeve nodded and unfolded the set. It was one that Ethan had cut the arms off—Ethan hated the arms on his sleep shirts.

Ethan started undoing the buttons on the shirt he wore with his trembling fingers. The constant shaking made it a lot harder to grasp, and Ethan couldn't help but be glad that Mason was helping him stay sitting up.

Mason helped him pull off his shirt. "I'll be back tomorrow morning to help you."

Ethan looked at him, narrowing his eyes. "Shouldn't you go to work?" But Ethan would need the help.

Before Mason could respond, Maeve spoke up. "I'll help you, Ethan." She looked at Mason. "I know you should be with your family and work and all that. I'm here anyway; I can do most of the stuff to help Ethan out by myself. I'm stronger than I look, and if you just write the medications and stuff down that he needs to take, I can handle it."

The three boys looked at her. Mason started to shake his head, but Ethan put a hand on his. "She's right, Mason. We can at least try it this way for a while. Between her and Mom, I'll be taken care of."

"Just leave me your number for emergencies," Maeve told him. "It won't be too difficult, I think."

Mason still hesitated, looking between them. Fallon nodded. "Mason, you've been caring for him constantly ever since he'd been hurt. Your family misses you a lot, and Owen will beg you to bring him over to see Ethan anyway; it's not like you'll be gone for long. Ethan is strong enough to stand on his own for a couple minutes. He'll be well enough with help from Maeve. She is a very competent young woman."

Ethan studied Maeve, sensing her uncomfortableness with the words. Ethan knew them to be true, there was plenty of evidence of it, but he wondered if she'd ever really been told so.

Ethan shook the thoughts from his head and reached for his pajamas. "I can do this," he said. He didn't really want to strip down in front of Maeve. "Fallon, can you get me…You know?" He didn't want to say undergarments so blatantly in front of a woman he barely knew. *Man, this was embarrassing.*

"Oh," Fallon nodded, turning to Maeve. "You can go out for this. We'll just help him get changed."

Maeve didn't move except to fold her arms again, a fire lighting in her eyes. "What, you think I wouldn't help someone just because it's uncomfortable? You wouldn't have left me—anyone—if they had gotten hurt." She started to stumble over her words, redness rising up her neck. "I mean, if I'm going to be helping you every day, I have to not be afraid of helping," she finished, less sure of herself. Her hands were tight on her arms, and her face was red with embarrassment. "I mean, it doesn't bother me, to help. Knowing your family, every one of you would have helped me if I'd needed it."

Ethan stared at her, mouth agape, suddenly sure that she *did* remember him from that night. She wouldn't meet his gaze now, suddenly uncomfortable; she had practically admitted he had helped her, though she changed it to a *would have*. He wanted to ask her, but he didn't know if she would appreciate anyone else knowing, and she looked so vulnerable at the moment.

Mason chuckled and teased. "That's true. You two expect her to help, but then suggest she shouldn't be here. Are you sure you don't want me to stay with you, Ethan? You can't be uncomfortable with your help."

Ethan cleared his throat, embarrassed. "Yeah, you're right. Sorry, Maeve; it's just weird."

Maeve nodded. "No, I…I understand."

Ethan looked at her and suddenly knew she truly did understand. She did remember that night, and she still felt embarrassed by it. Maeve's expression seemed to be asking Ethan if he would allow help in such a terrible situation because she still couldn't get past the fact that it had happened to her, and that he had been there to see it happen.

Mason got more serious after that though. "Ethan, if you're not comfortable with a female changing you, we can always make sure to be here, or mom, of course. She is willing to help, but that doesn't mean she has to."

"No, really, I'm okay. I've already had the nurses help me at the hospital anyway."

To his relief they helped him change as quickly as possible, and Mason started writing out instructions Maeve would need to know and any numbers that she could call if there was an emergency. Mason pulled her over. "This one is Mygyer's number, Ethan's boss. If there is any problem that's not medical, if you notice people following you or anything out of the ordinary like that, call him."

Maeve nodded in understanding. "Ethan knows all this, so you should be fine, but if you do have any questions, you can call either one of us. Make sure you check in on him a good amount, and make sure he tells you if he feels off—he'll probably try to pretend he's fine all the time, so you'll have to start paying attention to little things that give him away."

"Hey!" Ethan protested.

Mason waved away the interruption, smiling. "If he gets tired, make sure he rests. Don't let him walk around for more than a couple minutes at a time, especially by himself. He'll protest it, but if he wants or needs to go anywhere outside the house, we brought a wheelchair and a walker home that he can use. It would be good for him to use them even around the house, but my brother is stubborn, and I don't actually expect him to do so."

"I noticed that," Maeve confirmed, glancing at Ethan in amusement. Ethan wondered if it was because of all the details, or the fact Ethan had let out a gasp of offense, even though Mason was right.

Mason hesitated a moment, running a hand through his hair. "Now, I'm going to tell you this because I think someone who stays here should know. I don't think my mom could handle this if she knew, but I believe you're in control, you can handle the information."

Ethan looked sharply at his brother. "Mason, don't you dare!"

Mason waved off his complaint, looking at him. "Ethan, if I'm not going to be here, someone has to know."

Ethan shook his head, eyes wide. Maeve may look strong and like she can handle it, but Ethan couldn't forget her fear on that night. If she knew someone might try and find him…Could she handle it?

Mason peered into Maeve's eyes. "Some people might try and track Ethan here, Maeve. That's why I need you to pay extra attention to any suspicious people you see. Be vigilant. And don't be afraid to talk about anything you see."

Maeve blanched, looking at Ethan. "That's awful…Okay. I can do that."

Ethan sighed, deflating, suddenly exhausted. Maeve was playing it careful, not wanting to say anything. Right now, Ethan didn't care. He just wanted to go to bed and escape this day.

Maeve tilted her head, studying him. "I think he's ready for bed," she told Mason and Fallon. Both his brothers followed her gaze, then moved to set up the blankets and pillows for him to lie down.

They left soon after, each giving their own version of good night, and Maeve telling him her room was the guest room down the hall. Ethan was left alone to stare up at the ceiling, unable to sleep despite exhaustion. Sun filtered in, even with the blinds and curtains closed, and Ethan just couldn't get comfortable. The pain wasn't bad now, but he was just super uncomfortable.

Then he realized what the real problem was. Maeve continued to stay on his mind. Both the good and the bad—that night, the screams, but also, her gentleness and beauty.

How could she be so happy and independent after all that had happened?

He must have drifted off eventually because he awoke with a jerk, his hands flying to the side as he sat up. The sharp movement concerned him as his side gave a throb. His thoughts had followed him to his sleep, the screams continued to haunt him. He couldn't shake the picture from his mind. A whimper escaped him, and he rubbed his face before looking around. He'd slept for a couple hours; it was now dark.

There was a soft rap on his door. Ethan took a deep breath to calm himself before calling out a soft welcome.

It was Maeve. She peeked her head in first. "Just checking in. You okay?"

Ethan hesitated, suddenly unable to comprehend how this same woman was with him now. Why would God want her to be in his life some more, and vice versa? He was grateful to her, yes, but…why couldn't it be some other woman who took the job—one who hadn't been there that night. Every time he looked at her, he thought about what happened.

Ethan looked over to the clock, seeing with blurry eyes that it was now eleven at night. He'd slept longer than he thought.

"Ethan?" Maeve persisted.

Ethan blinked, forcing himself out of his thoughts. "I'm alright…could you do me a favor?"

"Of course." Maeve entered the room. "What's up?"

"In the hospital, they had me sitting up on pillows. It felt more comfortable sitting up like that. Do you know where my mom keeps pillows?"

"Yes." Maeve gave a little smile and nodded. "I'll go get some now." She went down the hall quickly, in the darkness. She must be good at navigating the house already. There was a light on in the bathroom down the hall, but the door was mostly closed.

She came back in mere moments with probably seven pillows. Ethan blinked—he'd been expecting one or two extras. Not seven.

She turned on the light, then noticed his expression and laughed. "I'm sorry—you said 'some pillows.' I figured I'd bring as many as I could carry, get you comfortable, and maybe have a couple others. I've found that having a pillow to grip helps me keep calm at night." She added the last part quieter, blushing, but meeting his eyes through her eyelashes, with a sort of half-teasing, half-serious tone. "Or you can scream in it if you want."

Ethan chuckled a little, knowing that's what she wanted, but really, he was disturbed. He opened his mouth to ask Maeve about that night, or about the obvious nightmares, but snapped it shut before he could. He wasn't ready to know yet, wasn't ready to open that wound.

"Thanks, Maeve," he told her instead.

Maeve nodded and brought the pillows around, starting to slip some around him in different positions, some behind his back, others behind his head, and some under his arms. He let her finish up, watching her finish her careful process. When she sat back on the bed, sitting on her legs, she smiled at him.

"Try that."

Ethan looked at her setup. "I don't want to mess it up," he joked, flashing a smile.

Maeve laughed. "Oh, trust me. You do. Just try it."

Ethan complied, somehow calmer now than he had been before she'd come in. Her very presence seemed to calm him.

He adjusted slightly, but then sighed. "This is heavenly," he admitted, looking over at her.

Maeve gave a little celebratory clap, happiness shining in her eyes. "Great!" Then she passed over one last pillow. "Now put this one on your chest and shoulder, but under your head like this." She showed him herself, then handed it to him. "Then, if you don't want your head straight back, you can rest if here, and it doesn't kink your neck."

Ethan hugged the pillow to his chest and tilted his head to let it rest on it. "Mmm…it feels great. Maeve, you're a miracle worker."

Maeve grinned. "I used to sleep with pillows around me like that all the time. I just know how to be comfortable." She frowned suddenly.

"What?" Ethan asked, concerned.

"I just realized I'll have to hunt for more pillows so I can give myself a throne as well." She pouted and poked his arm. "I know there are more in the bathroom closet."

"A throne?" Ethan snickered, squirming amongst his pillows. "I like it. Now, I am a king. Oh, won't you join me, My Queen?"

Maeve laughed. "Alright, sleep well, Your Highness. I should be getting to bed. You know, I've gotta keep up with the chores around the castle tomorrow."

"Isn't that the job of the servants?" Ethan asked, not even caring that he sounded childish playing along with Maeve. They were joking around, and it was calming him down, so he didn't care.

"Only of the incompetent queens," Maeve told him, tossing her hair over her shoulder. "Can I get you anything else before I get to bed?"

Ethan smiled. "No, I'll be fine. Thank you, Maeve. I feel a lot better now."

"Good." Maeve jumped off the bed. "Call me if you need me."

~8~

Maeve found herself sitting across from Ethan a couple days later, having built herself a "throne" at the end of his bed. Staring at him as he smiled and laughed, Maeve found it hard to focus on his words half the time. Her mind kept flashing back to that night she first saw him, and she had to force herself to focus on him now, not then. He was very nice, something she hadn't had much time to notice that first night.

Ethan sat up in his pillows a little, staring at her. "Think we can play a game?"

Maeve had been distracting Ethan by asking questions about growing up, though now it seemed Ethan ran out of things to say.

"Sure. What do you want to play?"

Ethan shrugged. "Just something fun."

Maeve nodded and quickly shifted off the bed to head for the game closet in the hall. Maeve couldn't help but feel comfortable around Ethan; he had the same charm as his mother, and she was pleased he hadn't mocked her about making him a "throne" and play-pretending that he was a king. Instead, he had played along with her. Amused, yes, but not dissuaded.

Maeve smiled to herself. She couldn't believe how much she got along with Ethan, not when she knew he was her rescuer, and she knew *he* knew. She was pretty sure he kept wanting to ask about it; he'd pause occasionally and open his mouth, but then shut it and ask her about something else. Maeve was relieved he didn't tell anyone else about what had happened to her and that he hadn't brought up the subject with her. It would be a lot harder to stay not awkward around him if he approached her with the conversation she kept dreading. She hadn't even called the agents who had suggested she move to Kansas, though one of the ladies at the hospital in Chicago had called just to ask if she'd had her monthly. Maeve still hadn't called back, but she planned to go to the hospital here to figure out why she hadn't had one.

She grabbed the first two-player game she saw, *UNO*. She hadn't played that game since she ran from her foster home. It would be fun to play with Ethan, and it was not a game that needed lots of instruction like the rest of the games in the closet.

Maeve went back into the bedroom to find Ethan standing on his own, leaning on the nightstand next to his bed.

"What are you doing?" Maeve gasped, throwing the game onto the bed as she neared the stubborn man. "You're not supposed to be standing up on your own."

Ethan waved away her complaint, smiling. "I'm alright, only be up a moment. I just have to run to the bathroom before our game." He looked at the bed. "*UNO*?"

"Would you rather something else?" Maeve asked him, coming closer and grabbing his arm. Ethan shook his head, eyebrows furrowing.

"*UNO* is fine." He met her gaze. "Did you know you're very beautiful?" he asked suddenly.

Maeve stepped back, eyes narrowing. "What?"

"You're beautiful," Ethan repeated.

"Uh…" Maeve swallowed. She didn't know what to say.

Ethan grabbed her hands. "Just wanted to make sure you knew that. Do you hear it often?"

"Well…" Maeve looked to the door. "Your mom has told me before, I guess. She's really sweet."

Ethan grinned at her. "She never lies. I'm glad you're here. You're just…great to be around."

Maeve cleared her throat, looking at their clasped hands, and then she awkwardly pulled her hands from his. "You better go to the bathroom before you lose your strength." Surely he was mistaken; she carefully touched her hand to her hair as Ethan turned to the bathroom. He held himself tall, but slightly to one side, and he moved slowly. Maeve knew she should follow him, make sure he was alright, but instead, she turned to the mirror on the dresser, looking at herself.

When she was younger, her parents had always told her that she was beautiful, but after they died, and she'd lost the only two who would encourage her, and she was left with lot of doubt. She would tell herself she was beautiful, but she slowly lost that faith in that.

Had she ever believed she was as stunning as Elisa and Ethan said she was? For years she had pretended to believe it, not wanting anyone to see her insecurities, but eventually she stopped caring.

Until she'd come to live with Elisa. Now, she knew Elisa thought of her as beautiful. But she was an old lady, and she was sweet. She'd say that to everyone. Now Ethan was saying the same to her…Could she believe it?

Her fingers were still in her hair. She studied the color, unsure. It was mostly blonde, with a bit of a red to it. Was it pretty?

She heard the toilet flush and water turn on, and she jerked herself out of her thoughts. It didn't matter if he did think she was pretty or not.

She pushed open the bathroom door. "You doing okay?"

Ethan looked over at her as he dried his hands on the towel. "Not going to tip over, if that's what you mean."

She laughed. "Good. I don't know if I can get you all the way up from the ground if you go toes-up."

Ethan snorted. Maeve felt proud when she made him laugh; it chased the shadows from his eyes, and showed his dimples that intrigued her.

She was planning to clean up the house today, but Elisa had told her she'd be out with some friends for dinner, and she wanted her to just keep Ethan company instead. Maeve had agreed, albeit reluctantly. She enjoyed Ethan and all, but the more time they spent together, the closer they'd get to talking about the man who'd attacked her and the rest of that night. Maeve still didn't understand what had happened to her, fully, but it had left her feeling embarrassed every time she thought about it.

Ethan stepped closer and plucked a hair that had fallen from her braid, pushing it back behind her ear. "Did you do the braid?" he asked, meeting her eyes. Maeve swallowed hard, suddenly dry mouthed.

"No. Your mom did. I told you, she's amazing; she can get it finished within a minute. I swear it takes me at least ten with all this hair." She picked up the end of her braid to her back and turned so she could slip under his side, since he was starting to tilt a little more again.

"I have a question," Ethan said.

Maeve's heart skipped a beat, worried—as she was every time he asked her anything. "What's that?"

"Could we walk in the garden for a couple minutes, and go sit out there on the benches?"

Maeve frowned. "Do you think you can handle the stairs with me? It might be better if I go get the wheelchair for the walk."

Ethan frowned. "Aw, come on. It's a short walk—I did more walking than that on the way to the house."

"You also had two brothers to pretty much carry you," Maeve pointed out. Ethan paused.

"Good point. But I'll be fine, Maeve. Come on, it's pretty outside in the garden. My mom still takes good care of it." He tilted his head and looked at her. "Or is that all you?"

Maeve smiled. "Nah, the garden is one thing Elisa likes to do herself still. She goes out every day to weed and collect anything that needs to come in. I help a bit, but I don't know plants much. For all I know, I could be pulling out strawberries instead of the weeds."

"I could teach you if you want," Ethan said in all seriousness.

Maeve poked him. "Doubt we have the time before your mom gets home. I'm sure she'll want to visit with you. And Mason said he was bringing Owen over, remember?" She personally didn't want to remind him of his limitations at the moment.

Ethan's face fell into a pleasant smile. "Oh, yeah. Are you sure you're up to us two rambunctious boys?"

Maeve snorted. "Yeah, right. You're not going anywhere."

Ethan pulled her close, looping her arm around his. Maeve nearly gasped at the movement but managed to keep it down. She was playful with Ethan, and Ethan only played back, but sometimes he startled her. It didn't help that she was already hard on breath with being as close as she had been, this position was far more romantic.

"Please, let's go on a walk," he begged. Obviously, Maeve couldn't say no. Not when he looked at her with his blue, begging eyes.

"Alright," she agreed reluctantly. "But if Mason kills us, he better kill you first so I have a chance to run."

Ethan squeezed her hand playfully. "He won't kill either one of us. He worries, but he won't bite. I think you're growing on him." He looked thoughtful. "Actually, I think you're growing on my whole family."

Maeve blushed. "I like them a lot." She changed the subject. "Do you want to change before we go out?"

Ethan looked down at his pajamas. "No. It's in the backyard anyway. I don't want to spend all my strength changing."

Maeve and Ethan spent the next hour or so walking the grounds, sitting on benches, studying plants, and talking about life. She redirected any questions that might lead to sharing more about the last few years of her life, which had been in and out of homeless shelters. Ethan learned about her parents' deaths when she was thirteen, about how much she loved them, but nothing more."

"To be honest, I've kind of forgotten how it is to be with people I care about," she admitted to him. "I loved my parents a lot, even though they were so busy most of the time. I felt like I barely saw them. Then, they were gone, I guess I was mostly on my own since then. Then your mom let me stay here…These weeks have completely changed me. I got a place to stay and a friend all rolled up in one. I can never repay your mom."

Ethan took her hand then, his eyes unwavering on hers. "I think my mom would say the same about you. I definitely do…We're so glad she had someone with her through all this, and now helping me…I am amazed by you, and I know I never could pay you back."

Maeve leaned back against the shed, staring at the trees. "I think that's it. We've been talking about how we can pay people back. When you do one thing for someone, you expect something in return, you know? But really, it's not about that. It's about sharing what you're good at with another person you care about. We don't have to worry about paying someone back because, in reality, you'll never be able to. Everything you do has a different 'price' depending on the person perceiving it."

Maeve wouldn't forget Ethan's eyes as she spoke, the admiration and understanding that he displayed. He didn't need to say a word.

At that moment, she wondered if she would ever have a chance with him. A part of her wondered why he would ever consider dating her, but the other part just prayed she would have a chance. Maybe when he was healed and wasn't relying on her for everything. And maybe if they could ever talk about their connected past.

Mason and his family found them outside about an hour later. They had found a bench with the shed as a backrest. Ethan wasn't too badly off, but he still leaned a little on Maeve—which she liked more than she would admit—and had seemed relieved when they sat.

As Mason's family drew close, a boy who looked about ten ran in front. "Uncle Ethan!"

"Owen!" Ethan scooted to the front of the bench so he could give Owen a big hug. "Man, I swear you've grown five inches since I've seen you!"

Owen laughed but stood tall, looking to his dad. "Have I, Dad?"

"Well, let's see here," Mason said, coming forward and laying a hand on Owen's hair, a thoughtful look in his eyes. "I think you have grown some." He winked at Ethan.

Owen beamed at Ethan. "Well, it's no surprise. I haven't seen you in ages!" Owen said. "Dad says you got hurt. How? Where?"

Ethan ruffled the boy's hair. "Sure did. I got shot." Mason's wife—at least, Maeve assumed—put their daughter on the ground.

"Go get Uncle Ethan," she murmured. Ethan heard the command, so he slid to crouch on the ground with a little wince and spread his arms wide for the little girl to crash into.

"Dang," Ethan said with some pain and plenty of amazement in his voice. "She's grown a bit too."

Mason helped him stand back up and Ethan hugged his sister-in-law. "Been awhile. I've missed you," he told her, then gestured to Maeve. "Have you met Maeve yet?"

Mason's wife looked at her and held out her hand. "No, but I've heard a lot about her. I'm Tyra."

Maeve stood and shook her hand. "Nice to meet you, Tyra."

"I'm Owen," Owen interjected, holding his out as well, though he held it high above him since he was small.

Maeve grinned and shook it. "Good to meet you, Owen. How old are you?"

Owen shook her hand enthusiastically. "Eleven, almost." Then Owen tugged on Ethan's shirt. "Where did you get shot? I want to see."

Ethan laughed. "You won't see much; I'm wearing a bandage."

"So?" Owen pouted.

Ethan shrugged and pulled up his shirt, revealing the bandage. Owen frowned. "But I want to *see* it." Maeve studied Ethan's chest, trying hard not to admire his body. *Fail.* She wondered if he had to be in such good shape for his FBI training or if he just tried to be anyway.

Ethan pulled Owen into a side hug and let the shirt fall. "I'll tell you what. When I've got to change the bandage, I'll let you see it."

"Ethan!" Tyra interjected sharply.

"What?" Ethan asked, looking at Tyra with a nearly identical look of bewilderment that Owen did.

"I don't need my son to see such things."

"Oh, come on, Mom! It's not like it's still bleeding or anything." Owen grabbed Ethan's hand. "Please?" Maeve fought a smile of amusement, meeting Tyra's gaze.

"How are you doing?" Mason asked Ethan, gripping his shoulder.

Ethan shrugged. "Better today. Maeve has been great company." He looked over at her, grinning and giving her a smile. "Been treating me like a king. Even made me a throne."

"Is that so?" Mason arched an eyebrow, looking at her. Embarrassed, Maeve blushed.

"Well, I mean, yeah. I made one for myself also," she said nervously.

"King and queen?" Mason asked, amused. Ethan gave a sort of nod.

"Oh dear," Tyra jumped in. "Get married without telling us?"

Ethan's jaw dropped. Maeve felt her face heat even further.

Mason chuckled at them, then turned more serious. "You haven't forgotten about your check-up tomorrow morning, right?"

Ethan paused, thinking. "Um…no?" he said unconvincingly.

Mason punched his shoulder softly. "At ten. Come on, Ethan. How am I going to ever leave you alone?"

Off-handedly, Maeve shrugged. "*I* remembered it." In fact, Maeve planned to get checked up at the same time—kill two birds with one stone. She really didn't want to, she didn't want the fuss, and part of her didn't even want to know if something was wrong, but she figured she better get it over with. She got nauseous a lot these days, and she was pretty achy.

Mason pulled her into a side hug, surprising her. "Good, at least Ethan has someone responsible with him."

"Hey! What's that supposed to mean?" Ethan asked good-naturedly.

Mason rolled his eyes. "Alright, Tyra. I suppose we better get going. Maeve, are you sure you're okay with Owen staying?" The worry in his eyes was surprising. Owen had really wanted some time with his uncle, but both Tyra and Mason had work. He had already asked her if she'd be okay with it.

"Of course, Mason. It'll be fine."

"Bye!" Owen rushed forward to give his mom and dad a hug, not giving them time to argue more.

Mason looked at Maeve again. "If these two give you too much trouble, call me and I'll ground them for a month."

"I'm already grounded to my bed if I don't have a supervisor," Ethan pointed out. "Does that disqualify me?"

"No." Maeve glared at him playfully. "I'll just retract any allowance of you leaving your room."

Mason and Tyra laughed, and a smile tugged on Ethan's lips. Maeve raised her eyebrows daringly to Ethan.

"Nevermind then," Mason murmured as he started away with his wife. "You don't need my help; you have this completely under control."

Maeve, oddly, found herself pleased.

As Mason left, Maeve turned toward Ethan. "Speaking of: It's about time to go in to change your bandages and give you your pills."

Ethan sighed. "Yeah, I guess so." But then he wrapped an arm around Owen. "Help your uncle out, won't you? I need a hand inside."

"Sure," Owen said enthusiastically.

Maeve smiled, amused by the little boy. Mason had asked if Maeve would be okay keeping an eye on Owen because the boy had wanted to visit with Uncle Ethan. Maeve didn't mind at all. She liked kids, and Owen turned out to be adorable, obviously adoring his uncle. And Ethan seemed to brighten around the boy.

Maeve slipped under Ethan's other side, shaking her head with amusement.

They made it back up to Ethan's room without a problem, and Ethan sat on his bed. Maeve grabbed the pills he had to take, poured some water, then moved over to Ethan and gave him both. Ethan swallowed them all down at once, then pulled Owen to his side. "Want to see?"

Owen looked sort of nervous but ready. "Yes."

"Maeve? Do the honors?"

Maeve gently pulled up Ethan's shirt, then pulled the bandage off before grabbing new gauze, tape, and the gooey stuff that Ethan used on it. Maeve didn't know what it was; it didn't have a sticker on it to tell her. But it essentially kept it clean.

"Whoa." Owen leaned forward, studying Ethan's stomach. He'd had a hole to the left, then a long gash down the center of his stomach, essentially traveling all the way down from his ribs to his belly button, now held together with the stitches. "That looks so weird."

Ethan grinned, tussling the boy's hair. "It does, doesn't it?"

"Why do you have two? The hole and the long slash?" Owen's eyes crinkled.

"The hole is from the bullet. The slash is where the doctors cut so they could get all the pieces removed from me and clean me up." Ethan closed his eyes a moment as Maeve changed the bandage, and Maeve knew that it stung a little from the tense expression.

"It's so crazy what doctors can do," Owen said. "To be able to get in you like that and help you…It's so weird. Kind of gross too." Suddenly Owen brightened. "I want to be a doctor! I want to help the good guys, like you, Ethan! I want to make people feel better after they've helped save the world."

Ethan looked amused, yet also honored. "That's a great career choice," he said. "A respectable doctor."

"Respectable?" Owen's eyebrows drew together.

"Yes. A kind doctor. One that listens and loves, you know?"

"Oh." Owen nodded eagerly at Ethan's words. "Yes, a respectable doctor."

"Okay, doctor," Maeve said to Owen. "How about you help me with this?"

Maeve looked between Ethan and his mom from where she sat in the back seat of the car. His mom was driving them to the clinic. Maeve was glad she wasn't taking Ethan alone because it would be way harder for her to disappear for her own check-up if she had to stay with him the whole time.

Elisa was maintaining the conversation in the front. Maeve didn't mind because she only kept worrying about what could be wrong with her.

She found herself tuning back into the conversation when Elisa started talking about the dinner party from last night. "Oh, I wish you could have gone, dear," Elisa said, reaching over to pat Ethan. "All the ladies were asking about you. A lot of them have heard that you'd gotten injured, about you getting shot while on patrol and all. They all wanted to make sure you're okay." Elisa squeezed his hand. "Sylvia, Kat, and Iris especially." Maeve felt a rush of alarm at the words, not liking the idea. She pushed the emotion away immediately.

Ethan groaned, looking at Elisa. "Mom, I know they're sweet and cute and all, but they're way too pushy! I don't like them like that."

Elisa laughed. "Oh, honey. I know you don't like them like that. But one of these days, you're going to find a girl who'll keep you out of trouble, won't you?"

Ethan smirked and met Maeve's gaze in the side mirror, but she looked away, toward Elisa. "I don't know. If I find someone, I guess. Right now, you and Maeve are doing a fine job."

Elisa winked at Maeve in the mirror. Jeez, she wasn't safe to look at either of them. "She is an amazing young woman, isn't she?"

Ethan looked back at Maeve as she felt herself blush. "Yeah. She is." He stared at her.

Maeve shifted uncomfortably, putting her hands between her legs. The way Ethan stared at her sometimes unsettled her.

Luckily, Elisa went right on talking, once again going into how when she and her husband had met, how it took a while for them to admit feelings, especially on her end. Since Maeve had heard this story a few times now, she kind of stopped listening as they drove. Instead, she found herself wondering where she would be if that man hadn't attacked her. If she hadn't been rescued by Ethan, she wouldn't have moved, found a job, and met his wonderful family. She'd likely still be out on the streets and in shelters. Being homeless had been both bad and easy at the same time. It hadn't been a good environment for her—wasn't necessarily good for anyone, but some people managed it better than others. But she hadn't had to try for anything except sit on the side and hold a cardboard sign, or wander and ask for odd-end jobs, or go between houses and shelters that the government and people let her use sometimes.

However, it had been a good learning experience. Would she go back and change it if she could? Now that she knew that it led to these people, she wasn't so sure. She had learned well how to watch out for herself—even if that hadn't helped her the night she'd been… raped. She had still been in shock and pain when they had talked; Maeve knew she didn't understand or even hear most of the conversation.

She had also learned that when she eventually got a job and a place to call home, she would always try her hardest so she could keep it.

Maeve blinked in surprise as she realized she *wouldn't* trade the experiences. She really enjoyed the family, and even looking back on that night, it was just…a change for the better after the downfall. She was starting to look at it like the night of the rescue, no longer the attack. The other man didn't matter anymore. Only Ethan and his family.

Maeve looked at Ethan, smiling. She never thought she would need a hero. She'd always been independent due to her time one the streets. She used to grimace at the idea of some hero sweeping in and rescuing her from the tower. She thought the characters were rather disappointing if they couldn't do things for themselves and needed a Prince Charming to save them. One reason she scoffed at so many romance books was that most of the time the girl became totally dependent on a man and had to be rescued in the end.

Now she realized that it doesn't matter what situation you're in, or how bad or good life is. You'll hit that downfall and need a friend to help you get back on your feet.

She relaxed against the seat, allowing the wonderment of what it might feel like to let herself fall in love with Ethan. Or, at the least, to let herself love this family.

But the thing was, she already had fallen, or was falling, in love with Ethan. Could she admit it aloud though? That part she didn't feel so sure about. And what if it was just some sort of hero complex?

But she wanted to admit it. It was so strange to feel love for and from others, and to feel like she belonged somewhere again. She hadn't shared about her parents dying with anyone for years, but Ethan listened to her, and the way he looked at her made her think she might be something more than just a caretaker or job to him.

The thought made her feel giddy.

Maeve looked out the window, relieved to see the clinic. She wanted to know what was wrong with her—she shouldn't have waited so long, and she shouldn't have lied about not having her cycle.

"Maeve, will you help Ethan?" Elisa asked as she pulled up to the front.

"Yep." Maeve nodded and slid to the other side, pulling her door open.

She went to the front as Ethan pulled open his door, to help him out. Really, Ethan did most by himself, even if he wasn't at his strongest yet, and he used a crutch for his injured leg. Maeve felt relieved that he seemed to be doing better, even if he was still slow and in pain.

Instead of slipping under Maeve, Ethan merely grabbed her hand, giving his small, amused smile. As soon as the door shut and Elisa pulled away to park, he spoke: "How many times have you heard the story of my mom and dad meeting by now?"

Maeve chuckled, glancing back at the car. "Maybe three times," she replied, leaning close and looking down. Her hair fell from behind her ear. "I don't mind. Elisa loves talking about it."

"That she does." Ethan chuckled, then winced. "Think the painkillers are wearing off."

"Painkillers suck," Maeve said decidedly.

"Yeah, but the pain may suck even more." Ethan thought for a moment. "My mom's not a very big believer in the medicine idea. She thinks they're too addictive for what they're worth. I mostly agree with her. But having this pain wouldn't be fun, so I'll take it anyway."

"They have too many side effects," Maeve agreed. "But you're right. Having to decide which you'd rather have, the pain or the drugs…" She stopped talking as they entered the hospital doors that slid open smoothly. She saw a sign near the front, directing them to the different places, and led Ethan toward the rehab side, eyeing the arrow for the women care as she did so.

Maeve waited as Ethan checked in and got him to the outpatient rehab facility. Elisa had gotten there just a couple minutes before he was called back, so Maeve smiled at them. "I'll be back a little later."

She left before they could comment, going out to the women's side. She'd had a chance to meet with a doctor and nurse when she first moved here, introduced as doctors she could come to from the agent that helped her get settled. She hoped they would remember her and that they'd be here.

The lady at the desk greeted her. "Hi. How can we help you?"

"I'm looking for either doctor Crance or Nurse Tiff—uh Tiffany, I think was her name. My name is Maeve. I came in once a bit ago, and they were…"

She didn't seem to mind her trail off. "They're both in, and I think they're free. I'll go get them for you. What are you here for?"

"A, uh… check-up."

The receptionist just nodded and stood, holding a clipboard with paper as she did so. "If you could work on filling this out the best you can while you wait, that would be great."

"Thanks." Maeve took it, then sat and started to do so.

After a couple long minutes, she heard footsteps and saw Dr. Crance step out. "Maeve, it's good to see you again. How are you doing? What can we help you with?"

"I was hoping for a check-up, doctor." She took a deep breath. "Agent Kinnik said I could come here if I needed to."

"Of course, let's head back," he agreed.

As soon as they settled in the room, Dr. Crance gestured for her to sit on the patient chair, and he to the rolling chair to sit in front of her. "What's seems to be the problem?"

Maeve decided to just jump straight into it, pulling every ounce of courage together in a hope that her voice came out steady. "I haven't had her menstrual cycle since I got to Kansas. A couple months now." *Not since I was raped,* was her frantic thought she tried to not let show.

"I see." Dr. Crance took a deep breath. "And how have you been feeling?"

"Mostly okay, but I have been feeling a little nauseous. Achy and tired…" She didn't let herself formulate why that might be.

"Is it a new thing? Is there any reason you didn't come in earlier?"

"It's been getting a little worse for about a month now." She rubbed her chilled arms. "I mean, I didn't even notice I missed a month, but I had an agent call to check up on me and she had me wondering, and…well…" She trailed herself off for a moment. "I've been so busy, so I didn't try to take the time to come in earlier, but I know I needed to."

"Alright, I think it'll be good to get you set up for a few tests then, and then I can answer any questions you may have."

Maeve agreed, anxious to get this over with and get back to Ethan. She suddenly wanted his soothing presence with her—he always seemed to dispel the sadness and worry in her.

"'Kay. Come with me." He nodded soothingly to her, and Maeve followed him to a room down the hall with a hospital bed. He had her sit as he called out the door for a nurse.

"You've met Tiff before. She's going to draw some of your blood, alright?"

"Sure." Maeve nodded shakily.

"Good to see you again, Maeve." Nurse Tiff said warmly, instantly calming some of her nerves. Maeve took a deep breath as she took her arm and gently slid the needle in the underside of her elbow. She watched as it filled with blood, her brain swirling as she thought of answers she didn't really want to have.

"Great. Tiff, could you get that to testing right away?"

"Of course." Tiff agreed, looking between the two of them before taking her leave.

Crance nodded, then went on explaining the use of the menstrual cycle, the reason for it. How it was her body's way of shedding the lining in her, prepping her. He was very matter of fact, which helped with any awkwardness, and it was more of an explanation than she'd really had before, but it didn't help with the dreadful feeling in her gut that she knew what was coming.

Before Dr. Crance could finish explaining, nurse Tiff came back into the room, holding a clipboard.

"Do you understand all of that?" Crance asked Maeve.

"Yeah, I do," she whispered. "But I just don't understand.... I mean, it was so quick, how could I..."

"Become pregnant?" Nurse Tiff was the one that finally said the words that terrified Maeve.

Maeve hadn't been trying! She hadn't wanted to bring a child into this world. How was it fair that she could get pregnant due to someone else hurting her?!

She felt as though all color left her face at the thought of that night, images flashing through her brain—she couldn't stop them.

Rape was so ugly—how could babies come out of such a situation?

Suddenly, Maeve started to cry. She buried her face into her hands as she sobbed. She'd been feeling so good, doing so good with these people. What would the Contens think if they knew she was pregnant?

What if this baby turned out to be like his father? What if he…she…it—was a murderer of hope, like the one who'd assaulted her? What if she couldn't raise the child? Her life had consistently gone wrong; what if she ended up homeless again, but with a kid?

Maeve heard movement but was barely aware of it. A hand lay on her shoulder, and she was pulled into an embrace. She didn't care to see who had left and who had stayed, she just let herself cry. She would have to pull herself together when she got back to Elisa and Ethan, but until then, she didn't know how to stop. She felt all the energy and happiness drain out of her.

After several minutes, she started to calm down. She looked up to see that it had been Tiff who had stayed with her—which she had kind of guessed from the size.

Tiff gave her a sympathetic small smile, her hands on each of her arms as she rubbed soothingly. "I know it seems like the end of the world, sweetheart. I know the last thing you want me to tell you is that all will be okay. But what I want you to know is that I'll be here for you every step of the way. Any questions you have, I'll be there to talk. Any time you feel off, I'll be there to check on you and make sure you and your baby are okay. You're not alone in this. Do you have family or anyone you can be with that you'll tell?"

Maeve hesitated, wiping her eyes. "Um…I don't know. I have some I can tell, but I…I don't know them well enough, you know?"

"Do you want me to break the news to them?"

Maeve shook her head carefully. "No. I need to figure out a way to tell them." She swallowed.

Tiff patted her hand and reached into her vest, pulling out a card. "Here, sweetheart. This is my number. I want you to call me if anything at all happens, or if you have any questions. Any time, don't worry about waking me up or anything, I will be here for you."

Maeve looked at her. "Thanks…a lot." She took the card and put it into her pocket as she stood. She felt her hands trembling, so she folded her arms.

Tiff stood beside her. "I don't know if you'll want to do this now, but we do need to get you in for a check-up so we can check on the baby, make sure it's all healthy, and then you can hear its heartbeat and stuff. Do you want to do it now?"

Maeve shook head. "No, I…I need to think about this for a bit," she said softly. "I'll…I'll call you when I'm ready to come in."

Tiff nodded. "Don't wait too long, sweetie. And let me know if I can do anything for you."

Maeve nodded, mostly numbly, as she walked to the door. She wiped her tears again, then prayed it wasn't noticeable that she'd cried—and that Ethan was still busy in his check-up. She would have to take a stop in the bathroom to see if she could gather her composure.

¤ ¤ ¤

Ethan didn't pay much attention to what the doctor was telling him—he should have, surely, but he didn't. Sometimes doctors forget that you're just the client and that you have no idea what they're talking about half the time. Elisa was paying far more attention than Ethan was. Ethan essentially just got "he's doing good" and stopped listening much after that.

He was too distracted. Maeve had come back into the room right before the doctor had, and he knew that something was wrong with her. Her eyes had a distant, shocked kind of look to them, and Ethan was positive she'd been crying. When he'd asked her, she put her guard up and denied anything being wrong. What had pulled Maeve away? And why had it upset her so much?

Now Ethan was paying more attention to her than what the doctor was saying. Maeve looked like she was paying strict attention to the doctor, though, and Ethan wondered if she was really hearing anything or just trying to avoid his searching gaze every few seconds.

When they finally left the hospital and they got in the car, Ethan turned just enough to see Maeve. "Maeve, what's wrong?"

"Nothing. I already told you that," Maeve nearly snapped, and she softened her voice as Elisa got into the driver's side. "I'm glad you're doing okay."

"Me too," Elisa added, putting her hand on Ethan's. "You seem to be stronger now. That's good. But remember not to push yourself too hard. You're still healing. You heard Dr. Destin."

Ethan grimaced. "Actually, I kind of didn't. I zoned out while he was speaking."

Elisa laughed, hitting him softly on the arm. "You're still that same kid I raised. You never did like to have a lot of information as to what's wrong with you. How are you ever going to live on your own if you don't start paying more attention?"

Ethan shrugged. "I don't know. I guess I'll have to learn to pay more attention," Ethan said, looking back at Maeve momentarily. She met his gaze and smiled. Ethan almost believed she was fine, but she couldn't hold it up for longer than a second. She looked to the window, shifted uncomfortably, and the smile disappeared. Her arms were still wrapped around herself.

Ethan opened his mouth to talk to Maeve again but stopped. She wasn't telling him, and he didn't want to overly worry his mom if he kept pressuring Maeve.

Ethan felt torn. He really wanted to know. He was starting to care a lot for Maeve, and he would hate for anything to be upsetting her. However, a part of him thought he needed to let Maeve have her privacy. Agitated and annoyed, he tapped his leg, turning his attention to the road in front of him.

Surprisingly, Elisa seemed to sense the tension or something, because the drive back to the house was quiet. Ethan couldn't stop looking back at Maeve. One of the times he did so, he saw a tear make its way down her face before she wiped it.

"Elisa?" Maeve finally asked amidst the silence.

"Yeah, dear. What's up?" Elisa looked at her in the rearview mirror. Her eyes were worried. She *had* sensed something wrong. Of course she had. She was a mother.

"I'd like to get an additional job. I'm grateful for the one you've given me, but I'd like to get another one so I can make some money to save." She paused a moment. "I'll still work for you and earn my stay, of course. When I'm not at work."

Elisa smiled, giving a little chuckle. "Dear, I understand. But you've long since earned your stay here, even if you no longer helped clean; I don't need cleaning terribly anymore. I just enjoy you living in my house. Now, about the job. I can help you find one. I know people who are hiring. In fact, Isabelle is looking for some help in her shop. She makes and fixes clothing, especially dresses and tuxes."

"That would be nice," Maeve told her, voice even. "Would she want me?"

"I can definitely ask," Elisa told her. Ethan sat there, quiet. Something was definitely up; Maeve was distancing herself. Why did she want this suddenly?

Mind swirling with possible reasons, Ethan looked out the window, shoulders falling. The idea of Maeve not being there with him during the day was strangely a sorrowful one. He wanted to protest, but he had no right to do that at all.

They pulled into the driveway and Maeve got out to help Ethan.

Ethan opened his door and stood to get up. His frustration suddenly snapped when Maeve reached underneath his shoulder.

"I can do it," Ethan told her sharply, pulling away quickly. He grabbed his crutch and swept past her, into the front door—aware of the hurt and pain in Maeve as her arms folded and she stood back to watch him.

Ethan regretted snapping as soon as the door shut behind him, but he had already been spread thin with his patience for himself. He felt angry that he had to rely so much on other people for everything and the fact that Maeve was upset but not being able to do anything for that either made him taut like a tightrope.

He sat down on the couch in the living room, waiting for the other two to come in. He knew his mom would be very upset with him for treating Maeve like that.

In only a couple minutes, Elisa came in alone. She saw Ethan and sighed. "Baby, what is it between the two of you?"

Ethan shrugged miserably, running his hand through his hair. "I don't know, Mom. It was fine when we got to the hospital, but when she came back in the room…She seemed upset. I only asked her what was wrong."

"And just then? Why did you snap at her?"

Embarrassed, Ethan looked at the ground without a response.

Mom sighed again and put a hand on his shoulder. "Ethan, I don't need to tell you this, but this young lady has already been through a lot. Losing her parents as she did when she was young. Even if that was the only thing that has happened in her life, she would be sensitive sometimes. I may not know her whole story, but I'm not an idiot. Maeve and you have a past that you're not telling us about, and she has a past that she's not even telling anyone. Be patient with her—and yourself for that matter. You're still healing."

Ethan looked carefully back up at his mother, wondering how much Maeve had told her. Did she ever mention being attacked—raped—by Santorini?

Suddenly, a new thought flooded through him, leaving him chilled to his bones.

But she would have told them if she was having issues—if she was hurt by Santorini more than he originally thought? He may never know everything that had happened to her that night, or any night before that.

"Mom, where did she go?"

Mom gave a small side smile, but it had no happiness in it. "She went on a walk. She said she wanted some time alone."

¤ ¤ ¤

When Elisa called Mason to get over to Ethan, Mason didn't waste a second. He left work, leaving word with his associates that he was heading out to be with his brother, and drove off as his mom finished explaining the situation.

"Mason, I don't know what to do for him—for either of them really. Ethan has been constantly in a cloud of mental, emotional, and physical pain since he's been back, but today…there's been some tension between Ethan and Maeve, and they've both gone out to be by themselves. Maeve is out walking, blowing off steam. I've never seen Ethan so down; he hasn't left the front porch since Maeve left, silently brewing a storm. He needs you; you know he looks up to you."

"Mom, take a breath. I'm on my way. I'll be there in about twenty minutes."

"I'm pretty sure Ethan and Maeve have a past that neither want to talk about…not like *lover* history, but something happened, I can almost guarantee that. Talk to Ethan, see if he'll tell you what. I don't care if you tell me, but he needs to talk about it. It's hurting him."

Mason tapped on the wheel as he passed a slow-moving car. He had known his brother was upset, but also knew that it would take time to heal.

"What about Maeve? What happened with her today?"

Elisa sighed. "Mason, I don't even know. She went out for a bit while we went for Ethan's check-up, and she came back…distant. Or upset? I don't know exactly what, but she was withdrawn. Something happened while we were there, and I have no idea what."

Mason frowned. "Alright, mom. I'll talk to Ethan. I'll be there in a few minutes. How long have they been like this?"

"Essentially since we got back from the hospital. It's been a couple hours. Maeve hasn't come back yet, and Ethan refuses to go inside— he's just sitting silently whenever I come out." Her voice caught. "I've never seen him so sad. Sure, he can be quiet; he's always been a quiet kid. It always surprised me when I would find him sitting out on the porch and not needing to say a word for hours, but now…now he is sitting and—like I said—brewing a storm."

"'Kay, Mom, just make sure he stays there. Let me know if anything changes. I'll come sit with him." Mason remembered finding his youngest brother sitting on the porch like his mom said. He'd find him staring at the horizon, a thoughtful look in his eyes, sometimes a little sad during the time he was sick, but grateful after he survived. He'd tell Mason that he was just enjoying the time that he had, grateful that God had helped him and given him this time. He'd talk about how he imagined heaven to be, how long he'd have to wait to meet God, and wonder if he'd done any good in the world.

Mason hung up the phone without waiting for his mom to respond. He knew she was panicking but also knew that sitting there brewing in it with him, saying the same things over and over, wouldn't help her calm down. Knowing that he was on his way should help at least a little.

Mason found himself praying. "God, please help Ethan…help me to know what to say and do."

And as he drove on, the only thought that kept coming back again and again was *be blunt. Get to the point. Talk it through with him.*

When he got to the house and saw Ethan sitting on the steps, Mason took a deep breath, prayed once more for guidance, and headed over to his youngest brother.

Ethan didn't look over at him as he sat. His mom was right; shadows filled Ethan's eyes.

Mason sat by Ethan, leaving half a foot for space, and put a hand on his brother's shoulder.

Ethan looked down at his lap. "Thought you're supposed to be at work," he muttered.

"I was," Mason told him gently. Taking a deep breath, he did as he'd been prompted to. "Ethan, what happened out there? What's got you fighting darkness all the time? What happened with Maeve?"

Ethan looked up at him from the side carefully, his eyes a flimsy wall. It looked as though he was trying hard to hide his emotions, but tears crowded his vision, completely ruining any attempt.

"I knew…I knew that going into this job, being an agent…it was going to be hard," Ethan finally murmured, voice catching. "I knew the terrible things…But I never should've taken the undercover job." He felt Ethan shudder.

Blinking a couple times, Mason rubbed Ethan's back. "What happened, Ethan?"

The dam broke. Ethan told Mason about Santorini, how he'd cheat people of their money, how he blackmailed innocent people, and killed people who got in his way. "I knew going into it that it was dangerous. They knew Santorini was a bad man, but they had no real proof. They wanted someone to go in. I offered to go—I just wanted to help—but then it took longer than I thought it would. They had warned me that it might even take years, but I thought that I would be able to get him earlier. But gaining trust takes a long time with the people in the mafia, especially since I couldn't break any laws. I eventually got Santorini to trust me enough to have me do errands and go with him on his deals…if I didn't know that what he was doing was wrong…I don't know. It was hard to become friendly with him but have to keep this barrier between us that only I could see.

"Then Santorini started treating me like I was his friend. He had me go with him nearly everywhere." Ethan folded his hands together. "And I enjoyed his company. When he wasn't being a criminal, I liked him. He was like a close friend to me…but a friend I knew I had to betray. It messed with me, to see both the good and bad of someone like that. To start to care for the jerk, even as he continued with his deals. And then…"

Ethan brought his trembling hands to cover his face, resting his elbows on his knees, and sat there in silence.

Mason licked his lips anxiously. Mygyer had warned Mason that Ethan may have taken the assignment badly, but Mason wasn't expecting such a raw anguish in Ethan.

Blunt and to the point, he reminded himself.

"And then?"

Ethan suddenly stood, using his crutch to pace back and forth on the sidewalk down the stairs, and glancing around himself. "And then Santorini decided to assault this young woman! To rape this lady as if he could do whatever he wanted; never mind the fact that she was begging and screaming. Never mind the fact that I was right there, I mean I walked in late for it, but still!" He tossed his free arm around the air, a fire in his eyes. A fire that was screaming, even though his words were still contained in a near whisper.

The brewing storm had broken free.

The words shocked Mason into silence. He drew back—he hadn't known about Ethan being there when a woman was raped.

Ethan stopped and deflated as if his energy already spent itself. "I wanted to help her—to stop it—so badly, but I couldn't…I didn't. I was undercover, I was told not to blow my cover, so I just stood there. I should have stopped it from happening. I should have killed Santorini then. I shouldn't have let it happen right in front of me without doing anything. Santorini and his men would have killed us both immediately, but not stopping it…I'm a coward, just as much a jerk as Santorini. And that woman…" Ethan closed his eyes, shaking his head as tears rolled down his face.

Suddenly struck with horrifying realization, Mason clenched a hand. "That woman…Ethan, was that Maeve?"

Ethan looked over at him, not verbally denying, but the pain in his eyes answered in the affirmative.

Mason breathed out long, wondering what to say now. He'd gotten to the root of the problem but didn't know what to say to help. He couldn't fathom having to watch a woman get raped, knowing that if he tried to stop it, both he and the woman would be killed. The thought of it happening to anyone made Mason's gut clench, but *knowing* both people—Maeve and his brother—made it that much worse.

Mason stood and moved over to his brother, putting a hand on each of his shoulders. Ethan let his head drop forward again, folding his arms around his stomach.

"Have you talked to Maeve about it?" he asked gently. "About what happened, and your feelings?"

"No." Ethan's voice caught. "I don't…I don't want to think about it—and I especially don't want to make Maeve have to talk about it. I just don't even know what I'd say. I want to apologize, and all that, but I just…I can't. I know she recognizes me, and if she wanted to say anything, she would have by now, right?"

Mason didn't answer the question. Instead, he nudged Ethan's face up. "You need to talk to her about this. It will be good for both of you."

Ethan shook his head, breaking his head away, and looked down again. Mason didn't try to argue with him, instead just pulled him into a hug. "I don't know the whole story, so I can't tell you what you should have done, or not have done, but you can't keep everything festering inside. I know it will be hard, but whatever the outcome, you need to see where Maeve and you both lie with what has happened. And from what it sounds like, you were late getting there, and it was a dangerous situation to walk in on."

Ethan took a trembling breath. "I hate it when you're right."

Mason forced a chuckle as he pulled away. Ethan still looked guilty and traumatized, and suddenly exhausted, but somehow there was a spark of hope in his eyes again.

Ethan continued. "But what if I scare her off? Mom really likes her, and I like…her company."

Mason smiled a little as he caught the tone, sure he knew what his brother was so reluctant to say. "Maeve is one tough girl. If she hasn't been daunted with the task of taking care of you, plus enduring Mom's chatter, and she clearly is still here even with her past, then I don't think she'll be scared off easily. And, as I said, you need to get this past the two of you for any healing to happen for either."

Ethan fell silent, looking down the road. "I know," he whispered. "Can you help me up to my room, Mason? I'm exhausted."

≈10≈

Maeve could barely get her eyes open the next morning. Crying seemed to do that to her, making her eyes puffy and tired. She just hoped it wasn't terribly obvious she'd been crying, even though she knew that everyone was already aware.

Last night was uncomfortable. When she came back home, Elisa had wanted to know if she was okay, and Maeve had been expecting Ethan to try pushing her about what was wrong. Luckily, he had been asleep when she got back, so she'd managed to escape to her room after a quick goodnight to her and Mason.

Maeve sat up in bed, rubbing her eyes. Unfortunately, she was feeling a little nauseous this morning. She planned to check in on Ethan before she went downstairs to clean. Just because she was trying to avoid talking to him about what was going on didn't mean she could justify not doing her job. Plus, he was her friend. She needed to make sure he was okay.

She looked at the clock, then felt her eyes widen. She had slept in way too late! Elisa would already be out, Ethan would probably be up—Maeve knew he was strong enough to get his medication, and do anything, but she didn't want him to push himself.

She quickly pulled a robe over her pajamas and went over to Ethan's room. When she knocked, she heard no answer, so she pushed into the room carefully.

Ethan was still in bed, sleeping. Previous days told Maeve that Ethan was a morning person. It was twelve, he should've been awake by now.

Maeve stepped closer. "Ethan?" she whispered, then shook her head, knowing that wouldn't wake him, she'd have to be louder. She stepped next to him, sat on the side of the bed, and put a hand to his forehead. His forehead was sweaty, his hair stuck to her hand, and the heat radiating from him worried her.

Maeve swallowed and shook Ethan slightly. "Ethan, wake up."

He gave little response, eyes opening, but he turned further on his side and pulled the blanket tighter as he shivered.

Maeve swore and grabbed Ethan's phone off the dresser, calling Mason.

Luckily, he picked up nearly immediately. "Hello?"

"Hey, Mason. Ethan's temperature spiked during the night. He's hot to the touch. What should I do?" Maeve felt her hand tremble.

"I'll call over someone to check up on him," Mason said, voice calm, but clear concern showing through. "And I'll head over in a minute. For now, could you get a cold damp washcloth and put it on his forehead?"

"Yes." Maeve sighed in relief; glad someone was telling her what to do. She gave one more look to Ethan, then left to get a washcloth from the closet in the hall. She washed it in the sink in the bathroom, then came back to the room and put it across his forehead. The movement woke Ethan a bit more.

"Maeve?" His voice was raspy, and he turned onto his back and met her eyes.

Maeve pushed back a loose hair of his. "How're you feeling?"

"Little cold…" He seemed hesitant. "You?"

She smiled a little, barely noticing when Mason hung up to call some help.

"You're cold?"

Ethan paused a moment, then nodded. Maeve grabbed the blanket from the edge of the bed and brought it over him. After a couple moments, his eyes closed, so Maeve sat with Ethan for many minutes, changing the towel a couple times, until Mason, and then some lady arrived to help. The lady waved them out of the room so she could work.

"Do you know her?" Maeve asked Mason, where they waited in the hall. She felt uncomfortable because he kept staring at her.

Mason smiled and shifted. "She's my mom's friend. She has her nursing degree and started medical school, but then she decided to go a more natural way. Essential oils, energy work…things like that."

"Huh." Maeve narrowed her eyes. "Do they work?"

"They seem to." Mason nodded. "I don't personally use a lot, but when my brother was sick a lot as a kid, they used some to help him feel more comfortable."

"What will she do for Ethan now?"

Mason looked at the door. "She likes to say she goes to the root of the problem and fixes it rather than just helping the symptoms. My mom trusts her more than any doctor because it was her who caught the problem in Ethan the first time." Mason said, smiling thoughtfully. "Hopefully she gets an idea of what's wrong, and if it looks like it's an infection or something, we'll take him to his doctor."

"I thought he was doing good," Maeve said, worried and biting her lip as she stared at the door.

Mason gave a sympathetic grunt and leaned against the wall. "I'm sure he'll be fine," he said, but Maeve heard the worry.

They spent a couple minutes in silence, then the lady came out to them, pulling off some gloves and closing the door softly behind her.

"How is he?" Mason asked before Maeve could, mostly because Maeve felt her breath stuck in her chest.

She gave them a small smile. "I think he's just pushed himself too hard, and his body is catching up. No sign of infection. I think he just needs some rest, and he should be better by tomorrow. If he does get worse, or his fever higher, you can take him to his doctor."

She took some bottles out of her bag and passed them to Mason.

"I have some oils that can help make him more comfortable, you can use them if you want," she told him. "I'll explain to you how much to do before I leave. He says he feels cold so it's okay to let him use blankets but try and keep a cool washcloth on his head to try to keep his temperature under control. Also, make sure he stays hydrated. You'll have to wake him up to get him to drink some water; he should be able to do that fine." Then she gestured behind her. "Try not to leave him alone today."

Maeve laid a hand on Mason's arm. "I can stay with him. I know you have work—I didn't want to pull you away from it."

Mason smiled at her. "Thanks, Maeve, but I wanted to come check in with him. If you can handle it, I'll go back to work, but don't be afraid to call me with any change, okay?"

"Of course."

Mason gestured for her to go down the hall first, then followed behind with the other lady. As much as Maeve had been trying to avoid Ethan yesterday, now she wanted nothing more than to make sure he was okay. She couldn't fathom going to the hospital until Ethan was better—if she was honest with herself, yes, of course she worried about Ethan, but really, she wanted Ethan's support when she had to go see or hear her baby, or whatever it was she had to do. Which meant that she really wanted to tell him; she just didn't know how.

For the rest of the day, Maeve sat with Ethan, changing his cloth multiple times and helping him drink down his medicine when needed. A little later in the day, Ethan was feeling well enough to talk a little, but she still didn't want to wear him out, so she just told him about the fishing experience she'd had with her father, his friend, and the friend's son that Maeve had had a crush on when she was young. After that trip, she'd been so mortified that she no longer had the crush.

"Wait," Ethan laughed a little. "You mean, the fish dragged you in the water?"

"Okay, first off," Maeve said sharply, even though she enjoyed his amusement. "I was ten, and teeny for my age. Second, I don't think it was a fish. I'm pretty sure my line hit on a passing boat or raft before I could pull it back in, and it dragged me in the river." She crossed her ankles. She had made herself and Ethan another throne, though she had not positioned Ethan as high this time.

Ethan winced. "Must have been terrifying. Especially with how young you were."

Maeve thought back to that day, smiling wistfully as she thought about her dad. "To be honest, it happened so fast I didn't even understand what was happening. The river was rather shallow, but strong enough that I couldn't stop myself. Luckily both our dads had thought to make us wear life jackets, even though we complained that no one else had to wear life jackets."

Ethan chuckled. "Dads are smart like that. So, what happened?"

"My dad came in after me. He was tall enough to reach the floor easy and so he used the current to help guide me to the bank." Maeve laughed at the memory. It was a bittersweet one. "The friend and son were waiting on the bank, and I was more worried that my crush had seen me than I was of the fact that I had almost drowned. Back then, I hadn't realized the severity of what had happened."

Ethan put a hand on his stomach, wincing, but smiling.

"Maeve…" Ethan's smile fell. Maeve felt her stomach tighten, knowing what was coming. Sure, she had decided she wanted Ethan to be with her, but she was still unsure and hesitant—and she didn't want to talk about anything until he was healed. She didn't want him to worry about her.

"Ethan, just don't—"

"No, Maeve…" His voice shook. "I need to say something. You don't have to say anything, but I just have to…" he looked away, and the tear that slid down his face shocked her entirely speechless. He cleared his throat but wouldn't meet her gaze. "I'm sorry. About what happened that night. I should have done something. I should have stopped Santorini from hurting you. I know you recognize me, but even if not, I need you to know. I know that night was terrible, and I'm sorry for reminding you about it, but I just…I'm sorry, I should have saved you. I let you get hurt, and I can't stop thinking about it. I don't understand how you can treat me so kind. You were hurt bad, and I couldn't stop it."

Ethan was crying silently but wouldn't look at Maeve. Maeve swallowed, letting the silence reign for a couple minutes as she tried her hardest to keep emotion in check. Tried and failed. Seeing Ethan cry sent her over the edge.

Maeve closed her eyes a moment, took a deep breath, then moved off her throne and sat by Ethan. *Twenty seconds of bravery. Let's see if this works,* she thought.

She grabbed his hand and waited until Ethan looked at her. "You're wrong." Maeve told him firmly, wiping his tears. "You did save me. I know now that you had a job to do, and looking back, yes, I had wondered why no one was helping me. But you came in, and you tried to get him to stop, and then I learned that it was you who called the cops and made sure Santorini didn't kill me when the cops arrived."

Ethan looked down. "The only thing it tells you is that I could sit and watch something like that and not do anything."

"No, what it tells me is that you're a very compassionate man who also knows how to think about the outcomes, and then be strong enough to get through the challenge, while keeping your job intact, and making sure we both didn't end up dead." Maeve smiled at him through her tears when he hesitantly looked back up. "I'm not going to say that waiting was the 'right' thing to do, or the easiest, or even the hardest. I'm not going to say that I wasn't hurt, by both them, and by not being rescued sooner. Ethan, I have scars, like I'm sure you do from it. I don't like thinking about it, but hey…there was one thing good that came out of that night."

Ethan licked his lips. "What's that?"

Maeve tightened her hand in his. "Ethan, you gave me a new life. You saved me, and that gave me the opportunity to come here and meet your mom and your family and come see you. I didn't know I'd see you again, and at the time I didn't really think I wanted to, but I thank God that I got the chance to help you like you had helped me that night."

Ethan still looked unsure. Honestly, Maeve found it a little amusing that she was the one reassuring him about what had happened, when it had happened to her.

She continued, however, serious; "Ethan, I do not blame you for what happened. Santorini made the decision to hurt me, and I'm glad you didn't get us both killed by acting too soon." Yes, Maeve hated talking about that night, it always brought up the reminder of her being helpless and alone, but somehow it seemed easier to talk about it when she was looking at it from Ethan's point of view. And Maeve knew as she spoke that they needed to get this out in the open. It had apparently been holding them both back.

Maeve didn't know if she had convinced him, but when he looked away a long moment, then finally met her eyes again, his didn't seem so sad anymore.

"How are you doing…about what had happened?" he asked her.

Maeve figured now would be a good time to tell Ethan that that assault had left her with a baby she didn't know how to raise. But somehow, she couldn't convince herself to, even still. She'd hate to be a burden, for Ethan to feel responsible for taking care of her or her baby. Yes, she liked Ethan, but she wanted Ethan to love her, not have a duty to her.

"I'm…" she hesitated. "I'm glad to be here. I still look back on that night and can't believe someone could be so cruel. And yet, I am glad to be here now. I still have some days that are harder than others, like yesterday, but otherwise I'm doing better than I have in years." She had a home now; a place she felt she belonged, at least to some extent.

"What happened yesterday?" Ethan asked carefully.

Maeve swallowed, and her mouth was evading once again before she could think of it. "It was just a hard day. I've just had a lot to process."

¤ ¤ ¤

A couple days later, Ethan was doing better again, which Maeve was relieved about. He was still weak and sore, but he was healing well. Maeve was with Ethan, except for when she was at work with Isabelle, or the occasional time with Elisa when one of Ethan's siblings came to spend time with him.

Ethan's sister was a sweetheart. It was no question she was Elisa's daughter; she had the same kind characteristics as her mother. She was talkative, but could listen too, or even work in silence.

Isabelle had set her up to manage the front desk mostly, and to help in the back with sizes and tailoring when her other assistant was out. Maeve hadn't really sewn before, unless you count some kid crafts she had done before her parents had passed away. She was learning a lot, and she enjoyed working in the shop with Isabelle.

Isabelle would do repairs on suits and dresses—or really anything someone brought in, but fancier items were the most common—and she would also design some clothes and have them in her store to sell. It was a small business, and part of Maeve wondered how she was still in business when there were so many slow days, but she loved it. The atmosphere was super friendly, and Maeve felt like she belonged. Also, Isabelle paid well.

"Maeve!" She heard Isabelle's voice calling for her. Maeve looked up to see Isabelle come in. "Someone is calling on your phone."

Maeve grabbed it from Isabelle, then turned it on silent and slid it into her pocket. It was the hospital. She knew they wanted her to come in so they could check up on the baby, but she didn't want to worry about it yet. Besides, except for a little cramping and nausea, she felt fine. Also, she had little money, and while she knew Elisa would willingly pay if she knew, Maeve didn't want to tell her. If she said she was pregnant, she'd then have to explain how.

"It's not important," Maeve told her. She put a hand to her stomach, hating how bad she'd been cramping lately. "I'll call back later."

Isabelle nodded. "I could use your help in the back then."

Maeve looked over to the door. "What if someone comes in?"

Isabelle laughed, eyes twinkling. "Don't worry, I have an alarm back there; if anyone comes in, it'll let us know and we can come back out here."

Maeve nodded and came out from behind the counter. "What did you need?"

"I'm going to pull some boxes down from the shelf. I'd like you to grab them from me. They're just boxes of some sewing stuff and old clothes I'd made for me and to sell." Isabelle led her to the back room, still talking. "I want to finally get it out to sell."

"Is it hard to sell?" Maeve asked, watching as Isabelle took the rungs of the ladder and climbed up. Maeve looked around the storage room. It was well lit but didn't look quite finished.

"Well, I mean. I'm sure people would like them. It's just something I'm super attached to, so I never could bring myself to get rid of any of it." Isabelle brought the box down and handed it to Maeve so she could climb back down. "Just put it on the front desk and we'll go through them."

Maeve nodded and went back out to the front, putting the box on the desk. Isabelle followed her and pulled the lid off. Inside, there was a tiny, yellow, frilly dress. Isabelle pulled it out, barely looking at it, and grabbed the clothes underneath. As Maeve realized what they were, her hand flew to her abdomen.

Baby clothes.

Isabelle rubbed the fabric between her fingers, and Maeve was startled when she noticed Isabelle's tears.

"What is it?" Maeve asked her.

Isabelle wiped her tears quickly but kept hold of the outfit with her other hand. "I had made them for my baby, my last one. He had been stillborn. I put them away because I couldn't see them, but I also couldn't give them away."

"Are you sure you want to now?" Maeve asked, picking up one of the outfits. "They're very nicely done. Really perfect for a boy." The one Maeve had grabbed was blue, with a little white bird pattern across the whole thing.

Maeve wondered what gender her baby would be. Suddenly she found herself more anxious than ever to go to that doctor's appointment she'd been avoiding.

Isabelle put a hand on Maeve's wrist that held her stomach. "Maeve. Do you have something you're not telling?"

Maeve pulled away, heart beating frantically. "What do you mean?"

Isabelle smiled softly. "Maeve, you've been sick a lot lately. You get nauseous at any strong smells, and you keep cradling your abdomen. You're pregnant, aren't you?"

Maeve hesitated, looking down at the baby clothes, then nodded and cleared her throat. That was an easier way to get the news out.

Isabelle held her hand again. "Does Elisa know?"

"No," Maeve whispered.

"Ethan?" Isabelle's forehead crinkled.

"No, I…I just found out last week. I was going to tell Ethan, but then he got his fever. I don't want him to worry about me too." Maeve cleared her throat, feeling a little shaky.

Isabelle frowned. "Who is the father?"

Uncomfortable, Maeve looked at the door. This part would have been easier to tell Ethan first—he already knew what had happened to her.

Swallowing hard, Maeve looked back and met Isabelle's gaze as strong as she could. "A man raped me, Isabelle. It's the man's baby."

She watched the shock fill Isabelle's eyes and she gasped, drawing her hand to her mouth, the other tightening over Maeve's. "That's terrible!"

Maeve nodded and looked away, feeling awkward. Her face felt hot.

"Do you want to tell me what happened?" Isabelle asked softly.

Maeve thought about the question, and suddenly realized that she did. Isabelle was sweet, and if Maeve could have any girl on her side, knowing what had happened, Isabelle was the girl. Kelly, the daughter of one of Elisa's friends, was sweet as well, but Maeve had barely seen her since the first time.

Maeve slowly nodded. "Do you mind?"

"Of course not!" Isabelle led her over to the round sofa, sat on it, and turned her knees toward Maeve.

Maeve looked at her, then took a deep breath. "I don't want to do a lot of details," she said, staring over Isabelle's shoulder and focusing in on that night. The room seemed to disappear from her view. "I was out walking at night, some guy pulled me into an alley..." A tear fell onto her right cheek. "I used to live in Illinois. Used to…live on the streets." She looked quickly at Isabelle at that. She hated telling people that she'd been homeless for years, but a load of stress washed from her shoulders.

Isabelle rubbed her hands. "That's terrible. How could someone do that?"

Maeve shrugged distantly, thinking about when Ethan stepped in. Some people may doubt that Ethan had done much to help her. He carried her out of there, yes, but that by itself wouldn't have done anything; it was the fact that he'd been so kind and encouraging when she'd most needed it. It had been his voice and worry that had gotten her through the hospital stay. And at the time, she hadn't known that it had been him who called the police.

"It was Ethan who saved me," Maeve told Isabelle softly. "He was undercover, keeping an eye on Santorini—the man that had attacked me. He convinced Santorini to let him take me out to the police who had arrived and spin a story to get him out of the mess. He's the one who called them."

Isabelle was silent for a long minute. "You two did seem uncomfortable the first time we saw you together." She thought for a moment, studying Maeve's gaze. "You like him?"

Maeve blushed but nodded. "I think I even knew the first night. When he held me, I just felt safe. And he was so worried about me—I haven't had many people care about me that much. And I think he might like me."

Isabelle smiled lightly. "I think you may be right," she murmured, then held both of Maeve's hands in hers. "You're a very special woman, Maeve. Thank you for telling me this."

Maeve didn't know how to respond, but Isabelle continued. "Maeve, if your baby is a boy, I'd love for you to have the baby clothes."

Maeve gasped. "What? I thought you were going to sell them."

Isabelle laughed. "No. Not if you'll take them. I'd much rather they be taken care of by someone I know and love. I was thinking about giving them to Riley for her baby, but she's having a girl." Isabelle quieted a little, eyes pleading. "Maeve, please say yes."

Maeve hesitated a moment. "Okay, I will if it's a boy." She put a hand to her abdomen. "I'm scared, Isabelle. I don't understand how I could even be pregnant. I wasn't prepared for this. And I don't want to tell anybody. I'm still ashamed that this happened to me, and I'm worried someone is going to hate me, or something." Her hand trembled.

Isabelle pulled her into a hug. "No one in my family will hate you, Maeve. Very few people are that cruel-hearted. We just all want what's best for you."

Maeve nodded.

"Are you going to tell Ethan and my mom?"

"I will…but not yet. I need to visit with my doctor first." Maeve took a deep breath, still holding her abdomen.

The sound of the front door chiming to announce a customer distracted them. They both looked over to see a man come in. He wore a nice tux, very expensive-looking leather shoes, and his hair was slicked back. "Hi," the man said, his voice a friendly rumble. "Do you guys do walk-in patch jobs?" He lifted his elbow to show them a hole about the size of a tennis ball. "I need a quick fix, and it's important that it happens now."

Isabelle rose immediately, shielding Maeve from his view long enough she could wipe her tears. As Maeve stood, Isabelle approached the man, holding out her hand to shake. "Of course we do. I'm Isabelle. This is Maeve. I'll have Maeve situate you while I go get some thread."

Maeve smiled and stepped forward to take the man's hand. "Hi, Mr…?"

The man took her hand. His grip was firm, but he took her hand and flipped it so he could kiss her knuckles. Immediately a feeling of insecurity flooded over her—it had been so different when Ethan had done it, and the fact that this man was quite clearly way older than her, made her extremely uncomfortable.

"I'm Aaron Calloway. But please, just call me Aaron."

Trying to keep the smile fixed on her face, despite his gaze on her, she gently pulled her hand back, gesturing to the side as she did so. "This way please."

Maeve felt itchy as she turned her back on the man. She had the terrible sense that she should never turn her back on this man, so as she walked, she tilted her body so she could see him as she moved over to the mirror and seating area. "If you'll hand me the jacket, I'll take it back so we can fix it." Maeve stayed her distance away from the man, and merely held her hand to him expectantly. The figure of this man seemed vaguely familiar. Why couldn't she remember where from, though?

The man smiled and shrugged out of his jacket. "I don't see a ring. Does that mean you don't have a man?"

"Um…"

"Come on, a lady as beautiful as you *has* to have found someone by now." The man was studying her intensely.

Maeve licked her lips as she grabbed his jacket. She was saved from having to answer when Isabelle came in talking. Maeve couldn't help but thank her silently as she scurried over to the desk so they could get the jacket fixed. She took a deep breath and exchanged a look with Isabelle. She seemed amused. Maeve's instincts, on the other hand, were telling her to *run*.

¤ ¤ ¤

Ethan felt super bored now that Maeve went to work for a couple hours every day. He always worried about her. He just wished he knew if she was okay. He'd been so used to her being there for him, and now that his fever was gone, she'd been working a lot more. Even though she had said she didn't blame him for what had happened, a part of him believed that she really did since she seemed to avoid him.

But then she'd come back and make him feel like everything had happened did so for a reason in God's plan. He found it hard to turn his thoughts away from her most of the time.

One of Ethan's friends had come over today to hang out; Ethan hadn't seen Brayden since he'd gone to college in Texas nearly a year before Ethan graduated to become a cop. They had been super close, but Ethan hadn't told him about what had happened, and they'd barely talked since Ethan had been undercover. He was only over now because he finished up school for the year and came back home to live near his girlfriend and friends. Apparently, Andrea and Brayden had gotten close while they went to college together down in Texas, which was slightly weird because Ethan and Andrea used to date.

"Let me get this straight." Brayden leaned forward in the chair. His hand was enfolded in Andrea's. "You didn't think of telling us when you got into the hospital?"

Ethan sighed, folding his arms on the table in front of him. "I thought about it. I didn't want to interrupt your schooling, and I didn't even tell my family where I was."

"You told Mason."

Ethan rubbed his arm as he leaned back. "Yeah, well…I kind of had to have someone as my emergency contact."

"What if you had died?" Brayden asked, eyes narrowing furiously.

"What difference would it have made? You would have just gotten the news that I was dead either way." Ethan looked at Andrea. Her face seemed pale from the news, and she was clearly clinging to Brayden's hand. Ethan decided that the two of them were a good fit for each other.

"Ethan, we would have wanted to visit you," Andrea said, reaching across the table and laying a hand on his. "You're our best friend." Ethan smiled as she said that, as if the two of them were one entity.

"I don't know, you two seem pretty close now," Ethan said, eyebrows darting up playfully. "And you haven't seen me in a while. I'm sure you would've found other friends by now."

Andrea blushed and let go, looking away awkwardly. Ethan looked at her, tilting his head, and Brayden followed his gaze, then let go of Andrea's hand. "Andy, can I talk to Ethan for a couple minutes?"

Andrea looked between the two of them. "Promise not to wring his neck?" Ethan wasn't sure who she was asking the question to, but both the boys smirked and met eyes. Andrea rolled her eyes and left without waiting for that promise.

Brayden waited a couple moments, then lowered his voice. "Ethan…I want to ask Andrea to marry me."

Shocked, Ethan's breath hitched. He hadn't realized how much had changed while he'd been gone. "Really?"

Brayden nodded. "I know you used to like her and she you, but we've gotten really close. She hadn't wanted to upset you by being so upfront about our relationship, and I know you had been kind of upset when she decided to move to Texas and go to college with me instead of staying here, but…"

Ethan cut him off. "It's fine, Brayden. I'm really happy for you two."

Brayden studied him intensely. "Are you sure? Ethan, I don't want to cause contention between us. You're still my best friend. I know we didn't talk much over the year, but you're still the friend I grew up with, and the closest I have."

Yes, Ethan was slightly weirded out about them being together, but he really found himself happier for them than anything else. And warmed that Brayden still considered him to be his best friend. Ethan smiled. "No, Brayden, really. I'm happy for you two."

Brayden seemed to relax. "Do you still like her?"

Ethan thought for a minute. "As a friend, yes. But…To be honest, I really like someone else now."

Brayden brightened. "Who?"

Ethan looked away. "I'm not ready to push anything right now, Brayden. I mean, it's still too close to my assignment, with what had happened."

Brayden nudged him. "I just want to know who."

Ethan fought a smile. "So, are you planning on proposing soon? Have you talked it out at all, or asked her dad?"

Brayden leaned back, looking uncomfortable with the change of subject. "I'm going to talk to her dad when we see him in a couple days. And I've hinted at it with Andrea. I think she wants to marry me too." He hesitated. "I'm really nervous about talking to her dad. What if he says no?"

"He won't say no! He loves you," Ethan admonished.

"I'm just worried," Brayden told him softly. "Really scared. I don't want either one of them to say no to me."

Ethan was going to respond, but the door through the mud room opened. Ethan looked over to see Maeve come in. Maeve noticed them and smiled. "Hi."

"Hi." Ethan nearly stood to greet her but stopped since she stepped quicker than he'd be able to get his body to move.

"How're you feeling?" she asked. She looked at Brayden curiously.

"I'm doing good today." He gestured to his friend: "This is Brayden, my best friend. Brayden, this is Maeve."

Maeve stuck out a hand. "Hey, Brayden, nice to meet you. I help out around the house."

"Understatement," Ethan murmured. "She does practically everything, including taking care of me." He winked at Maeve. She merely laughed and softly punched his shoulder.

"I'm going up to take off my shoes and such. I'll be back down in a minute." As she left, Ethan suddenly became aware that her face seemed tense, as if she was in pain. He nearly called out after her to ask if she was alright, but she was out of the room quickly—and Ethan figured she'd hate it if he made a big deal out of it.

Brayden was studying him. "She's cute," he said calculatingly, an eyebrow raised.

Ethan leaned back, staring warily at Brayden. That seemed to give Brayden what he wanted, as his smile suddenly grew. He lowered his voice. "You like Maeve, don't you? That's your new crush?"

"Shh!" Ethan hissed quickly, glancing over his shoulder. "Please don't."

"Why don't you say anything? Ask her on a date or something."

Ethan gave him a half-skeptical and half-annoyed look. "Brayden, please. I can't even walk for very long by myself yet, let alone take her on a date. Besides, our relationship is…complicated."

"More complicated than…" he gestured between himself, Ethan, and the door Andrea had disappeared through, indicating how they both had dated the same girl.

"By far." Ethan sighed and felt his shoulders fall.

Brayden stopped teasing immediately. "What is it?"

Ethan swallowed hesitantly, unsure if Maeve would appreciate him telling his friend, but ultimately, he couldn't keep it from him any more than he could have his brother. He told a brief summary of what he felt like he had repeated a million times already. Brayden whistled as he finished.

"Man, that's a crazy coincidence. She seems to have adjusted pretty well. Has she been in to check up at the doctors? She hasn't picked up anything?"

Ethan shrugged, feeling unsettled at the thought. "Honestly, I don't know. She won't talk to me much about it." Ethan looked toward the door. "I'm worried about her."

Brayden stood and put his hand on Ethan's shoulder. "You should go talk to her. I'm going to go find Andrea."

"She probably slipped out to the garden," Ethan suggested, knowing that she loved the garden.

"Probably, yeah." Brayden's eyes twinkled, as he turned away.

Ethan sighed, wondering if he should go after Maeve. The tabletop became subject to his tapping fingers as he thought, then after a minute or so, he decided to go find her.

He grabbed his crutch and used it and the table to help himself get up. His side still hurt a lot, but Ethan had decided to slowly work his way off the painkillers—he hated how easy it was to get addicted to them—so it seemed to hurt a lot more now. He instead used some oils his mom's friend had suggested, and just had to hope they would work.

He moved out of the kitchen and into the family room, heading to the stairs. Out the window, he could see Brayden walking quickly into the garden. A second later, Andrea walked into the family room from the bathroom.

Andrea smiled nervously at him. "Where's Brayden?"

"He went out to the garden to find you."

She laughed. "Man, if I hadn't had to go to the bathroom, he would have been spot on."

Ethan opened his arms to give her a hug. She brightened and dashed in for it. "I'm really happy for you, Andrea. Truly. Brayden is great."

Andrea smiled up at him, kissing his cheek. "You are too, Ethan. Thank you." She looked out the window. Ethan grinned and nudged her forward.

"Go find him."

Andrea nodded and took off, nearly skipping.

Ethan chuckled and worked his way to the stairs. Before he could get up them, Maeve showed up on the top and started down. She tilted her head at him. "Please don't tell me you were about to get up these on your own."

Ethan smiled. "I've done so a handful of times already."

Maeve stepped on the stair right above his. "What if you hurt yourself and tumble down?"

Ethan winced at the image. "That would hurt."

She grinned playfully. When she stood on that step, she was just at Ethan's height. Ethan nearly kissed her. Maybe would have if Maeve's face didn't suddenly scrunch up in pain and she gasped.

Ethan grabbed her as she leaned forward, arms wrapping her stomach. "What is it?" Ethan asked frantically.

Maeve shook her head. "Just been feeling a little sick today," she said stiffly, nonetheless accepting his help down the step.

Ethan nodded, unable to help much, but keeping a hand on Maeve. "Can I get you anything?"

Maeve didn't answer for a minute, then she slowly straightened and relaxed. "Some water would be nice, please."

Ethan hesitated to let go, but since she did seem to be doing better, he decided he wanted to help her. "Okay, I'll be right back. Do you need to sit?"

"I'm alright now," Maeve told him, smiling shakily.

"Okay." Ethan quickly moved to the kitchen, limping on his leg with the crutch, and grabbed a glass to fill with water.

As he was pulling it away, he heard a loud noise back where he'd left Maeve. Panicking, Ethan went back to the room as fast as he could. "Maeve?" he shouted.

He found Maeve kneeling on the ground, one arm to her stomach, the other braced on the end of the coffee table. Ethan came and crouched next to her, pushing the cup onto the table, tipping it over in his haste. As water poured out, Ethan grabbed Maeve. His heart was beating frantically, and his ears seemed to ring.

He pulled her near him, and she didn't resist; she fell limp into his side.

Ethan turned Maeve in his arms. "Maeve? Maeve?" His voice turned pleading. "Come on, answer me." Desperately, he brushed her hair back, feeling her clammy skin as he did so. "Brayden!" His voice cracked, he felt like he had never screamed louder.

Maeve's eyelids fluttered. Ethan patted his pockets for his phone but knew before he did so that it wasn't in there. He had left it on his bed. He nearly swore.

To his relief, the back door opened in moments. Ethan looked up frantically and saw Brayden and Andrea come in, holding hands.

Brayden noticed what happened first, his eyes widened, and he let go of Andrea's hand, rushing forward.

"What happened?"

"I don't know!" Ethan said frantically. "She just…she collapsed! Call an ambulance!"

Andrea dug her phone out of her pocket, dialing quickly. Brayden crouched beside Maeve, checking her pulse.

While Andrea talked on the phone, Ethan couldn't bring himself to do anything except hold Maeve, praying that she would be okay, and saying her name over and over. Maeve didn't answer.

"There's blood," Brayden said suddenly. Ethan followed his gaze, noticing the blood on his own abdomen. At that moment, Ethan was flooded with pain.

His wound had torn, but somehow his first response was relief it wasn't from Maeve.

≈]l]l≈

Brayden and Andrea sat with him the entire time. Ethan hadn't yet been able to stop panicking; his hands kept shaking, and his fingers or feet kept tapping. Sure, his abdomen hurt a little—they had to put stitches in again. At least it hadn't torn open completely, only a few stitches. But that meant they had to dress it and clean it again. After they had finished with that, Brayden came into the room to sit with Ethan. Andrea had followed soon after—she had taken a couple minutes to call Ethan's mom.

His mom got there soon after that, coming in with the evident worry in her face and a hug for Ethan.

"I'm fine, Mom, really," Ethan murmured when she inquired of him, her hands framing his face as if to search for any lingering pain. "I'm only worried about Maeve."

Elisa nodded. "Me too. Have you heard anything yet?"

All three of them shook their heads. Elisa thought for a moment, then seemed to come to a decision. "Okay, I'm going to see if I can catch a nurse who might know, and then call Isabelle." She kissed his forehead, ruffling his hair, then smiled at Brayden and Andrea on her way out.

Brayden was studying Ethan with his intense gaze. Ethan knew he wanted to say something but was just trying to figure out how. Andrea seemed to catch on and stood to leave. "I'll be back in a couple minutes, hon." She stood, and Brayden took a break from staring long enough to give her a quick kiss.

"What?" Ethan asked, squirming when Brayden's eyes wouldn't leave his face.

"You really love her, don't you?"

Ethan swallowed heavily, looking away. "Brayden…I do like her, but please don't—"

Brayden smiled at him. "I'm not going to force you into anything, bro. But think about it. Would you rather her not know, and you have not told, and then have this possibility of her being gone?"

"She's not gone!" Ethan snapped, the words flaring his desperation again. Brayden raised his hands soothingly.

"I know, bro. You know what I mean."

The stupid part was, Ethan did. His shoulders fell, and he looked toward the door. He wanted to know how Maeve was, the thought of her hurt nearly broke him inside—or maybe it had. Ever since he'd first seen her, he couldn't take his mind off her, whether good or bad memories.

Brayden leaned forward. "I'm sure she's fine, Ethan."

Ethan met his gaze, hating how desperate he felt.

As time wore on, Ethan became glad that he had been given a bed so that he could rest the new sutures. He leaned back on it, getting comfortable, even though his mind was on edge.

Visiting hours were over before they heard about Maeve. Ethan was only still in the hospital because they wanted to make sure his sutures stayed in. His friends and mom were told to go home for the night. One of the nurses took pity on Ethan and assured him that as soon as they knew anything, they would tell him. Ethan made her promise that she would wake him up to tell him if he happened to fall asleep.

It was about ten when some news came.

The door opened and that same nurse came in. She smiled as she saw he was still awake. "Maeve is sleeping now," she told him. "But she and her baby will be okay."

Ethan started to sigh in relief, but the las part of the sentence made it stick in his throat. "Baby?" He managed to choke out, thinking horridly of Santorini.

The nurse looked at him, startled. "Had she not told you?"

"No." When had Maeve learned? When she'd disappeared from Ethan's last check-up? Is that why she had been so upset? Why hadn't she told him?

All these questions and more swirled around his head, but he voiced his main concern. "She's okay, though? Can I see her?"

"She's fine. We'll probably keep her here a few days to be sure, but she's fine."

"And the baby…Is it okay? How did…" He trailed off, unsure how to ask. He knew how she'd become pregnant, but his mind couldn't wrap around the idea of it. And he wanted to know more about what happened with her, but knew he wasn't immediate family, so he would have to ask her.

She smiled sympathetically. "The baby seems to be healthy. Ethan, you get some rest. In the morning I'll get you over to Maeve's room to visit with her."

"Thank you." Ethan said softly as she left. He felt relief that Maeve was okay, but it took a long while for his mind to stop asking questions and swirling in thoughts in order for him to sleep.

¤ ¤ ¤

Maeve woke up to an unfamiliar voice, and an unfamiliar room. She was staring at a white ceiling, and it seemed the rest of the room was white too. *Ah, crap. What happened this time?*

Slowly, she realized someone was trying to talk to her. She blinked and looked over to see a nurse hovering over her. She smiled as Maeve focused on her. "Hey…How're you feeling?"

Maeve thought about that. She felt a little nauseous. She did not yet understand why she was here, and she didn't know why she felt groggy.

"Where's Ethan?" The last thing she remembered was Ethan as she came down the stairs.

The nurse's smile seemed to come again, even though it hadn't disappeared in the first place, it just became even brighter somehow. "He's just in a different room. I'll send for him in a few minutes. I wanted to check on how you're doing first."

"What happened?" Maeve asked, struggling to sit up.

"Are you uncomfortable?" Now her smile turned into a concerned frown.

"A little. I mostly just want to see." Maeve strained to sit up. The nurse stepped forward and pushed a button that lifted her upper body, adjusting the pillow so it stayed under Maeve's head.

As she moved, she was struck with some pain in her abdomen. Remembering how bad the pain had been before she had awoken here, she looked at the lady. "What's wrong with me? Is my baby alright?"

The nurse nodded. "I'm Dixie. Your baby is fine. In fact, amazingly so after what happened."

Maeve thought about asking what had happened, but her mind was so foggy, she doubted she'd be able to understand anything anyway. Instead, she just nodded and closed her eyes. "Ethan's here?"

"I'll go get him now." She hesitated a minute. "A few stitches of Ethan's wound had reopened when he was trying to get to you. He had to have those redone. I'll help him get in here."

Shocked, Maeve nodded mutely. Dixie gave her one last encouraging smile and left to find Ethan.

Maeve wondered what she'd say to him. Did he know about her baby now? Did someone tell him?

Anxious, Maeve ran her hands weakly through her hair. She felt tangles but felt too weak to brush them out. Instead she sighed and closed her eyes, leaning her head back on the bed. She hated that she hadn't had a chance to talk to Ethan before this happened.

She fell asleep before they got in there, and when she jerked awake, it was because of a sound to the side of her. She looked over to see Ethan sitting on the chair beside her. He must have been there at least a couple minutes because the nurse wasn't in there anymore.

Ethan paused—he had been grabbing a tissue from the table in between them but had knocked off a water cup.

"Sorry," Ethan said. "Didn't mean to wake you." His eyes furrowed in concern. "How are you feeling?"

"I'm okay. Little tired." She hesitated, swallowing. "Did they tell you?"

"About the baby?" Ethan looked at her, seeming sad. His voice was soft. "Yeah, they did."

Maeve looked away, swallowing.

"Sorry you tore your wound open again," she said after a moment.

She could hear some amusement in Ethan's voice. "That doesn't matter, it will heal."

"Not if you keep tearing it, it won't." Maeve looked back, unable to resist a small smile.

Ethan looked at her, then carefully leaned forward and grabbed her hand. "Maeve, why didn't you tell me?"

Maeve's hands trembled. She blinked back tears. "I don't know. I was scared. I didn't want to believe that I was pregnant and telling you…it would make it seem real."

Ethan rubbed her hand. Maeve felt tears slip down, and Ethan moved closer, wiping her tears. He winced. Oddly, his pain made her feel comforted. He was hurting too, but still wanted to be there for her. If that didn't make her feel special, nothing could.

However, she was still concerned. "Ethan, you're hurting."

Ethan smiled softly. "A little. But I'm fine. Right now, I'm worried about you, Maeve. What can I do for you?"

Maeve thought about it, feeling loved. "Just sit with me."

"Want me to build you a throne as well?" he asked teasingly, raising his eyebrows. The joke made Maeve laugh. She gave a sigh of happiness.

"I love you so much, Ethan," she said, grinning. Then she froze suddenly, noticing her words. "I mean, you're a really good friend. I mean, I'm glad you're here with me…you always seem to make me feel better."

Ethan's face went serious and intense, his hand reached up to wipe her tears gently. Suddenly, Maeve felt her breath catch. Everything focused on Ethan and his gentleness. Without saying a word, she knew that he really wanted to kiss her—and she wanted him to kiss her.

At the same time, her mind recoiled. She'd already been used; Santorini had ruined her for any future with a man. No one wanted a broken girl—not for long. Ethan would lose his interest in her.

She looked down, breaking the intimate connection she felt between them. Ethan ran his hand across her cheek, pushing some hair back. "I love you too, Maeve."

Her shoulders fell from her tense position at the words. A wave of awareness washed through her; she was no more broken than he was—than anyone was. Ethan had seen terrible things as well. Strength seemed to flow into her. She leaned forward and wrapped her arms around Ethan, hugging him, but careful of his wound. She felt his firm arms around her, much like that night they had first met. How far they both had come since then.

Ethan ran his hand through her hair as he pulled back. "You're beautiful, you know?"

Maeve scoffed and wiped away new tears. "I'm sure I'm not so pretty in this gown."

"Nonsense." A smile played once again on Ethan's face. "Haven't you heard? Hospital gowns are the new trend."

"Oh yeah, I bet that open slit in the back is a great endearment along with the flashy white and blue color. And look at that, it does well on men too." She scanned her eyes down his body, trying to act somewhat sincere.

Ethan laughed so hard he immediately winced and grabbed his abdomen, still chuckling.

"How do you do that?" Maeve asked him suddenly.

"Do what?" He looked confused.

"Always make me happy again."

Grinning, Ethan met her gaze. "I don't know, but you always make me feel better too." He took a slow breath. Maeve knew he was struggling to keep sitting up. He was probably in pain again.

Maeve put her hand on his. "You should go sit back on your bed. You're hurting."

Ethan looked sideways at her and turned his hand into hers. "I was worried about you."

"What happened to me anyway?" Maeve asked. "I was going to ask the nurse earlier, but I was super tired."

It was that moment nurse Dixie stepped back in, overhearing. "I can tell you what happened now, if you don't mind Ethan hearing as well."

"He can stay."

You had something called pancreatitis that caused an infection." His grip tightened a moment. "You'll have to stay here for a couple days to fight off the infection, we gave you antibiotics, but otherwise you'll be fine since we caught it. You and your baby are both fine."

Ethan was silent for a moment as Dixie finished and started checking over all her wires and clipboard, then he gently cleared his throat. "Have you seen your baby yet? Know if it's a boy or girl or anything?"

Maeve shook her head. "Honestly, I was going to today or tomorrow. I am finally okay with the fact that I'm pregnant. I was really resistant to it at first. Now I think I might be a little excited about it."

The corner of Ethan's mouth quirked up. "I'm glad." He paused a moment. "Aren't you worried?"

Maeve answered honestly. "Yes. Terrified. But I've always wanted to have kids. It didn't happen the way I was expecting, but I guess God just really wanted me to have this child."

"Maeve, I…" Ethan bit his lips a moment, then forged ahead. "I just want you to know, you don't have to raise this baby alone. I'll be there for you. I'd love to act as if a dad, you know what I mean?" He stumbled over his words. "I don't want to see you doing this alone. Everyone needs help. Me and my family will all be there for you."

Maeve smiled. "I appreciate that, Ethan. Let's just see how it goes, and what you think later."

Ethan nodded, looking sad for a moment, then he forced a smile and carefully sat back. "Are you okay with me in here too? I didn't want you to be alone, but if you want to be, I'll let you."

"No, I'd rather you be here." Maeve relaxed onto her bed, body weary again.

"Good. I really don't want to fuss about moving right now. They forced me to sit in a wheelchair."

¤ ¤ ¤

Anthony frowned, chin to his palm as he thought. Big Paulie thought he could pull one over on him? just dissolve Anthony's soldiers? He didn't put so much work into his crew just so Paulie could throw it all out and move them to other groups. Anthony had some loyal people; they'd never switch so easy, not most of them. He had only picked the best.

Anthony thought about the streets of Chicago, how easy it was to hide there. So many people could go missing and no one would notice. In Kansas, it wasn't quite so likely. It wasn't as busy.

Standing, frustrated, he started pacing as he thought.

He knew Bullet Oscar was in jail now, along with Peter "Specs." Anthony had no idea if they would get out, but that didn't matter. Now, Paulie, their Capo, wanted to dissolve Anthony's group and add them into the few other groups—and make Anthony a soldier again? No, he wasn't going to be downgraded after his hard work. This was his business. And being replaced by "The Con." No way. William "The Con" Tocco didn't know the first thing about this business. It was only because he was Paulie's son-in-law that he even thought he had a chance at being a street boss.

Anthony narrowed his eyes. He'd have to break off from Paulie. That would cause war, sure, but sometimes he had to do what he had to do. If Anthony was to get higher on the scale, he'd have to do things his own way.

He'd have to talk to his under in command, tell him the plan. But first, he had a date. His first since arriving in Kansas. After this, the police would know for sure he was here and he was on the move again, but they'd never have enough to get him in. He would enjoy this; he missed the thrill.

The girl didn't know what she was in for.

Anthony paused from his pacing when his phone rang. Slightly frustrated with the distraction, he answered swiftly, noticing it was Derek "Devil" Harris as he did so. One of Anthony's men that was still down in Chicago.

"Devil, what?" Anthony snapped.

"Got news. Remember that man, Alley Ice, who slipped in and stole your first promotion in Chicago?"

Anthony rolled his eyes. "Sure, I remember him." His voice went dry with annoyance. Anthony had a personal vengeance against the man. Ice swept in and took the title right under him, and Anthony was kicked to Kansas. Who cared about Kansas? But he built the best he could in this place, and now it was his.

"Right, of course. I heard something that I think will spark your interest."

"What's that?" Anthony indeed felt his interest pique.

"Ice turned out to be a traitor, working undercover for a branch in the FBI. Nearly died. Apparently, he lives in Kansas, and his real name is Ethan. He is currently injured, so he should have some information in a hospital."

Anthony felt a smile pull at his lips. Idiot Bullet. He and Paulie had a habit of getting too close to people, becoming vulnerable. Anthony wasn't stupid enough to trust anyone like that. "Is that all the info?"

"He has two brothers and a mom still. One of the brothers is named Mason. Ethan had two bullet wounds, if that helps. That's about all I've been able to gather. Also, Dase has some people looking for him as well; they have their own score to settle. Might do well to work together."

Anthony scowled at the mention of Dase and the idea of working together. There was nothing more that Anthony hated than a traitor. Dase was supposed to be a dependable lawyer, but he was actually a part of the mafia. He wished people would just pick a side, but people like Dase just went where the money was. And it turned out, Ethan also had lived the double life. No wonder Anthony had never liked the man.

But at least one traitor had to be annihilated.

≈12≈

Maeve's hand entwined in Ethan's as they slowly walked the gardens. Emphasis on the slow, since Ethan was now *carefully* using his crutch again, and Maeve herself was weak. Part of her was annoyed with the slow pace, the other part just enjoyed being with Ethan so much and loved the peaceful stroll as Ethan pointed out flowers here and there.

"That's the begonia. Don't tell my mom, but that flower is my favorite." He pointed to a pink and red flower to the side of the sidewalk, in the dirt. Maeve smiled and crouched to smell the flower, then sat beside them, feeling the soft petals.

"I really like this one," Maeve said, smelling it again. "I love the look of it, the almost spiral, but almost looking like a rose too…kind of like a…man, what's that one, the one you told me earlier?" She looked up at Ethan, shielding her eyes from the sun with her hand. Ethan was smiling down at her.

"Geranium, maybe?" Ethan asked. "That's what they remind me of."

Maeve thought for a moment, thinking back on the orange- and brown-looking flower. "Yeah, but a different color. It's super pretty and unique too. You know?"

Ethan grinned, then made it slowly to the floor next to her. "Yeah, I do." He studied the flower, then her. "I think it would look very beautiful in your hair, but I'd hate to kill such a beautiful gift God has given us."

Maeve tried not to smile as she felt that giddiness rise in her stomach. Mentally, she told her giddiness to *shut up*. "I agree. I love it, but I'd much prefer coming out here and looking at it, rather than killing it and putting it in my hair where I won't see it anyway." She jerked when Ethan adjusted his crutch, accidentally hitting her leg in the process.

Ethan looked mortified. "I'm sorry," he said quickly, reaching for her arm.

Maeve reassured him quickly with a little laugh. It hadn't been a hard hit, just surprising. "I'm alright, just jerked me is all." At his touch, she remembered how he had been with her the entire stay in the hospital, even when she'd gone in to check on her baby. She closed her eyes, remembering the awe in his eyes when they showed the baby, or the gestational sac, in the photo, and he had reflexively grabbed her hand and squeezed it. Maeve herself had been feeling excited about seeing her baby, and knowing Ethan was there with her made it that much better. She wouldn't be alone.

This baby would have a mom, and hopefully by then, a father that could be counted worthy as being one. Not to mention the whole support system of the rest of the Contens and their families. They had all come to see her and Ethan. Came for *both* of them, not just Ethan.

Looking back, Maeve still thought it was super ridiculous, both of them being hurt in the hospital. But Maeve preferred not being alone, and if he hadn't been admitted, they would have probably forced him out after visiting hours. She liked having him there with her in the same room.

Ethan leaned over and wrapped an arm around her, almost tentatively. Maeve leaned into him, enjoying his presence.

"It's really pretty out here," Maeve said, looking around a little, then relaxing with a sigh.

"Yeah," Ethan agreed.

Maeve felt the vibrating of Ethan's phone before it started to make a sound. Someone was calling him. She pulled away from him so he could answer.

Ethan looked at her in apology and pulled it out. He hesitated a moment before answering the call.

"Hey, Mygyer. What's up?" Ethan asked, his voice carefully even. Maeve could see the darkness flooding into his eyes again. It did so almost every time he thought about being undercover.

Ethan's hands tightened into fists. "Are you sure? How long? Do you think they will?" Ethan listened for a minute, then took a trembling breath. "I don't think so, Mygyer. I mean, they wouldn't be able to…"

Ethan trailed off, looking at Maeve. "Okay, I'll be sure to keep an eye out. Not like I go out much…that's true though. Okay, yeah, I know. Thanks." Ethan hung up and looked away from Maeve, eyes scanning the garden.

Maeve put a hand on his back. "What's wrong, Ethan?"

Ethan hesitated, not meeting her eyes. "Well, I'll be able to get back into training for work again soon," he said slowly. "And it seems Santorini has contacted some people…has people looking for me here in Kansas." Ethan's voice fell flat, but Maeve could see the nervousness in him as he looked around the yard again.

"They won't find you, right?" Maeve asked, her grip tightening. She didn't want to have a chance of losing Ethan now that they'd grown so close.

Ethan looked at her. "I…don't know. I hope not." He grabbed her hand and took a deep breath.

"And about going back to work? You're not strong enough to be back out there." Maeve rubbed his hand with her thumb.

Ethan tried for a smile. "They won't have me out in the field again yet. It's more, they want me to start seeing a counselor and stuff. I refused it at first, just wanting to be home, but to get back into work I have to pass some tests—and I'll have to get back to work eventually."

"Oh." Maeve frowned. It may do some good for Ethan to start with some counseling; he needed something to help get him back on his feet, for sure. "It would probably be a good thing."

Ethan looked at her hesitantly. "Yeah. That's what people keep telling me. I just…I don't know. It still scares me." Ethan swallowed heavily. "I don't like the idea of talking about all these things to someone I don't know."

Maeve hesitated, then moved closer, sort of in front of him. "Talk to me about it then."

Ethan looked at her, eyes unsure.

"Come on, Ethan. You're letting it haunt you. When your family talked to me, they said you've lost your happiness. They want *you* back, and if talking will help you come back, then I think you should do it." Maeve grabbed his other hand too, peering into his eyes.

"I'm alright, Maeve," he said unconvincingly. Then he sighed. "It's just…I just feel so confused now."

"Why is that?" Maeve asked gently.

Ethan let go of her hands and leaned back, looking to the sky. For a moment, Maeve felt put out that Ethan had let go, then realized that it was his way of letting go of his pain. He was opening himself up.

"I've always tried to be honest. Maeve, it would kill me to have to lie to people. I hated the feeling I got, even as a kid. Then, when I got to be an agent, I thought it would be an honest job. I thought it would be a good thing. And I suppose it started off that way. I would see a lot of others lying and hurting people, and that would bother me a lot, but I also was able to stay the good guy in a way.

"I started as an undercover agent because I wanted to help people." Ethan continued, slowly stretching his legs out in front of him. "I knew that Santorini was doing terrible things. I figured I had nothing to lose, and I might be able to help some people in the process…" He hesitated, looking at Maeve. "And I guess I did. I just didn't realize how much of myself I would lose along the way."

Maeve was silent—she didn't know what to say. Maybe it would be a good thing to talk to someone who was trained in this. "What do you think you lost?" Maeve asked after a couple of long moments of silence.

Ethan met her eyes for a moment, then looked away. "Trust. In myself mostly, but even with other people. After living such a long lie, I don't know what's right anymore. After betraying someone who seemed so good most of the time, I feel like the bad guy. Now I just don't know what's true, or who to trust. I don't know if the person beside me is actually on my side. And I especially don't trust myself. If I was put in that position again, I don't know if I'd have the strength or courage to do the right thing. I don't even know if I'm sure what is right and wrong right now."

Maeve swallowed and narrowed her eyes. "Okay, so let's start very simple," she said. Ethan looked over at her, seemingly with a spark of hope, or at the very least, interest. "What and who do you like?"

"My family." Ethan answered almost instantaneously. "And you, strangely enough. And I like helping people still."

Maeve nodded. "And your family? Do you trust them?"

Ethan looked thoughtful. "Yes, I do. I know they care for me and would never intentionally harm me or do anything wrong."

"And you trust that you would do anything to protect them, right?" Maeve asked.

"Of course, I would. And for you too, Maeve." Ethan smiled softly at her, but it didn't last long.

"Sometimes you just have to start with the simple things that you know, Ethan," she told him. "Build up from there…Do you trust that God has a plan?"

Ethan looked warily at her. "Yes."

"Do you trust He can help you get through this if you let Him?"

Once again, a hesitant affirmative. Then Ethan elaborated. "I know He can, but…I don't know if I can let Him. Does that make sense?"

Maeve nodded. "Why do you feel that?"

Ethan threw a hand in exasperation. "I don't know. Stubbornness, I guess."

Maeve waited patiently. Mostly because she didn't know what else to do.

Ethan's shoulders fell. "Because I don't think I should let go of it. Because I feel like I need to get over this."

"By yourself, you mean?" Maeve pointed out.

Ethan nodded. "I know it's ridiculous, Maeve, but I can't let go of that thought. I've tried pushing past it. *Obviously* I need God's help, but I can't. I don't know how."

"Ethan! Ethan!" Childish yelling interrupted them. Maeve looked over Ethan's shoulder to see Owen running at them at his fullest speed. Behind him stumbled two little girls, both of whom waved their hands enthusiastically. "Grandma told us to come out and get you! Dinner is ready and the family is all here!" Owen tossed himself into Ethan's awaiting arms for a big hug.

"Why didn't you call us in when you first got here?" Ethan asked, confused but holding his other arm out for the two girls. Lila got to him first, then the other girl.

"Grandma says you guys were having some time together." Owen pulled away and looked at Maeve, giving her a little wave, but looking too shy to give her a hug too.

"Hey, Lila, Zee. How are you two doing?" Ethan asked them as he started to stand with his crutch. Maeve stood as well and helped steady him.

"Look at the picture I made," Lila told him, holding up a picture with blobs that look sort of like trees.

"Good job, Lila. It's beautiful." He lifted Zee onto his good side since she was pulling on his shirt. She put her head on his shoulder immediately. Maeve worried that he would hurt himself with holding her.

Lila beamed and ran back toward the house. Owen grabbed Ethan's hand and started walking in slowly with his uncle. Maeve smiled and followed behind, wondering if she should offer to take Zee. But Ethan looked at peace while holding her.

They made their way slowly back inside. When they got in, Ethan's whole family was already gathered at the dining room table. The family tried to get together at least once a month for dinner. Apparently, they had been out of the habit of doing it until Ethan had been injured and came back home. Now they all felt more desperate to have the time together. One good thing about this trial: it's brought the family together even more.

The family greeted them both as they came in, Fallon taking Zee from Ethan almost immediately while his wife, Jessica, started scolding Ethan about holding a kid while injured. Ethan just gave his sister-in-law a hug, smiling. Maeve had the feeling he just did some things to get a rise out of people.

She couldn't help but smile as Elisa's family greeted her, asking how she was doing, and if she was planning on coming to Owen's birthday. At the question, Maeve looked to Owen, who was still gripping Ethan's hand, as well as his own fathers, but was looking in Maeve's direction. When Maeve looked, Owen looked embarrassed. Maeve found it amusing since she had spent the day with him and Ethan, and he had seemed fine most of the time then, only a little shy when she asked him a direct question.

Tyra leaned closer. "Owen really admires you," she said softly. "You and Ethan. I think it's because he knows what you've done for Ethan, and Ethan has always been close to his nephew."

"Of course I'll come!" Maeve admonished, looking at Owen again. Owen grinned, this time looking relieved. He slowly moved away from his dad, and Maeve crouched, holding her arms out to show that he could come. He took the invitation, jumping into her arms—probably a little too rough with how weak she was. She laughed, though, hugging him tight. He was a cutie.

"Thanks, Maeve," Owen whispered, then ran over to take his chair.

Tyra put a hand on her arm when she stood back up. "You're really amazing, Maeve. Thank you."

Maeve smiled at her even though she couldn't find a response. She felt relieved when Elisa came in, announcing dinner was ready and to have them all sit.

"Uncle Ethan, Aunt Maeve, sit by me!" Lila gestured for them, bouncing in the seat she had been placed in.

Maeve felt her eyes widen as her face darkened. She couldn't bring herself to look at Ethan or Elisa.

Tyra caught onto their uncomfortableness, though Mason and Isabelle laughed. "Babe, Maeve isn't your aunt."

Lila looked at her, confused. "Sure, she is. She's here all the time."

Tyra looked apprehensively at Maeve, but Maeve forced herself to calm down, waving a hand dismissively. Surely, Lila only meant for it as the fact that she's seen Maeve a couple times here with the family.

Tyra smiled, seeming relieved. When Maeve sat next to her and Lila, Tyra leaned closer. "Thanks. Sometimes it's hard to argue with her; when she gets an idea in her head, she's convinced of the truth of it and won't change her mind. Are you sure you're okay with sitting by her?"

"Of course." Maeve nodded, smiling at Ethan over Lila. Ethan smiled back at her as he pulled a chair out to sit. His eyes had turned thoughtful, and she could feel his gaze on her, even when she turned away.

"Fallon?" Elisa asked as they all settled down together at the enlarged table. Maeve looked around, once again finding herself amazed that she had all these caring people in her life. Though explaining what had happened to her to the family was hard, it was ultimately worth it. "Will you say the blessing, please?"

~13~

Anthony ran his hand down his jacket, annoyed with the rip down the side. He had just gotten this same jacket fixed on one side from a little tailor shop, and now the opposite side had ripped.

Anthony took a deep breath, calming himself. The rip itself wasn't so much what bothered him. Meeting with Mr. Dase was what bothered him. The man had called and wanted to meet about finding Ethan, sure that Anthony would have heard something about it by now.

Then he offered Anthony the position Ethan had been given, but with more benefits, if only Anthony would help Dase find Ethan and his family. He was tempted, for sure.

Anthony narrowed his eyes, looking into the mirror. It's not like Anthony didn't want the help; he liked the idea of finding Ethan one way or another and would hate to miss out on revenge if he refused to help Dase and Dase ended up being the one to find the man. All in all, it wasn't a bad deal.

Anthony nodded at himself, then opened his office door and yelled out. "Big Dig, call Dase and tell him he's got a deal, and if he does find Ethan, he better call me before he does a thing about it!"

"Yes, sir," Big Dig shouted back to be heard over the sound of construction right outside their door. Usually the construction bothered Anthony, but right then, he hadn't noticed it at all.

Anthony looked momentarily in the mirror, then made a split-second decision. He needed his suit patched up again, and that girl who had helped him last time, though shy, was a beauty. Today he determined he'd break through her shell and convince her of a date. His last date had gone flawlessly, her body now marred the alley, or maybe the cops had found her by now. He planned out his course perfectly, not wanting to make any mistakes of being caught on camera.

Whistling, he left the room, passing Dig as he talked on the phone.

A part of him couldn't believe he even considered working with Dase, with how much he hated the man. It almost felt as though he was betraying his standards to get back at another man. But this would get him to the top, so he thought it worth the risk. Besides, once he made it under Dase, it wouldn't be hard to either kill or set the man up for prison and have that traitor out of the way as well. That thought cheered him up as he walked, his hands in his pockets. He nodded at the passing people, oddly excited to go see the two ladies in the shop. This was his day.

When he got to the shop, he opened the door and saw two females in there. One was the married lady he had seen last time. The other, Anthony didn't recognize.

Great. How was he going to tell if the other girl was there without showing too much interest?

He didn't have to try and figure it out. At the sound of the bell, the third lady, the one he wanted, came out. When she saw him, her foot paused mid-step and her hand gripped the wall beside her. He merely smiled, curious as to her nervousness. Was it because she was just uncomfortable around men? Or was there something else?

Isabelle looked up and smiled politely at him. "You're back. Is there something wrong, sir?"

Anthony headed toward the desk she stood behind. She was sorting through some baby clothes. "In fact, nothing is wrong. You see, you fixed up this side of the suit jacket the other day." He turned and showed her the well-done side. "Quite beautifully, I must say." He then turned to the other side. "But now, you see, it had the gall to rip on me on the opposite side while I was at work." He didn't say that he had to dislocate an arm while at work last time because this imbecile thought he could betray him. That was when it ripped on him.

Isabelle smiled and came around the desk. "I see. Maeve, dear, could you go get me some thread?"

"Of course." The girl who had come from the back said, quickly disappearing.

Maeve. Unique name. He smiled in the direction she disappeared, wondering how he would get such a hesitant woman to go out with him.

"Let me see your jacket," Isabelle said, starting to walk him to the couch. He shrugged out of it and handed it to her gently. He didn't trust many people with his suits; he had been very hesitant to come into this tailor, but they had done a good job with it last time, and he wanted a good excuse to see this woman, Maeve, again.

Instead of sitting, he decided to stand, walking slowly after Isabelle. He knew Maeve would have to go over to Isabelle when she came out.

"So, Isabelle. Is this your shop? It's rather well-put-together." Anthony looked around. He knew compliments made it harder for girls to say no.

Maeve came out from the back and walked over to Isabelle as she responded.

"Yes, it is my shop," she beamed. "It's pretty small, just us girls, but we don't need more than that in this small town."

Anthony nodded his head in her direction. "Right you are. And I see you're married. Does he live near here?"

"Oh, yeah. Right around here." Isabelle started threading the needle, her mind now more on her task.

Anthony turned to Maeve. "And what about you? You live close by?"

"About half an hour out," Maeve answered, seeming uncomfortable.

"And what about you?" Anthony raised his voice slightly, inviting the other girl into the conversation. It was obvious that she was younger, maybe still in high school, even. Maeve looked maybe twenty-five. Isabelle in her thirties probably. Anthony himself was nearly forty, but he also knew that he looked handsome—and most young ladies only cared about handsome and rich. He felt that Maeve might be an exception to that, which would make this a challenge. He always liked a challenge.

The younger girl looked up momentarily, shocked. "Oh, not far. Otherwise, my mom wouldn't let me work here." She smiled, blushed, and looked back at her work. Anthony smirked in amusement.

Anthony paused a moment, wondering what to say next. "Well, I am glad you're here. Can't believe I ripped my suit up twice already while being here. I'll say it's a new record."

"You just move here or something?" Isabelle asked distantly.

"No, visiting. In fact, I finally have a free night to enjoy some of this town. I've been busy in meetings all this time." He stopped talking as the bell rang, signaling someone coming in. He felt a flare of frustration. Maeve took the chance to step away and greet who came in.

"Hey, Charles," he said.

"Hey Maeve." Charles hugged Maeve. Anthony felt himself frown, swallowing frustration. Isabelle looked up, then lowered her voice to Anthony.

"I'm sorry, sir," she murmured. "That's my husband. Mind if I see him a moment?"

Relieved, Anthony nodded. "Of course."

Isabelle ran to Charles, throwing her arms around him. Charles laughed and twirled her. "How's my beauty?" he asked.

"Feeling beautiful," Isabelle told him flirtatiously. "How's your day? I'm so glad you were able to get free." She looked behind her, to Anthony.

"It's good," Charles told her. "How's Ethan doing? Any better?"

Anthony felt himself stiffen at the name.

Ethan.

Maeve put her hand on Isabelle's shoulder before Isabelle could respond. "Go see him for a while. I can finish up the sewing."

Isabelle nodded. "Thanks." She seemed to miss the panicked look Maeve gave Anthony. Did Maeve sense the tension in him when he'd heard the name? Was this the same Ethan that Anthony was out to find? Did they happen to know him?

"Ethan a brother?" Anthony asked, turning away as if to show his lack of intent interest.

Maeve didn't answer the question, just walked around the counter. "You don't mind if I finish up the sewing, right?" she asked instead. She looked at the other girl in the shop, her eyes nervous.

Something was definitely up. "No, of course not." Anthony smiled smoothly at her. "So, Maeve. You up to anything later?"

Maeve didn't meet his gaze as she sewed. Unlike with how Isabelle had been almost entirely focused on the sewing, only giving a little portion of her attention to the conversation, Maeve seemed the opposite. Her shoulders seemed tense, and eyes almost *too* focused, as if she was trying not to look at him.

"Yes, in fact. I have a date with my boyfriend," she said stiffly. Out the corner of his eyes he saw the high school girl look sharply at Maeve. Anthony doubted Maeve told the truth, but he couldn't force it without making anyone suspicious.

"That's truly a pity," Anthony said as she finished up the final couple stitching's. He grabbed the jacket when she cut the string. "I hope to be seeing you guys later. Thank you for your service." He paid the high schooler, then left. He walked down the street, turned a corner, then made his way to a place across the street in a roundabout way so he could keep watch over this little shop. He debated calling Dase to have some help with following the other two. It would be faster, but Anthony wanted to be sure first.

He planned on following all three of the girls to see which one led to Ethan, starting with Isabelle.

¤ ¤ ¤

Patricia frowned as she glared at Mygyer. "I told you someone was here stirring up trouble," she said sourly. She was frustrated that he hadn't taken her seriously. Okay, yes, he had plenty of reasons not to investigate it. With Ethan injured, and the court happening with Santorini, plus the million and one other cases he'd had to keep an eye on. He was the Director over the Crime unit in Kansas and was working with the Chicago Crime unit on this case, and Patricia was just the Liaison between the two. But now this young lady was killed—with all the signs of a crime boss that used to live in Illinois—in an alley here in Kansas. In Kansas! Patricia knew the mafia weren't common here. They had some here and there—even more so in the bigger cities—but almost no one in the smaller towns.

Patricia paced in front of Mygyer, the pictures of the dead girl to her side. She had already seen the pictures; she refused to look at them again.

Mygyer studied the pictures, his eyes holding onto a sadness that wouldn't leave. "Do you think it's from a family here in Kansas, or one coming over from Chicago?" he asked her, leaning back in his chair and watching her pacing.

Patricia grabbed the folder and tossed it in front of the director. "I'd been following up on a lot of leads these last few months. The stupid thing is, they're all being very careful, so even the things I got I can't be a hundred percent sure about. A lot of it could be false, I know that, but I'm grasping at straws. And now we know that at least one more boss is down here, one who we thought had died or something down in Chicago. He's coming out again, and I don't think I'm ready to try and meet him. I've been trying to follow this jerk for years now, and so have many people on the team. No one has been able to get him in the action. We don't have any concrete proof of who it could be." She sighed, paused, and put her palms on the table as she took a deep breath. "I'm sorry. Mygyer, I know I shouldn't—"

Mygyer waved away her apology. "I know why you're upset, Patty. I should have looked in on this earlier." He sighed as he flipped through the pages, then closed it up as he finished. "I just don't know what we will do when we have so little substantial evidence." He held the folder up, then let it fall to the table as he put fingertips to his eyes. "Who found the girl?"

"Officer Damon." Patricia sighed and sat in the seat across from Mygyer. "He's a little shook up."

"Don't blame him." Mygyer looked at her. "And how're you doing, Patty?"

Patty shrugged. "I don't know. I'm okay, I guess. Sometimes it's hard." She looked at the folder and pulled herself together with the help of that scene from *Incredibles* flashing through her brain *"Pull yourself together, you are Elastigirl!"*

"Well, Mygyer. What should we do?"

¤ ¤ ¤

Maeve couldn't help but breathe a sigh of relief as she watched that man, Aaron, stroll around the corner. Must be staying somewhere close by if he was walking.

The nasty feeling she'd had with the man last time had come once again, amplifying. She felt it was unsafe to talk about anything around him, and she really hated how he continued to hit on her. It's not like she was even that friendly with him or anything. Why did he keep trying?

She smiled suddenly, wondering what Ethan would think of having been called boyfriend. She wondered if there was anything romantic between them at all, then realized that she knew for a fact there was. She couldn't stop crushing on him and thought of him almost all the time. Whether or not Ethan had any feelings for her that would last longer than a couple months, she didn't know.

She turned around and saw Timmy's gaze on her, eyes wide.

"What?" Maeve asked, walking toward the back.

"I can't decide if you were scared of him or the thought of becoming his girl," the high schooler murmured, smiling a little.

"How 'bout both?" Maeve told her, disappearing into the back, but talking loud enough for the teen to hear. "He makes me feel super uncomfortable."

"He's kind of hot," Timmy said, matter-of-fact.

"Sure, but I felt as though he was undressing me with his eyes." Maeve felt herself shudder. Timmy was right, the man had good features, but in a rough, worn type of way. In a way where he knows he's hot, so he flaunts it. As if he's so confident, he knows he'll get what he wants.

But why did he want Maeve so badly?

Timmy laughed from the other room. "He's definitely older than you though, so that's a little weird that he was trying so hard."

No kidding. Maeve reminded herself to call Mygyer or let someone know about this man.

"Don't you have school?" Maeve asked as she came back out with a box, wanting to change the subject.

Timmy shrugged. "Yeah, but not for three days. The school has some things that need maintenance, and they need students out of there. I offered to work here; it's more fun than waiting around at home. Though I wonder at times how often they use excuses because the teachers just want a break from us students." She chuckled.

"I see." Maeve put the box on the counter and opened it. More stuff that Isabelle was ready to sell. "Man, she has made a lot of things."

Timmy looked at the new box. "I'm sure she didn't make it all. Some of them are old clothes from her kids she had bought. She thinks it's time to get rid of old, and if she happens to have another child that needs clothes, she'll start with new."

"Oh…That makes a lot more sense." Maeve opened the box. More baby clothes, but slightly bigger this time. Maeve couldn't help her hand as it fluttered to her stomach, cradling. She could feel a barely imperceptible bump. It filled her with warmth.

She was going to have a baby.

And, thank God, a family to help her. She wondered if Ethan would end up caring for her still and wanting to be this baby's dad. What if she had been assaulted and not been removed for her and Ethan's protection? What would she have done if she was still in Illinois on the street, alone?

Timmy chuckled. "A lot of these are still in good shape. But some of the more well-worn clothes will have to be given away or something."

Maeve nodded, starting to sift through the clothing and separating them into piles. It might be a good thing to separate in the back, so customers weren't there when they did so, but they all preferred to be in the light, and today it'd been slow. Honestly, it was pretty slow anyway; Isabelle could only afford to keep this shop open because her husband was a manager of some big business Maeve forgot the name of. Isabelle kept the shop open because she loved it, and it was a space that she could sew in.

And the clothes Isabelle made were always so beautiful and heartfelt. Timmy was working here because she wanted to get a homecoming dress and didn't have the money, so Isabelle thought of something else. Maeve was convinced that Timmy would have the prettiest dress out of everyone there. Isabelle had shown her it, and it was stunning. Timmy herself wanted to be surprised, so she refused to go into Isabelle's office.

Isabelle was so nervous that Timmy might not like it as much as they both hoped, but Timmy would only smile.

"I trust you," she'd say, then blush and turn away.

"Your dance is coming up soon, right?" Maeve asked, looking at her.

"Oh." Timmy swallowed heavily. "Uh…Yeah." She sounded upset. Maeve paused and put a hand on her arm.

"What's up?"

"Well…" Timmy bit her lip, then tears ran down her face. Shocked, Maeve rubbed her arm and stepped closer.

"What happened?"

"The boy ditched me," Timmy sobbed. "Dylan, I was going to go out with my crush. He finally noticed me, and I felt so happy. Then yesterday he pulled out. Said he'd only done it on a dare, and that he didn't really like me. He decided to ask this new girl out instead—this drop-dead gorgeous girl—and left me to be alone. It was a jerky thing to do. I haven't even told my parents."

She sobbed and covered her face in her hands. A moment later she was wiping her tears, trying to calm down. "My parents have always encouraged me, trying to tell me that I'm beautiful—that I don't need a guy to define me. I usually believe them, but there's got to be a reason he pulled out on me, and I keep coming back to the fact that I'm just not pretty. Maybe if I tried harder, if I wore makeup and did my hair in the mornings, maybe it would be different. Maybe he would like me. I hate that my natural beauty isn't beautiful to others!" She exploded with frustration.

Maeve put both hands on her shoulders. "Is this your natural beauty?" Maeve asked her gently.

Timmy nodded, wiping her eyes again. "Sure."

Maeve hugged her. "You're beautiful, Timmy. I wish I'd had your beauty when I was your age. Dylan sounds like a jerk—it's better to have known it before he did something worse. I know it's hard to see a boy completely block you out like that. I'm sure you feel completely humiliated. But Timmy, it'll pass. That might not be what you want to hear, but trust me. Sometimes bad things happen for a reason. You will find the right guy for you."

Timmy nodded against her shoulder, then managed a small laugh. "You sound like my parents." She pulled away, looking slightly better.

"Good?"

"Yeah, I think so." Timmy sighed. "I don't want to tell Isabelle—I mean, she's worked so hard on my dress, and I worked so hard to pay for it, but now it's worthless."

Maeve narrowed her eyes, looking toward Isabelle's office. "Nonsense. You can still go to the dance, can't you?"

Timmy looked down, shrugging. "I don't know if I'd want to."

"Timmy, don't let one boy ruin your night. You go there, blow your ex-date's mind with your beauty, make him regret letting you go. Then show him you don't need him." Maeve raised her eyebrows playfully. Timmy snorted, then burst out laughing and crying at the same time. Maeve held her another couple minutes, then she heard the door open again and Timmy ran for the bathroom in the back.

Maeve turned and saw Isabelle come back in with Charles. She had seen Timmy run back.

"What's wrong?" Isabelle asked, concern in her eyes. She dragged Charles closer since her hand was in his.

"Timmy's date pulled out last minute to go with another girl to the dance," Maeve told her. "She's devastated. She hasn't wanted to tell anyone because she feels so bad that you made the dress for her already, but now she doesn't want to go."

Isabelle's concern grew. "Oh dear." Her eyebrows drew together angrily. "I hate it when boys are jerks like that. She's still going to go, isn't she?"

"I'm not sure," Maeve told her. She looked over at Charles, seeing the tightness in his jaw. He seemed mad as well, but also slightly amused.

"She should." Isabelle let go of Charles' hand and went to the back, following Timmy. Maeve stood there awkwardly. Sure, she liked Charles well enough, and had given him a hug because she knew

Charles liked hugs, but she didn't really know what to say to him. Especially right now.

"I wish I was her father so I could go beat the living tar out of this boy," he admitted after a moment, making Maeve smile. It sounded like something Maeve's father would have said.

"That age can be hard," Maeve said. "Those feelings in general. I know for me those feelings lasted a while, and I still fight them. I'm not sure any girl can really get over it."

"Any guy really either," Charles admitted, then he blushed. "Don't tell Isabelle I said that."

"I already know, dear," Isabelle said in a singsong voice as she came back out with Timmy. Timmy smiled a little, but ducked her head away from Charles, as if embarrassed. "Now." Isabelle turned toward her, putting both of her hands on Timmy's arms. "I have something to show you."

Timmy wiped her eyes. "What?"

"Close your eyes." As soon as Timmy closed her eyes, Isabelle looked at Maeve as she also covered the teen's eyes. Maeve somehow knew exactly what she wanted and nodded. She went directly to Isabelle's office.

Isabelle had finished the dress last night and had shown Maeve to see what she thought. It would be the perfect thing to cheer Timmy.

She opened the door quietly, glad that the serviceman had come in only days before to grease the hinges.

The dress was a light blue, almost a mix between sky blue and aquamarine. The top part around the torso was lacy with an under coat of peach color. It had capped sleeves, but they were done so they moved easily. The bottom had a thin, sheen, layer of that same color, then a thicker piece underneath so it wouldn't be transparent. It was simple, but stunning. Perfect for Timmy's character.

Maeve brought it back out, lifting it up so the wheels of the mannequin thing didn't make any noise. Charles came over to help her settle it in front of Isabelle and Timmy.

As soon as Maeve and Charles stepped out of the way, Isabelle let go. "Okay, open your eyes." Isabelle released her hands.

Timmy did as she said, then gasped as she caught sight of the dress. "It's so beautiful!" she said, squeezing and hugging Isabelle tightly. "Thank you so much."

Isabelle nodded, looking into her eyes as she pulled back. "Timmy, I want you to go to that dance as confident about your beauty as you know your parents believe about you. You're stunning, and it's okay that you're not going with Dylan. You will find your guy." She grinned. "Now how about you go try this on and we'll see how it fits?"

Timmy nodded eagerly, eyes shining. Isabelle quickly untied the back and slid the dress off, then handed it to Timmy so she could go around the screen to change.

Charles stepped forward to grab Isabelle's hand, lacing his fingers in hers. "I'm really proud of you, babe," he whispered. "You know how to make a girl feel like the princess they are."

"Sure, she got it from her mom," Maeve inserted, remembering how Elisa had made her feel confident in herself within weeks.

"When is the dance?" Maeve asked a little louder so Timmy could answer.

"It's Friday. Not tomorrow Friday, but next Friday." There was a pause. "Could someone help me tie the dress?"

"Sure." Maeve jumped at the opportunity, stepping behind the screen. Timmy was turned away from her, holding her hair out of the way. Maeve gently tugged at the ribbon until it was smooth and tight.

"How does that feel?"

"Perfect." Timmy turned to her, throwing her arms over her shoulders. "Thank you, Maeve."

Maeve hugged her back, then followed behind Timmy to see Isabelle's reaction.

Isabelle covered her mouth with her hands. "Oh, you're beautiful, Timmy."

Charles smiled. "You haven't even done your makeup and you're a beauty, imagine the reactions when you do both."

"I'll be drop-dead gorgeous." Timmy smiled in Maeve's direction. "Undoubtedly."

≈14≈

A storm rolled in. When it first came, it was so sudden, no one had time to prepare. Kansas, well known for their tornadoes, had little warning this time. Elisa's family had been together for dinner when Ethan noticed the sky swapping colors to a dull green and dusting the air outside. They then spent the next couple minutes checking that all the windows were shut and moving down into the cellar.

This time, while all his family was there with him, was the best time to be trapped underground. He listened to the sound of thunder, then the hard rain, or hail, that started to pound down a moment later. He always loved to listen to the sound. His family pressed further into the shelter, some to play pool, some to sit on the couches; Ethan chose to sit on the stairs and leaned back to listen to both the storm and his family. He'd never been out during a tornado warning for longer than a half an hour, so he's never seen a full tornado touch ground. Some people have asked him if it was scary, but to him, it was just a common thing in his life, and when he hid in a cellar and listened to the sounds above, he was more fascinated than anything else.

He sat there for a handful of minutes, alone, then heard footsteps come closer. He didn't open his eyes, but the sound of a sigh as he felt someone sit beside him told him that it was his mom. He smiled.

"How're you doing?" she asked, leaning beside him. Ethan finally opened his eyes.

"Good, Mom. You?" He looked at her.

"Good." She paused, then looked him in the eyes. "You seem to be doing better, happier again."

Ethan didn't answer right away. "I am, I think." He grabbed her hand. "I mean, there are still some hard things, obviously, but…I have lots of support. I'm grateful to see you, and to be here. And when I think of the really bad experiences, I…I feel more at peace, you know? Like, God really does have a plan for everything that happens. I still am mad at myself for what I did, and didn't do, but…I'm trying to forgive myself, and to get past what happened. Maeve has helped me a lot with that. She is so strong, and she keeps things in perspective. It's so easy to forget how angry I was at myself when I'm with her."

Mom smiled softly. "Maeve is amazing. And I'm glad, Ethan. I think you both need each other."

Ethan nodded slowly, looking away. "I just don't know how much, yet."

"You don't need to know yet. Right now, you both need each other's friendship, and that's as far as it needs to extend." Mom patted his hand. "I'm proud of you."

Ethan smiled a little, face down even though he looked at his mom out the corner of his eye. "Why?"

"Nothing ever keeps you down. It makes me proud to be your momma."

Ethan looked at her, grinning. "I had a good momma to teach me."

Mom laughed. "Sometimes I wonder, even when you were little, how you got through all of your sicknesses."

"I mean, I had you back then too."

Mom pulled him in a half hug. He wrapped his arm around her lithe body and they both sat there in silence, listening to the storm a while. Finally, she patted his hand and stood, kissing his forehead before going into the other room.

Ethan was left alone for a while after that. He leaned his head against the wall next to him. He never understood why he loved to sit there in quiet during the storm. When he was younger, he loved it when the tornados came so he had an excuse to be still.

It sounded bad out there, but Ethan sat in a cocoon of peace, knowing that he was safe. The feeling he'd had in church earlier came back tenfold. It was amazing how God knew what Ethan needed, just another storm to get through.

He knew now that he could make it through these trials. He *could* be happy again. He could forgive himself. But the moments where he felt sure of that were rare the last few months. The fact that God gave him this moment of stillness in the storm, as well as such a great family, made him feel very loved and known. Oddly, Ethan felt that the storm had been brought specifically for him.

Ethan sighed, looking at his lap. "God, help me let go of my anger toward myself. Help me forgive myself." He took a deep breath and released it slowly.

He heard movement again. Looking up, he saw Maeve in the doorway. She smiled and tilted her head at him, coming closer.

She sat next to him, silent, grabbing his hand. Suddenly Ethan felt his shoulders fall; there was his answer. How could Maeve forgive him, but he deny forgiveness to himself? She was right; he had done all he could to help, even if he wished he could have made it there sooner.

"How has your week been?" Ethan asked her quietly, enfolding her hand into the two of his.

"Good," Maeve told him. "You know the girl we work with, Timmy?"

Ethan thought back. "Yeah, I've seen her around."

Maeve frowned, nodding. "We gave her the dress. She'd had a hard week; her date for the dance dumped her pretty much last minute."

"Oh man," Ethan scowled. "My mom taught me to never do such a bullheaded thing."

"Apparently his momma either didn't, or he just didn't care. I was pretty pissed."

"Don't blame you." Ethan shook his head. "If I were there, I'd knock some sense into the boy."

Maeve laughed. "That's pretty much Charles' reaction." She shook her head this time, amused. "It's so funny how boys react that way, and women react another."

"Whoa, why are we boys, not men, but you're women?" Ethan turned toward her, studying her playfully.

"Because that's exactly how you react," Maeve told him with a shrug. She leaned back, her eyebrows furrowing with worry suddenly.

"What's up?" Ethan asked, turning toward her. The movement gave him a slight pang in his abdomen.

"I just remembered I had wanted to call Mygyer."

Ethan frowned, concerned.

"Why?"

"There was this man at work that unsettled me," Maeve told him. Her fingers tapped. "It's probably nothing, but I got a weird feeling around him. Just wanted to know if Mygyer has learned anything else."

Ethan looked at her, concerned. Whether or not he was someone Mygyer needed to investigate, he didn't want Maeve to have any men around her that made her uncomfortable.

Maeve gestured that it was fine. "I can handle myself. It's not like he did anything, just tried to ask me out a couple times. I told him I had a boyfriend. I hope you don't mind."

Ethan felt his heartbeat speed up suddenly. "Of course not."

"Good. It's the only thing I could think of that would make him leave me alone." She leaned her head on his shoulder.

Ethan swallowed heavily, looking at the door to the other room. "Hey Maeve?"

"Yeah?" She lifted her head to look at him.

"Will you go out on a date with me?" At her surprised look, he continued quickly. "I mean, I feel like I know you pretty well, but it would be nice to go out on a date, with you, alone…" He trailed off, feeling his face hot with embarrassment. Why did he have to say anything? If this didn't work out, Maeve would feel forever uncomfortable with him, and his mom would hate it if he scared Maeve off.

Maeve smiled softly and rested her head on his shoulder, sending him into relief. "I'd love to." *This is Maeve we're talking about. She doesn't get scared off easily.*

Ethan relaxed, closing his eyes while taking a deep breath. "What would you want to do?"

Maeve shrugged. "I don't care." She shifted. It took Ethan a moment to realize that she had reached for her abdomen.

"You okay?"

"Oh." Maeve looked down. "Yes, I am, I just feel better holding like this. It's like a comfort."

Ethan hesitated, with his hand reached out slightly. "May I?"

"Uh, yeah, sure." Maeve seemed a little hesitant, but she still grabbed his hand to gently put it on her stomach.

"Have you felt anything yet?"

Maeve looked like she was fighting a smile. "No, they said closer to four months I'll start feeling it. They said that while I was getting checked; did you miss it?"

Ethan blushed. Once again, he had drifted into thought. It had probably been when he had been listening to the heartbeat of the baby and couldn't stop thinking about how the kid would turn out. He also couldn't stop thinking about Maeve. He wanted to be there for her. He felt an uncanny attraction to her—who wouldn't? She was amazing.

"I guess so."

Maeve grinned teasingly. "How did you ever manage to be such a great agent when you zone out so much?"

"I don't know. I guess I just wanted it bad enough and knew many people's lives depended on it." He suddenly felt the same pull to get back into the action that he'd had to first get him started. A pull that had been missing for months.

"What is it?" Maeve asked, shaking him slightly.

Ethan looked at her, realizing that he had gone quiet and was staring at nothing. "Oh, I…I think I'm ready to start going back to work again."

Maeve went silent a moment. "That's good, I guess. And yet it worries me."

Amused, Ethan pulled Maeve close. "Oh yeah?"

"Yeah. I know you need to be working and all. You love it. But it makes me nervous to have you go back to work." She put her other hand over his and ran her fingers back and forth. "Do you think you have enough strength to go back yet?"

Ethan nodded. "Mygyer would only have me work a couple hours to begin with, and most of that time would be meeting with a counselor or paperwork." Ethan knew he couldn't do much more than that. His abdomen was still healing. And his leg for that matter. But he was ready to help people again; he yearned for it.

Maeve grinned suddenly and looked back. "You want to go back to paperwork? I heard it's awfully boring."

Ethan laughed. "True that. But I'd only stay in paperwork for a bit."

Maeve pulled away and turned toward him. "Thank you, Ethan, for being such a great support to me."

"Ditto." Ethan took his bag off his shoulders. They had each packed up a light bag of the most important things and some clothing while waiting for the storm to pass. Maeve's bag was smaller. She must not have wanted to bring that much. Probably didn't even have that much.

Ethan threw his bag onto the ground in front of him and rolled his shoulders. Sometimes he could get so distracted and not realize that the way he was sitting or holding something was hurting him. He thought back on Maeve's question and found himself agreeing with her. How *did* he manage to be a cop when at times he couldn't seem pay attention for more than five seconds?

¤ ¤ ¤

Isabelle smiled as she put her phone down. Maeve saw the smile and gave her a questioning look. Happily, Isabelle skipped back over to the desk. "Charles just called, said he has enough time during his lunch to make me a lunch and bring it." She loved when she got to see her husband; he worked so often and left town enough that it felt as though she barely got to see him.

Maeve looked over to the clock and Isabelle followed her gaze. Only another hour, maybe less if she was lucky.

Isabelle's kids were in school. They had two, both double-digit ages, though her younger was barely so. After the loss of their third child, she had been told it would be too dangerous for them to have another baby. Though she had wanted to have more kids, she was grateful she even had the two. She adored them like nothing else. And she'd been given a great man. Charles was supportive of everything she did.

"That's great," Maeve told her as she pulled out another piece of baby clothing and separated it into a different pile according to size.

Timmy was doing some homework on the desk, taking up the seat. Curious, Isabelle grabbed a shirt and looked at Timmy. "Have you found someone else to go to the dance with you?"

Timmy blushed as she looked up, nodding. "Yeah, actually." She hesitated a moment, then grinned. "To be honest, I think I'm more excited to go with this boy than I was Dylan."

"Who is it?" Maeve asked, at the same time Isabelle asked, "Why's that?"

Timmy took her time answering, grabbing a shirt as distraction. Isabelle threw a shirt at her, for her stalling, and Timmy laughed. "Well, I mean…" She paused again, sighing. "Dylan was my dream, but you know when you have a dream and it seems so great as this distant thing, but when it actually comes down to it, you don't think it's worthwhile."

"Like…" Maeve narrowed her eyes. "Like the idea of playing the piano. It seems amazing to think about it, but you have to decide if it's actually worth it to learn."

Timmy grinned. "Exactly. And I don't think Dylan is worth the effort I would have to make to try and please him. Isaac though…"

Isabelle jerked toward her. "Isaac Beatren?" she inquired, surprised. Timmy looked up nervously.

"You know him?" Timmy asked her.

"Yes." Isabelle felt herself smile. "You're going with Isaac?"

Timmy nodded shyly. "Do you think he's a good kid?"

Isabelle thought back on the teenager. That boy had serious anxiety, always thinking about the worst possible things that could happen. He had always had financial insecurity, despite being a great budgeter, so he asked Isabelle if he could work for her or anyone she knew. She knew that he could think of every possible scenario that could go wrong—but also knew that he was confident he could get out of most of those terrible things because he would study what best to do if it ever happened.

But strangely, Isabelle couldn't imagine Isaac going to the dance with any other girl *except* Timmy. Timmy could handle a boy like that, and maybe even get the boy to look on the bright side a little.

"He's definitely a good kid," Isabelle told her. Timmy seemed relieved.

"A lot of people have teased me about accepting the invitation to go with him," Timmy told her, relaxing and sorting the clothes. "I mean, sure he's a little strange; last class period in lab we were partners, and he went through every disaster that I ever could have thought could happen while at the dance, then at the end, he asked if I would go with him to it."

She chuckled. "It was the best thing ever, I swear. There he was saying, "or an earthquake could happen, and all the decorations could come toppling in on us and we would have to get out of the building, or under something secure—and by the way, did you want to go with me to the dance?""

She shook her head, then burst out laughing. "I was so surprised by the question. I'm pretty sure he had to ask twice, and by the second time, he had started to get really nervous." She sighed in contentment. "I think I might enjoy his company a lot, and if something terrible did happen, I now know exactly how to act, or at the very least know that *he* knows."

Maeve laughed. "Sounds like an interesting boy. Does he seem responsible?"

Timmy nodded. "I'm pretty sure he had nearly talked himself out of going to the dance; this would be the first event I've seen him at. He sits by me in a couple classes, and he noticed I was down. When I told him that my date dumped me, he then went on that rave about the dangers of such a dance and proceeded to ask if I wanted to go." She paused, looking thoughtful. "But he is very responsible. He walks his youngest siblings to school before he comes to high school. I'm pretty sure he does so only because he worries about all the possible scenarios that could happen if he *wasn't* there."

Maeve laughed even harder. Even Isabelle laughed at that.

"Sounds like a wonderful kid," Maeve said, squeezing her arm affectionately.

Timmy nodded, grinning, then looked down at her homework. "Think you guys can help me? I'm no good at Calculus."

Maeve snorted. "Yeah right. I never finished high school, and I suck at math too."

Timmy looked at her, curious. "Why didn't you finish?"

Maeve hesitated, then looked at Timmy. "I ran away from a foster home at fifteen."

"That's crazy," Timmy said, looking shocked. "And scary. Why were you in the foster home? And why did you run?"

"My parents died when I was thirteen. I had no other relatives, and I never got adopted. But I got tired of going between really good homes and really terrible ones for the next three or so years, so I decided to make a home myself." She frowned, distracted. Isabelle didn't want to say anything, afraid Maeve would stop talking. Timmy didn't wait though.

"What was it like, living on the streets?"

Maeve looked at her, then looked past them both, to the window. "Well…I was definitely wrong when I tried to 'make a home for myself.' It didn't work because I moved around even more, obviously. I enjoyed it sometimes, except when it got cold at night or got hard to find food. I saw a lot of bad on the streets, but I also saw a lot of beauty, a lot of kind people. I guess it all depends on what you look for because I know plenty of people only see the bad, and others who taught me to look for the good. Those people and teachings are the only reasons I made it through some of the hardest times in my life."

"Is that what got you through, you know, Santorini?" Isabelle asked. As she did so, she immediately regretted it. Timmy didn't know about that, plus she'd hate for Maeve to get uncomfortable.

Maeve paused, swallowing heavily. "Um…sort of. I mean, when it happened, I couldn't believe that someone could be so cruel. At first, I was alone with Santorini, or at least I thought I was, but then I saw two figures. A couple minutes after that, Ethan showed up. I saw him start to interfere. He kept begging him to stop, but he seemed at a loss. At the time, it was Ethan who got me through it. Just knowing that in that terrible time there were still people who wanted to help, even if they didn't know how to."

Timmy looked confused. "What happened?"

Maeve put a hand on Timmy's shoulder, but before she could speak, the door opened. Isabelle looked over, then found herself frowning in surprise. It was that man, Aaron Calloway. It was the third time she'd seen him in the last couple weeks.

Forcing a smile, Isabelle skirted the desk. She knew Maeve was uncomfortable with this man, and this being the third time coming made Isabelle feel uncomfortable as well. What did he want? Was he starting to do it just to come?

She heard Maeve's breath hitch behind her, but focused on the man as he came in.

"Aaron, is it?" Isabelle asked. "What can I do for you this time? Your suit didn't have another mishap again, did it?"

"Actually, I recommended the shop to one of my coworkers." Aaron chuckled and gestured behind him, then seemed to realize no one followed him. "Oh, well he was right behind me—there he is." Isabelle saw a man in the window, walking in.

Maeve had followed Isabelle, now Isabelle heard Maeve draw another sharp breath, and when she looked back, she saw the color flee from Maeve's cheeks, and her hands clenched as she stared at the new man coming in.

Isabelle wasn't the only one who noticed; Aaron seemed to as well, even though he continued as if he didn't. "I figured I could show him the place, since I had nothing better to do." He smiled. If Isabelle wasn't so nervous, with Maeve's reaction, she would be convinced of the story Aaron told.

Timmy had stayed over by the desk. As the new man entered, she looked up from her studies, then eyed everyone as if she recognized the tension.

"Um…Okay." Isabelle cleared her throat and turned to the new man. "What can I do for you?" She forced another smile.

The new man looked at Aaron with a glare, then around the room. "Are you the only three who work here?" he asked after a moment. At seeing Isabelle's confused gaze, he continued. "I mean, I guess I expected something bigger; most places where I came from are bigger."

"I see." Isabelle chanced a look at Maeve. She still looked pale, and her eyes seemed scared. "Well, yes. What can I do for you? Maeve, can you go get my sewing kit?" She needed to get Maeve out of there, both because Maeve looked like she was about to have a panic attack and because she wanted someone to be able to reach a phone easily.

"That's not what we need," Aaron said, and he was suddenly pulling a gun out from under his trench coat and pointing it at Maeve. Isabelle took a frantic step back, closer to Maeve, and Maeve's hand flew to a tight grip on Isabelle's arm.

"Look, man, we have nothing good here," Isabelle told him, taking another step back and wishing she could reach for her phone. Or that Timmy would be smart enough to call the police from behind the desk.

Aaron grinned. "I don't know. Three hot girls in one store."

The other man scowled but looked more intently at Maeve and suddenly smiled. "Oh man, this is great. Santorini's gal. Ethan bring you back here for himself then, huh?"

Isabelle frowned, finally catching on to what was happening, sort of. Maeve had been attacked by Santorini; Ethan had saved her. That meant someone was here for Ethan and had ended up finding Maeve first, it seemed.

Maeve's breathing went shallow, yet she stepped slightly in front of Isabelle. "I am not Santorini's gal," she said stiffly.

Aaron was looking at the new man, curiosity in his gaze.

"Let's take them both," the new man told Aaron. He nodded, but it was his turn to look disgusted with the other man.

"What are you doing?" Maeve asked shakily. "Why do you want us?"

"We want Ethan," the man corrected. "This is just an easier way to get him."

"What about the girl?" Aaron nodded toward Timmy. Isabelle had hoped they had forgotten about her. She looked back to see Timmy, her eyes wide.

Suddenly, Aaron swung the gun and shot at Timmy. Timmy screamed right as the gun swung her way and ducked. Isabelle wasn't sure if she was hit or not, but the bullet went through the building near where she was, and she didn't see any blood, so she hoped at least.

Isabelle prayed for interference. She wanted her husband, but worried that if he came, he'd be shot at too. *Help us, God.*

"Get the girl," the man said. "Leave a message and get out of here." He brought out his own gun and gestured to Maeve and Isabelle to head out. Isabelle shared a frantic look with Maeve before they were ushered out. She gave one last look toward the desk Timmy had ducked behind, praying she hadn't been shot and that Aaron wouldn't harm her.

¤ ¤ ¤

Ethan looked at the caller ID, then felt himself frown. Mygyer.

Sure, Ethan was planning on coming back to work, but it made him feel nervous to receive calls from his boss. Also, he was kind of exhausted today. He wouldn't tell his brother, but Mason had dropped off his kids to let Ethan spend the morning with them. Fun, yes. Exhausting, for sure. But he enjoyed them, so it was worth it. He was glad that Mason had come by to pick them up by then though.

He took a deep breath, then forced his voice to sound chipper. "Hey, Mygyer. What's up? I was going to call you about coming back to work next week."

Mygyer's voice was grim. "Ethan, you may want to sit down."

"What? Why?" Ethan's nervousness rose. Ethan was already sitting in the family room, but he sat forward in his seat.

"Isabelle and Maeve were just taken from work."

Ethan felt his breath catch at Mygyer's words.

"We don't know a lot of details, but we found Timmy tied up, and she said these men came in and took off with the two of them, leaving her behind. They seemed to know Maeve and seemed to be looking for you. She heard the name Santorini a couple times, and…"

"And what?" Ethan asked stiffly.

"You remember that man you told us about, Anthony, who you practically stole the job from at the start of the mission?"

Ethan scowled. "Of course—" he cut off as fast as he started, his hands clenching. Bullet had sent Anthony to Kansas. Ethan stood with the help of his crutch and quickly made his way to the front door, grabbing the keys off the hook. "Mygyer, please tell me…"

"He has them, Ethan. He and another man. Anthony left a mark on Timmy. *His* mark, that's why we know. He left a message with her."

"Mygyer, I'm on my way. Are you all still at Isabelle's shop?"

"We are, but Ethan, I don't think you should…"

"Don't stop me, just tell me what I need to know." Ethan's jaw clenched. "How is Timmy doing?" He remembered the young lady.

Mygyer sighed. "Terrified. Her parents are on the way. They'll probably get here about the same time as you. She's in shock, surely. She's only said a couple of coherent sentences, just enough to let us know about that. They're trying to get her to calm down now, but she doesn't want to go to the hospital, and she won't let go of Charles, and she just wants her parents."

Ethan could imagine. "Wait, Charles? He's there?"

"Yeah, he said he had come to give lunch to Isabelle and the girls, made it a bit late for the action. He's beating himself up about it." Mygyer's voice quieted a little, as if he was close to others or something. "Ethan, hold on a minute…" Ethan was put on mute as he pulled out of the driveway in his mothers' truck. Hopefully she wouldn't miss it, but this was an emergency.

Ethan couldn't drive the best with his hurting leg, but he didn't let that stop him, just carefully had it out of the way and used the other leg. It took him fifteen minutes to get to Isabelle's shop, and Mygyer hung up on him after a couple more minutes to see how Timmy was doing. He also beat Timmy's parents there.

Ethan grabbed his crutch and painfully scooted his way out of the car. His tiredness seemed to vanish, but with working his body so hard, it would be back later.

The caution tape surrounding Isabelle's shop brought more of a crowd than there'd usually be, as pedestrians came to investigate. Plus, media trucks. Ethan pushed his way through the crowd and was nearly stopped by another cop before the man recognized him and ushered him through.

"I'm sorry about your sister," the man said as Ethan went toward the center, to Timmy and Mygyer. Ethan nodded vaguely at the man but was already focused on the scene.

The glass at the front door of the shop had been broken in. Timmy looked a mess. She had blood drenching the front of her shirt and a pair of paramedics were working on bandaging her chest, where "AAC" was cut into her right below her collarbone. Her eyes had a distant but alarmed look. Charles was holding her to his side, her hand gripping his tight.

Timmy's parents were right behind Ethan; he heard the mother shout her daughter's name, and watched as mother and father flew past and gathered Timmy in their arms. Timmy started to cry as she held onto them.

Ethan frowned as he watched the reunion. Thank God Timmy was okay, but where was Maeve and Isabelle?

Charles saw him. His eyes darkened and he made his way to Ethan, hands curled into fists. "What the heck, man? Where did he take them?!" He was practically yelling, his eyes blazing. Before Ethan could blink, he was punched in the jaw hard enough to make tears rush into his eyes. As Ethan stumbled, he felt pain flash in his gut and leg, but fought not to show it. He didn't blame Charles for his anger, so he waved off the couple of officers as he fought not to put a hand on his jaw. "Why did you have to get her into this? They took Isabelle!"

"I never would have purposely endangered anyone. I didn't want any of this," Ethan said calmly, putting his hands in front of him. "I'm sorry, Charles, but I'm going to find them both, and whoever took them." Ethan had to stop himself from calling these guys any swear words that he knew his mom would be disappointed to hear him say. It was hard.

He glanced at Timmy.

Really hard.

He took a deep breath, meeting Charles' haunted gaze. Charles suddenly sobbed, curling slightly forward. "What am I going to tell the kids?" he asked in a choked voice, miserable. Ethan quickly took the two steps and put a hand on Charles' shoulder, trying to offer comfort. Charles just pulled him into a hug and buried his face in Ethan's shoulder. Having just been punched by his brother-in-law, he was slightly surprised, but he pulled him close anyway. Charles had always been a hugger.

"I'm going to find them," Ethan murmured in his ear. "I promise, I will. I know at least one of them who took them. I know the guy won't kill the two of them, at least not until he has me." Ethan patted Charles back and pulled away, turning to his boss while keeping a grip on Charles' arm. "Mygyer, have you identified the other man yet?"

Mygyer was standing just a couple feet away, looking both overwhelmed and concerned. He stepped forward as Ethan spoke. "No. I haven't seen the man before. I've sent it out to the police in Chicago and other places with known groups under Santorini. Thus far I've found nothing." Mygyer sighed. "We watched the camera. The second man avoided the cameras like the plague, can't get a good look at his face. Want to take a look?"

Ethan nodded but turned to Timmy. He crouched beside her and her parents as carefully as he could with his abdomen and put his hand on her shoulder. "Timmy, I know this is difficult for you." He waited until she looked up at him. "Are you able to tell me everything you can about what happened?"

Timmy hesitated, grabbed her dad's hand, then nodded. "Think so." Her breath shuddered. "I wanna help find Isabelle and Maeve." Her eyes went distant as Ethan gestured for Mygyer to come closer.

"First, the one man came in. He called himself Aaron…Aaron something. I can't remember his last name, but it started with a C, I think. He's been in the store a couple other times, I guess, because they welcomed him in by his name, but also with surprise. I'd seen him once before, and Maeve seemed a little uncomfortable with him. I think he was trying to hit on her before."

Timmy eyes furrowed. "This time, he said he brought back his friend because he liked our service. I was kind of just getting back to doing some homework, so I didn't hear everything. Then the next man came in. It was weird, he looked in different places and seemed more tense than the first man. I didn't really like him that much, his eyes were…like, angry." She shuddered. "When he came in, Maeve seemed to recognize him. Her face was pale, and that's when I started worrying more.

"Then Aaron pulled a gun out and pointed it at Maeve and Isabelle. I got out my phone to call the police as soon as I got over my initial shock." She closed her eyes. "I think Aaron saw me move, because he turned the gun in my direction and shot at me. I didn't get hit. I think because I had dropped to the floor as soon as he looked at me." She started laughing, almost hysterically. "I remember, that's one of the things Isaac said to do if someone pointed a gun at me."

Her mom rubbed her arm, eyebrows furrowing, and Timmy calmed back down enough to continue. "Then they took Isabelle and Maeve out, and Aaron came over and tied me up and cut me." She put her hand over her wound and curled into her dad's chest, trembling as he held her tight.

Ethan felt anger flood his veins. He knew Anthony, knew he was a terrible person, but Ethan still couldn't understand these crimes people were capable of doing. These were good girls, good, innocent people.

But then it was anger directed at himself.

Ethan clenched his jaw, took a breath, then rubbed Timmy's arm encouragingly. "Thanks, Timmy." He started to move, but Timmy caught his arm. She couldn't meet his gaze, though she tried.

"Also, he told me…" She swallowed heavily. "Told me to tell you…"

"What?" Ethan frowned, trying not to look at the blood covering her or the half-done bandage.

"Said if you couldn't figure out where they went or what to do then you're not worthy of being a mafia or an agent." Then she started to cry again. "He said you couldn't involve the cops, and that I couldn't tell the cops about what he said, but I'm so scared. What if they hurt them because I told you?"

"Shh…It's okay, Timmy." Her mom soothed next to the girl's ear. "We've got you. You're safe here."

Ethan stood and moved to the shop, studying everything with an intense gaze. The only thing that seemed out of place was the broken window.

"Did they break this?" Ethan asked Mygyer.

"No, I did," Charles told him, voice hard, carefully set to hide emotions. "I came to bring lunch and the door was locked when I got here. I knew Isabelle wouldn't have locked the door, and no one answered when I knocked and called, so I broke it." Charles followed him into the building. "Timmy was tied up to the chair behind the desk." He shook his head. "She was completely breaking down when I got to her, probably about half an hour after the attack. As soon as I got her free, she wouldn't let me go. It took me probably ten minutes for her to calm down enough to tell me that my wife and Maeve were taken."

They were silent as they looked around. Then Charles spoke again. "But I don't get it. What does the AAC stand for?"

"We're not sure," Mygyer answered. "We've been working on uncovering that for a while now. Initials maybe?"

"Maybe he goes by Anthony because it's his middle name," Ethan suggested, his analytical brain clicking on. Good, he needed it to find them.

"Then Aaron could be his first…And whatever his last name is that starts with a C." Mygyer suggested thoughtfully.

"Maybe," Ethan agreed. He wandered in the back of the store as he felt tears prick his eyes.

"You okay, Ethan?" Mygyer asked.

Ethan's anger at himself overpowered him and he slammed the curl of his fist into the wall loud and hard. "I never should've come home!"

It was silent for a moment, then Ethan heard some footsteps come up behind him and a hand lay on his shoulder. "Ethan, don't think like that," Charles told him gently. "Isabelle had been completely distraught when you'd been injured. She always worried about you while you were in the field. She would barely sleep when she wondered if you were okay." Charles rubbed his back. "It's not your fault."

Ethan glared at Charles through his tears. "They wouldn't have found them if I'd stayed in Chicago." He pulled away and went into Isabelle's office instead, to the computer. He sat on the seat and played the tapes, escaping back into his analytical brain. He needed to stay in that until he found the girls. He couldn't think about his sister being with Anthony. Couldn't think about Maeve scared, but this time without him.

He skipped until he saw Anthony enter the room, then played it at regular speed, watching it play out. He could see the nervousness in Maeve when Anthony entered the room, then the absolute fear when the next man entered. Mygyer was right; he did keep his entire face away from the camera, but Ethan still knew exactly who it was, cursing under his breath.

"What is it?" Mygyer asked. "Do you recognize him?"

"Yes." Ethan leaned back in the chair, still watching, feeling washed with weakness. This was bad.

"Ethan!" Mygyer snapped suddenly. Ethan realized that his director had called him multiple times already. "Who is it?"

"I don't know his real name, but they called him Dase—or Mr. Dase—in Chicago." Ethan didn't look away from the screen as he answered. He felt his hands tremble, so he tightened them both into fists. His wound was pounding again now that he took a moment to pause, and taking a slow deep breath didn't do anything to help.

Mygyer frowned. "I'll see if we can get anything on him."

Ethan nodded but couldn't get any words out. Mygyer's firm hand rested on his shoulder. "Ethan, do you want to come with me to search files on Anthony? I had Patty pull everything out."

Ethan hesitated a moment, then nodded. He couldn't bring himself to move, mostly because tears had darted down his face at Mygyer's touch. How could Ethan have lost both of them? He'd just thought he was getting away from this assignment, and now it was coming back to haunt him and hurt his family.

I never should have come back.

His thoughts kept coming back to that. He had to force himself not to think like that, instead telling himself that he would find them.

Come on, God. Please…

≈15≈

Maeve only wished her stomach would stop churning. Well, that, and she wanted herself and Isabelle free, of course. The permeating smell made her feel sick near constantly, and seeing Isabelle there with her made her feel sad. This wonderful lady should not be in this situation.

Isabelle was strangely calm despite her worry. As Maeve shifted uncomfortably again, wishing she had use of her hands, which were tied above her head, Isabelle turned her gaze to her. "You okay?" she whispered.

Maeve nodded, letting her head lean against her arm and the wall behind her head and wondering if any part of this actually made her at all okay. Outside this hidden room was Aaron's office, and beyond that, they were in a meat factory. That's where the smell came from. All the dead meat, some slowly becoming jerky, others cut into pieces or ground up. There was quite a rottenness to the smell, and she had to wonder if some of the meat went bad before they could get use out of it.

"Just nauseous," Maeve said at last, more truthfully. She breathed through her mouth to avoid the stench. Unfortunately, the smell was so bad it was as though she could taste it. "I'm sorry, Isabelle."

Isabelle cracked a smile, though she winced. Anthony's associate had slapped her when she'd tried to resist, resulting in a large bruise on her cheek. Maeve still had to swallow down her anger when she thought of it.

"It's not your fault, Maeve," Isabelle told her.

Maeve didn't believe her; Anthony's associate had known her, and she him. He was one she'd seen the night Santorini attacked her, the one who watched her and even stepped in front of Ethan to stop him from doing anything. Somehow, he had found her. And Ethan.

Maeve had known Ethan was in trouble. Mason had warned her on that first day, but she hadn't realized that it would be like this. She didn't like how Isabelle was here, and that they were trying to bait Ethan. Didn't like how that somehow put the rest of his family in danger as well. And she wished she too was safe at Elisa's home.

Maeve shifted uncomfortably as the smell suddenly became more piercing and her stomach seemed to roll inside her. She quickly moved to sit on her legs and got to her side, hating the vomit that arose.

As soon as she finished puking, she rested her head on her arm, which gave extra weight on her wrist in the handcuffs, but she couldn't pull away.

She felt movement on her thigh and opened her eyes. Isabelle had reached out her foot to try and soothe Maeve or get her attention. "You okay?"

Maeve nodded, wiping the tears on her arm. "I…I wish we were not here."

Isabelle frowned. "I know. Me too. But I'm glad we're together, at least I know you're safe." The *for now* was left unspoken. Isabelle rubbed her leg with her foot. Maeve couldn't help but laugh at the movement, the attempt to cheer her up. Seemed to work since she laughed. Isabelle smiled at her.

"Are you okay?" Maeve asked Isabelle after a moment, putting her mouth to her arm, hating the lingering taste.

Isabelle smirked. "I'm scared to death," she said honestly. "However, when I get nervous, I go through everything that I'm grateful for."

Maeve found herself smiling as tears filled her gaze. "Can you tell me?"

"Tell you what I'm grateful for?"

"Yeah." She needed something to distract herself.

Isabelle thought for a moment. "Well, first off, that we're together. That the man who hit me didn't break any bones or anything else he could have done. That they placed us close enough together to touch…But I guess mostly, I'm grateful that my family is still okay, and that Ethan is still free, and officers and Ethan's team will be looking for us. I know Ethan will find us. It's what he does. I don't know how long it'll take, but I believe in him. And I know Charles will be right behind him." Isabelle shifted with a wince. "And I'm really glad you puked on the opposite side."

Maeve laughed. "Ugh, I hate that I feel so sick."

Before either of them could say anything else, the door swung open, letting in a stream of light and a larger stench. It wasn't entirely dark in there, but Maeve's eyes had adjusted to the near darkness. Now she had to blink many times, and then just close her eyes, to get them readjusted.

As she still fought the light, she saw that it was Aaron. Maeve immediately felt as though her insides were squirming. She didn't like either of her captors, but Aaron had a stupid uncanny attraction toward her, as if she were a prize to be won or a dog to be disciplined. It made her want to sink into the floor to hide.

Aaron moved closer and put a plate he was holding on the floor between Maeve and Isabelle. On the plate was some meat—mostly raw meat, Maeve would guess. Aaron's nose scrunched up. "Not feeling the best, my beauty?" Though disgusted by the puke, he put some gentle fingers to her chin. Maeve pulled away from him, but that seemed to anger Aaron since his hand instead went around her neck and pushed. Immediately she found she couldn't breathe. Her head hit the wall as he moved closer to her. She tried to squirm out of it, to get free.

Aaron was glaring at her. "You will respect me," he said, inches from her. Maeve tried to take a breath, but instead started to feel lightheaded and her mind went into a momentary panic, sure he was going to kill her. The panic rose along with disgust as he kissed her. Her brain became fuzzy, and her body screamed for air. Suddenly she was released. She gasped and slowly the fuzziness disappeared. She heard a shout of pain from Isabelle and forced the darkness away faster. She saw Aaron holding Isabelle's foot far out in front of her in an awkward angle.

Aaron let go and stood back up. "It looks like you both need more time to learn how to be docile," he said. "Maybe you'll be ready by breakfast." He left with the plate.

Maeve herself couldn't have cared. Sure, she was hungry—she guessed it had been two days with little food and water—but the gross meat would never make it down her throat while she felt like she did.

Isabelle was biting her lip as she dragged her leg closer to her body. "Are you okay, Maeve?" she asked.

Maeve nodded, throat aching and still kind of coughing. "What happened?"

Isabelle shrugged, managing a small smile. "I kicked him. Think he sprained my ankle or something." She winced as she sat up.

"I'm sorry," Maeve told her again, feeling bad.

Isabelle shook her head. "Maeve, if you say 'I'm sorry' again, when it's not your fault, I will have to kick you. And trust me, it will hurt me far more than you." They both grinned. Maeve shook her head and nearly apologized again.

Instead, a sudden sob shook Maeve. Isabelle frowned. "What is it?"

"I thought he was going to kill me," Maeve said, wishing she could hold her neck. "I'm so glad you're here. I don't think I can make it without you. How is any of this happening?"

Isabelle didn't answer right away. "I don't know. But we'll make it out of this. Ethan will find us."

Maeve knew that, but she wondered what state she'd be in by the time he found her. She hated being so dependent on another for her life, but right now she had no choice. *Please hurry, Ethan.*

¤ ¤ ¤

Mason didn't know what to do when Ethan left the room, limping with his crutch. Elisa was sobbing on the couch, overwhelmed that both her daughter and practically adopted daughter had been kidnapped. Riley and Fallon were there as well. Mason hesitated, torn between comforting his mother and comforting his brother. Riley approached their mother and shot Mason a glance, freeing him to go console Ethan, who was heading for the garage door.

Mason caught the door of the garage. "Ethan?"

"What?" His voice was hard, and he kept for the truck. Mason knew how Ethan felt. He wanted them back too.

"Where are you going?" Mason asked.

"I don't know. For a drive." Ethan coughed to clear his throat as he pulled the car door open and hopped in. Mason knew his younger brother was capable and all, but Ethan had also been stretching himself thin, going back to work during the day until Mygyer had to send him home, then continuing researching when he got home. Mason wondered how much sleep he'd had. If anything like Mason, not much.

"Can I come?"

Ethan just shrugged and shut the door. Mason took it as a yes and jumped in the passenger side. He wouldn't have let Ethan go by himself anyway.

They both stayed silent as they drove. It was dark out—not crazy dark, but the sun had mostly disappeared on the horizon. It also looked like another storm might come their way, but that was far in the distance if at all.

The silence stretched far longer than Mason liked, especially when tension was so high. He hated watching his brother stew silently because he knew that unless pushed, Ethan wouldn't talk about anything that bothered him. But Mason didn't know if Ethan was ready to talk yet. Mason didn't know if he was ready to hear.

At last, tired of wondering, Mason sighed and saw Ethan tense. "Ethan…What are they going to do with them?"

Ethan's hands adjusted on the steering wheel, and he looked out the window nervously. "I…don't know," he admitted. "They want me. With Anthony there, it makes me think he'll keep them alive until they have me. But with Dase…The problem is, I don't really know who is in charge of this situation. If either one of them is, or if they're just following instructions. I never expected them to work together; they hate each other. If Anthony is working with Dase, then there must be something in it for him." Ethan wiped a hand on his head.

Mason frowned, not liking the odds. These men wanted Ethan, so they kidnapped two innocent women. If they didn't get Ethan, they'd probably kill both Isabelle and Maeve, but if they got Ethan, they'd surely kill Ethan, and maybe all three.

"What are the chances they'll let them go, whatever the case may be?"

Ethan shrugged. "One in a hundred, I'd say. I know what you're thinking, sacrificing myself for them sounded like the best option at first, but even if I knew how to find them, they would never let any of us go."

"I never suggested you turn yourself in," Mason said sharply. "*No way* will I let you do that. No way. But there has to be something."

Ethan looked over at him. "At this point, it might be our best chance," he murmured. "If I ever find out where they are, we might want to send in bait to make sure they're okay, assess the building and safety, then get a bust on." Ethan shook his head. "I don't want to risk their lives. Isabelle has never been in this type of situation, she wouldn't know what to do, and Maeve's been in far too many terrible situations, I just wish I could help them."

"I know. Me too." Mason put a hand on Ethan's shoulder. "That's what we're trying to do."

"Just feels so useless and slow when you know the person." Ethan frowned. Mason silently agreed. They drove on quietly. It was only a couple of minutes later that Ethan slammed his hand against the wheel.

"What's wrong?" Mason asked quickly, alarmed and grabbing onto the dashboard in front of him instinctively.

"I think I've got it. I think I know where they're keeping them."

Feeling a spring of hope, Mason leaned forward. "Where?"

"Bullet sent Anthony to Kansas once and asked him to keep watch over a meat-packing factory. I don't know if the girls will be there, but Anthony might." Ethan's fingers tapped on the wheel. "Mason, call Mygyer."

Mason grabbed Ethan's phone from the center console and quickly put the password in, then found Mygyer. The phone connected to the car Bluetooth.

Mygyer answered practically instantly. "Ethan, I was just about to call you."

"What did you find out?" Ethan asked him.

"We've interviewed some of the women recently assaulted in the area. There's been a couple that have described a man like Anthony.

One even has the carving of Anthony's signature." Mygyer spoke quickly, though he sounded exhausted. "She's an escort though, and she didn't report it, fearing getting in trouble. Anyway, add on top of that, we've searched the database for an Aaron Anthony C. Plus the names by themselves a bit with other things we know about him. We've come up with a few but none of them match any descriptions. Would you want to come take a look at them?"

"For sure," Ethan said smoothly. "Could you do me a favor?"

"Of course."

"Run the names with any meat-packing factories here in Kansas."

"Meat-packing factories?" Mygyer seemed bewildered. "Okay. Did you figure something out?"

"Maybe. I remember Bullet and Anthony talked about it. I missed most of the conversation, but Anthony was to come down and take care of something to do with it." Ethan tapped his fingers on the wheel. Mason took a deep breath, hoping for the best and praying to his God for such. Mason was surprised to hear Ethan swear a moment later. He looked over at his younger brother and saw the anguish as he suddenly hunched forward. "We got to get them out of there."

"Ethan…" Mygyer's voice pained.

"We'll find them," Mason said firmly. He couldn't believe anything else.

"We did find something on Dase," Mygyer said after a moment. "It's not a lot, but guards at Santorini's prison recognized Dase possibly as the lawyer who visited him a couple weeks back. I'll keep digging."

Ethan frowned suddenly and looked down where Mason put his phone back. Now Charles was calling.

"Mygyer, thanks. I've got a call coming." He hung up and switched it over to Charles. "Hello?"

"Hey Ethan. Just wondering if you've learned anything new yet." Charles voice was a forced chipper. Mason heard voices in the background and knew Charles was with his kids. Ethan seemed to realize it as well, as there was a forced optimism in his voice.

"Well, we've got a new lead, so it should get us closer to finding them."

"See kids? Momma will be fine." Then the phone went quieter, and Charles took a moment before lowering his voice. "Are you close?" His voice was somber, completely heartbroken. "Have you figured out where they are?"

"I think I might know where they are, sort of. I mean, I have an idea. I just don't know exactly where it is, but we're figuring that out. I'm praying they are there."

Charles sighed. "Okay, I…I guess I'll let you go. Call me if you have any news, Ethan."

"I will," Ethan responded, then they ended the call. He sighed and looked at Mason. "Thanks for being with me, Mason."

Mason put a hand on Ethan. "I know you're worried, Ethan. Just remember God will be with us to find them."

Ethan swallowed heavily, then nodded. "I just…I don't want to lose them. I mean, I love Isabelle. I can't imagine anything happening to her. And Maeve…I just wish I could save her."

Mason knew what Ethan was having a hard time saying. He saw the vulnerability in his eyes every time he thought about Maeve. He wondered what sort of relationship they'd grow given a chance, either unbreakable because of all the trials they went through, or a very rocky one because of the same thing. Thus far, they seemed to get along well.

Mason put a hand on Ethan's shoulder. Having Isabelle missing was one thing—Mason understood that because she was his sister too. However, Mason couldn't imagine the woman he loved being in the hands of someone he knew was so evil. Not like both Ethan and Charles were currently experiencing.

"I know, Ethan. We're doing everything we can. She's strong. She'll make it through this. They both are, and they both will."

Ethan nodded and took a turn. Mason finally realized that he had no idea where they were heading and looked around. "Where are we going?"

"Cedar Bluff," Ethan said shortly.

It was one of Ethan and Mason's favorite places to go. Truly, their entire family loved it there.

"Sounds like we're getting somewhere, at least," Mason said, referring to their conversation.

Ethan nodded. "Yeah, hopefully." Mason noticed Ethan hunch over his hurting side, and one hand went to his wound as he took a breath.

"You alright?" Mason asked quickly.

"Yeah." Ethan tried to sit back up but couldn't seem to. "Just tired of holding myself up."

"Pull over," Mason ordered. "We'll switch seats, and you can lay back. I'll drive to Cedar Bluff."

Ethan hesitated, looking at Mason, but nodded and moved to the side of the road. Ethan sighed as he stopped but opened the door almost immediately.

As they got driving again, Mason realized that Ethan fell asleep within minutes, leaning back in his seat. Mason drove in silence for nearly another twenty minutes, finding it interesting that they were going there so late. But it was peaceful there, and obviously they both could use some peace.

~16~

Ethan crossed his arms as he waited for Mygyer to come in with the rest of the team. He was sitting alone in the conference room. Mygyer didn't want Ethan to spend so much energy, so he was only allowed to work in the office a few hours each day. But Mygyer had called him and told him to come in, which made Ethan sure he had a plan or at least enough information to get the girls back.

At least, Ethan hoped so. He missed them both and was starting to feel overwhelmed that they might not make it in time. It had already been three days, though it felt a lot longer than that. Why hadn't Anthony tried to reach out to Ethan by now? What had he meant, that if Ethan couldn't figure out where they were, then he wasn't a true mafia or agent? Was he supposed to know? Did they want him to find them, or were they content with just making him sweat for now?

It took another five or so minutes for Mygyer to come in. Next came Patty, then Cameron, Liz, Daniel, and Sarah. Ethan sat forward immediately. "Mygyer, what's the news?"

Mygyer gestured for the rest of the team to sit, then turned to Ethan. Mygyer had a bit of stubble hair on his face, which showed Ethan he was worried and tired.

"We've found the connection between the factory and Anthony." Mygyer put his hands flat on the table. "Santorini's son-in-law owned it. However, he died just last year, so he sent Anthony to keep an eye on it essentially. We believe this son-in-law was murdered because he and his wife betrayed the mafia, then went into hiding. Obviously, he was found. Santorini now owns the factory but didn't want ties to it, so he sent Anthony to it.

"From what you've said, Ethan, it doesn't seem he wants that responsibility, but he still took it on. We believe Anthony might be working with Dase to get back where he wants to be: the streets of Chicago." Mygyer pulled away and passed the file he had in front of him to Cameron. "Ethan, you know all that's in this already; I'm letting the rest of the team in as well. I have a plan as to how we'll get the girls out, but it's not solid yet."

"What's that?" Ethan pressed. They needed to make it solid—soon.

Mygyer spared a look at him, seeming to tell Ethan that he understood, but they better not rush anything. Ethan merely narrowed his eyes, just wanting Mygyer to get to the point.

"Since we've found Anthony, we want to follow him to the most likely place he's keeping Maeve and Isabelle are. I'm hoping the factory. The man I sent to follow Anthony has reported that the places most common for him to visit is the factory and his house, so it makes sense. And Ethan, you said Anthony was the one trying for Maeve's attention in the store before the day they were taken?"

Ethan thought back to the videos, not liking to remember that Anthony had been so close to Maeve, trying to vie for her attention. "Yeah, that was him."

"Then I believe he would be the one to keep a more hands-on approach and might lead us right to the girls. I'm going to send Daniel in as a scout under the vise of an inspector. He is still technically one even though he doesn't work often in that career."

"But—" Ethan started, but Mygyer shut him down immediately.

"No way am I sending you on the field, Ethan. You're still on a crutch and we haven't gotten you tested. Also, we both know they'd recognize and kill you in a heartbeat." Mygyer waved off Ethan's next attempt at protesting, leaving Ethan frustrated. He wanted to be there for Isabelle and Maeve. Mygyer seemed to have seen his look, as he continued a moment later. "You will be with us when we get the girls, but in no way are you allowed in until we declare it safe."

Ethan swallowed down his frustration, knowing arguing was going to get nowhere, and that if he kept pushing, they might keep him off entirely. He wanted to hear the rest of the plan.

Mygyer continued, turning his attention from Ethan. "Part of this will be loose, depending on where and how we find them."

"It's not like they'll keep them in the open," Cameron said.

"We know that." Mygyer sighed. "But maybe someone has seen something. And I'm working on getting a warrant to search the whole factory. Should know by tonight. I thought it would be good to get a layout before we go in, which is why I think Daniel would be great to send in first. This time we have proof that they've done something wrong, so I believe it will work out alright."

"Are you just going to arrest Anthony when you see him?" Ethan asked, forcing himself not to let any emotion through his voice. His hands shook as he thought about what that may be doing to Maeve—Isabelle too, but Anthony had fixated on Maeve.

"As long as we have the girls, I will. I don't want the chance of not being able to get Maeve and your sister." Mygyer paced. "Like I said, I really don't have too much of a plan yet; I need to know more details and get some layout before we can decide for sure, but we'll be in by tomorrow, Ethan."

Ethan nodded, feeling a flare of relief. Tomorrow still felt so far away, but he knew it was the best they could do.

¤ ¤ ¤

Isabelle's hands felt numb. She tried to adjust her arms, lifting them, but her shoulders were so sore, the movement didn't really happen. She wished her hands to be free. Dase and Aaron had let their hands go long enough to feed themselves or use the restroom occasionally, but each time, Isabelle was barely given enough time to try and grasp the food to get it down, let alone gain her feeling completely. At least with them being numb, she didn't feel the pain from the handcuffs digging in.

But the pain from her foot she did feel. She didn't know what was wrong with it, but it hurt like crazy. As if someone was insistently shoving a dagger into her ankle.

Maeve had managed to fall asleep in the last hour. Isabelle could tell she wasn't doing well; she became sicker with every passing day. Though Isabelle was fairly certain it was morning sickness mixed with the smell and taste of the meat, Isabelle would prefer to know with a surety. Maeve continued to say she was okay despite her obvious discomfort, determined to be brave. Isabelle understood that.

The worst part was the smell. If the raw and rotting meat wasn't bad enough, no one had cleaned up the vomit, and they weren't free to use the restroom often enough, so those both continually stunk their dark room.

Realizing she was sinking into despair, she fought for a distraction. Listening to Maeve's breathing for a moment calmed her mind until she could think about something beautiful. Her family. Her husband and two children. She knew her kids would be missing her, and both were old enough to understand what was happening. Charles would be devastated by her disappearance, but she knew he would care for the kids. That was the kind of man he was. He would be pestering the police station or Ethan's FBI team unceasingly until she was found. If he knew where she was, he would barge in—then probably try to carry both her and Maeve out at once.

Those thoughts cheered her up. She found herself grinning, but a sob shook her at the same time. "Oh Charles, I miss you," she murmured quietly. She wanted to go home. As time went on, she became less and less sure that they would be found. She tried to continually believe it, and, in her heart, she still did, but her mind doubted. When she thought about her family, it made her determined to make it out of here. Even as pain pounded her body, and doubt plagued her thoughts, and fear dragged her down, she knew she couldn't give up.

Her butt was hurting. The hard floor seemed as though it was digging in. It probably was just her bones and muscles getting tired of being sat on, but the sharp twang running through her butt and traveling up her back made her feel very uncomfortable. She wanted to sit on her feet, but her ankle would scream at her even more if she did so.

After a couple more uncomfortable moments, she made up her mind and shifted her not hurting left foot underneath her, gritting her teeth with the movement that happened in her right foot because of the shifting. If she kept it still, the pain was manageable. Otherwise she wanted to scream.

She exhaled long as she relaxed, then stiffened as a scraping sound of the door opening and a brilliance of painful light filled the room. She blinked and saw Aaron. She felt herself shudder and tried to look past Aaron, wishing for someone else to be there.

He seemed different this time, grinning, but there was an underlying edge of anger in him that made Isabelle even more nervous.

When the door opened, Maeve had awoken. She seemed immediately wide awake as she caught sight of Aaron.

He put a plate of food on the ground between them, then undid one of Isabelle's hands. Her hand flopped to her side, and it took her a couple moments before she got enough strength and feeling to pull her hand back on her lap.

He then turned to Maeve and took both of her handcuffs off. Isabelle frowned as Aaron dragged Maeve to her feet. "Don't try anything," Aaron said. "Walk in front of me and do as I say."

"Where are you taking her?" Isabelle managed to say, seeing the terror in Maeve's eyes.

Aaron grinned, eyes displaying a cold triumph. "I've got something special planned for her," he taunted, touching her face. Maeve pulled her face away from him, looking nauseous. As she did so, Aaron frowned and tossed Maeve toward the door. Isabelle tried to reach toward them, but the restriction of the other handcuff and her weak hand made it impossible.

"Please don't," Isabelle begged, knowing he wouldn't listen. Aaron just exited the room with Maeve, slamming the door behind him. This time, however, the door didn't shut all the way. It came back open about an inch, giving the room a little bit more light so she could see better.

Isabelle felt tears clog her throat as she was left alone. With Maeve there, it had been a lot easier to act hopeful. Alone now, she felt as though the darkness was even more overpowering, even though more light filtered in.

Fighting for a distraction, Isabelle reached for the small cup of water left for her. Her hand felt as powerless as the rest of her; she could barely grasp it. As she took a sip, a sob shook her shoulders. She prayed for the cops to come, for her family. For someone. She didn't want to be there anymore. The meat looked horrid; she couldn't even think about getting anything down right now.

"Please, God. Please, save me. I just wanna see my family. And please protect Maeve." She continued to pray silently for a couple minutes. Then, suddenly, she heard a knock.

Then a voice spoke, "Mr. Colloway?"

Isabelle didn't recognize the voice. She thought briefly, then realized this man may be her help she'd prayed for. Too bad it had to be after Maeve was already taken.

Usually the room was soundproof, but with the door slightly ajar, she could hear, even though it was muffled. Taking the chance when no one responded to the voice, Isabelle tried to scream. Not much came out—her throat was dry. Panicked that he would leave, and she'd miss her chance, she tossed the cup in her hand at the wall with all the strength she could muster, and it shattered with a piercing loud sound.

"Hello?" The voice turned even more cautious but seemed to come closer. The door opened hesitantly, then a gasp from the new man as Isabelle sat blinking in the light.

"Please help me," Isabelle managed to say. And the man seemed to hear it as he came closer and crouched beside her and swore. His eyes were wide with horror.

"Hold on just a moment, miss. I'll be right back," the man promised. Before Isabelle could protest, the man was back out the way he came, nearly running. Once again, Isabelle felt the pressure of being alone, but now she could see anything that came her way. She forced herself to stay calm, knowing that help was on the way—praying that it was.

Only minutes later, the man came back with another person who appeared as shocked as his coworker. They both obviously worked in the factory; they had symbols representing such on their uniforms.

"Miss, can you talk to me?" the new man asked. The former tried to get her hand free of the handcuffs, but he stopped when he realized it would be harder than it looked.

Isabelle nodded and sobbed. "Please, I just want to go home."

"We called the police and sent for an ambulance," the first man told her, pushing her hair back from her cheek and inspecting the bruise there. Isabelle had been unable to see how bad it looked. She also knew that she had multiple bruises, particularly a bad one on her hip from a kick. "They'll be here soon."

A gunshot sounded in the rancid room, and Isabelle jumped as the first man jerked forward and a bullet ripped through his shoulder. Dase came into the room, his eyes dark with anger. Isabelle gasped in horror, then started crying harder, scared that Dase would shoot them all. Every ounce of composure seemed to leave her in that moment, which gave Dase a momentary pause as he looked at her.

"Where is Maeve?" he asked her harshly.

Isabelle shook her head, sobbing. The other worker had pulled himself slightly in front of her and Isabelle gripped onto his sleeve desperately. *Please don't let him kill anyone else.*

Her prayer was once again immediately answered. A shout sounded, a warning of police, right before Dase spun and another shot sounded. That shot didn't come from Dase. The bullet hit Dase almost exactly where Dase had hit her rescuer, making him lose grip on his gun.

"Funny," the officer said to Dase as he approached. "I was wondering the same thing." He kept his weapon trained on Dase as Dase swore and grabbed hold of his arm. "Is everyone okay?" he asked as he kicked the gun far from Dase's reach.

Though Isabelle had a hard time stopping her tears, she looked to her first rescuer, who now was shot and half laying against the wall, trying to push himself up. As the scene became secure, the other man approached his coworker and grabbed his shoulder. "You alright, Collin?"

"I'll be fine," Collin muttered. "It's not bad, just stings." He reached Isabelle with his uninjured but bloody hand. "It'll be okay, miss. Don't worry."

Yeah right. Isabelle sniffled. The police officer spoke into his radio, reassuring them that the scene was safe, but one woman appeared to be missing. Isabelle waited minutes until more men entered the room. Other officers, and then, to her biggest relief, Ethan.

Ethan pushed past everyone else, shoving through despite the crutch he still leaned on. He collapsed next to her and knew what she needed as he grabbed her hand. "It'll be okay, sis. I've got you."

Isabelle sobbed and nodded. Another officer came in with big wire clippers and cut the handcuff from her wrist. As soon as she was free, she threw her arms over Ethan's shoulders and hugged him as tight as she could. Ethan hugged her back, his hand running through her hair gently. She noticed that he was trying to calm her by shushing her and talking softly, but it took a moment to realize it because she was sobbing uncontrollably.

Finally, Isabelle pulled away, wiping her eyes. "He took Maeve…Aaron did, he took her out just about ten minutes before I was found. I don't know where they went." She sobbed again and Ethan grabbed both of her hands.

He was crying too. That kind of shocked her. Ethan didn't cry very often.

Isabelle looked toward the other officers and realized they had already taken Dase out of the room. Isabelle shuddered but felt an overpowering relief that she would never be hurt by him again.

Then she realized she had not yet thanked those who had been her rescuers. When she looked for them, they were both gone.

"Where…" she sniffled. "Where did the other two go? The two who found me?"

Ethan looked inquiringly at the officer behind her. The officer cleared his throat and came closer. "They went out. The ambulances are here, but I wanted to wait until you were ready."

Isabelle felt new tears run as she gave a small grateful smile. "Thank you." She turned to Ethan. "I'm ready now."

Ethan nodded and the officer came to help both her and Ethan get up. As soon as she was up, Ethan wrapped his arm around her and helped her stay up as pain flared back into her ankle, making her gasp.

"Where are you hurt?" Ethan asked instantly, brows furrowed.

"I think he sprained my ankle or something. It hurts when I put pressure on it." Isabelle hopped, but upon hearing it, another officer immediately slipped under her other side and took the weight off. Even still, the movement was hard, so she was relieved when they got to the ambulance outside and she could sit on the side. The sun was bright but sinking low into the sky. Probably about seven or eight at night.

Ethan sat next to her but made sure to give the paramedics room to work. "I called Charles. He's heading down here to see you."

Isabelle felt a sigh of relief wash off more of her fear. "Thank God." She craved to see her husband. "Ethan, what about Maeve?"

Ethan stiffened with the reminder, and his eyes darkened. "We'll find her. We have some people interviewing any possible witnesses. I don't know any news yet, but I hope they find something quickly." He grabbed her hand. "I don't want you to worry about that right now. Just focus on you."

Isabelle looked down at their hands, marveled that God had answered her prayers to rescue her. "I think it's easier to worry about Maeve than it is think about what happened," she said. "And I can't not worry about her. Especially when I know how you feel about her, and how I feel about her." She met his gaze sideways. Ethan looked away after a moment as tears pricked the color, turning them brighter. She squeezed his hands. "Go get news on her, please?"

Ethan swallowed, then his eyes sharpened. Isabelle looked over and saw that Charles was heading right toward her. She stood despite the paramedics, right as he got there. Even as she was wrapped in her husband's embrace, she felt herself fall from the pain that flashed up her leg. Charles held her strong, his hands running frantically through her hair as she sobbed.

"Oh, Isabelle, I've missed you so much. I was so worried," Charles murmured. He pulled away slightly and kissed practically every inch of her face. She closed her eyes as peace and love nearly overwhelmed her. "I'm so sorry…I should've been there for you, my dear."

Isabelle opened her eyes as she heard the guilt in his voice. She pulled away enough so she could look into his eyes. "You are with me, Charles. You are, right now. Thank you. Besides, they might have killed you had you been there." She put her head on his shoulder and refused to let go, even though the paramedics were waiting to fix her up, and she saw Ethan walk toward that one agent Isabelle figured might be the chief or something.

When she finally pulled away, Charles gently ran his thumb across her bruised cheek. Anger flared into his eyes. "They hurt you."

Isabelle brushed Charles own cheek, still unable to believe the nightmare was over and wanting to hold onto him as long as she could. "I'm okay, Charles." Finally, she sat back on the ambulance with Charles so the paramedics could finish their assessment.

"How're the kids?" she asked after a couple minutes of silence. Isabelle just enjoyed the feeling of being free of that room and with her husband, but she needed to know how her kids were.

Charles tried to smile, surely for her sake since she could still see the worry in his eyes. "Worried about you. They missed you. They're both at home with a babysitter right now. I called Cassy over last minute when Ethan told me they knew where you were kept. They had surveillance on this place mere hours before the man called and said he found someone locked in a secret room. That's how Ethan and I managed to get here so fast."

"I'm glad. I'm glad you're with me."

"Me too." Charles rubbed her hand.

The paramedic at her feet, working on her ankle, looked up at them. "Miss, it appears your ankle is sprained. I don't think hospital will be necessary unless you feel as though anything else is wrong with you, but I can wrap your ankle and tell you how to care for it."

Isabelle was relieved it wasn't worse. "No, I think I'm okay otherwise," she told him. "Just wrap it, please."

The man nodded and gestured for another EMT to grab the roll of gauze. He spent the next couple minutes carefully wrapping her ankle as his coworker explained how to handle her foot, telling her to ice it and keep all her weight off it until she started doing better. And to go get checked out at your primary care physician if anything gets worse.

"I can shower, right?" That was one of the first things she wanted to do. She wanted to sleep also, but she felt too dirty to climb into bed like this. Even more than that, she wanted to snuggle with her kids and husband and watch a movie or something. She just wanted to be home already.

The man wrapping her foot hesitated, then nodded reluctantly. "Just be careful and wrap the bandages. Probably don't shower alone so you don't slip and tweak something."

The rest of the night left her drained. After the paramedics finished wrapping her ankle up, an agent, clearly from Ethan's team, asked if she could answer some questions, introducing himself as Cameron. Charles, Ethan, and Director Mygyer stayed as she answered question after question. She hated reliving it but knew it was necessary—especially in finding Maeve.

After that, she was asked if she could answer the media's questions as well. Not feeling the best in the first place, she declined but gave permission for the cops to give any information they deemed necessary to them. Before she left, she asked what they had on Anthony—apparently Aaron's name was truly Anthony—and Maeve. They only told her that they were working on it.

She also sought out Collin and his friend, Peter, to thank them for being there for her and finding her. Collin's arm was wrapped and in a sling, but he grinned softly at her and gave her a hug. Charles shook both of their hands.

By then, the sun was sinking down. Isabelle said goodbye to Ethan, told him to keep her updated on Maeve, then Charles carried her to their truck. As he walked around to get in, she lifted the middle compartment up so she could sit in the seat right next to her husband. One of his arms wrapped around her shoulders as he drove, and she fell asleep with her head on his shoulder.

¤ ¤ ¤

Ethan sat to one side, unable to get his mind off Maeve. Isabelle told them how sick Maeve was, and now that she was separated and taken by Anthony…

He watched Mygyer walk over to another officer who was interviewing a worker. They talked for a couple moments, then Mygyer approached Ethan, sighing as he got closer.

"No one is sure, Ethan, but we should really get you home. You look exhausted."

Ethan could feel his entire body trembling; he knew Mygyer was right, but he couldn't imagine going home. Ethan looked past Mygyer without responding, but as he sat beside Ethan, he looked back.

"We'll get her."

Ethan's head sunk into his palms. He'd been losing faith in it before they found Isabelle, and now that they had his sister but not Maeve, he wasn't sure how much faith he had anymore. He felt that she was still alive—he hoped she was.

"Ethan." Mygyer put his hand on Ethan's shoulder. "I need you to take a deep breath and unscramble everything in your brain that you know about Anthony. Every little thing he's said or you know about him."

Ethan sighed and sat up in frustration. "I've already told you everything."

Mygyer gripped his arm. "You want to find Maeve, don't you?"

"Of course I do!" Ethan snapped.

"Then *think,* Ethan! I don't care if it's big or small. I don't even care if it helps us entirely, but we need more. No one knows where Anthony lives or where he would have gone. There's got to be something in that brain of yours worth looking into!" Ethan could tell by Mygyer's voice that he was getting tired of this search—and probably even tired of Ethan's attitude.

Ethan continued shaking his head, then paused. His mind flashed back to the day he'd first met Anthony. When Bullet told Anthony to move to Kansas to take over the business there. The factory. Anthony had hated the idea of moving, even voiced his frustrations.

"I don't want to go to Kansas! There's no one there! I like living in the big cities, with people around."

Bullet had shrugged. "Someone has to take it over, and you're the only one I can trust to take care of everything I need. Besides, there are big cities in Kansas too. Right outside the factory."

Ethan jerked out of the memory. "Big cities. That's what he said. Back then, he didn't want to move to Kansas because he liked being among people. If he still feels the same, then we should check the busiest places close to here and keep an eye out for the car."

Mygyer nodded and stood. "Keep thinking, Ethan. I'll get Cameron started on it." He walked back over to the young man, and Cameron nodded before taking off to their surveillance van. Ethan tried to do as

Mygyer asked, forcing any thoughts about his family and Maeve away and doing as he was trained to do. *Focus on the job,* he thought. He had to erase all parts of the real him to analyze all the information he'd received.

The name he'd been trying for the last couple day finally came to him.

Liz Santorini, his daughter. The one who had betrayed the family. She'd gotten married to Averis. Liam Averis. What did they change their names to when they went into Witness Protection?

That he didn't know. He did know, however, that Mygyer could get the details with his contacts. Ethan stood up and walked over to Mygyer, interrupting him and the media. Mygyer promised he'd be back and followed Ethan a few feet away.

"I know this is not new," Ethan murmured quietly. "But Averis, the man who'd died—Santorini's son-in-law…Was his wife also killed?"

"No. She was once again forced into protection." Mygyer folded his arms. "Look, I'm not supposed to talk about this, and I don't even know much."

"I know, but I want to know what she knows about her father's businesses down here and how she betrayed the family." Ethan coughed lightly and suddenly realized he'd had no water since being here. "Do you think we can get ahold of her somehow?"

Mygyer frowned, hesitating. "I'm not sure. I'll try though. Go get a drink and rest, Ethan."

He didn't plan to rest necessarily, but he was thirsty. So, as Mygyer turned to make some calls, Ethan looked around, then headed toward a small café down the street. The walk was slow, but it was a relief to step away from the chaos to think and relax a little.

He entered the café and his eyes immediately drew to the plants everywhere. Seeing them, Ethan found himself relaxing, and he sunk into a booth when he saw that it looked like someone would come to take his order. He hunched his shoulders forward even as he looked around, eyeing the plants. While typically he could probably name them all, he didn't even want to try today.

He sighed and leaned forward, burying his hands in his hair. Why couldn't any of his information be useful for finding Maeve now?

Someone cleared their throat. "Sir?"

Ethan raised his head to a young man—probably still in high school—with the nametag "Darrick."

"Can I do anything for you?" Darrick asked nervously, his notebook in between his hands. He seemed worried.

"Uh…Some water please." Ethan muttered, leaning back in the seat.

The boy nodded but didn't move away. "Are…Are you with the police?" he asked quietly.

Something in the tone of the boy's voice caught Ethan's attention. "Yes, I am." *FBI, but close enough.*

Darrick hesitated, looking over his shoulder momentarily. "Sir…I really need to talk to you."

"Okay, what about?" Ethan's interest was caught.

"Not now." Darrick shook his head. "I have break in twenty minutes. Meet me at the bookstore down the road. My grandpa owns it, that's where I usually have break. I'll go get your water." He scurried off before Ethan could ask why all this caution was necessary. Ethan thought about it for a moment, then at last shrugged and decided he would know soon enough.

Darrick came back in moments with the water. "Did you want anything else, sir?"

"No, this will be fine." Ethan took a sip of the water as he watched the clock. He spent almost ten minutes just sipping on his water, then he left and headed toward that bookstore. Alan's & Books.

Original.

Ethan pushed the door open and was greeted by a shrill little bell. He looked up to see an actual bell there.

The bookstore itself was small enough that Ethan felt it should be out of business by now, with the mismatched furniture and every book they could gather. Ethan loved bookstores, and books, so he immediately felt at home.

Between the café with the plants and the bookstore, he was feeling slightly better.

"Hello." An old man came from behind the counter. He was lanky and had a curve in his back that made him bow a bit forward. But he was spirited, if his grin was any indicator.

"Hello," Ethan echoed, forcing a smile. It felt unnatural.

"What can I help you with?"

"Well..." Ethan didn't know if the teen had wanted anyone to know Ethan was there to talk to him. "Are you Darrick's grandfather?"

The smile became brighter and wider. "I sure am. You know him?"

"Briefly. He told me this was your store." As Ethan turned, the grandfather caught sight of Ethan's badge that rested on his belt.

"Darrick's okay, right? He's not in some sort of trouble?" The man reached toward Ethan but withdrew before he touched. Ethan saw the worry in the grandfather's eyes.

Ethan shook his head. "No. At least not that I know of. He said he wanted to talk to me while on break in another five minutes." Ethan looked at his watch to confirm the time. "That's it though, sir." Ethan stuck out his hand. "I'm Ethan."

The man smiled and shook. "Alan, if you can't tell." He gave a hearty laugh, the twinkle in his eye back. He looked at the door. "Seems my grandson is off early."

Ethan followed his gaze, relieved to find him coming.

Slightly impatiently, Ethan waited for Darrick to enter, trying not to move closer when he finally did.

Darrick looked toward his grandpa for a moment, then around the store. "Anyone else here?"

"No."

"Okay. Good." Darrick looked at Ethan, shoving his hands into his pockets. "I don't know how important this is, or what you're doing at the meat factory, but..." Darrick paused. "It was a little strange to me."

"What was?" Ethan asked, slightly impatient.

"Just a little before the police came, this man came to my boss. They didn't know I was there. I was taking inventory. The man was threatening my boss, wanting to use the café truck." Darrick swallowed. "My boss gave in, and the man took off."

Ethan took a step closer to the kid. "Did you catch a look at this man?"

"Well, yes. I mean—sort of. I saw him, but it was such a quick look, and I panicked, and I was not *super* close to them."

Ethan pulled out the folded picture of Anthony and gave it to Darrick, who took it hesitantly. "Was it him, do you think?"

Darrick didn't answer right away. "Um…I think. It looks like him, at least. But he was in shadow and wearing bulkier clothes I think." Darrick handed the picture back. "My boss would kill me if he knew I told you."

"Why's that?" Ethan folded the picture back into his pocket, the words leaving a harder idea in his mind than what Darrick probably meant for it.

"The other man was threatening my boss's daughter." Darrick grabbed Ethan's arm. "My boss never would've let the man borrow the car if he knew or thought the man would use it for bad. Well, I mean…" Darrick sighed and ran a hand through his hair. "Okay, so my boss has this thing about others driving his car—he doesn't let anyone, not even me. When he agreed to the other guy driving it, I was surprised, but then I heard a little bit more of the conversation, and I understood."

Ethan calmed Darrick. "What does this truck look like, Darrick?"

"Typical, I guess. Just a white utility looking van. Except it has our café name on it, of course. TerraFood." Darrick shrugged. "What happened over at the factory anyway? I've heard a couple things here and there from people that keep coming in. Something about shots been fired and some women injured, but other than that, I don't know."

Ethan hesitated, wanting to get the information to Mygyer quickly. However, this young man may have helped them, so Ethan gave them the quickest summary that wouldn't interfere with the ongoing case, asked a couple other questions, and took back off to Mygyer.

~17~

Isabelle was surprised (to say the least) that her shop looked good as new since Charles had said he'd broken the glass to get to Timmy, and that Timmy had also been scarred by Anthony. She'd expected blood and glass everywhere.

Instead, it looked like how she left it. Except the clothes she'd been sorting were now finished.

"Who has been in?" Isabelle asked her husband. Charles put his arm around her waist.

"Timmy."

Surprised, Isabelle looked at him. "Didn't think she'd want to."

Charles met her gaze. "She hasn't kept the store open, but she wanted it to be nice for you when you got back. She kept the door locked and she wasn't alone." He looked at the clock. "She said she wanted to come and see you."

"I'd like to see her." Isabelle squeezed Charles and stepped away with her crutch. She went into her office, looking around. Charles followed her at a distance, giving her a little space but not wanting her out of his sight. She felt herself smiling a little, loving him even more every second, and glad that she was with him. It turned somber a second later as she remembered how Maeve was still trapped.

Isabelle paused, then turned back to Charles, folding one arm across her chest. Charles was leaning against the door frame. "Charles…Have you heard anything new about Maeve?"

Charles shook his head. "Not yet." He looked concerned, but Isabelle wasn't sure if it was more for her or Maeve.

Isabelle sighed and moved back over to Charles, standing in front of him. He pulled away from the doorframe and put his hands on her hips. "You feeling okay?"

Isabelle nodded and let herself be pulled into a hug. "I'm just worried about Maeve."

"I know," Charles sighed. "I love you."

Smiling, she looked up at him and gave him a quick kiss. "Love you *more*." Before Charles could continue with any sort of "love you" competition, the front door to her shop opened. She dodged around Charles to see Timmy and—surprise, surprise—Isaac come in.

Timmy took off at a run to give Isabelle a hug. "I'm really glad you're okay," she whispered in Isabelle's shoulder. Isabelle hugged her a couple long seconds, then squeezed slightly and stepped back.

"I'm glad you're okay too. I had no idea what Aaron did to you." She ran her hand down the girl's hair and caught sight of the bandage on Timmy's chest. "Are you okay?"

Timmy nodded. "I'm alright. I was really scared when it happened. Then I didn't want to go to the dance because I had the bandage, but Isaac convinced me otherwise." She smiled at him as he slowly came over. "I think I owe him my life. While Aaron was here, talking to you and Maeve, I could only think about the scenarios Isaac had told me about, and what he said were the best ways to get out of them. That's how I ducked behind the desk so fast."

Isabelle smiled at Isaac as he hesitantly threaded his fingers in Timmy's hand. "He also helped me out at the store here after; he's been a really good friend," Timmy added.

"I keep trying to tell her that it's dangerous to come back," Isaac joked—or as much as Isaac ever joked. "Both mentally and could be physically. She didn't care. She said everywhere was dangerous, including the dance—as I regret pointing out now." He shook his head and looked around. "I don't understand how you guys can come back so soon."

"Me neither." Charles put one hand on Isabelle's back as he approached but stuck his hand out for Isaac. "I'm glad you're taking care of Timmy. She's an amazing young lady. And Timmy, you found a great young man."

They both blushed, which made it hard not to laugh.

Suddenly Timmy beamed. "Oh, you wouldn't believe it! Guess what?"

Isabelle studied her. "What's that?"

"Oh, I wish Maeve was here. She'd get a kick out of it." She chuckled, though her eyes were sorrowful. "She was right. Dylan was extremely jealous. He kept trying to get me away from Isaac. However, I think he wanted me more because he wanted details about what happened to me, not because of how I looked, but still, it was hilarious. I turned him down flat, and I didn't even feel weird about it. It's like my crush on him disappeared when he backed out."

She looked at Isaac. "I mean, I know I'm too young to have a boyfriend—like, I don't want a boyfriend yet—but Isaac is a really good friend, and I enjoy hanging out with him. I don't know if it will go anywhere else in the future, but for now that's okay."

Isabelle felt as though she was eavesdropping on a conversation that Timmy and Isaac should have had alone, but she didn't care at the moment. She was just so glad Timmy was alive and okay. She didn't care if she talked her mouth off.

"I'm really glad he didn't hurt you worse, or break your spirit, Timmy," Isabelle told her truthfully after a moment of silence. Timmy looked back at her, her smile fading a little as she licked her lips.

"Yeah well…I mean, I don't know how I could let him bring me down. It's my attitude, not his, that will rule my life." She put a hand over her bandage. "It's hard, and it hurts, and I hope the scar fades *really* fast. I was really scared when it first happened. I don't think I could have made it if Charles wasn't there when I was found." She looked gratefully at Charles.

Isabelle looked up at her husband, also glad that he had been here. He'd been amazing.

Charles kissed her forehead, then laughed suddenly. The sudden change surprised Isabelle, she looked at him in confusion.

Charles stopped laughing, but still smiled and shook his head.

"What's so funny?" Isabelle asked him, pulling away so she could peer into his eyes.

"Nothing. You'll be mad at me."

"I'm sure I won't," Isabelle protested, wondering what he could have done that would make him think she would.

He shrugged. "I punched Ethan."

"What?" Isabelle was shocked. She couldn't imagine Charles punching anyone—except maybe Aaron and Dase now, and Dylan, who had been a jerk to Timmy. She also couldn't imagine Ethan letting himself get hit. Ethan had fast reflexes, though he was injured. "Why?"

Charles pushed a loose hair behind Isabelle's ear. "Because I was worried about you." Then he kissed her. Isabelle sank into it, cherishing him being there again.

Then she remembered they had company and pushed him away, smiling a little. "But I don't get it. Why did you punch Ethan?"

Charles sighed. "I don't know. Because I knew the people were after him, and I hated how they took you to try and get him." Then he frowned, probably at her face. "You don't believe me."

"Well, I mean, I can't imagine you being able to punch Ethan. Sure, you're strong and all, but Ethan has had special training." Isabelle shook her head, half teasing him.

"For your information, he can't move that fast with a hurt side." Charles looked at Timmy. "Jeez, I sound like a jerk."

Isabelle laughed but turned her attention back to Timmy. "So, your parents let you out of the house? I kind of expected them to hoard you in your room."

Timmy grinned and shrugged, looking at Isaac. "I was, for about a day, then Isaac came over because he was worried and wanted to know how I was and if I wanted to stick with the dance. At the time, I had said I didn't want to, but a part of me knew if I didn't go, I'd regret it. I think he saw that in me. He convinced my parents to let me go with him."

"I see." Isabelle smiled. But as her gaze caught on the baby clothes that she told Maeve she could have, she frowned. Where was her friend?

◻ ◻ ◻

Someone knocked on the door to Ethan's hotel room. After last night, he hadn't wanted to drive back home. He couldn't face his family after failing to find Maeve, and he couldn't think about possibly getting further from her either. He would stay in the city until they knew where she could be.

Ethan sighed and let his head fall to the side to look at the door, hating how he had locked it behind himself because he didn't want to get up now and open it. After the knock resounded, though, he finally forced himself to his feet.

It was Cameron. He practically shoved his way in. "Get dressed, quickly," he said.

"What's going on?" Ethan asked, narrowing his eyes.

"I'll talk while you dress. Well? Get a move on." Cameron paced the room. Bewildered, Ethan did as he asked.

"We found that truck your kid was talking about. Abandoned on the side of the road. Nothing to help us there, as of yet." Cameron noticed Ethan struggling to get his pants off and came over to give a steadying hand. "However, your girl—Maeve—called the police about fifteen minutes ago."

"What?" Ethan felt startled. "Is she okay?"

"Well…Doesn't sound like she had much time to say." Cameron shook his head. "The call was cut short. She seemed more concerned about making sure you had Isabelle's location than her own, but she also didn't know her own other than it was at the big hotel." Cameron released Ethan as he finally got his pants on. "However, the call was long enough to track Anthony's phone. He's on the move. I don't know if Maeve will be with him or at the hotel, but we have a location for both. Mygyer is waiting in the car out front for you."

"Why didn't you start with that?" Ethan inquired, annoyed that it had taken him so long to get dressed. He may have been more motivated if he knew Maeve was on the verge of hopefully being rescued. As it was, he tore his shirt off and quickly put on a white button up, starting to walk with his crutch as he did his buttons with one hand. Cameron grabbed the door for him and led the way to the car.

Mygyer barely greeted him as he got to the car before they were pulling out of the hotel, sirens on.

"Cameron, track Anthony. Ethan, hotel or after Anthony?"

Ethan thought for a moment. Which would get him to Maeve? How would Anthony act?

"He'd want to keep her as a pawn as long as possible," Ethan finally told him, leaning forward in the seat. "After Anthony."

Mygyer nodded. "Cameron, keep us on him. Other officers are already heading to check out the hotel the call came from."

"Yes, sir," Cameron said, reaching between the two front seats and messing with the touch screen on the dashboard. Within minutes, a map popped up with two dots. "Blue you, red him," Cameron said as he sat back. "You are on the fastest route to intercept him." He said it similar to how the phone would say it, with such a straight face that Ethan wondered if he even noticed he was doing it.

"Does anyone else have a visual on him yet?"

"No sir, not yet." Ethan glanced at Cameron quickly, grateful to the other man. His hands were trembling in fear and tightened them into fists, not sure how he would have managed life the last week or so without his team.

"Have some faith, Ethan. We'll find her," Mygyer told him, giving him a side look. Ethan nodded, taking a calming breath and watching the road, though he didn't see much of it.

Mygyer tapped his fingers on the wheel in front of him, seeming concerned as he bit his lip. Ethan hesitated to ask what the problem was, but finally cleared his throat.

"Mygyer? What is it?"

Mygyer sighed. "I just don't know how many people know where you and your family live. Even if we get Anthony, we have the problem that he may have told people where you guys are. We'll have to get some people watching and protecting your family, or go through the Protection Program, but that will be a hassle with all your family." He shook his head. "I don't know what they'll try next."

Ethan swallowed nervously. He didn't know either. Once again, he felt guilt wash over himself for coming back and putting his family in danger.

He tapped his foot, praying silently. *God, please, this was my mistake. Let Maeve be okay.*

He felt like he'd been doing nothing but praying lately.

"Take the next right," Cameron said from the back. Ethan looked at the screen and noticed they still hadn't closed much distance. Anthony was heading toward a freeway while they didn't even have any visual on the car. They could lose track.

Cameron swore suddenly. "We lost connection. He must have figured out we were tracking him somehow."

Mygyer swore as well, and Ethan felt tempted to follow suit. He took a trembling breath instead as they continued in the direction they'd been heading.

After a couple minutes, Ethan sat forward suddenly, catching movement on the side of the road. On closer observance, he saw Maeve standing on the side, hands wrapped around herself. As they approached, she stepped closer.

"Mygyer, stop! That's her!" He didn't even need to say it; Mygyer had already started pulling over. But Ethan couldn't let Anthony get away again. "Just keep going, Mygyer. Get Anthony."

Ethan didn't even wait for the car to stop fully before he was out, his heart pounding in relief and anxiety. He slammed the door behind him and was relieved that Mygyer kept going.

Ethan held Maeve's arms, peering at her. "Are you okay?" he asked frantically, checking her body over. Maeve merely nodded, seeming kind of hesitant or something. She was wet, her hair was dirty, and she smelled like puke. Ethan pulled her into a hug and ran his fingers down her hair, unable to think about letting her go.

Maeve held her arms close to her chest for many long minutes, then buried her fingers in his shirt, starting to cry.

"I've got you," Ethan whispered, crying too. *And I'll never let you be hurt again.*

They stayed that way for many minutes, then Maeve finally pulled away. Ethan reluctantly let her go, but not all the way. He pushed hair back from her face and wiped away some tears. "I was so worried," he told her.

"I missed you," Maeve said softly. Then she tried for a smile and used her wrist to wipe tears. "Our ride is gone."

Ethan gave a rough laugh. "They'll be back," he promised.

"I smell really bad." She tried to take a step away, but Ethan didn't let her. "I've been sick all week…and in a meat processing factory."

"I'll take you clean or dirty. I'm just glad we found you." Ethan rubbed her hand with his thumb. "We can get you a shower at my hotel."

She sighed. "Thank God. I hate feeling so gross." She squeezed her eyes shut and trembled.

"Did he…hurt you?" Ethan didn't know how to ask—how to check what he needed to do for her.

Maeve shrugged. "I guess. He didn't, like, *touch* me or anything…yet—he was going to, but something happened that freaked him out." Then she stiffened and paused. "Isabelle? Is she okay?"

Ethan cut her off before she could panic herself. "We found her. She's back home with Charles. When Anthony got you, the door didn't shut all the way, so she attracted the attention of a worker when he came in for Anthony. She's doing okay now, I suppose. Just a little traumatized, but surprisingly okay." He rubbed her arms, but before they could say anything else, a police car with its sirens on came close and pulled up beside them. The passenger window rolled down, and the closest cop gestured for them to get in.

"Mygyer told us to come fetch you two and take you wherever she needs to go."

Ethan hesitated, looking at the two men. He didn't recognize them, but he did want to get Maeve to a hospital or anything she may need.

He exchanged a look with Maeve, and when she nodded, they both climbed into the back. As he did so, he made sure the lock and handle could be manipulated and that there was no child lock on the door. He'd been trained to be cautious.

He also shot a text Mygyer's way as soon as they settled in to ask him if he did send some men to get them.

Ethan wrapped an arm around Maeve, and she lay on his side. "Maeve, should we take you to the hospital?" he asked her gently.

Maeve shook her head. "The hotel first, please," she said, then closed her eyes and relaxed against him.

Ethan nodded to the driving officer and told him the hotel, taking some seemingly first full breaths since this entire ordeal started. His worry vanished to be replaced with relief she was okay—here.

Her breath deepened within minutes, falling asleep as he held her.

¤ ¤ ¤

Maeve let the water run off her face, cleansing her body from grime and the soap. She stood there for a while. It helped clean not only the filth but also the fear of Aaron from her mind. She found her breaths coming more fully.

She took a couple more breaths, then shut off the water. She grabbed one of the hotel towels and dried off, careful with some of her bruises.

When she finished, she wrapped herself in the hotel bath robe. She didn't have any clothes here yet.

She opened the door and went around the corner, finding Ethan sitting on the bed, head in his hands. As she stepped out, he looked up, then stood. "How're you feeling?" He came close to her and found the bruises on her neck, tilting her neck slightly to see the coloring.

She let him look for a minute, then looked back at him. "I'm fine, Ethan." She hesitated a moment, then stood tiptoe to kiss him. She had liked him for a while, and the entire time being trapped, the only thing she knew was that Ethan was going to save her, and that she wanted him. He seemed surprised at first, then he kissed her for a couple seconds before pulling away quickly.

"Maeve…" He pushed her hair back. "Are you sure…"

Maeve nodded and put her forehead on his chest. "I've been hesitant, but after this week…I just don't want to wait for things that are important to me. You know what I mean?"

Ethan brushed her hair back and bent below her face. "I do." He pulled her into a hug. "I really do." He held her for many long minutes. When he pulled back, he still held onto her shoulders. "Shall we get you home?"

Maeve looked at the ground. "Are we allowed to leave yet? Do I have to give a statement or something?

Ethan shook his head. "Mygyer called me just barely. They didn't get Anthony yet. He said to head home and instruct some officers through watching my family until they catch him and close this case." Ethan sighed, looking down and hunching his shoulders.

Maeve grabbed his hand, noticing her scratched wrists and feeling relieved that she no longer wore the handcuffs. Ethan had cut them off with these huge clippers. "Let's get back then."

"Are you ready to?" Ethan asked her gently. His eyes held his concern.

Maeve nodded. "Yes. Especially since we need to take care of your family." She smiled at him, then looked down. "Could we go to the store to get clothes first?"

"Cameron said he was going to bring some by for us," Ethan reassured. "How did you get free? Did he let you go?"

Maeve smiled softly. "He was frustrated because I kept fighting him. I kicked his wheel a couple times, then he checked his phone and realized that I had called the police. He threw the phone out the window and finally kicked me out, I think to distract you long enough to get away." She felt her shoulders relax. "I'm really glad you were right behind; I was only out there for two minutes or so." Then she frowned. "Did stopping for me make it so you didn't catch Aaron—I mean Anthony?"

"No," Ethan turned her to the door as he shook his head. "We were still a couple minutes out."

Maeve felt her eyes narrow, but she turned under his arm, reassured and protected at his side. She stay still until there was a knock, then Ethan answered the door for Cameron who held the bag of clothes out to Maeve.

"Here you go. I'm glad you're safe, Maeve."

"Thanks." She smiled politely and felt glad when he left without anything else.

"I'll step outside, just come out when you're dressed, and we'll get going."

"Thanks."

Maeve spent the time driving home drifting between sleeping and explaining what happened to Ethan, and conversation about the family. When they got to the house, she couldn't convince her body to drag itself out of the car, so Ethan carried her in. She vaguely wondered how he had the strength to do so, knowing his side wound and leg. It had been getting better, but she was surprised at how much. She heard Elisa greet Ethan as they came in, her voice quiet. Maeve put her hand out toward where she knew Elisa would be, wanting to greet her, but unable to open her eyes back up. Elisa put a hand on her shoulder as she also grabbed her hand and kissed her forehead. "Get some rest, Maeve," she told her softly. "I'll see you in the morning."

≈18≈

Ethan's chin dropped from his fist, jerking him awake for what seemed the fiftieth time that morning already. His eyes were so heavy, and his mind so tired, that his dreams and thoughts were mixing as one.

After he realized, quite dimly, that he was sitting at the table in the kitchen, teacup in front of him with barely touched tea, his eyes closed again. His mind scrambled once more, trying to figure out if he was thinking about possible confrontations with more mafia, worrying about Maeve, or sleeping in his bed.

A hand lay on his shoulder, jerking Ethan awake again. He turned slightly to see his mom behind him, in her robes still for the morning hour. "Dear? You feeling alright?"

Ethan nodded, not really thinking of the question. Grabbing his tea and taking a sip, he realized it was cold already. Didn't he just barely pour it out to let it sit? Must have been asleep longer than he thought. He sure felt like he hadn't had any sleep.

Choking on the tea because of the unexpected cold and bitterness of it, he shook his head and pushed it away from him.

Elisa sat next to him, putting a hand on his. "Did you get any sleep last night?"

"Not really—not much." Ethan sighed and leaned back in the seat to study his mom with heavy eyes. "You?"

"More than you, I'd guess." She squeezed his hand. Ethan turned his hand to hold hers. "How's Maeve?"

"Still sleeping, last I checked," Ethan replied. He looked at the clock, but his brain couldn't focus to even remember when that had been, or even when he had gotten up this morning. "Strangely, she seems to be doing pretty good. A little nervous, but as she was telling me her story, she seemed proud at how hard she fought and that she practically got herself free. I'm going to take her to the hospital when she wakes up."

Elisa shook her head. "You're not taking her anywhere unless you get some more sleep, Ethan. You can't even sit here without falling asleep. I'm not going to let you drive."

Ethan thought about arguing, but he knew she was right, so he resorted to smiling at her instead. "Well, she does need to go for a check-up. When she wakes up, please wake me up."

"Fine, but I'll drive the two of you." Elisa hesitated, then. "What happened to Maeve? Did they hurt her?"

Ethan paused, wondering how much to say. "Well…A little. Mostly a couple bruises here and there, and a burn or two, but she said that part was kind of her fault." Ethan yawned, then rubbed his face and looked at the tea. "I can never make tea right."

Elisa smiled at him. "I'll make you some later. Get some more rest, Ethan."

Ethan didn't move at first, but at last nodded and stood. Mom stood with him, and he gave her a hug and a kiss on the cheek before making his way back upstairs. He peeked his head in on Maeve, realizing as he did so that his mom had followed him upstairs.

He heard a gasp from Maeve, then her voice trembled in the near darkness of her room—he had closed the curtains so she could sleep as long as she needed. "Ethan?"

"Yes?" Ethan stepped into the room.

"Would you lay with me?"

Ethan hesitated, looking at his mom. The rule in her house was no men and women sharing a room unless they were married.

But her look now told her she was far more worried about Maeve than her rule. She nodded with a small smile.

"Of course," Ethan answered, coming closer as he mouthed a thanks to his mom. He slid underneath the blanket, a foot and a half away from her, but Maeve scooted closer, back to his chest, and lay down on his arm. Ethan stiffened a moment, but then wrapped his arm around Maeve and sent thanks to God for keeping her safe as she drifted back to sleep.

It was strange how natural it was to hold Maeve in his arms, but he had merely seconds to think about it before he too was asleep.

When he woke back up, he felt a lot better, despite being groggy still. He saw Maeve staring at him, and when she noticed, she smiled. "Hi."

"Hi. You doing okay?" Ethan pushed back her hair. She closed her eyes and took a breath.

"Yeah. Thanks for staying with me." She grabbed his hand. "Really, I appreciate it. It's easier with you here."

The words worried Ethan. He frowned, studying her face to see what he could do or say. He hated seeing her hurt, and he was worried about her.

She smiled a little. "I'm alright, really. It'll be a little hard, obviously, but I can get through it. Especially with you and your family here for me. You guys are all amazing."

Ethan smiled a little, thinking about his family. "Yeah, I love my family. They've always been amazing." Ethan looked past Maeve, to the clock. "Holy crap, we slept forever."

"What time is it?" Maeve asked but pressed closer to him to stop him from moving.

"Nearly four in the afternoon." It only halfway surprised him. He'd been exhausted, and so had she. But four was crazy late.

Maeve shrugged. "That's okay. You needed it. We both did." She closed her eyes. "Though I'm groggy now."

Ethan nodded. "We should get you in for a check-up now, Maeve."

Maeve huffed a little. "Yeah, I suppose you're right." She shifted to get up, slowly, her movements stiff. "Ugh, I'm sore."

"I'm sorry." He frowned, stood up, and wrapped his arms around her from behind. "Can I help you?"

"Don't think so." She breathed in, then bent to get her shoes on. He frowned, catching sight of her bruised and scratched arms. Her abuse may not have been terrible, but it…was. It could have been worse, but he hated it anyway.

Ethan swallowed hard to wash down his anger. Maeve stood back up as she finished putting her shoes on, sighing, and let him guide her to the door as she put her head on his shoulder. He wished he could have caught Anthony, to give him what he deserved. That type of thinking—that anger—kind of worried Ethan. He didn't want to get into the mindset that his old mafia "friends" had been in. He didn't want to always be angry or worried that they may come back, always seeking revenge.

Downstairs, his mom came close immediately, putting the book on the end table beside her and approaching Maeve. "Oh, my dear." She pulled Maeve into a hug. "I'm so very glad that they found you, that you're safe. How are you feeling?"

Maeve shrugged against his mother. "I'm alright, Elisa. Thank you."

Mom put her hands on Maeve's shoulders when she pulled away. Ethan was pleased to see how much they cared for each other—he really liked Maeve, and he wanted his mom to like whatever woman he ended up with.

"Are you ready to go get your check-up?" Elisa asked her, looking back at Ethan as well. They both nodded, and she tugged Maeve's hand to lead her to the car. Ethan followed them, watching. He bit his lip as he thought back on his and Mygyer's conversation. Anthony hadn't been caught yet—but they knew where he wanted to be. Back in Chicago. No one knew those people more than Ethan. Ethan felt the best option was to get back to Chicago with his team to find the culprits.

Ethan fought a sigh. He didn't want to go back to Chicago. It was very dangerous, and he wasn't quite ready to work in the field, let alone in the place that had almost killed him—nearly breaking his spirit.

However, there was no way he could just sit by while they tried to come after his family again. So, he would pass all the tests to get back out on the field, then work on convincing Mygyer that he needed to head back there with them all—even if he did have to work behind a desk or as bait.

Ethan didn't believe that acting as bait would work well; they wouldn't believe he'd be that stupid. But Ethan had to find a way to get these people behind bars before they hurt others.

"Hon, you alright?" Elisa asked him, her eyebrows furrowed in concern. Ethan caught up with the two of them and grabbed the door.

"Of course, Mom. Just a little bit tired." He smiled at her, trying for reassurance. He didn't know if he succeeded necessarily, but hopefully she thought that he really was just tired.

He knew his mom was proud of him—with following what he felt he needed to do and becoming a police officer. She was proud of all her children because she knew each one of them had found their way to do something important to them. It wasn't the job that made her proud, but that they followed their passions.

However, Elisa always had a concern about his desire to help by becoming a cop. She wanted him to do it because he loved the work, but it made her worry constantly about him. Because of this, he didn't want to tell her that he was going to try and get back to the field.

Ethan cleared his throat as he shut the door behind them, trying not to meet Maeve's gaze. As they drove to the hospital, he kept his eyes closed, hoping they might think he was merely too tired to join in with any conversation. His mind told him that he needed to let them go. He was going to find Anthony, and Ethan had no idea what would happen next if that was the case.

He wanted to pursue marriage—or at least dating—with Maeve, but he couldn't leave this case open. Maeve would understand that, right? He didn't want her to be waiting on him forever though, and what if he never came back? What if he left her and her unborn child to take on this world without him to help?

Then he realized that Maeve *would* have help. Elisa would help—and surely Maeve could find another kind guy, right? Though that tore him apart as well.

He realized he knew what Maeve would say to this; she had already sort of told him when they first talked about Santorini's attack on her. She knew his character, his ability to see all he had and still keep a level head in order to catch the bad guys. He had to try to do this job right.

What happens next?

¤ ¤ ¤

Maeve frowned at Ethan, wondering why he was so quiet. He'd been doing fine since she was free—a little more protective of her and worried, yes, but seemingly happy and wanting to be with her. Now, and for the last day or so, he'd been a little distant. She wondered if something was worrying him, or if he was done with her now that she was out of danger.

"Are you okay?" Maeve asked him, for what seemed to be the fifth time in the last hour.

He looked over at her, then nodded, trying for a fake smile. "I'm fine, Maeve. You?"

"Yeah, I'm fine." Maeve swallowed. "Is work worrying you?"

Ethan frowned. "No. It's fine." He was withholding something, but Maeve wasn't sure what. She wished he would open up to her. He'd been doing so good.

"I'll be back, Maeve," Ethan said, excusing himself. He left before she could respond. They were waiting for the rest of his family to get home so they could eat dinner with them—since it was Sunday again. Maeve had seen most of them since she'd been out, but she looked forward to seeing them again, especially Isabelle who felt like a sister to her.

But she could barely think about that. Ethan's recent distance made her heart ache. Maybe she could talk to Isabelle about it. Isabelle was a wonderful listening ear. Plus, she knew her brother; she might be able to help her decide how to approach him.

Was he still mad at himself? That she wouldn't doubt. What he'd been through was terrible, and she doubted he could have just gotten over it, but he refused to talk about it now. That made it hard to get close to him.

She looked out the window, waiting anxiously for the others to arrive. It took a while—she got the tea ready before someone knocked on the door. She heard Elisa answer, but Maeve didn't leave the kitchen. In minutes, Isabelle found her in there to pull her into a hug.

"Oh, my friend. I'm so glad to see you," Isabelle greeted. Maeve couldn't help but smile—she had been in to work with Isabelle a couple days ago, but Isabelle acted as if it was a pleasure to see her every time they got together.

"I'm glad to see you too," Maeve told her, hugging her close. But she felt her smile disappear as Isabelle pulled away. Maeve got back to making the tea, putting the tea bags into the water.

Isabelle tilted her head. "What's wrong?" She pulled Maeve's hands to a stop.

Maeve looked around, checking for listening ears, then lowered her voice. "Ethan seems different, Isabelle. He had seemed so happy to have me back, but then this last day or so he's been distancing himself or something. I mean…" She trailed off a second, then found herself admitting: "I really like him, Isabelle. But he doesn't seem to like me anymore…not now that I'm out of danger. It feels like he only likes me as the damsel in distress." She wiped a loose tear. "I don't want to lose him."

Isabelle frowned. "Oh, hon, be patient with him. He's still struggling."

"I know." Maeve waved her hand to dismiss her tears. "I thought about that, and I know that may be true, but why is he pulling away now? He hadn't done so before, not even when I first got to know him."

Isabelle thought about it. "I'll try and talk to my brother, Maeve. But don't worry. It's probably just a hard day for him. I'm sure he'll be fine. I doubt that he's lost any of the care for you that he had."

Maeve sighed but nodded. That would be for the best. Isabelle knew how to approach conversations. She tried to turn her thoughts away from Ethan. It was hard, but she managed to lose herself in Ethan's family during dinner—even with Ethan's sullen silence during the meal.

But when he left the room right after they finished, her thoughts immediately flew back to him and wouldn't leave.

Isabelle followed him out of the house, a concerned look on her face. Now she had seen what Maeve meant.

It's her turn to try now. Maybe Isabelle could do a better job at getting him out of his shell.

It was quiet around the table for a couple of minutes, some silently eating, others sitting back and watching the door where Ethan had exited. Maeve was one of those avoiding looking at anything. As much as she tried not to, she just kept coming back to the idea that Ethan only liked her when she was somebody to rescue.

Tyra grabbed her hand, and when Maeve looked at her, she noticed a reassuring smile on her face.

Maeve squeezed her hand, thankful to her. Really, Maeve was grateful to all of Elisa's family, but the women were especially sweet. Maeve was still uncomfortable around some of the men, but she trusted that they'd be there for her if needed.

She looked around at all the family. Charles looked uncomfortable, as if he was barely managing to keep himself sitting. He probably wanted to go after Isabelle. His wife had told Maeve how he had been hesitant to let her out of his sight.

Owen had started to stand, but Mason stopped him, saying some quiet words, and Owen sunk back in his seat with a sigh and frustrated glance.

"Does he seem to be getting worse again?" Fallon asked his mom softly.

Elisa sighed. "Well…He's been doing better. It's just been this last day, ever since he went to investigate the happenings outside Isabelle's shop." Elisa hesitated. "He went in to start work again."

Mason immediately put down his fork, leaning back in his seat. "He can't have," he protested.

Elisa arched an eyebrow. "Try telling him that. He's already passed the testing. They've started him on paperwork. I don't want him to, but he is starting either way. He told me he's not going on field yet, but..." She sighed. "I'm worried about him."

Maeve heard a murmur of agreements as she followed Mason's gaze to the door. A couple minutes later, Isabelle pushed her way back in. When she saw questioning looks, she shook her head.

"He went for a walk. Said he wanted to be alone for a bit." She stood behind her seat, gripping it with tight fingers.

Riley noticed the tension around the table and nudged her husband. Scott peered over his glasses at her; he reminded Maeve of a very handsome nerd. He was a little nervous around people, typically quiet, yet he seemed like he'd be the first person to offer to help with anything. In fact, he often was. He usually volunteered to do the dishes and clear the table.

Scott pushed up his glasses, glancing at Riley, then immediately seemed to know what she wanted. "Kids, come with me. You too, Owen." Scott stood and held out his hand. Lila did so automatically, smiling. Andrew and Mallory, Isabelle's kids who were both older, seemed frustrated, but Andrew grabbed onto his Zee's hand as they all left the room.

"Can we color?" Lila asked.

"Of course," Scott nodded, lifting her and Zee in his arms. "Come on, Owen. The adults want to talk."

Owen sulked, looking at his dad. When Mason nodded at him, he sighed and slowly moved to his feet to follow Scott out.

Lila giggled. "Aren't *you* an adult?"

Scott smiled and winked. "That's debatable." He looked back at the rest of the adults before the door shut. Riley gave him a grateful look. As did Isabelle.

"What do you think?" Fallon asked Isabelle, grabbing onto Jessica's hand. Maeve hadn't had a lot of time getting to know Jessica yet.

"I know he's not ready to start up work again. I don't know what he's thinking." Isabelle shook her head.

"Well, it's obvious what he's thinking," Fallon commented. "He doesn't want us hurt. These people keep getting too close for our comfort." He stood, pacing the room. "I mean, for heaven's sake, we have officers on guard, watching us day and night! That's not a way to live life, and Ethan knows it. He's trying to stop these guys; he knows them the best after all."

Mason sighed. "That's the problem. He may know them, but it doesn't mean he should be out there. He's not taking his own well-being into account. He's just worried about us."

"I'm worried about us too!" Fallon snapped. "*All* of us—Ethan included. But if he doesn't go out there to find these guys, we may be watched for the rest of our lives, however long those lives may be." Fallon deflated and sat. "I just wish there was a way I could help him find these guys."

Jessica rubbed her husband's back. "We all know this is a part of Ethan's job," she said softly. "And sure, we might not want him to go back or think he's ready, but we all know Ethan will do what he knows is best. We just need to remind him to pray about it."

They were silent for a moment. Jessica was right. That's one thing Maeve had noticed about Fallon's wife; she always had this calm demeanor, and when she spoke, it was thought out and honest.

"What if he does do it, and he's not mentally prepared?" Maeve asked. "I mean…He may do it because it's right, but it could make *him* worse." Or something…or he could very well die.

"We'll be there for him," Elisa said. "We all will. We know this will be hard, whatever happens. But we're all a family, and he needs to know we'll be there for him." She met each of their gazes. Most nodded in agreement, some looked away.

Charles leaned forward. "I don't want anyone to be hurt or taken again. If Ethan is ready to go back to work and find these guys, then I want him to. I already almost lost Isabelle, and I know none of us want to get into any trouble. It'll be difficult, but we know it needs to happen."

Maeve didn't say anything. She didn't want Ethan to start up work yet—she knew he wasn't mentally, emotionally, or even physically there. She doubted he was spiritually there. It worried her, to see the darkness in his eyes half the time. He'd try to act happy for her, to be there for her, but this last day, he'd been even worse than all the time she'd known him. Honestly, Maeve wasn't sure how Ethan had managed to pass the psychological test, or why Mygyer was letting him back on the team already.

When it fell silent again, Maeve stood and followed Scott out of the room. Part of her wanted to stay in there with them, the other part of her couldn't handle this line of conversation anymore.

She found Scott in the library with the kids. He was reading a story in theatrical voice, with Zee on his lap and Mallory beside him. Lila was on her stomach, coloring in a book. Owen was looking out the window, but as Maeve entered, he looked over and gave a small smile. Andrew wasn't in there.

Scott broke off his reading. "How's it going?"

"Fine," Maeve told him for the kids' ears. "How about in here? Where's Andrew?"

"Good. He went to the bathroom," Lila said in a sort of humming voice. She kicked her feet and tilted her head as she drew. "Look, Aunt Maeve, I colored the kitty." She scooted, telling Maeve she wanted her to sit with her. Maeve crossed her legs as she sat, still amused that Lila had convinced herself she was her aunt. Maeve hoped that one day she truly would become her aunt—if Ethan really wanted to be there for her. She was too scared to ask.

Maeve peered at the picture and gave Scott an amused look. "It looks great," she told Lila. "Doesn't it look great, Scott?"

"It sure does," Scott agreed. Maeve had decided she really liked Scott. He had a calming presence about him, despite his nervousness. He was the type of person who would make jokes and completely surprise everyone in the room with them. He liked joking, he just seemed so nervous that she hadn't imagined he'd be so funny. "Maybe you'll become an artist like Aunt Riley."

Lila grinned at him. "I like Aunt Riley. She does good pictures too!" Then she went all serious-like: "but sometimes she doesn't do bright colors."

Scott laughed. "Oh no?"

"No, some of them are sad looking." Lila kicked her feet again, then turned to the next page to color that one. This time it was of a dog.

Maeve fought not to laugh, exchanging an amused look with Scott before Zee complained that he'd stopped reading, and he returned to his animated voices with the story.

Maeve took another couple of seconds beside Lila, then stood and moved to sit beside Owen. "How're you, bud?" she asked him quietly.

Owen looked at her, then his lap as he shrugged. "Fine."

Maeve cocked an eyebrow. "Owen. What is it?"

Owen shrugged, looked at his sister, then lowered his voice. "I'm sad that Ethan isn't doing well."

Of course. He absolutely idolized Ethan. Seeing him so down must be hard on him.

Maeve pulled him into a side hug. "Ethan will be okay, Owen." But Owen didn't seem convinced. Making up her mind, Maeve stood and held out her hand for Owen to grab. "Come here."

Owen hesitated a moment, looking at her, then nodded and took her hand. As soon as they left the room, Owen peered up at her. "Where're we going?"

"To see Ethan a moment." She walked to the front door, hoping that Ethan was nearby.

Her simple prayer was answered—she found Ethan sitting on the front steps of the house. As they exited, Ethan looked over his shoulder, then smiled a little as he saw Owen. "Hey, bud."

"Hey, Uncle Ethan." Owen sat beside his uncle. He paused a moment. "What are you doing?"

Ethan pulled him to his side. "Enjoying the sunset."

Maeve followed their gaze to the horizon, amazed by the colors. She was tentative to sit next to them though, not with how distant Ethan seemed to be. She didn't want to make him uncomfortable. So, she stood by the door, shutting it quietly behind her.

Ethan rubbed Owen's arm. "You doing alright?"

Owen nodded. "Yeah," he hesitated. "You seem sad."

Ethan didn't meet his gaze. "Well…I guess I am a little," he admitted. After a minute he finally looked down. "Some days are hard, Owen. But don't worry. I'm fine." He smiled. "Just because someone is sad doesn't mean they can't be okay too. Does that make sense?"

"Um…I guess. Mostly at least." Owen laid his head on Ethan's arm. "So, you're okay? For sure?"

Ethan nodded, glancing at Maeve over Owen's head. "Yes. I'm okay." He kissed his nephew's head. Though he answered Owen, Maeve wondered if the answer was also directed at her. He knew she worried about him.

After a couple more minutes, the door opened. Maeve looked behind her to see Mason, Tyra, Fallon, and Jessica come out, all with their kids. Jessica smiled at Maeve and gripped her arm. "We've got to head out, Ethan. Get these kids to bed," Tyra told him, laying a hand on his shoulder. Ethan scrambled to his feet—Owen following a bit more reluctantly.

Ethan hugged Tyra tightly. "Thank you," he told her. "Have a good rest of the night."

Tyra cocked her head at him, seeming a little surprised by Ethan's heartfelt hug. "I will. You as well. I love you." Tyra pulled Lila from her father and grabbed Owen's hand. "Come on, let's get in the car."

Owen resignedly followed her after his own hugs.

Next was Jessica. She gave a hug with Zee in her arms. "'Night, Ethan. See you later."

"You too." Ethan gave her a smile. Still looked a little forced to Maeve. She stayed back though, crossing her arms.

Fallon and Mason faced Ethan now. "Ethan, you know we're there for you and we care for you?" Fallon asked softly, grabbing his brother's arm. Maeve was slightly surprised to hear the words come from Fallon. From what she'd seen of him, he was the one least likely to share personal feelings with the family. On the lovey side, anyway. Totally fine to share times of worry and exasperation.

Ethan managed a weak half-smile. "I know, Fallon. Thank you. A lot." He pulled his younger older brother into a hug.

Fallon did the weird pat on the back hug that half the men seemed to do. Then Mason was left with Ethan.

"Ethan, do you have time to go out to lunch tomorrow?" Mason asked him.

Ethan hesitated, then shrugged. "I don't know. I guess."

Mason took the hesitant answer as if it was a positive affirmative, slapping his hand down on Ethan's shoulder. "Good. See you at noon. Shall I pick you up?"

"I'll just meet you. Where?"

"DeRose Café." Mason hugged his brother. "Make sure you're there."

"Okay." Ethan nodded, and as soon as Mason walked away, Ethan headed back inside, practically ignoring Maeve.

Hurt, Maeve decided not to follow Ethan back in. Instead, she folded her arms, standing there a moment to watch Ethan's brothers and sisters leave.

Tyra waved at her as they pulled out. Maeve forced a smile and a small wave, then she pulled her sweater to cover her hands a bit more and continued to stand a while longer, wondering…Hoping.

≈19≈

"Ethan, you can't go," Mason said, eyebrows pinched in worry. "You're barely walking as it is, and Chicago is dangerous for you. They'll kill you if they see you."

"No one knows them better than I do, Mason. I need to help them find Anthony." Ethan tapped his fingers on his arms, getting worried because he knew that Mason was kind of right. But Ethan wouldn't back down. He was going. He just hated making Mason—his family—worry. But Anthony had left Kansas after this last fail and Dase getting captured, and Mygyer figured he would be heading back to Chicago to pull together Santorini and Dase's men and putting himself as their new head.

Mason leaned forward. "Please, Ethan. Think about it. You know this is dangerous, and what if something worse happens? And without you here…Well, Mom needs you, and Maeve will be devastated if you leave. Come on, bro. I know you always think you have to go out and save the world, but you don't need to do this. If you really want to help, stay here and start work here instead."

It was getting hard to argue. Mason hit good points, yes, but that's not what made it hard. Ethan had already thought about these points, he knew the risks, but he needed to do it anyway. No, the hard thing was that Ethan knew his brother cared for him, and only wanted him safe, and Ethan was giving him a huge reason to worry.

Ethan took a breath and looked out the window of the DeRose Café. Mason, probably thinking he was winning the argument, pressed on. "Ethan, the officers there know what they're doing. If they haven't caught wind of Anthony yet, how will you? It's not like you can just waltz into a base like you used to and poke around. They'll know you, and they'll kill you if you're caught."

Ethan's shoulders shrunk. "Mason, you don't understand," he whispered. "If they're not found soon, they're going to move all of us into protection—at the very least, me and Maeve and Isabelle, since that's who Anthony knows most about. It's either I go back there now, or I live my entire life—until they're found—hiding. And I make so many other people live the same. The force here can't stay guarding you guys forever. Eventually they'll pull officers away, and then people might come back to hurt you guys, and I can't let that happen because of my mistakes."

Mason got teary-eyed. "It's not your fault, Ethan. It's not your mistake. You were doing your job."

"A job that I messed up on. Mason, I already told you what happened—I screwed that night up."

"Exactly, you did tell me. There's nothing else you could have done that night. Nova found you out. You did what you could to get out of there." Mason grabbed his arm. "Ethan, I don't want that to happen to you again. *Please.* Just stay here. You can work behind scenes here, research and work *from here.*"

Ethan was shaking his head before Mason even finished getting the words out. Frustrated, Mason stood, drawing looks from the surrounding tables.

"Selfish jerk," he muttered to Ethan, throwing his napkin onto the table and striding out the front door quickly. Ethan stared after him a couple moments, then let his head fall for a moment, fighting his own tears. He knew the conversation was going to be hard, but he hadn't imagined it like that.

Ethan leaned his head on his fists, trying hard to keep it inside. He wanted to stay here with his family so bad it hurt. Ethan felt that he was doing the right thing, going to find this guy. It's not like he was just jumping into the idea. He'd taken a lot of time to pray about it, until there was no doubt in his mind that he needed to go after Anthony.

But he desired to stay here.

If he did, what would that make him? He knew staying here would destroy him, day by day, always wondering what could happen. Always looking over his shoulder and needing someone watching his back. He would hate it. He couldn't do it.

But a part of him also couldn't bear to leave. Especially not Maeve right now. She really would be devastated. Mom wanted him here, but

Ethan knew she didn't need him as much as Mason tried to make it seem like. Mom was strong. She had family to look out for her.

Maeve had people to look out for her, but she had stated her opinion on the matter. Ethan knew Maeve would hate it if Ethan went out again.

How was he going to do this?

Ethan was startled when he felt a hand on his shoulder. He looked up to see Mason again. He had returned, eyes shimmering. He took a couple long seconds, staring at Ethan's face, then he closed his eyes and sat in the seat right next to Ethan.

"I know you need to go, Ethan," he whispered. "I know…but I wish you didn't."

Ethan's shoulders fell. "Yeah. Me too." He sighed. "Mason, I know Mom will be alright. She'll miss me and worry constantly—obviously…but what about Maeve? What do I do? I don't want to leave her—I really *really* love her. I mean, she's strong and all, but what will happen if I leave?"

Mason shook his head slowly. "I don't know, Ethan. But whatever you do, don't leave anything unspoken between the two of you. Tell her about your feelings for her. Tell her what you need to do and why. Tell her that you may not come back. Don't try to keep her from the pain of any information because it's not going to work."

Ethan looked down. Again, he knew his brother was right. He needed to talk to Maeve about everything. She might hate him for leaving, but he needed to stay true to himself. He wanted her. Desperately. So much that the thought of leaving her killed him more than the thought of leaving anyone else. He wanted to raise her baby as his own, and to ask her to marry him. But that wouldn't be fair of him until he returned home.

Ethan had been trying to distance himself a bit with Maeve. He didn't want her to get attached to him. It hadn't seemed to work, however; she just became more upset every time he saw her, and he knew it was because of him.

He nodded, taking a deep, slow breath. "Come on, Mason. It's time I go have that conversation I guess."

¤ ¤ ¤

Charles had joined them in the shop today. His business was going so well, he could take weeks off at a time and still make the same money—he'd set up a good team. After everything that had happened, Charles was very reluctant to let Isabelle out of his sight, and whenever he left her, he had her call him—or at the very least, shoot him a text about every ten minutes. Isabelle seemed slightly annoyed by her husband's requirements, but she also knew that Charles just loved her and wanted her safe, so she abided by his set rules. For now. Really, Isabelle was the type of girl who wouldn't do something if she really didn't want to, but she loved her husband.

Charles eyed the clothing and toys Isabelle separated. "I don't understand why we're going through all of this," he told her.

Isabelle looked at her husband lovingly. Maeve wondered briefly if she would ever get the chance to get that close to Ethan, but she forced the thought away, not wanting to dwell on something that hurt.

"Because, dear, it's time I got rid of it."

Maeve could see the pain in Charles' face, and thought she knew why. The clothes and toys would have gone to their miscarried baby.

Isabelle grabbed his hand. "It's been years, Charles. You know as well as I that I won't be able to have another baby. If we decide to adopt or something, I'll just buy new clothes." Charles grabbed one of the toys, staring at it for a long moment before sighing and putting it in the toy pile. "I'm tired of holding onto things that I don't need anymore—other people need it more than I do."

"Like who?" Charles asked, his voice slightly bitter.

Isabelle looked at Maeve but didn't betray her secret. Maeve appreciated that, but with that, Maeve decided it was time to let other people know.

"Like me," Maeve told him softly, looking away, to the door, as she felt heat flush up her neck.

Movement stopped, the air was silent, and she could see Charles look at Isabelle from the corner of her eye.

"Maeve…? What do you mean? Did Ethan…no, of course he wouldn't." His voice fell into confusion. Maeve felt sure her blush became even more evident with his words. Had Charles guessed her growing love for Ethan? Wouldn't be surprising.

Maeve took a moment to calm herself, then looked back to Charles. "No. Definitely wasn't Ethan—he would never do something like that." She swallowed heavily. "I was raped. Before I met you guys." She debated telling him that Ethan had been there; however, she didn't want to tread on Ethan's toes by revealing something he might not want everyone to know. She'd already told a few people.

Charles stared at her, his eyes shocked; worry, pity, and understanding floating around in the small expression changes. "Oh." He seemed unsure of what to say; he looked once again at his wife.

Maeve didn't know what else to say either, so a very awkward silence descended upon them. Maeve looked back down and went back to sorting. A moment later, the shop door opened. Relieved with the distraction, Maeve stood to see who it was.

An old familiar lady came in to greet them. Mrs. Dowery. Maeve felt herself smile. This old lady came nearly twice a week, bringing treats and new requests for clothing for herself or one of her family members. She seemed to have an endless supply of money and kindness and was probably Isabelle's best customer.

"Mrs. Dowery! So good to see you!" Maeve rushed forward, eager to take the basket from her. She put it on the counter with barely a glance at the contents, then hugged her.

"Good to see you as well, Maeve." Mrs. Dowery hugged her back, then pulled back and patted Maeve's cheeks gently. "Oh, you're looking pretty good for where you've been. I was sure worried about you two." She looked behind Maeve to include Isabelle. "All this craziness happening." She shook her head.

Maeve smiled. That's one thing she loved about this lady—she wasn't afraid to say what she thought.

Mrs. Dowery hugged Isabelle, then Charles when he came out as well, then got to business. "Now, I know you girls are fine if you're back to work already—I'm sure proud of you two—I have a big project if you're feeling up to it."

"Of course, Mrs. Dowery," Isabelle told her. "What can we do for you?" She walked off with the old lady to the couch and Mrs. Dowery got started showing her designs from the book she'd brought in. Mrs. Dowery was amazing at designing the look of clothes, just not the skill to bring it to life like Isabelle.

Charles was studying Maeve. Feeling uncomfortable, Maeve smiled at him, then headed back toward the storage room to get back to sorting. Charles followed, speaking quietly. He reached out as if to touch her, but then stopped. "Maeve…Thank you for telling me. I'm sorry for what happened to you, but I'm amazed at how you're handling it."

Maeve felt a warm glow inside. She smiled—more sincerely this time. "Thank you, Charles." It felt good to be told that.

He nodded, but once again they were interrupted by the door opening. This time, Maeve was surprised by who it was.

Ethan.

Her body reacted in two ways at once. Her vision narrowed to just Ethan, wanting desperately to go to him. At the same time, her body seemed immobile, staring at Ethan and not daring to hope…unsure of why he was there.

Heart deflating, she realized it was probably for his sister, or maybe the case.

Ethan's eyes seemed to flick immediately to Maeve. He paused as well—she wondered if he was feeling like she was.

After a long moment, Ethan stepped forward. "Maeve, can I talk to you?"

He was here for her! Maeve felt her heart pound. "Uh, yeah…of course." She stumbled over the words. Face growing hot once more, she left Charles' side and headed to Ethan. "Here?"

"Out there…If you don't mind taking a walk with me." He stuffed his one free hand into his pocket, his other gripping the crutch under him more tightly.

"Yeah." Maeve nodded, approaching a little slow, worried. What did he want to talk about? Was he going to tell her what had been bothering him?

She hoped so.

Ethan opened the door and held it open for her. His gaze seemed vulnerable as he watched her walk out. They walked together for a couple minutes before Ethan let out a sigh and turned toward her.

"Maeve, I'm going back to Chicago."

Shocked, Maeve stared at him. That was not what she'd been expecting. "What?"

Ethan looked down. "I…I need to go find Anthony. Not to mention, I need to testify against Santorini. I have a job to do."

Maeve closed her mouth when she realized her jaw had dropped. "No…you can't."

Ethan winced, as if he really didn't want to have this conversation. "Maeve, I have to."

"You can't!" Maeve raised her voice. "They'll kill you, Ethan! You can't go back there. Please, I can't lose you." She lowered her voice in with the last words. "*Please.*" She grabbed onto his arm, frantic. "You don't even know where Anthony is—if he's even in Chicago. Other officers can testify against Santorini. You can send in your testimony or something. You don't have to go. Please don't leave me."

Ethan continued looking at the floor. Maeve took a step closer so he would be forced to look at her. "Ethan, you can't do anything there anyway, they'll kill you if they see you, so undercover work won't work."

Ethan ran a hand through his hair, sighed, and avoided her eyes again. "Maeve, I don't want to hurt you, but…I need to be in Chicago, where I can get news right away, and help them find Anthony. We've been after him for a while, and we need to find him before he hurts someone else."

Maeve felt tears start to flow. A part of her was dismayed that she was showing emotions so easily, the other thought that they might help her convince Ethan to stay.

"It's too dangerous." Her voice cracked. She couldn't bear to see him leave.

"It's too dangerous to leave him free."

"But you're too close to the case. And you told me how this case had nearly destroyed you. I know you have feelings about what happened, and they can't have gone away." Maeve tightened her grip. "Ethan…"

Ethan pulled away and started to pace with his crutch. "Maeve, I have to! I know you don't want me to, I don't really want to either, I just want the bad in the world to stop already, but it's here, and I can help out. I need to do my part. I know you may not understand, but I've prayed about it a lot, and I know I need to do this. If I don't, I'll be looking over my shoulder everywhere I go, always worrying, always wondering if I did the right thing. I couldn't live with myself if I refuse to go." Ethan wove a hand through his hair again. With every word spoken, Maeve felt as though she understood him a little more. "I know I can't expect you to understand this. The hardest thing is leaving you, Maeve. After everything you've been through, you deserve someone you can trust to be there with you forever, not someone like me—"

Maeve took a quick step, pulled Ethan to a stop by grabbing his shirt, and pulled him down to kiss him. He felt as safe now as he did the last time she'd kissed him. She felt like she finally found home. But this time, there was also a sorrow, an anguish, and a hunger. He seemed to want her as much as she wanted him. Neither wanted him to leave.

But they both knew it needed to happen.

Maeve broke off the kiss, too quickly, yet too late. She closed her eyes, hugging him a moment as he put his lips on her forehead. "I do understand, Ethan," she whispered.

Then she ran.

She did understand. His job would come first. He had something great to live for—a purpose in his life, of helping others. She had been his damsel in distress, and he'd rescued her, but he would always feel as though there was something more for him to do. She would never be enough.

Part Two

~20~

"Alright, come on! We can't let him get away," Ethan muttered, staring at the screen, frantic. Cameron glanced back at him but didn't say anything. He knew Ethan was just anxious to get this guy behind bars.

Manning Rodiez, street-named El Dios, had been pursued for years, but these last few weeks, they'd gotten a tip that he'd started working with Anthony. The news had surprised them; Dios was not one to work well with others unless those others were under him. Anthony had become partners with this man—or at the very least, they were rivals with the same end goal. To bring their mafia family to the top.

The one good thing was with Anthony's attention diverted to creating the best family in Chicago, he didn't care for small revenges at the moment, so Ethan's family were left alone so far. The downside was with it being months after the attack, the police force back home debated pulling the extra officers from Ethan's family. That's one of the main reasons Ethan was so desperate for this raid to work. El Dios had hurt a lot of people, and it would be one step closer to getting Anthony.

Ethan paced behind the chair, stealing glances at the raid until Cameron huffed in frustration. "Please sit down, Ethan. You're distracting me."

"Sorry," Ethan murmured, sitting in the seat next to him. He was frustrated that Mygyer refused to let him come with them on the raid. Ethan's wounds were pretty much healed, to the point that he no longer needed crutches, and his side didn't hurt unless he overextended. He was doing fine, but Mygyer still wouldn't let him back in the field.

Ethan leaned forward, watching closely as they heard El Dios accept the cash. "Now, jeez, come on already. He's admitted it." They had given Ethan a headset to hear what was going on, but Mygyer hadn't given him a mic, so no one could hear him. Probably a good thing—if he was distracting Cameron, he sure would be distracting everyone else.

Cameron took a moment to look at him, then shook his head. He seemed annoyed.

"What? This is why I need to be out there; I'm much better on the field."

"Obviously, for you to still be alive," Cameron told him shortly. "But you seriously need to shut up. They're doing what they can."

Cameron's temper was short today. His daughter had kept him up all night the last handful of nights, then last night he had flown in to do this bust, and he hadn't gotten much sleep then either. His exhaustion became obvious when something annoyed him—and everything seemed to annoy him when he was exhausted. Usually Cameron was a nice guy, someone Ethan could call a friend. Today, Ethan had to fight down his own annoyance at the man as he turned back to the screen.

Cameron sighed after a moment. "I'm sorry, Ethan. I know you're worried. I'm just tired."

Ethan looked at him, smiling. Cameron had always been one to realize his mistakes and try to do better. "It's okay. I understand, Cameron. How's your wife and daughter doing?"

Cameron smiled a little. "Good, mostly. Missy is exhausted also, with staying up with Kammy. But she never complains." He didn't tear his gaze away from the screen and after a moment, he touched the button on the mic. and leaned forward to speak. "Alright, head in now," he instructed over the mic. Ethan wished he knew this side of the bust like Cameron did because he never knew what they looked for as an opening…He usually just went in shooting when told, so to speak.

Ethan turned his attention to the action, praying that nothing would go wrong.

¤ ¤ ¤

Maeve walked arm-in-arm with Kelly, looking at the sights of the town. Ever since Ethan had left, she'd become very close to Kelly. Perhaps Maeve's best friend, with only Isabelle and possibly Tyra in competition with that role. Maeve loved all of Elisa's family, but those were the two she had become closest to.

Still, Kelly was the friend who helped Maeve escape everything, mainly the pain that Maeve felt when she was with Elisa's family.

Maeve knew it to be pathetic, but she missed Ethan desperately. She never thought she could miss someone as much as she did him. He had saved her in many ways, but the biggest was by showing her that she could care about someone like she did him, and that someone could care for her too.

Being around the family was hard because she only constantly wanted Ethan there in the home with them, talking with her. She remembered their final kiss, months before now. Two and a half months. It seemed forever ago, yet as if it happened two seconds ago. She felt like she could still feel it on her lips sometimes.

As the time wore on, Maeve's doubts continued to grow. She felt sure that Ethan was off saving more damsels in distress, and that each one of them was falling in love with the handsome gentleman…and where would that leave Maeve? Would Ethan still care about her when he finally got to Anthony? Or would she just be a girl in the past to him?

Realizing that her thoughts had wandered back to Ethan, even with Kelly, she forced herself to pull away and focus on Kelly's skirt for a minute, watching it flutter as she walked. Kelly noticed the look and stopped, pulling Maeve next to her. "Maeve?"

With the one word, Maeve knew what she was asking. She pretended she didn't. "Yeah?"

"You look sad again. I don't like it when you think about Ethan. It's always with sadness. Can't you remember the good you had with him, or at the very least, with his family?"

"I do remember the good," Maeve said defensively. "The bad too, but they come together now." Maeve sighed. "I'm sorry, Kelly. Ethan called Mom today, and it has me focused on him again." *Not that I'm ever not focused on him.*

Maeve had taken to calling Elisa "Mom" lately, since that's what she was to her.

Kelly pulled her into a hug. "I know it's hard, but Ethan will be back."

"But how long will it take? And what if he doesn't love me by then?"

Kelly pulled back and gave her a look; one eyebrow raised, as if she couldn't believe the question. "Come on. Who would move on from you? Ethan wouldn't be able to forget you."

Maeve put her hand on her belly. She had grown a bit the last couple months—not much, but enough to notice a bump if she touched it. What if Ethan didn't come back before the baby was born? What if, even after what Ethan said, he didn't want to raise the baby as his anymore?

She shook herself very forcefully from the thoughts, frustrated that she couldn't stop the doubt.

"What about that gentleman you said you were dating?" Maeve changed the subject.

Kelly's face lit with a smile. "I met with him again last night." She sighed in contentment. "Oh, Maeve, he's just amazing. You have to meet him. I need your approval."

"My approval?" Maeve raised an eyebrow.

"Well…" Kelly blushed. "I mean, I really like him. You're my best friend. I'd like for you to see what you think about him. I don't want to put you in an awkward position, but it would mean a lot to me. Maybe when Ethan gets back, we could double date, or I can bring him over to Elisa's house for dinner or something when I come one of these nights. Trust me, you'll love him. He treats me like I'm a princess, but…but a very independent one. Does that make sense?"

Maeve bit her lip, trying not to laugh. It made perfect sense—that's how Ethan made her feel.

Automatically, the laugh seemed to turn into tears. She nodded and pulled Kelly into a hug to hide the fact that she was nearly crying and forced the emotion down. "I'm super happy for you, Kelly. He sounds amazing."

"He is, he truly is." Kelly pulled away and they started walking again. "Oh Maeve…I know life has its curveballs, but it really is amazing if you take a step back to look at it."

That was very true. Maeve thought about all her life's curveballs. She had told Kelly quite a lot about her own life, and Kelly had shared hers. They had grown quite a bond. "Yes." Maeve took her hand. "I'm glad I've got you as such a wonderful friend."

"Ditto." Kelly squeezed her hand, then walked toward the aquarium—their destination.

Maeve loved animals. She had never before known she was such a big fan—granted the usual animals she'd seen were rats and stray dogs, both of which scared her more than anything else. But now, she'd learned that she loved animals—especially water animals. She loved the otters at the zoo, and octopus and stingrays from the aquarium.

They entered through the front door and gave the workers their passes to be scanned, then they walked in. They spent a fair share of time at each exhibit, watching the water creatures and commenting on how they looked, how they swam, and laughing with other people that were there when the animals did something interesting. Maeve thoroughly enjoyed visiting, and when she got some time alone on one side of the stingray's pool, she reached in to touch one, relishing the simple beauty of the moment. Kelly was right…take a step back and you can really see the beauty in life.

The texture of the stingray felt almost like rubber, but slippery. As she touched it, it changed directions and skirted away from her fingers. She smiled, watching it swim away. A moment later, a bigger one approached and seemingly tried to eat her fingers. Maeve laughed.

Kelly neared and stroked the top, laughing as well. "It likes you."

"I like it," Maeve said, waiting until the stingray left, then pulling her hand out of the water. Sighing in contentment, she walked to wash her hands, Kelly on her heels. "They make me so happy."

"Me too," Kelly agreed. "Shall we go see the octopus now?"

Maeve nodded eagerly. She loved to spend time with the octopus.

They made their way that direction, making small talk about the animals they'd seen and that they passed on the way.

The octopus seemed to like to show off—or it didn't like to be locked up in the small tank so long and was getting restless. Maeve wouldn't be surprised by either possibility.

She put her hand on the tank. "Hey, boy." She smiled and watched it squeeze into the helmet in there. It stayed in there for a couple of minutes before coming out because the workers opened the top to feed him.

Maeve and Kelly spent the feeding time watching the octopus before eventually moving away.

All in all, the day at the aquarium had been a wonderful time. Maeve was dropped off at home by Kelly. She was surprised to see that Mason's car was in the front.

Maeve followed voices into the family room and saw Mason on the couch with Tyra. Their kids weren't with them currently, and Maeve wondered about that. Elisa was on the other couch.

Tyra smiled and stood to greet Maeve, all conversation ending when she entered. Maeve smiled and hugged her. "Hey, Tyra. Where are the kids?"

"Daycare and school." Tyra smiled.

"Did you have a good time at the aquarium?" Elisa asked her.

"Yes." Maeve went over to hug her surrogate mom, then Mason. "What's going on?"

"I just came to say goodbye," Mason told her. "I'm heading up to Chicago. I'm gonna visit Ethan, see the improvement…All that."

"Oh." Maeve hadn't known that. The desire to see Ethan felt overpowering and Maeve looked around. "You flying?"

One nod. Before Maeve could think further, the words were out of her mouth. "I'd like to come with you."

The three of them were silent, then Elisa leaned forward. "Maeve, I know you miss Ethan too, but I don't know if that's smart. Not with your history there. Not with the danger."

"There's danger for Mason too, and Ethan. Besides, I'm not going to let my past interfere with my future. I'm going to live my life." Maeve folded her arms.

They still looked hesitant. Maeve rolled her eyes. "Look, I'm an adult. You really can't stop me. Mason, am I going to fly with you or am I going to have to find my own flight?" She loved Elisa and her family, but sometimes they treated her like she was fragile. She may have been through a lot, but that made her tough and determined, not fragile.

Tyra chuckled then, as if she read Maeve's mind. "No one's doubting your capabilities, Maeve. We're just worried about you."

Maeve softened. "Yeah, I know. Thank you. But I'd really like to see Ethan." She needed to see him and to know if she should wait for him, if he wanted her at all.

"I can get another ticket," Mason told her after a second. "If you're sure."

"Yes. I'm sure. I'll get the cash." Maeve left before Mason could protest—like he'd probably do, knowing him.

She ran up to her room. She didn't know how much she'd need, since she'd never bought herself a ticket before, but she grabbed it all from her desk drawer. About two thousand.

When she entered the room, Mason was talking to his mom again. "I'll be gone for about a week, I think. I have some business while I'm there anyway." Mason looked at Maeve as she came closer. "You don't need to worry about it, Maeve. I can get the ticket."

Maeve merely smiled and grabbed her cash. "How much is a ticket?"

Mason shook his head, an amused smile flitting on his lips. "Just give me five hundred of it. If it's more, I'll cover it. If it's less, I'll repay you."

Maeve handed it over. "But I can pay you back if you end up paying more," Maeve told him, frowning. She liked being financially independent. "When are we leaving?"

Mason pocketed the money. "Tonight, at seven. I'll have to call Ethan to let him know you're coming too, so he can get everything he needs to set up." Mason stepped away, looking like he didn't want to do the task. He went into the kitchen, leaving the three women alone.

Tyra grabbed Maeve's hand. "You sure about this?" she asked gently.

Maeve paused, searching deep within herself, then nodded. She felt as though she desperately needed to do this; for herself. It felt *right*.

Tyra nodded and squeezed her hand, smiling. "Just be sure to stay safe. I would hate for anything to happen to you. I worry about you just as much as Ethan." Tyra paused, looking at Elisa. "We'll be praying for you."

Maeve smiled. Over the months, Maeve had grown to love their testimonies, and even their church.

"Thank you." Maeve grabbed onto Elisa's hand as well. "Don't worry too much. I'll be careful, and I'm sure they'll have an officer tailing my every move there as well." *Even more so there, I'd think,* Maeve admitted to herself. She wouldn't tell the others, but she felt scared about going to Chicago again. There, her parents had died, and she'd been homeless most of her life. She had been raped there. That was where she'd been told she would have to move for her safety.

But she needed to face this fear she had about it. And she needed to know where Ethan was at—whether he still cared for her; more than just a friend or a job.

Maeve swallowed and forced a smile at them, then escaped after Mason.

Mason was on the phone. He looked at her while she entered. "Yeah, well I tried that." He sounded annoyed. "Think I'm an idiot? But you can't stop her—she's right that she can make her own decisions..." He huffed after another moment. "Well, you tell her that then." Mason handed the phone off to Maeve. Maeve took it hesitantly, worried. What if Ethan didn't want her there because he didn't even like her anymore?

"Hello?" Maeve asked softly.

"Maeve?" Ethan's voice sounded in her ear. His face flashed in her eyes, and she felt her heartbeat speed up.

Dang, that was annoying.

"Yes."

"Maeve, please tell me you're not coming up here," Ethan told her gently.

Annoyed, Maeve felt her defenses rise. "Well, why not? You'll be so busy you'll barely see me anyway."

Ethan paused a moment, then his voice pleaded this time. "Maeve, that's not it. I can't see you hurt. I can't see you taken again. If Anthony or the other man from that night recognizes you, I don't know if I'd be able to protect you. No one cares enough to go after you guys in Kansas anymore—at least not right now—but they won't hesitate to pick you up if you came here. You'd be in danger."

Maeve crossed her arms. "No more danger than you're in," she protested, refusing to back down.

"More," he insisted. "You're a woman, more appealing to them, and smaller, so you're an easier target. You don't even know how to defend yourself." Ethan's voice was still low in the tone of pleading. The softness in his voice made Maeve wonder if she might have a chance with him after all.

"Actually, I do." Maeve reassured him. "I've been taking self-defense classes since you've left. I'm no pro at it or anything like that, but I know how to decently take care of myself."

That made Ethan pause. "Maeve…that's not enough. Please, you've got to see—"

"I understand your concern, and I thank you for it, but you're not persuading me not to go. I'm coming, and that's that." Maeve used her no-nonsense tone.

"Not if I call and tell our officers that you're not allowed to leave the town." His voice was low with warning, almost cold.

Suddenly panicked, Maeve tightened her hold on the phone. "You wouldn't do that—you couldn't."

"Don't make me," Ethan told her.

"Ethan, you can't," she pleaded, feeling like she was suddenly suffocating. She couldn't be locked down like that. She refused to be. After all the time's she'd been in foster homes, held captive, or injured, Ethan should know how that would make her feel.

"Please stay there, Maeve. I'm begging you." Ethan sighed. "Please put Mason on the phone."

Maeve went out to find Mason in the living room without replying to Ethan, handing the phone off silently, then rushing up the stairs to her room. She was relieved Tyra and Elisa had been in the family room, not the living room, so they hadn't seen her run up.

Maeve shut her door and locked it behind her, trying to get some semblance of control back in her as her entire body shook with a stupid fear.

Ethan was practically threatening to keep her under lock and key. She knew he worried about her, but that was crazy. He couldn't do that, could he? The other officers wouldn't allow that.

Well, she didn't know for sure. The officers might fully agree with Ethan on keeping Maeve "safe," but why couldn't they understand that she didn't feel safe even with those cops following her around all the time, let alone if she was forced to stay somewhere?

She paced inside her room, shaking out her hands and biting them intermittently. She already felt like a caged animal, and Ethan hadn't even done what he'd threatened yet. Memories flashed in her mind. Being locked away as everyone she loved tried protecting her.

Could he really do that to her? She didn't think he could—she thought he would be one to understand her, if anyone could. But how desperate was he to try and keep her safe?

She made up her mind. She wasn't going to stick around to find out. She pulled her phone out of her pocket and headed to her closet, pulling out a backpack as Kelly answered on the other end of the phone.

"Maeve? Everything alright?" Kelly's concerned voice sounded.

"I need a favor," Maeve told her quickly. "Please don't ask questions yet—not until I see you. Meet me at our spot at seven."

¤ ¤ ¤

Mason watched Maeve run up the stairs and frowned, pulling the phone back up to his ear. "Ethan, what did you say to her?"

"What do you mean?" Ethan asked, his voice still holding concern, but also a wariness. "I just told her I wanted her safe. I told her to stay there." Ethan cut off abruptly. Mason knew he was withholding something; he knew his brother, and he knew Maeve would not have reacted like that for nothing.

"Ethan." Mason's voice went firm.

Ethan sighed. "Mason, I just told her that I'd have the officers keep her there if she kept refusing to stay, that's all. I'm just worried about her. I don't want her up here. It'll be too dangerous and too complicated."

"I don't see how it's any more dangerous for her than it is for you or for me," Mason said. "But that's not what you mean, is it? It's complicated because you just want to catch these guys, but you don't want here there, and you're worried about her because you love her." Mason grabbed onto the back of a chair as he entered the kitchen again.

Ethan paused a moment. "You're making me reconsider even letting you come down."

Mason ground his teeth in frustration. Mason hated that he had to have officers following him, or at the very least be watched on camera in his own work and home. He was a freaking grown man, he didn't need babysitting or monitoring. Ethan was being paranoid. Sure, these guys can come after any one of Mason's family, but if they really wanted him, they would get him, and there was nothing he could do to stop it.

Even more than that, Ethan's worry was blocking him from seeing others' feelings about the situation. He didn't see how much it hurt each of them that they couldn't see him. He didn't see how telling Maeve she couldn't leave felt just as bad as locking her up. Mason may not know her the best, but even he could tell she felt locked away.

Mason rubbed his head. "Ethan, you cannot do that to her. You can't do it to any of us, but especially not her."

"I can, and I will if I need to, to protect you guys."

Selfish jerk. Mason found himself thinking. It was hard to think of his little brother this encumbered, angered, and controlling. He had no right to step into their lives in such a way to tell them what they can and can't do.

"You don't understand—" Mason started, but Ethan cut him off.

"No, *you* don't understand!" Ethan snapped. "I can't see you guys get hurt. Not by my mistake. Not by these men, and not like this."

They both fell silent a couple of long moments, nearly a minute. Finally, Mason spoke, very softly.

"No. Instead you're going to hurt every one of your family members, and every person that you love, because *you're* too scared and selfish to consider what we may be feeling. Stop being a jerk and realize that *you're* not the only one in this world—it's not all about what *you* want, and you cannot control everything just because you are an agent." Mason hung up and nearly tossed the phone onto the counter in his frustration.

Mason wanted Ethan back, the old Ethan, without this paranoia and desire for control. But until Anthony was caught, Mason didn't know if that would happen. He understood where Ethan was coming from. But he also knew Ethan was just grasping onto any straws he could.

It was a sad way to see his brother. Something had to snap him out of it.

Mason took a couple calming breaths, wondering what to do now. With how his brother was acting, going to visit him didn't seem as appealing, but Mason knew he couldn't just leave his brother alone over there, even if he was frustrated with him.

Sighing, Mason forced himself to release the back of the chair, then made his way in the direction Maeve went. He knew she had gone up to her room.

Her door was shut. And locked. He knocked lightly. "Maeve?"

He waited a couple moments before Maeve showed up at the door, cracking it open slightly. "What?" she whispered, but didn't let him in. Mason noticed the nervousness in the flutter of her hands, and the fear vivid in her eyes.

Mason reached into his back pocket. "I don't think I can get you the ticket right now." He held her money out to her. Maeve hesitated, then opened the door wider to take it. As she did so, Mason put a hand on her shoulder. "Whatever you end up doing…stay safe, alright?" He somehow knew that after the conversation with Ethan, she was going to do something. He couldn't and wouldn't stop her, but he prayed that she would take caution.

A brief look of relief filled her eyes, and she flung her arms over his shoulders for a hug. "Thank you, Mason. For everything. You stay safe also."

Mason nodded, hugging her tight a moment, then smiled as he pulled away. "Maeve, I know you've grown feelings for my brother. I love having you here, and I know the rest of my family agrees. However, I know there is something stopping you from fully settling down here. I wish you luck in finding out whatever it may be. Just promise me you'll be safe and stay in contact, alright?"

Maeve nodded, tears running. "I promise, Mason…." She retreated to her room.

Mason stood there a couple moments, trying to get his bearings. He knew most of his family would hate him if they knew what he'd just told her, but he didn't care. Of course he wanted her there, but he knew she would never settle. She needed to figure out her life, and as much as she loved it with Mason's family, she wasn't going to find it by hiding from the past like he believed she was.

Mason made his way back down the stairs, finding Tyra waiting in the living room for him. His mom was gone.

"What's going on?" Tyra asked him, sensing his mood.

Mason shook her head and pulled his wife into his embrace. He didn't know how to tell her what he suspected of both Maeve and Ethan, but he knew that if anyone could make sense of it, she could. He took a couple minutes to explain it to her quietly as they stood there.

~21~

Maeve's dreams disturbed her. She relived Santorini taking her, using her, leaving her unworthy. She dreamed of Kelly, of their last parting hug. Of the tears that ran down Kelly's face, but the numbness in Maeve's heart that stopped her from feeling the same emotion as her best friend. She thought back on the hopelessness and fear she'd felt when her parents had died. The fear of living in a foster home with people she didn't know. Her confusion as Ethan kissed her, but then turned around and left her feeling unwanted.

Unloved.

Unworthy.

Trash.

She woke, disoriented and trembling in the hotel bed. The windows were dark; it was night. Midnight, according to the clock.

She gasped in a breath, then held her hand to her chest.

She forced her breaths to deepen, thinking back on the peace she'd felt with Elisa and her family, and the religion and God she'd become dependent on entirely this last half a week. Mason's parting words echoed in her mind. He knew there was something she needed to find out for herself. She knew it too. She wanted to push it aside, but it was persistent, especially now that she'd acknowledged it.

She wasn't going to let Ethan stop her, no matter how much she loved him. He could not put chains on her. She refused to let anyone do so. Not again and not like that. Especially not someone she loved. It was expected from a bad guy, but it was not expected from her loved ones…she still couldn't believe that Ethan had threatened her with that.

She slowly sat up, taking stock of her situation. She'd found a bus and ridden it for a while, then hitchhiked with family in their RV, and now found herself in Weston, Iowa. She hadn't wanted to take a direct route to Chicago, but she was slowly heading in that direction.

Why did she feel as though she needed to be in Chicago? Besides Ethan, of course. Something had been drawing her back, even before she'd met Ethan. Was it just because she'd lived there for so long?

She felt there was something incomplete back in that city.

She blinked a couple times, wanting to go back to sleep, but she hesitated to do so. Feeling a rush of urgency, she finally stood up. She clicked on the light in the bathroom, trying to keep the light at a minimum in her hotel room. She didn't know if anyone would be following her, but she wanted to make it as hard as possible for anyone to do so.

She checked her reflection, brushed through her hair and teeth, then slipped on her shoes. She dug out a granola bar, stuck it in her pocket, then turned off the light and cracked the door to the hotel room open. She didn't see anyone out there, so she slipped out and headed to the bus stop, munching on her bar as she did so.

She felt like a criminal, sneaking around like this. It was hard that one of the reasons she had to be secretive was because of someone she loved.

She sighed as she finished up the bar, and then saw the bus start to pull up. She ran the last bit to catch it and was relieved when she climbed aboard that there were only a few people on it.

She relaxed onto one of the seats, staring out the window. Though she tried to stay awake, as the time went on, she drifted to sleep…

She jerked awake awhile later to someone sitting beside her. Maeve looked around. It was morning now, and there were more people on the bus. So many that it was time to share rows. She looked around, looking around for information as to where she was. She didn't recognize the town.

She turned to the lady that sat next to her. "Ma'am, I'm sorry, but do you know where we are?"

The lady smiled at Maeve in understanding. "We're pretty close to Mt. Pleasant, Iowa."

Maeve nodded and thanked her. She didn't really know where that was, but she knew it was closer to Chicago. She needed to check that map again.

She pulled it out of her backpack, then unfolded it enough that she could see Galesburg, Illinois and searched for Mt. Pleasant. However, she didn't know if this bus would take her there.

For the first time in years, she let herself think back on the details of the night her parents died. She hated thinking about it, but she knew this portion of her past had to be faced if she were to ever move on or be able to settle fully with anyone. She knew she would have mental scars on her forever, and hiding it would never allow her start to heal.

She remembered her mom locking Maeve into her room, warning her to stay in there, as dad went to go answer the door. It wasn't unusual that she was sent to her room when guests came over, but it had been different when her mom had locked the door that night.

Maeve, at the time, had just shaken off the movement to play with her toys.

Until she heard the gunshots from downstairs. Two of them.

She'd froze, unsure what to do after that, then she ran to her door, trying to open it. When she had no luck and heard the front door open, she ran to the window to see who was leaving. She'd only gotten one quick look before the killer was gone.

Maeve bit her lip, debating a moment, then she finally decided to go talk to the driver. She had to get to Galesburg. It was at her old home, in her old town, that she would try to discover the truth of her parent's deaths.

¤ ¤ ¤

Patty watched Ethan pace the floor, reminding her of a caged lion. He was angry, worried too, obviously, but the anger seemed to show more than the worry for now. Or maybe his worry was showing up as anger?

"And we haven't heard from her at all?" Ethan asked, his voice strained. The concern heard in his voice about this "Maeve" made Patty frown. His constant worry about her made Patty realize that the chance she wanted with Ethan wasn't bound to happen.

Forcing down her disappointment, she got back to work.

"No," Mygyer told him. Mason, Ethan's brother, sat two seats down from Mygyer. Cameron had claimed the seat next to Patty. Will, their newest member, was a nervous boy. Boy, meaning, he was only a year out of high school, but amazing with the technology aspect of everything.

"Maeve is capable of taking care of herself. She's done it her entire life," Mason told him, putting his fingertips together on the table in front of him. He seemed a little cautious about speaking, but his voice was firm when he spoke to his brother.

Ethan gave Mason a look, then stopped his pacing and put his hands on the end of the table, his anger seemingly flooding from him and a vulnerability rising in the sag of his head to his chest. "I never should have threatened her."

Mygyer jerked up. This was obviously new information to him as well. "You *threatened* her?" His voice was incredulous. Sort of angry too. They were all short-tempered with being on this case, but especially Ethan and Mygyer. Will seemed to be the only one holding onto any shred of cheerfulness in whatever he may be doing.

That's not how it used to be. At the beginning of the undercover work Ethan had been the cheerful one. Now it seemed all he could think about was getting Anthony locked away…or dead.

Ethan winced and sat in a seat. "I didn't mean anything by it. She just kept saying that she was going to come down here, and I didn't want her to be here—not while it's so dangerous. I told her I'd make sure the police kept her there if she didn't stop pushing on coming down here."

Patty folded her arms, strangely hurt by what he said. "I cannot believe you said that," Patty said, keeping tight control on her anger. It looked like Mygyer had been going to say something, but Patty had beat him to it. He and the other two members of the team looked at Ethan like they were looking at him for the first time.

Patty continued, her voice scorning. "'Too dangerous' my butt. That's a pathetic excuse in this line of work, and you know it. I understood keeping the police on your family, that makes some sense at least, but you have Mason come up here, then as soon as a woman is in the picture it's suddenly 'too dangerous'?" She snorted derisively, realizing why she didn't like what he said. Even still, there were a lot of people who think a woman couldn't get the job done as well as a man. Patty wasn't usually intent on bringing that fact to attention or anything, but she could not believe her ears.

Ethan avoided everyone's gaze, messing with his hands. "Maeve's not trained like you are, Patty. You've been in this work for years. Maeve doesn't know how to defend herself." The way he spoke told Patty that there was a hidden *"and I love Maeve,"* or something in there as well.

Patty scowled. "Maeve has lived on the streets for years. She knows how to handle herself well enough."

Mason shook his head on the other side of the table. "Maeve was going to leave eventually," he told them quietly, interrupting any other argument they could make.

They all looked at him in surprise. "What do you mean?" Ethan's voice was pained. "Why would she?"

Mason looked at them all. "She really likes the family. I can see that. However, haven't you noticed how she hasn't even unpacked her backpack yet? She always has it partially packed, as if ready to leave at a moment's notice. She's never bought a lot of things. And when she talks, she usually avoids talking about herself—at least her past. Do any of you even know how her parents died? Or why she was homeless? Or why she never left Chicago?" Mason sat back in the seat, taking a heavy breath. "She has something she has to figure out. I don't know what, or why, but it's been weighing her down as long as I've known her."

Mason looked at Ethan. "Then you snapped and told her she can't come up. Ethan, Maeve really likes you, everyone can tell. She has already had a hard time letting people love her, and loving them in return, then you came in and she wanted you, but you left. She doesn't know if she can trust her heart out to anyone."

"Did she tell you this?" Ethan asked softly, his eyes finding Mason's with a strange gentleness.

Mason shook his head. "She didn't need to." He sighed. "Then you told her you'd lock her up, essentially, and she couldn't take that. She ran for it while she could." He shook his head.

They were all silent for a couple minutes, then Ethan stood and left the room. Patty hesitated a moment. She hated seeing Ethan hurting. Having the crush on him made her care about him—and he may never care about her like she wanted him to, but she knew he could have a happy ending.

"Ethan!" she shouted down the hall, walking quickly after him. He slowed slightly but didn't stop. "What are you doing?"

Ethan put his hands into his pockets and shrugged. "Don't know. Back to finding Anthony, I guess."

Patty frowned. "But what about Maeve?"

Ethan slowed even further. "Don't know what I can do about her. I don't know where she is. And even if I did, she wouldn't want me anymore. Not after what I've done to her." He looked so miserable that Patty put a hand on Ethan's shoulder and stopped him.

"From what I've heard, Maeve has to be pretty forgiving and open to have fallen in love with you after your history. She may not know if she can trust you, but she *wants* to trust you. Don't let her down now. Apologize."

"But how can I if I can't find her?"

Patty snorted, smiling a little. "Ethan, are you seriously asking me this right now?"

"What?" He studied her.

"You're a freaking cop! An undercover agent! If you can't find her, no one can." She shook her head. "Put the pieces together, dork. Where has she stayed? Chicago. Where did she used to live? Here. Why would she come back? What happened to her parents? Search for what could've happened to her parents and where she used to live. Follow your instincts." Patty smiled at him as she saw a little hope spring forth. "I know you love her, Ethan. And that's great you've found someone. Don't let her slip through your fingers. Not if she loves you back."

Ethan grinned at her. "Thanks, Patty. You're amazing. Thank you." He pulled her into a hug, then walked away, a little skip in his step now, like how the old Ethan—when she knew him as Derek—had been.

Patty watched him walk away, feeling a little piece of her ache. That was that.

Someone came up behind her. She felt a hand on her shoulder softly, and somehow knew it was Mygyer without having to look.

"Patty," he said softly. "Isn't letting Ethan go, letting him slip through your fingers, exactly what you told *him* not to do?"

Patty sighed. "Yeah…but there's a difference."

"And what's that?" Mygyer asked.

"He doesn't love me back."

⁓22⁓

This feels more like it, Ethan thought as he walked through the city. Being out and about, not stuck behind a desk. Inside work wasn't what he enjoyed at all. He knew there was paperwork involved in all field work, but that was worth it for the chance to be out instead of always behind the computer. He didn't know how Will and Cameron did it.

Mygyer had been convinced Ethan shouldn't go out on any of the cases they had of Anthony or any of the mafia families due to the high risk of recognition, and for months, that had been what Ethan had been solely focused on.

Now, though, he felt that familiar handgun strapped under his shirt.

He'd asked Mygyer to give him a small case—something that had nothing to do with Anthony or the usual case. Mygyer had agreed, though Ethan was under Chicago Police jurisdiction currently as he worked the case with them. They'd needed extra hands.

He'd needed this.

It was good for Ethan to step away a little. It had been a grueling process, these last couple months. It had consumed him. Stepping away, he'd realized that. What felt even more stimulating was the tough words Mason had spoken to him, and the encouragement from Patty. Mason was right. He had been trying to protect everyone, even at the cost of all of them being miserable. Ethan had been trying to carry the guilt all by himself.

As Ethan walked to the house and took his place on the side of it, watching the windows that the chief expected the criminal to take if he realized he was being surrounded, Ethan realized he'd been trying to carry the burden of guilt alone. Pridefully thinking he could finish this case on his own.

That's not how he was raised to live. First off, his family was all there for him, to talk to at the very least. For help, when possible.

Secondly, Ethan had been raised in a church that fully believed that his Savior would take all the guilt and pain—if Ethan would let Him.

That gave Ethan a pause. No, Jesus would not take it if Ethan *let* Him. The scriptures clearly stated that He carried the burden for *every* person. He had *already* carried it, now the question was whether Ethan would let go.

Ethan had a sudden image of himself hanging onto the end of Jesus' cross, getting dragged. That did two things. It made the going rough on Ethan, as he got beat up on the floor, trampled by the crowd. Even more so, it made the burden heavier for Jesus.

A voice in Ethan's ear, a warning that the bust was about to start, stopped Ethan's train of thought and focused it on the task on hand, but an intense warmth filled him suddenly.

Peace.

Glass shattered around Ethan, the window breaking. Ethan raised his gun as the man that had jumped out made a run for it to the back of the house. Ethan nearly swore as he took off after the man, giving warning through his headpiece for the people in the back to be prepared.

As Ethan nearly rounded the corner, he saw a new movement that stopped him. The cops at the back of the house went after the first guy, but a second guy was slipping out the window. When he saw that Ethan noticed him, he moved faster, jumping the fence to the right. Ethan spoke into the headpiece about this second man, then took after him, jumping the fence. The movement was hard. His wound was healed, but it wasn't untouched, so to speak. The movement pulled a little at his scar, giving a pang, but it didn't make him stop.

The man led Ethan on a chase over a couple more fences before ending up in a backyard with a family. The mother and one of the daughters screamed as the man got over the fence, but before the family could make it inside, the man grabbed one of the teenage boys and put a gun to his head. Ethan was still a good ten or so feet off.

"Stop or I'll shoot him," the man shouted at Ethan. Ethan scrambled for a stop, breathing heavily, his gun pointing at him, but the tightening of the man's finger made Ethan hesitate to even try for a shot.

The dad tried to take a step closer to his son, panic in his eyes, but the man swung in his direction slightly and took a step away. "Stay back! And put the gun down, officer, or I'll blow his brains out." He situated himself more firmly behind the teenager, backing up slowly.

"Please don't hurt him!" the mother sobbed, grabbing her youngest children and pulling them behind her.

"Put the gun down." The man's voice had calmed. He wasn't the irrational criminal anymore; he had gathered himself as he felt a sense of control over the situation.

Ethan hesitated a moment, then lowered the gun. The teenager met his eyes, one hand low at his side, instead of at the man's arm—where it typically would be whenever one was held hostage with an arm around the neck. After a moment, Ethan realized the teenager was trying to give some sort of signal—a countdown.

The information barely processed before the teenager elbowed the man, tossed up his hand to knock the gun away, and flipped him over his shoulder quickly.

Ethan reacted on instinct, running forward to cover the man with his gun. The father pulled his teenager out of harm's way as Ethan kicked the gun.

"Are you okay?" Ethan asked the family, but mainly the teenager who had been grabbed. He saw the nods but didn't focus on them. He pulled the man to his feet, forced him against the fence, and quickly slapped cuffs on his wrists. "You're under arrest."

At that same moment, officers rounded the corner of the fence. A few saw he had it under control and checked on the family. Ethan handed the man off to someone else to state his Miranda Rights and take him to the station.

Ethan smiled as he turned back to the family. "You sure you're all okay?"

Their dad nodded, pulling his teenager against his side. Mom put a hand on her son's back.

"Thank you," the father said, holding his hand out for Ethan. Ethan took it but shook his head.

"No—thanks to your son." Ethan smiled at the teenager. "Nice trick you got there. Glad you managed it safely. It could have gone wrong."

The teen nodded. "I know, sir, but I had to try something." He looked at his mom. "Man am I thankful to those classes now, Mom."

His mom nodded. "Me too." She gave a long shuddery breath, as if trying to calm herself.

Ethan smiled at them, nodding once more. "Sorry to interrupt your dinner. I hope the rest of your night is peaceful." He started to turn away, but the teenager stepped forward and grabbed his arm.

"Wait. I just…" He hesitated, then hugged Ethan, surprising him. "Thank you. I was really scared," he said quietly.

Ethan tilted his head as the teenager pulled away. "Anytime, kid."

"Won't you eat with us? Something we can do to thank you?" The mom slid under her husband's arm as she spoke.

Ethan looked back at the chief, feeling awkward. He'd never been asked that before by a victim.

Chief Carter laughed. "Go for it, Ethan. Just remember you have paperwork when you get back. Just because you got the guy doesn't mean you can get away without doing it." He turned and ambled away, a smile on his face.

Ethan turned back to the family. The parents, the teenage boy, one teenage girl, and two younger kids. When he looked at them, Ethan couldn't say no. He was hungry, but even more than that, the idea of eating with a family again appealed to him suddenly.

The parents got the kids sitting around the table, then shakily went back to finishing up the meat on the grill. The man hesitated. "Looks like some of them were burned." He picked them up with his tongs, turning them over.

"We'll pick around it, hon," his wife told him. She stuck her hand out to Ethan. "I'm Amanda. My husband over there is Orson. My oldest is Danny." She pointed to the teenager that had been nabbed. "My second, Vanessa, my third, Gerald, and my last, Kinzy." She pulled her youngest daughter to her side.

"Nice to meet you all," Ethan said. "I'm Ethan. Thanks for inviting me to eat with you."

Ethan spent the evening answering question after question about being an agent, and he ended up staying a lot longer than he expected. As Ethan made his way back to the station, he relished the memory of peace that had come over him this evening.

The day seemed perfect, but there were a couple more things he had to do.

He pulled out his phone as he got to his car, surprised to find that he had a couple of missed calls. He had left the phone silent during the bust and hadn't cared to check it since.

Mason had called him twice, and Mygyer three times. Frowning, Ethan called Mason back first.

He answered on the third ring. "Ethan, hi. Are you okay?"

Ethan furrowed his eyebrows. "Yeah, why?"

Mason sighed in relief. "Thank God. We didn't hear about you after the bust, and Anthony killed again. This time he left a message for you…well, for the police. I was worried he'd already gotten you."

Ethan gripped the wheel. "What was the message?"

"Just get to the station, now," Mason told him. "We're all here, and no one will tell me more than that."

"Is the family okay?" Ethan asked. "And Maeve? Have you heard anything from her?"

"I called all the family. They're doing fine. And no, nothing substantial on Maeve yet." Mason's voice lowered. "Ethan, I don't understand all that's happening, but it's getting tense down here." It was probably worse being a bystander. Mason knew more than most would, but he wouldn't be included in all of the investigation.

"I'll be there in a few, Mason. Stay there for me."

"I'm not going anywhere," Mason promised. "Love you, Ethan."

"Love you." Ethan snapped the phone shut and started his car. Ethan worked on bringing back the feeling of peace, but it was hard.

Please, God, I know I can't hold onto control anymore, but help me do what I need to.

¤ ¤ ¤

Maeve knocked on the door. She hated the fact that it was getting late, but she knew she couldn't wait any longer. She needed a place to stay, and she needed to know if this man would help her.

The door opened a couple minutes later, and a light flickered on, nearly blinding Maeve for a moment. She blinked a couple times, seeing a silhouette of a large man in the doorway.

Even before she saw his face, she knew she was at the right door.

She held up a hand to block the light and squinted at the man in front of her. "Carl Lassing?"

The man paused, staring at her. "Yes?"

He didn't recognize her. No surprise, she hadn't been here since she was thirteen.

"It's Maeve Foundry," Maeve told him quietly. Her last name felt entirely unfamiliar. Strangely, Maeve realized that Elisa's last name seemed more fitting than her real last name.

The man gasped, then opened the door wider. "Come in, Maeve." As soon as the door shut, the man pulled her into a hug. "What are you doing here?"

"I have to talk to you," Maeve told him, still talking quietly. "Do you have time?"

The man looked back toward the kitchen. "We're about to start dinner. Will you join us?"

Maeve hesitated, but she knew she had to eat, so she nodded. "If you're sure that's okay."

"Of course," Carl told her, ushering her toward the kitchen. "Chrissa, we have a guest."

Chrissa looked up as Maeve entered, and her face immediately broke into recognition. "Maeve! I'm so pleased to see you." She rounded the table to give her a hug. "I've been so worried about you."

Maeve smiled. "I've missed you."

"Come, sit down and eat, and tell me what you've been up to." Chrissa went to grab an extra plate set. Relieved, Maeve sat in the seat. They were receiving her well. That made it easier to approach them about the hard subject.

"I can't stay long," Maeve told them. "I'm actually doing pretty good right now. I found a wonderful lady who is letting me stay with her. I have a job now, and I absolutely adore her entire family."

"How were the foster homes?" Chrissa asked as she put the plate down in front of her. "Did someone adopt you after we lost touch?"

Maeve frowned. "No…Didn't get adopted, just kinda… phased out of foster care." *Close enough to what happened.*

The Lassings' eyes held shock. "You could've come back here at any time. You know we would've helped you."

Maeve nodded and looked at her lap. "I was…I was scared to come back. After what happened with my parents."

Chrissa nodded in understanding. "But you came back now. Is there something you need?"

Maeve hesitated. Carl caught onto her nervousness and put a hand over hers. "Chrissa, let's all eat before we push for any information," he decided. Maeve felt a flush of relief. She really was hungry, and even the idea of asking them made her stomach sick with horror.

"Thank you," Maeve told them sincerely.

They chatted about small items of their life. Carl was now retired from the Chicago police force, been so for a couple years. That news bummed Maeve out since she had needed access to her parents' case, but she'd address that problem when she came to it.

When they finished, they moved to the family room. The room was oddly familiar to her, even though it was moved around and there was new stuff everywhere.

Maeve looked around, then admired the set-up on a table halfway down the hall. There were pictures of a little boy Maeve remembered, one that had been ten or so when Maeve had last seen him. The later pictures showed that he had grown into a very handsome young man. Then it showed him in Army attire.

"Daniel went into service?" Maeve asked, remembering how obsessed that boy had been about every aspect of the war, but especially the planes and boats. Then she saw a folded flag and a plaque. "Is he…is he gone?" Maeve asked softly, voice nearly trembling. She had really liked Daniel; she couldn't say dead.

"Right before I retired," Carl said, his voice as emotional as Maeve felt. Maeve thought about asking how it happened, but Carl and Chrissa's sorrow stopped her.

Maeve sat on the couch across from them. "I hate bringing this up, Carl, but…I need to know everything you know about my parents' deaths. As far as I know, the case was never solved."

Carl looked hesitant, but as if he knew this conversation would come one day. "You're right. It never was solved. We just didn't have enough information to keep any suspects in. You said that they seemed familiar with your parents though, right?"

Maeve nodded. "Yes, as Mom was taking me upstairs, I heard them talking to my dad. Both my parents seemed nervous though, and Mom locked the door behind me, which, thinking back on it, was strange." She bowed her head. "I should have realized it then. My mom would never lock the door—even when I was grounded."

"It wasn't your fault, Maeve. And I'm glad she locked it. Who knows what would've happened to you if she hadn't?" Carl smiled reassuringly at her, though it seemed sad.

Well, that much was true.

Maeve took a deep breath. "I want to reopen the case. I want to try to find these guys."

Carl shook his head. "I can't help you there. I'm not an officer anymore. Besides what more will you find out that we haven't already tried?" Though the first sentence was firm, the second seemed to imply that if she gave enough reason, he may consider it.

"I'm not sure," Maeve told him honestly. "But I'd like to know everything about the case. My best friend is a FBI agent, and he might help me get to the bottom of it. Sometimes a new pair of eyes can see something that hadn't been caught before."

Carl thought for a moment. "I really don't have that much power over the case, Maeve. I would talk to the new chief, but he and I never really got along. I had always thought he was a little too power hungry, and I had tried to stop his promotion. Ever since then, he's held a grudge against me."

Maeve thought for a minute. "I may be able to convince him to let me. If I do, will you help me?"

Carl sighed and ran a hand down his face. Chrissa looked concerned as they exchanged glances. But after a second Carl turned toward her and nodded. "You know I loved your parents, your family. If we can find this guy, then yeah, I'll do everything I can to solve this case."

"Let's talk about this more tomorrow," Chrissa told them. "You seem exhausted, Maeve. We have an extra room; won't you stay here for the night?"

Maeve hesitated, not wanting to be in the way, but ultimately, that would be better than what she had planned for. "That would be great."

"Wonderful." Chrissa showed her to the room, and the bathroom that was attached. "You can use whatever you need." Then they left her alone for the night.

Maeve chose to shower and get ready for bed, then grabbed her phone. She had turned it off to save battery for her travels, but now it was time to contact Ethan.

With trembling fingers, she turned it on. As it loaded, she got loads of messages and voicemails. Mostly from Elisa, Isabelle, and…Ethan. Maeve opened the texts.

Mason had texted her only once, knowing that he was the only one who knew she had left—besides Kelly—Maeve checked his first.

"Maeve, I know I told you to go out and figure out what is bothering you. I support you in that, of course, but I want to give you some warning. Anthony is on the move again, and he gave Ethan a warning. Please stay safe and let me know when you can if you are. I'd hate for Anthony to get his hands on you."

Maeve digested the text for a couple moments, thinking back on Anthony. She sure didn't want to be caught by him either.

Maeve looked at the other texts. Elisa's and Isabelle's were very similar, wanting to know where she was, if she was okay, some very upset messages. Maeve shot them both identical texts. *"Thanks for the love and support, love you. I'll contact you when I can.* With a heart emoji. Then she went to Ethan's. He seemed more guilty than anything else, apologizing and asking if she was okay.

Maeve called him.

The answer was nearly immediate. "Maeve, where are you?"

Maeve took a deep breath. "Ethan, I won't answer that. However, are you free tomorrow? I'd like to meet up about noon for lunch to tell you some things and ask for a favor."

"Of course I can meet," Ethan told her, then his voice turned pleading. "Please, Maeve, just tell me where you're at. Tell me you're safe. Obviously, you're here somewhere, to meet up for lunch. I can come tonight, set some watch on you."

"No." Maeve shook her head, though he couldn't see her. "I know you mean well, but I refuse to be locked away. I promise, I'm safe now as I ever have been. See you tomorrow, at the restaurant Trezeros. I love you." She hung up before he could reply, then she shut off her phone and plugged it into the charger.

Maeve felt a lot more refreshed now that she was clean and had a chance to talk with the people she loved, brief as it was.

~23~

Ethan's hands were shaking. What if Maeve didn't show up? It was ten past noon. She should've been there by now.

He looked behind him, to the entrance, watching for Maeve. Mason was more relaxed next to Ethan, arms folded against his chest. He was eyeing Ethan.

"You look better," Mason finally said, bringing Ethan's attention back to his brother.

Ethan smiled. "I am, a bit. It was good for me to step away from the case yesterday. And what you told me…Thanks." Ethan thought about telling Mason about his thoughts the day before that had helped the peace come over him, but it was still a little new, and Ethan wouldn't want to do it in public.

"I'm glad. I was about ready to punch your face," Mason told him honestly, making Ethan chuckle. "I don't want you to be that high-strung ever again, alright?"

Ethan nodded. "I mean, I'll try. No promises, obviously." The phone from Ethan's suit jacket pocket started to ring. Ethan slipped it out, wondering if it was Maeve, but it was only Mygyer. Ethan leaned forward as he answered. The warning from last night flashed into his brain. *"Better watch your step, or you'll slip in the Ice that you made."*

"Hello?"

"Ethan, we have a problem. Anthony has started getting bolder. He's killed another woman and marked his initials. This time, he did it with a man in the vicinity, nearly killing him as well. We also caught two kids who say they're soldiers for Anthony."

Ethan put a hand to his head as he stood to step away from the table. "Are we sure they are?"

"Well, the evidence is pretty condemning, as they also have signature *AAC* cut into the wrists." Mygyer's voice seemed angry. "These boys say they joined up on a whim, then got tagged and threatened before they could decide if they wanted to stay with it. Now they're scared to death they'll be killed for wanting to get out."

Ethan sighed. "They very well might." Ethan looked around as he heard the front door to the restaurant open. Maeve entered. "Mygyer, I'll call you back later. Maeve just got here."

"Stay safe, Ethan; he might be after you." Ethan hung up, a chill racing down his spine, but headed back to the table.

Mason gave Maeve a hug that she readily returned. As Ethan approached, he heard her thank him.

Ethan hung a few feet back, wondering if he'd be welcomed with a hug also. He'd missed Maeve, and if she could see inside his mind, she would know that he was so very sorry about what he had said, but she may have a grudge against him still.

When Maeve pulled back, Ethan saw the tense set in her shoulders, though her eyes were bright with a sort of happiness. Ethan wondered what had caused the differing emotions.

Maeve looked at Ethan, and they kind of stared at each other for a long moment. Ethan had time to think that she really was angry with him, and his hands had started to twitch into fists, then she flung her arms over his shoulders and pulled him into a tight hug and Ethan realized that this was Maeve they were talking about.

Ethan hugged her just as tightly, shoving his face in her neck. "I'm so sorry, Maeve. I was a selfish jerk. I never should have told you that you couldn't come here."

Maeve pulled back, giving a little crooked smile. "I know you're worried about me, Ethan, but I'm only going to tell you once. I will not be locked away."

Ethan nodded. "I know. I shouldn't have threatened you about that. Jeez, I was such an idiot. Please don't disappear like that again, though. I was scared to death."

Maeve seemed amused. "I'm a big girl, I can take care of myself." She sobered a little. "I needed to come back. I have some stuff that I have to figure out."

"What's that?" Ethan asked her.

Maeve hesitated. "I'll talk to you as we order and eat." Maeve promised, moving to an empty chair. Ethan jumped forward to pull the chair out for her, then tucked it back in as Maeve sat with a thanks.

Maeve grabbed her menu and glanced through it quickly, then she smiled and closed it and looked around at the restaurant. "Man…I haven't been here in ages."

"You lived near here?" Ethan asked, in a sort of stated way.

"Yeah, pretty close, I guess. This used to be our favorite place to eat. I would get the same thing every single time. When I was younger, I thought I was the only one who ever ordered what I did. I would have so much food, it would be leftover for the next meal." She smiled at the memory. Her wistful smile always did a number on Ethan. He grabbed her hand before he realized it. He was going to pull away as he fought embarrassment, but Maeve just tightened her grip on him and smiled softly.

Mason was watching the two of them, a lazy smile on his face, but he hid behind his menu when he noticed Ethan's gaze, for a false sense of privacy.

When the waitress came, they were all ready to order. Ethan was doing a last minute read through of the menu to make sure he knew what he wanted, so he missed what Maeve ordered. But when Ethan glanced up to say his decision, he saw the waitress staring at Maeve, surprise in her eyes.

"Maeve?" The older lady put her paper down.

Maeve blinked and looked up, then grinned. "Annie!" She jumped up and they hugged. Ethan watched the reunion, a little surprised. She had never seen such exuberant joy from Maeve. Coming back here did seem to do her some good.

"I knew it was you." The older lady grinned. "You looked a little familiar, but I couldn't put my finger on it. Then you ordered! I swear, I've never had someone order what you do and in the way you do. Oh girl, I've missed you so much." She held Maeve at arms length, eyes going over her, and touched Maeve's hair. "And after your parents…" She shook her head sadly.

Maeve but her lip, eyes shiny. "I miss them."

"Me too, baby. Me too." Annie rubbed her arms. "I've missed all you guys. I'm so glad to see you. What are you here for?"

"Actually…" Maeve looked over to Ethan and Mason. "It's what I came to talk to these gentlemen about. I'm here to figure out who killed my parents."

Ethan saw the surprise on Mason's face that reflected Ethan's own. After it absorbed, however, Ethan realized that it made a lot of sense.

Annie looked shocked as well, and worried. "It happened so long ago, Maeve. Will anything be forthcoming?"

Maeve shrugged. "I don't know, but I have to try. And now I have new eyes on the case, and I'm older, I might be able to connect something that I may not have thought was important when I was younger."

"Honey, I won't stop you, but please…You're walking a dangerous line, coming back and asking questions about this. Promise me you'll be safe." She hugged Maeve again, then turned to the brothers. "And what can I get you two?"

Ethan looked at the menu, having forgotten what he'd been going to order with their conversation.

They ordered, then Maeve sat back down and faced the two of them with a deep breath. "Not exactly how I wanted to tell you," she told them.

Ethan leaned forward. "Is that what you wanted as a favor? To look over the case?"

Maeve nodded, staring at the table. "I don't have access to the case, and I don't have training to look over them either. I thought maybe we could look over it. Even if I can't figure out who killed my parents, it will at the very least help me realize that the police did all that they could. I just feel like I have to reopen it, you know?"

Ethan scooted his seat closer and put a finger on her chin, nudging her to meet his eyes. "Why didn't you say anything before?"

She looked like she was trying not to cry, but didn't quite succeed. "Because I tried not to remember it," she whispered. "It was hard for me to think about it. I've always thought that I should have done something more to help my parents."

Ethan hesitated, then brushed his fingers back, tucking her hair behind her ear. "Tell me what happened?"

Maeve nodded and told the story.

"I just feel like I should have noticed that the door was locked. I should have called the police when I heard them fighting." She shook her head, the loose hair falling loose from behind her ear.

Ethan grabbed her hand. "No. You couldn't have done anything, Maeve. Don't worry about that." He rubbed her hand soothingly, and she sighed.

"I know that logically, but it still sticks with me. That's why I want to figure this out."

Ethan nodded. "I understand, Maeve. So, what's the first step?"

He didn't really know if they could even open the case again, let alone find anything new so many years later. If Maeve could remember what the guy looked like and pointed him out, that would be helpful.

"I need to reopen the case, or, at the very least, get details of it, if I can. I know it's a long shot, but it'll be worth it. I will need to talk to the new chief of this station in town."

Ethan nodded. "Well, I may be able to help with that. Turns out the chief in Chicago is good friends with the chief from Galesburg. They may let us look into it." Ethan stretched his back as the food got there.

Annie smiled warmly at them, but Ethan felt there was a wariness to her look. She didn't speak except to tell them to enjoy the meal, then she left them.

They ate without talking about their missions here, instead about how Ethan's family were doing at home.

"They're all worried about you," Mason said to Maeve, then included Ethan. "About both of you."

As they finished the meal, Mason dismissed himself to the bathroom. Ethan had a feeling he was giving him and Maeve a moment.

Ethan studied her. She was stunning. "I'm glad you're here," he told her softly.

Maeve laughed. "That's why I don't listen to you, Ethan. Where would I be if I had?"

Ethan grinned. "I truly am sorry. I just worried about you. But Mason said some things to me that made me realize how stupid I was acting, and then I took a step away from the case a little yesterday, and that helped me."

"I'm glad." Maeve smiled, then let it sink off her face. "Ethan, I want to ask you something."

"What's that?" Ethan tilted his head and leaned closer.

"Do you think you'd still want to… I mean, are you still in this? Us? Do you think that we may have a relationship in the future?" Maeve's cheeks burned bright red, and she wouldn't meet Ethan's eyes.

In answer, Ethan scooted closer, pulled her up into his arms, and kissed her. He'd meant for a brief one, but his body betrayed him. All worry fled him in that moment, as he held her close.

That is, until he heard a muffled crash coming from the back. Ethan jerked away, his instincts reacting instantly. Both the bathrooms and the kitchens were back that way, and it may have just been some plates or something breaking, but Ethan wasn't going to take any chances— not with Mason being in the back.

He pulled his gun as he moved, but as he walked past one of the other customers, Ethan felt his hand with his gun get knocked, almost making him drop it, and the man jumped to his feet, trying to armlock Ethan. He heard Maeve gasp, but he swung his foot out to the man, tripping him and tearing his arm free. He tightened his hold on his hand with the gun to swing it around, his insides starting to panic. If Ethan was trying to be stopped, then there was no doubt the trouble was with Mason.

Some of the customers started screaming as the man on the ground aimed a gun at him, and Ethan shot him in the leg, kicking the gun from his hand when he howled in pain.

Ethan started for the back again but saw more movement out of the corner of his eye. Another man headed toward him. Before Ethan could do anything about that, the man Ethan had just shot kicked the back of Ethan's knee, knocking him down. Ethan barely avoided the table with his head, and a shot went off wild toward the ground.

The second man reached Ethan, stood on Ethan's wrist and hand, and jerked the gun out of his hand, stuffing it in his pants, then he and the shot man worked to get Ethan onto the ground, punching his face a couple times. Ethan felt his vision darken by the third, and he was tasting blood almost immediately as pain arose in his jaw.

Don't pass out, Ethan told himself, practically begging as worry for his brother continued to rage.

Ethan managed to get one hand free, and he punched the hurt guy in his already-shot leg. That movement distracted him with pain long enough for Ethan to get his legs free. He arched his hips away from the floor, knocking the second guy off him. He had to catch himself with his hands to avoid landing on his face, giving Ethan some breathing room from the punches.

Ethan quickly grabbed one arm and pushed up with his hips again, dragging the guy underneath Ethan. Ethan punched his face a couple times, trying to blink past the darkness that still wanted to take over. Because of the darkness, he didn't see the hurt man get up again, tackling Ethan into the table, which then collapsed. Ethan felt that there would be a large bruise on his back later.

Dang! They're not good fighters, but they're resilient!

Ethan's muscles seemed to fail. The vision he'd started to get back nearly sent him into unconsciousness. Yet, he still heard a gun.

He didn't feel any pain, which was strange for a moment. Then he worried that someone else had gotten hurt.

"Get away from him," a voice said.

Maeve.

Ethan started moving before he even got his vision back, trying to get to his feet though he didn't know where he was on the floor, so it took a moment to get his bearings.

Ethan heard running and felt hands on his body. "Ethan, Ethan, please tell me you're okay," Maeve said frantically.

"Mason." Ethan groaned and blinked, catching sight of a fuzzy Maeve. "Got to go check on him."

Maeve shook her head. "I'm sorry, Ethan. They already took him out the back way. Mason was passed out—they were gone before I could get the gun off that man who had been hurting you."

Ethan stumbled to his feet, mostly feeling his way to the back door. Maeve handed him his gun back and Ethan checked the bullets as his eyes finally focused a bit.

As Ethan got the back door open, he saw a car race out of the alley. Ethan got off a shot at the wheels before they turned the corner, speeding away. Ethan had barely managed to see the car, let alone get a glimpse at the license plate.

Ethan cursed as he hit the wall next to him. His legs nearly gave out on him as his head pounded at the protest. Maeve quickly caught him. "Ethan, come on. Let's sit down," she murmured.

"Got to go after him, Maeve."

"I'm sorry, Ethan. They're gone. You're barely standing. Please, let's just go back inside and wait for the police and ambulance to arrive. The police will help us find him."

Ethan heard sirens. His brain clicked on, though his body felt beat. They needed to get some people to find that car. Ethan may have been half blind, but he knew it was a black Altima.

Ethan moved back in. As he moved this time, his eyes scanned the area. Blood drops were coating the ground. Ethan wondered if it came from himself or Mason.

He moved toward the bathroom, leaning on the door frame. One of the mirrors was shattered all over the sink and floor, and blood stained the spot.

The lunch suddenly didn't sit well with Ethan. It wasn't as though Ethan was particularly squeamish, but when it involved his brother, he couldn't bear to look.

Ethan left and went back toward the front of the restaurant as cops filed in, checking the scene, then coming to Ethan and Maeve and the couple of workers that had hidden in the kitchen for the action.

"What happened here?" the cop asked, coming closer to Ethan and Maeve, and eyeing the blood that had to be running down Ethan's face.

"You've got to get after this car," Ethan groaned, barely managing to blink past the migraine pounding behind his eyes. "A black Altima. Some people came in and attacked me and my brother. They took off with my brother, Mason."

The man radioed in those details. "Did you catch sight of the license number?" he asked.

Ethan shook his head, but the movement hurt. He put a hand on his head and one catching the table next to him.

The man steadied him. "Let's get you out to an ambulance," he said.

Maeve followed quickly. "I think I caught a couple letters on the plate. There was an eight and a T. The T was the first letter, and 'eight' was somewhere in the middle."

Ethan looked at Maeve, astounded by her observation. And thankful. She had no idea how much that would help.

Paramedics rushed up to Ethan, and the officer helped guide him to the ambulance as he continued the questioning. He could barely keep up with the rush of words. He put his hand to his head, trying to stop the trickle of blood before it got to his eyes.

As he got outside, Ethan tried to catch a glimpse of the car, though logically he knew it was gone. He shivered. The Illinois air was chilly, even with a coat on.

"Maeve." Ethan tried to turn out of the grasp but was unsuccessful. Maeve came to the front instead, so he didn't have to turn.

"What, Ethan?"

"Call Mygyer. Tell him what happened." The longer they walked, the harder it was for Ethan to keep steady. It was a relief when they got to the ambulance and had him sit on the edge. "We've got to get eyes on that car. On Mason."

¤ ¤ ¤

Maeve watched Ethan as she grabbed the door behind them, and he moved over to the edge of the hotel bed. He was still shaky from the hits he'd received, but he hadn't wanted—or needed—to go to the hospital. He wanted to get right to work with finding Mason.

Maeve bit her lip. She wanted to find Mason also. She hated that Mason was taken while they were helping her. If she hadn't called them to meet her, would they have all been in danger? And was the danger from Anthony, or was it from something from Maeve's own past?

The only thing that Maeve could think was that Anthony's guys were probably following Ethan and Mason, not her, so it couldn't have been her fault, could it? She wasn't sure.

Maeve gave a little sigh. She had called Mygyer; he was on his way down with the rest of the team. They wanted to see the crime scene and what they could do to find Mason.

Ethan still wasn't a hundred percent. He had a concussion, which Maeve believed was the only thing stopping him from going after Mason. He couldn't really think straight yet.

Maeve moved over to the bed and put a hand on Ethan's arm. "You okay?"

Ethan shrugged and put a hand to his head, grimacing. "Man, my head hurts so bad."

Maeve frowned. "Let me get you some Advil or something."

"Tylenol," Ethan told her, laying down and burying his face into his pillow. "And please block the light. It kills." Ethan shuddered, then moaned. "I should be finding Mason."

"Mygyer's on his way. Just get some rest until he gets here." Maeve closed the curtains and turned off the light, then grabbed the phone and called down for some Tylenol. As she waited, she got some water ready so when it got there, she just gently nudged Ethan awake to give it to him, then gently ran her fingertips down his arm as he fell asleep again. She'd been told that the concussion wasn't severe, and she could let him sleep, as long as she woke him up every hour or so. She wanted to be careful with his head and back. He had a lot of bruises.

Maeve closed her eyes, leaning against the headboard. It had terrified her to see Ethan getting beat by the two men. At first, Maeve didn't know how she would be able to help, but she knew she couldn't just watch Ethan take the two men by himself—especially when he had obviously been more concerned about getting to his brother than he was of taking care of himself.

Then when Maeve saw the gun in the man's waistband; she knew she had a slim chance of helping Ethan. She'd snuck closer, slipped it out of the pocket, and shot the man hurting Ethan, then threatened the one already injured. She knew the one she shot had bled out, but she couldn't be sorry for doing it.

Maeve gave a deep sigh. She was so exhausted of this, of always being in danger and looking over her shoulder. She'd been doing so since she was thirteen. Wasn't it time for some peace in her life? Yet, she knew that wouldn't happen until Anthony was caught and her parents' murders were figured out. She just had to take this one day at a time until then, but it was hard; she hated how long these things seemed to take, and how dangerous they could become.

Maeve laid down next to Ethan, wanting to sleep after this long morning, but also be able to monitor how he does. Concussions were scary; part of Maeve thought he should be in the hospital to be monitored. The other part was just glad she got to be with him.

"I'm so sorry," Maeve whispered into the air, the words barely making it past her lips. She felt tears block her vision, and she wept. Having been taken by Anthony once herself was bad enough. She knew what that man was capable of, and she also knew that his grudge had grown against them.

As she lay there, trying to block images and terrible ideas from her mind, she suddenly realized that no one had told Tyra yet unless the officers called, but Maeve didn't know how they would. Maeve bit her lip and reached for her phone from the nightstand. She didn't know what she would say to Tyra—how would she explain it? Just straight out, "Your husband got kidnapped?" Was there a right way to do it?

Maeve turned on the phone and went around the corner of the room, to the bathroom, to avoid disturbing Ethan. She didn't want to leave the room. Not only did she want to monitor Ethan, but she was also scared that Anthony's goons may come back, and if they did, she wanted to be with someone as a witness, and some sort of block before they snatched her or Ethan.

When Tyra answered, the first words were of relief. "Maeve, you have no idea how worried we've been. You just up and disappeared; I thought Anthony may have caught you again."

"Tyra, are you sitting?" Maeve asked, keeping her voice quiet and one arm wrapped around her stomach. She didn't want to share the news.

Tyra hesitated. "Maeve…you're scaring me. What is it?"

"I don't…" Maeve sobbed, then put a hand over her mouth to keep anymore in. Her shoulders still shook.

Tyra's voice rose a little. "Maeve, please, just tell me. Did something happen to you? Did you catch up with Ethan? Is there something wrong with him? Just tell me what happened!" She was nearly hysterical, not even knowing the news.

Oh God, how do I tell her?

"Tyra, it's Mason…" Continuing on when she heard Tyra gasp, "We were out to eat. He went to the bathroom. They were at the restaurant…maybe some of Anthony's followers. They grabbed Mason. When Ethan tried to get to his brother, two more fought Ethan, keeping him away, then Mason was taken to a car. They got away with him. I'm so sorry, Tyra. I'm so sorry!" Maeve couldn't help the sobs. From the sounds of it, neither could Tyra.

"No…No, they can't have. Mason told me he'd be careful. He told me…" She broke of unable to form any words. They cried together on the phone for many minutes before Maeve managed to get out more of the story.

"I called Mygyer. They should be here soon. They're trying to get sight of the car used to escape. We're hoping to find him fast, but I knew you needed to know, Tyra. Jeez, I wish I could've done something more to save him."

"What's wrong, Momma?" Maeve heard a voice in the background and knew it was Owen. Maeve took the chance to get off the phone.

"Tyra, I'll call you as soon as we get any more information on Mason, I promise. Pray for him." The last bit was a flash of inspiration.

"Of course, I will." Tyra managed to gasp out. "Please be careful, Maeve. And let me know."

Maeve hung up the phone, but sat on the ground where she stood, tucking into a ball, and trying to keep her crying soft.

His brain felt like a million pounds of lead was weighing it down, crushing him. Mason blinked, groaning. The pain was so intense, it took Mason many minutes before he realized he was tied at the wrists above his head. He couldn't focus on the surroundings, but he felt hot air and the sweat covering his chest and back…of which were bare. No shirt.

*What the…*he winced, confusion whirling in his brain. *Where am I?*

Mason squeezed his eyes shut for a moment, then tried his vision again. This time, he could make out the rough wooden floor underneath his bare feet. His feet could barely touch the floor with his arms being tied the way they were.

Red seemed very bright in his eyes, and he realized that blood had made trails down his torso.

*Jeez…*Mason thought weakly. He felt so crappy.

He couldn't bring his head up; even as he heard the door open, and a gust of cold wind made goosebumps break against his skin. A weird sound started up, like a low-frequency, piercing sound. Mason had heard something similar once from a video, but that had been a frequency that killed rats or something like that. Now, with Mason's pounding head, it felt worse.

His eyes closed without him noticing, until the man approached and lifted Mason's head up. Mason thought he looked vaguely familiar, but he couldn't think of how he knew him.

The man smiled. "Hello, Mason."

Warning bells seemed to fill Mason's mind. He needed to get out of here. Where was Ethan? He wasn't exactly sure what had happened, but he was pretty sure he'd been with him. He hoped his brother was okay—preferably out searching for Mason.

"Glad you're awake. We have some business to attend to." The man held a long stick, like a walking stick in his hands. Mason shuddered again, then tried to move his hands. He could barely feel them and wasn't sure if they did so or not. The only thing he could really feel was the pounding in his head. Slowly Mason began to remember that he had been out eating with Ethan and Maeve and had gone to the bathroom when he was attacked.

Mason licked his lips, tasting blood. With this man holding his head up, he could see that it looked as though he was in a shed or a shop of some sort. It was about the size of a family room. He tried to see if there was anything that would help him identify where he was, but ultimately it was bare except a table, two chairs, and a stereo projecting the odd high-pitched sound. The door at the front was left open, letting the cold air wash over him and making it hard to stop shivering as the humid darkness seemed to invade.

"Now, tell me about your brother and his little girlfriend."

Mason eyed the man's pole, preparing. He figured that the man already knew about the two of them and doubted there was anything he could say that would help this man, but there was nothing this man could do that would make Mason tell him about his brother and Maeve.

"There's nothing to tell."

¤ ¤ ¤

Ethan felt defeated. It was as though every time he got some sort of semblance of peace, something more was thrown his way, and he wasn't sure he had anything left in him.

But there had to be. Mason's life depended on it.

A very real weight settled over Ethan's shoulders, he couldn't even draw his gaze up to look at the team surrounding the table as Maeve told her side of the story. Mygyer was watching Maeve as she spoke, but he could sense the worry from the director to Ethan's wounds.

Patty's eyes were assessing the two of them, worried, yet also careful. Cameron and Will were listening, but both on the computer, still trying to get tabs on Ethan's brother.

Cameron whistled as Maeve got to the part of how she'd pulled the gun from the man. "That was dangerous."

Maeve merely shrugged and continued the story. "And Mason was already gone by then," Maeve finished, voice lowering in sorrow. Maeve grabbed onto Ethan's hand under the table. Ethan barely felt the warmth and comfort of it, but he didn't pull away either. He felt a little better knowing she was here with him, and that she hadn't been taken as well.

Ethan closed his eyes. The light still made his eyes water because of his head.

Ethan remembered that just a couple days ago, he had been pacing away the carpet under his feet, frantic to find Maeve. Now, though the desire to find his brother was strong, all faith that they'd figure this out and find Anthony had left him. Anthony could hide away forever; they may never find him until he makes a mistake. And who knows how long that could take—Mason may not have that much time.

Two days after the attack, they were back at the station. They had told Mygyer this already, when he came down a couple hours after it had happened, but it was new to Will and Cameron. They searched for two days the best they could, then headed back up here to Chicago, where they had more utilities at their disposal. Ethan swallowed heavily, feeling the sorrow tighten his chest. They needed to find Mason.

Two days and nothing. If anything, the trail is getting cold.

Ethan hated the overwhelming defeat that crushed him. He wanted to hope he'd find Mason, but it was so dang difficult. He'd already been through this with Isabelle and Maeve. He truly didn't know how much more faith he had in him.

Come on, God, Ethan begged. All his pride and confidence had left him, leaving him a broken man.

Mygyer stood and came around to put a hand on Ethan's shoulder. "We're doing everything we can to find him."

Ethan nodded, not looking up. That's what he was worried about, yet grateful for.

Before any of them could say anything else, the door to their conference door opened after a knock announced the person. Someone Ethan didn't recognize entered.

"Sir, I have an envelope for you," the man said, rushing forward and holding it out. Mygyer took it immediately.

"Thanks, Isil." Mygyer dismissed the man and opened the envelope, then blanched. "Ethan, Maeve, get out."

Ethan jerked in surprise. "Is it about Mason?"

"Out, Ethan," Mygyer said forcefully. "You know you're too involved in this right now. I'll bring you back in in a minute."

"You can't kick me out now," Ethan said, voice rising. "I've been on this case since the beginning. I need to know where my brother is!"

"That's an order, Ethan. I'll let you back in within a couple minutes, so stay close." Ethan didn't move right away, glaring at Mygyer, then he blinked as he realized the director wasn't going to back down and that tears had crowded Ethan's gaze again.

Ethan left the room quickly with Maeve, slamming the door in his wake. After spending a couple minutes fuming in the hall, Maeve put a hand on his arm. "Ethan…You've got to have faith. Everything is in God's hands. Mason will be okay, we have to believe that."

Ethan swallowed and grabbed Maeve's hand, gripping it like it were a lifeline. He couldn't speak.

They waited another ten minutes or so before the doors opened and Patty stepped out, looking disturbed. She softly shut the door and moved to Ethan and Maeve. "Maeve, can we talk to Ethan alone?" she asked gently.

"Oh…Yeah." Maeve looked at Ethan, seeing if that's what he wanted. Ethan nodded and hesitantly let go of her hand.

"Just stay right here," Ethan begged her. She nodded.

Ethan walked with Patty back to the door. She turned to him before letting him in. "Ethan, Anthony sent hostage photos. It's not pretty, but we think you need to see it, to see if you know where he is. Looks like he's in a storage compartment or shed. Something like that."

Ethan's jaw tightened, horror making his blood cold. He didn't want to see this—maybe Mygyer was right to send him out. Ethan grabbed the handle to the door, panic making his hand slippery.

"Can you do this, or do I need to tell Mygyer no?" Patty touched his arm but withdrew quickly. Her concern and words told Ethan that he had to get this together. If it would help find Mason, he *had* to do it.

Ethan took a deep breath, then shook his head. "I can do it."

Patty nodded and opened the door, looking back at Maeve a moment.

Mygyer turned toward Ethan as the door shut, folding his arms. Will was staring at the photos, his eyes wide with horror. Cameron had turned back to his computer, but his jaw was locked, which told Ethan he had seen something he hadn't liked and refused to look again.

Ethan forced himself to relax, trying to get into his analyzing mindset and not to allow emotions through. *It's just another case,* he told himself.

Ethan took one more breath as he approached, then forced himself to look down.

The first emotion that poured through him was horror at seeing his brother as he looked at image after image of him, bruised, tied, bloody. It looked as though his lips had turned blue, his fingers looked cracked, bloody, and swollen.

Then anger nearly made him throw the pages. He put his hands flat on the table to control the urge, studying the pictures meticulously. He hated looking, but he couldn't look away.

Mygyer put his hand on Ethan's shoulder again. Ethan didn't look up, going over to the warning that had been sent with the pictures. *"Time is running out, and the Ice is creeping in. Your brother doesn't have much longer. Come and bring the girl if you want to see him again. Bring the cops, and I'll have to blow his head off."*

Ethan turned his attention back to the envelope, looking for some address. Nothing. Why would Anthony send something to Mygyer if he only wanted Ethan to come? Did he not know how else to get it to Ethan? That would be the most obvious reason.

Ethan turned his attention back to the pictures, but to the background. The walls. The ceiling disappeared into darkness with the upward shot at Mason's tied hands. In one of the pictures he saw graffiti, which turned his blood cold and his fingers trembled. He clenched his hands and stood upright quickly, taking a step back.

"Do you recognize the place?" Mygyer asked him softly.

Ethan shook his head. "No. I mean, I'm not sure. I think I've been there before, but I can't think of when or where." Ethan shrugged off Mygyer's hand and quickly left the room.

The lie felt heavy on Ethan, but he didn't care. He needed to go rescue his brother. He had to get him out of there. Maeve tried to stop him, but Ethan held up his hand to stop her. "I just need some time, Maeve. Please…" he told her, sweeping past. There was no way he was going to let Maeve get back into Anthony's grip.

Maeve stopped immediately, biting her lips in concern. Ethan felt as though he couldn't breathe, something was squeezing him.

He got to the car before he identified it as fear. He gripped the wheel as he shuddered, tears forcing their way out.

It was all his fault his brother was caught, but Ethan would get him free. Ethan started the car and was going to pull out when he realized a figure was standing behind the car. A second look made him realize it was Cameron.

Ethan gestured for him to move, but Cameron shook his head. Growling under his breath, Ethan pulled the door open and got out to face him as he rounded the car.

"You recognized the place, didn't you?" he asked, as more of a statement.

Ethan folded his arms. "I already said I didn't."

Cameron narrowed his eyes. "You're not going there alone, idiot. You'll get both you and Mason killed. Don't you want to help him?"

Ethan put his fingertips to his head. "Get out of the way, Cameron." He started to get back in the car, but Cameron grabbed his arm.

"Ethan, I'm not going to let you get yourself killed," Cameron said forcefully, his hand tight. Ethan pulled free harshly and pulled his gun from his pants, pointing it at Cameron.

"Get out of my way." Ethan's eyes were blurring. Because of that, Ethan didn't see Cameron's hand grabbing his wrist, forcing the gun away, then wrapping around so he was in an armlock. Ethan gasped at the movement.

Ethan broke free, turning and pulling the grip. Then Ethan stomped on Cameron's insole and brought Cameron's hand above his head. Cameron cursed. "What the crap, man. Ow, ow." He moved onto his toes, trying to direct the sharp pain Ethan knew he would feel in his shoulder to somewhere else.

"Ethan!" a loud voice snapped. Ethan released Cameron immediately as he saw Mygyer walk toward them. "What is going on?" he asked, eyes blazing.

Cameron grabbed his arm, rubbing it. "Ethan, I think you need to come look at something I just found," he said. "Something about the case. Trust me, you need to know this, no matter what we decide to do." His eyes stared deep into Ethan, and Ethan was thankful Cameron understood Ethan at least enough that he didn't tell Mygyer that he had been going to give himself up.

"What happened here?" Mygyer asked again, then shook his head. "I don't know if I want to know. Whatever is wrong between the two of you, figure it out, then get back inside so we can brief. Ethan, I'm sorry about your brother, but don't be doing anything stupid." He shook his head once more, then moved back inside.

Ethan waited until he was gone, then bent over with a sigh to pick up his gun. "I'm sorry, Cameron. I shouldn't have pulled a gun on you."

"No. You shouldn't have," Cameron responded shortly. Then he sighed also, letting go of his arm.

"I never would have shot you." Ethan needed to make sure his teammate knew that.

Cameron cracked a smile. "I know. We're a team. I know you'd never hurt me on purpose like that." He put a hand on the car, leaning closer the way he does when he's about to say something important. "I mean it, Ethan. We are a team. Whatever foolish plan you had, get rid of it. We'll figure something out, but we're going to do it together. That's the only way we're all going to get out of this alive."

Someone cleared his throat. They both turned to see Will standing there. In Ethan's opinion, he still looked far disturbed about what he'd seen—no surprise there. "Cameron, it finished loading. What's going on?"

"We're coming to an understanding." Cameron approached Will, putting a hand on his shoulder. "Will, how're you doing?"

Will nodded, stepping back quickly. "I'm fine, Cameron," he said stiffly. "I'll, uh…I'll be inside."

Cameron sighed, looking after him until Ethan approached. "You know what's wrong with him?" Though Will and Ethan had worked together a bit these last couple months, Ethan hadn't gotten close to him. He'd been far more worried about finding Anthony.

Cameron shrugged. "Not particularly. I think he didn't expect to see such…" He trailed off a little, glancing at Ethan, but he already knew what he was going to say. He felt his hands twitch, trying to tighten into fists again, but he didn't let them. He needed to keep his emotions distant or Mygyer wouldn't let him stay on the case. But man, it was hard.

Part of Ethan felt urged to go off alone, but he knew he had to learn what Cameron found out, and even more than that, Cameron was right. They had to work together if they all were to get out of this.

Cameron put his hand on Ethan's shoulder. "We're going to get him, Ethan."

Ethan nodded, but his throat was closing with emotion.

Maeve met Ethan inside the door, tears in her eyes. "Ethan…"

Suddenly vulnerable, Ethan was glad when Cameron patted his shoulder and left him alone with Maeve.

Ethan practically stumbled to Maeve, and she wrapped him in her arms as he started to cry.

"Mason is in God's hands, Ethan. Take comfort that God is with him, and no matter what, he'll be okay," Maeve said after a couple minutes, smoothing down his hair gently, then pulling back to wipe his tears. Ethan nodded mutely, but thought that at times, that felt like such an empty platitude, like someone didn't know what else to say so they clung to hope. And yet, Ethan needed that hope. "Now let's go find him."

They walked to the conference room. To Ethan's relief, the pictures had been cleaned. He didn't want Maeve to see them.

"I can wait out here," Maeve said, loud enough for the whole crew. Mygyer hesitated, then waved her in.

"You're a part of this too," he said regretfully. Ethan pulled a chair out for Maeve, but felt too antsy to sit himself, so he stood behind her chair, letting one hand lay on her shoulder for his comfort.

When they all settled, Mygyer turned to Cameron. "Alright, what have you got?" He sat slowly in the seat across from Ethan.

Cameron tore his eyes away from the computer. Will sat at his side, though the younger man didn't look up from the screen. "Unless we know where that shed thing is, we won't be able to get to Mason," he started, not even glancing at Ethan. Ethan interrupted, staring evenly at Cameron.

"I do know."

"Thought you said you weren't sure," Mygyer questioned.

"I lied." Ethan didn't try to explain or excuse it. Just gestured for Cameron to continue.

Cameron opened his mouth to do so, but Patricia cut him off, glaring at Ethan. "You were going to do as the note said, weren't you?!"

Maeve looked up at him, and he bristled. "Of course not! I'd never bring Maeve into that kind of situation again!"

"What kind of situation?" Maeve asked quietly.

Patty rose from the table. "Oh, so you were just going to try and trade your life for your brother?"

Ethan went cold. He removed his hand from Maeve. "If that's what it took, yes."

Maeve grabbed his hand back quickly. Patty looked at their clasped hands, and suddenly the fight went out of her. She sank in her seat, looking hurt.

Maeve looked suddenly uncomfortable. Mygyer sighed and ran a hand down his face. Will looked as though he was trying not to smile.

"I can't stand the tension anymore!" Cameron finally snapped. "Can we all just be honest for a minute?" He glared at Patricia. Patty blushed dark. "For example, I've lied, my wife is divorcing me! She hates the hours that I work and decided she doesn't want to make this work. The only thing good out of this, is that I get to keep Kammy. My poor baby has been screaming her head off, wanting her mom, and I can't get her to calm down to sleep." He folded his arms and sunk in his seat as he finished, his face burning red, and Ethan knew the other man hadn't actually wanted to spill everything, but had reached the end of his rope. He wouldn't meet their eyes, and Ethan didn't know what to say.

Will finally cleared his throat and tentatively raised a hand. Ethan was amused at the motion, which reminded them all that the kid had just come out of high school.

"I hacked into the FBI servers before you guys recruited me. I thought I was in trouble when you approached me at that technology booth, but then you guys said you were impressed with my presentation and decided to hire me as an intern. To be honest, I've always waited for the other shoe to drop, thinking you knew and just weren't saying anything."

"You what?" Mygyer swiveled his head toward the young man, while Cameron just chuckled and put a hand on Will's shoulder.

"Why doesn't that surprise me?"

Will stared at them a moment, looking a little nervous at Mygyer, but pleased by Cameron's proud tone. "My mom found out I'd been, uh… hacking stuff. I couldn't tell her that I've been working for you guys—I didn't want her to worry, and you told me to be careful who I told—but she found out the other things. She kicked me out of the house."

Astonished, Mygyer leaned forward. "Why didn't you tell your mom? Or us?"

Will shrugged. "Didn't want to worry her. I didn't know if I could tell her, anyway." He looked down.

"Go back and tell her!" Mygyer told him sharply. "She's sure to be worrying more with you out of the house and knowing you could be getting in trouble. I'll even come with you to tell her."

Will stared at him, indecision fighting in his expression before he finally nodded.

Cameron gave Will a friendly nudge and a smile. Mygyer looked at Cameron now. "Why didn't you tell us either? About your wife?"

Cameron sighed. "It's embarrassing. I don't know what I did wrong, and we were so busy trying to figure out where Anthony was." He looked at Ethan. "I owe you an apology. I knew why we were looking for Anthony. He's dangerous and all, but I was kind of angry with you because you were so focused on trying to get him, you didn't even notice my issues—not like you usually do. You barely even noticed Will had joined the team. And you haven't even asked about Liz."

Ethan felt a bit defensive for a moment, but looking at his team, he realized how much he'd hurt all of them. That made him feel guilty.

"I'm…I'm sorry," Ethan murmured, looking down. Ethan needed to find Anthony before he hurt others, but he hadn't realized how much he'd pushed aside all his friends and family.

Cameron shook his head. "It was childish of me to be mad. You've been there for me ever since I joined this team, but the one time you needed us, I was just mad at you."

"No, I haven't been a team player," Ethan admitted. "Sure, what you said may be true, but I should have been better at being a part of the team." Then Ethan noticed Patty. She'd been staring at Ethan, the hurt still evident. "And you, Patty? I've done something to make you mad also." She had been there for him this entire Chicago case, for being a liaison between the two teams, she'd done a great job at feeling like a part of the team, and has helped coordinate their efforts with the Chicago team very well.

He could feel Maeve slip her hand free of his as he spoke to Patty. When Ethan looked over at her, Patty stood and quickly left the room.

"I think you need to talk to her," Maeve told him, with a nod after Patricia. Ethan nodded and took off after her, hearing the conversation between the rest of the team start up.

"Patty." Ethan caught up to her quickly. "I'm sorry for whatever I did."

Patty stopped and shook her head. "You didn't do anything," she told him. She was crying, and as he watched, she wiped her tears angrily. "It was me. I met up with you during the time we were undercover, and I let myself fall in love with you. Then after you got back, I thought maybe we could go on a date or something, but you showed no interest in me at all. Like I said, it wasn't anything you did, it's just what you can't give me." Patty shrugged off his hand. "I'll help you find Anthony, Ethan, but please don't expect me to be happy yet…I just can't."

Shocked, Ethan didn't move as she walked back toward the conference room, wiping her eyes as she moved.

That, he didn't expect.

¤ ¤ ¤

Maeve watched Ethan and Patty come back in. Patty had been crying, but none of them commented on it. Ethan looked like someone had slapped him…the shocked expression was kind of amusing, but she was too worried to laugh about it.

Ethan came to sit back by Maeve, grabbing her hand under the table, but looking more uncomfortable than he had before.

As they all settled once again, Cameron leaned forward. "Okay, moving on. Ethan, where is Mason being held?"

Ethan snapped back to attention. "It's at this guy's house, El Dios. The one we nabbed," Ethan sighed. "Mason is probably part revenge for Dios being taken, as well as revenge for Santorini and Anthony's plans being spoiled. It's the shed in the backyard."

Cameron nodded, as if he'd already pieced part of that together. "This is where it gets weird. This guy who lived there was never known as El Dios—he hid that part of his life well, or something. However, he was a suspect on the list against your parents." He nodded to Maeve.

Ah, so that's why she was allowed in there for the moment, they wanted to see if she recognized the guy or the name.

Maeve felt herself freeze. Ethan looked at her, his eyes equally surprised and concerned. Cameron kept reading. "There was no substantial proof against him." Then he paused. "No, this isn't the same man." He turned the screen. Maeve tried compare it with the image of the man fleeing the scene and finally shook her head.

"That wasn't him."

Cameron nodded and got back to what he was saying. "It's not under the same name either. Huh. I think your Dios guy just used the house. It's really under this other guy named Victor Olit."

Cameron turned the screen again. This time Maeve couldn't tell, so she didn't say anything. "I can't find anything connecting the two of them, so either it was under the table, or Olit didn't know about the usage. However, Olit is dead now, as of five years ago. It went under his son's name. The son had some minor charges as a teenager, and mid-twenties, but seemed to clean up his life since then. He has two kids and a wife."

Cameron whistled. "A hot wife. Also, his mother works in Galesburg, actually. At that restaurant you guys ate at. Annie Maureen-Olit."

Maeve felt Ethan stiffen under her fingers, but Maeve couldn't move. She was trying to process the words. Trying to think what Annie had to do with this all.

Maeve narrowed her eyes and turned to Ethan. "She wouldn't have lied to me, or set up Mason to be taken, would she?" The pain must have been evident in her voice because Ethan scooted closer to her and wrapped an arm over her shoulders.

"I don't know. She may have," he told her honestly. "But let's not jump to any conclusions. She may not have known anything. Her family might not even be in this at all."

Maeve nodded, appreciating his words but not believing them. There were too many coincidences. Too many connections. What had happened the night her parents died? What would happen to them all now?

Maeve relaxed into Ethan's side. She was slightly embarrassed that Patricia so evidently had a crush on Ethan, but Maeve had decided long ago she wasn't going to waste any more time, and she wanted comfort.

"You know Annie?" Mygyer asked.

"She's the manager there. She used to work there before my parents died. She actually offered to keep me, but her husband didn't have the funds to do so at the time. Or something like that." Maeve narrowed her eyes. My family and hers were friends."

Mygyer nodded, looking thoughtful. He finally sighed. "Okay, we know where Mason is. Right now, he is our top priority, getting him free. Hopefully with the bonus of getting Anthony while we're at it. But we have to play it as safe as we can." He looked at Ethan and the rest of them, ran his hand through his hair. "I have a rough idea. You're not going to like it." He was looking at Ethan as he spoke.

Ethan tightened his hold on Maeve, and his expression turned cold. "No way." He picked up on it immediately.

"What?" Maeve pulled away to look into his eyes.

Ethan and Mygyer had a staring contest, and in it, a seemingly silent conversation. "It may be the only way to save your brother, Ethan."

Cameron seemed to have picked up on it as well. "It would be dangerous to try that, Mygyer. Maeve's not experienced."

Maeve gasped. They were talking about her, and she wasn't even sure what they were saying!

"What are you talking about?" Maeve asked Ethan, nudging his side.

Ethan looked down at her, pushing a hair back. "He wants us to give Anthony what he wants. Me and you."

Maeve looked at Mygyer, feeling chilled. "What?"

"Not for real, of course," Mygyer soothed. "We need someone to scope the inside, see how many people there are. You two would be the only ones who'd make it inside without immediately being killed."

Ethan shook his head. "He wants me dead, and Maeve for who knows what. He'll likely kill me as soon as we step foot in there."

"You had been ready to storm the place half an hour ago," Cameron pointed out. "By yourself. This way, you guys will have backup."

Maeve was glad they hadn't asked her opinion on it yet. She couldn't make up her mind. She would never want to be in Anthony's hands, and anything could go wrong. But she also knew she would do anything to help Ethan's family, and she did want to have a chance to help Mason.

But as powerful as the idea of saving Mason was, it was overpowered by fear. There was no way she could face that man again, not with knowing what he had wanted to do with her.

Ethan gave her a glance and shook his head even more forcefully. "It's not an option. If she were trained, it would be something different maybe, but not with Anthony, and not when we don't know what we're walking into. Just send me in. I can scope it out just as fine without Maeve there."

"But he asked for both of you. He'll know something's up if you don't both go," Mygyer ceded.

Ethan looked determined. "No, he already knew I was going to involve the cops. He wouldn't have sent this to you if he wasn't anticipating that I'd involve the whole crew. He's not an idiot. He's trying to confuse us, and because he'll expect us, who knows what he's really doing." Ethan put hands to his head. "Okay, think," he told himself quietly. They sat a couple minutes in silence as they watched Ethan.

Finally, he nodded. "Okay. This is just speculation based off what I know about Anthony, which isn't much. Anthony had always been annoyed by little trifling problems. He would want to be finished with them as soon as possible. However, if those things got in the way of him accomplishing his higher goals, he wouldn't waste time with them. Personally, I think he has something bigger in mind than worrying about me and Mason; this is just to keep us on our toes and distracted. He wants us, but he's not going to go out of his way to get us unless it helps his overall plans." Ethan tapped his hands quickly on the table. "I don't know what his overall plans are, though. That's the problem."

Mygyer cleared his throat. "We think it's to build up another family. He'd have to get strong foundational ties."

"What would give him good ties? Who would he go for?" Patricia asked.

Ethan buried his face into his hands at Patricia's questions.

"I don't know. Anyone smart wouldn't attach themselves to him, since he's already gotten himself into trouble in Kansas. Most should know that."

"Well, what about the Ricardii family?" Will asked quietly. "They've been falling apart this last year because of a couple moles. Would Anthony try to gain ties with them and rebuild?"

Ethan looked up at him, surprised. "That's a confidential case. How did you know that?"

Cameron grinned. "Let me guess, that's one of the files you hacked into?" he asked, as if a proud parent and Will gave a sheepish smile.

"Which he won't be doing again," Mygyer added, giving a stern look.

Will nodded quickly to appease Mygyer.

Ethan looked thoughtful, hand rubbing his jaw. "Actually, Anthony is obviously patient enough to rebuild. He did it in Kansas, and has been doing it with whatever was left of Bullet Oscar's since he came back while staying underground. We know where Ricardii is, we can send someone to check it out."

"I'll go!" Will volunteered immediately, looking as though he'd jump out of his seat.

Mygyer nodded. "Yes, okay, you and Patty can try to talk to him, see what he's been up to. Not that he will be likely to say anything, but just get a feel for him. But what are we going to do about Mason then? You really think he won't be guarded?"

"I don't know. Can't be sure. But I think he'll have only a few people there." Ethan looked worried. Maeve knew he wanted to ensure Mason's freedom, but also to figure out what Anthony was up to.

Maeve put a hand on his arm. "Trust your instincts, Ethan," she whispered.

Ethan finally nodded. "Yeah, Mygyer. I think that's right. I just don't know why Anthony would do it this way. Why he would take Mason only to practically set him free?"

"Maybe as a distraction. Or a warning. A lesson," Cameron suggested softly.

Looking at Ethan's drawn face, Maeve thought, *lesson learned.*

~25~

Ethan felt antsy. He was worried that they might get to Mason too late. That his gut instincts were wrong. That something big might happen.

Tyra had flown up. Ethan had tried to convince her she didn't want to be a part of this, but she refused to take "no" for an answer. She convinced Mygyer to let her stay in the cars while they scoped the place out and got Mason out of there. She was super worried, but she had full faith that God would save her husband, and therefore wanted to be there for him. Ethan didn't want to be the bearer of bad news, so he prayed that Tyra's feelings were accurate. He trusted in God, but he wasn't sure himself that this would be God's will.

Maeve sat next to Ethan, her hand squeezing Ethan's. Tyra on the other side of Maeve, held onto Maeve's other hand. She seemed calm, so sure in her God, yet concerned. They may save Mason, but in what condition would they find him in?

They pulled a couple blocks away from El Dios' home and Mygyer, Cameron, Liz—Ethan hadn't seen Liz since she and Cameron had saved his life. She'd been on leave, back with just hours to spare before their bust. A few other Chicago agents and officers had joined them for planning, and they were finally, hopefully, going to get his brother back.

Ethan opened the door, but with feeling Maeve's hand over his, he couldn't resist pulling her for a kiss quickly. He was scared he may never be able to do so again.

Ethan broke it far sooner than he wanted, but her kiss lingered on his lips as he walked out. They didn't speak—they didn't need to; they had already made the plans before they left. Ethan kept the earpiece in his ear as he walked, alone, toward the shed. He kept his gun at the ready and moved quietly so he didn't alert anyone. The darkness helped hide him, as did the humidity. The humidity made the night seem that much colder, seeping into his skin. He shivered, but Ethan wasn't sure it was because of the chill.

The door to the shed was open. If Mason was as shown in the pictures, Ethan suddenly knew where Mason's blue lips had come from. The chill was deep, and Ethan had layers on.

Ethan took a breath, preparing himself mentally, then stepped into the threshold, lifting his gun.

What he saw surprised him.

Only one man and Mason. The man jumped back from Mason as Ethan entered, a glass falling to the floor and shattering. Ethan covered him, preparing to shoot, but the man—kid? He looked like a teenager—didn't reach for a weapon, just kept his hands raised in surrender. "Please don't hurt me."

"Get on the ground," Ethan snapped, then held the button on his earpiece. "Only one teenager inside. Check surroundings, make sure there's no ambush." Ethan scanned the inside, checking for any traps or bombs. Nothing drew his attention, except his brother.

And this loud piercing sound. Ethan narrowed his eyes, wondering what could be causing it, and his eyes drew to a stereo.

"Draw away from him," Ethan told the teen, heading toward Mason as the teen scrambled away. "And turn off that sound."

"Are you Ethan?" the boy asked, turning off the sound and cowering on the ground.

"Yes." Ethan kept an eye on the boy but was more concerned about Mason. Ethan didn't see any breath from him. He looked worse than the pictures had shown. Blood and bruises covered him. Ethan knew he would need help getting him down.

"I need help in here," Ethan said into his earpiece. It only took a couple moments for footsteps to sound and Cameron, Mygyer, and one other man, whom Ethan knew was a decent medic, entered.

"Safe out there?" Ethan asked, trying to wake his brother. No response. Heartbeat? Maybe. Ethan couldn't quite tell.

"As far as we can tell." Mygyer moved to Mason, studying him and walking around. He swore. "Okay, Ethan, I'm going to get a knife and cut him down."

The medic shook his head. "Be careful with him. He has hypothermia. You two hold onto him as Mygyer cuts him down." He gestured to Cameron and Ethan. "Try not to let him move quickly. Keep him upright, and keep his hands above his head, then slowly lower them to his side. If you aggravate him too fast, you can upset his heart. Just keep it slow." The medic shifted out of his coat as the three of them did as he asked. Ethan adjusted to hold his brother as Mygyer released him. It was hard, in that position, to hold his arms and body up at the same time, but between him and Cameron, they managed.

As soon as they had Mason's arms down (slowly, as the medic cautioned them many times throughout), the medic threw his coat over Mason. He had apparently called for a gurney, because a second later, one came in the doorway and him and the new paramedic instructed them how to get Mason without aggravating him.

Then they were off with the gurney, leaving Ethan flustered. That was far too easy.

Ethan followed behind, eyes scanning wildly, leaving Mygyer and Cameron to get the kid.

Ethan knew Tyra would want to see her husband right away. He hoped Maeve and Tyra both kept their promise to stay in the car until it was safe. They'd see Mason at the hospital.

Ethan hopped into the back of the ambulance right as they closed the doors.

The paramedics were in a state of chaos inside the ambulance. To Ethan, it seemed as though everyone was talking at once, though that may have been the blood rushing in his ears and the fear as he looked at Mason. Ethan couldn't tell how bad he was.

Burying his head into his hands, Ethan sat on the bench on the side, far away so he wasn't in the way of their work.

We got him back...Please, God, help him get better. Let him live.

¤ ¤ ¤

Maeve craned her neck in the car along with Tyra, trying to catch a glimpse as the paramedics rushed back out of the shed and into the ambulance. As they lifted Mason in, Maeve caught a quick look, but just enough to see the blood. Ethan climbed on in after, covered in a little blood as well. His face was in his worried frown.

"Did you see anything?" Tyra asked, slumping down as the ambulance drove off. Maeve sat back next to her, eyeing the lock on the door. Maeve hated being locked in there, but she also couldn't have stayed behind at the station, and this was the compromise. She took a breath, then shook her head.

"Not much, just a quick glimpse." Maeve looked at the lady. "But he came out on a gurney, not a black bag."

Tyra nodded once. "I know he's not going to die." Her voice was calm and sure, though her hands were shaking. Maeve grabbed her hand.

"How do you know? How are you so sure?" Maeve looked into her eyes.

Tyra smiled at her. "Because I prayed to God, and I got the overwhelming feeling that Mason would live." Her eyes went distant. "I know he's hurt. I don't know to what extent, or how hard it will be to get him back to full health, but I know he'll be alright."

Maeve stared at her for a couple moments. Her faith was incredible.

Tyra looked out the front window, leaning forward. Maeve followed her gaze to see Mygyer come out, a scared-looking teenager with him. He and Cameron were talking to him.

Tyra pulled the door open, surprising Maeve. She thought the doors had been locked.

Tyra caught her look and smiled. "I cracked the door." Before the driver, with the window in between them, could see, they both slipped out.

"Hey!" The driver shouted as they shut the door. He scrambled to get out.

Tyra didn't even look back, her stride purposeful as she moved toward Mygyer.

Only the teenager noticed her before she was a few feet off, bringing Mygyer's attention around. Mygyer's eyes widened, and he moved to intercept her. "I thought I told you to stay in the car."

Tyra stepped around him. "You told me until it was safe. Obviously it is if you've stopped to talk, so I'd like to be in on the conversation." She stopped a few feet away from the boy, folding her arms. "What was done to my husband?" She used the same tone she did on her kids when they did something naughty. It seemed to work with this teen as well, he ducked his head.

"I was just told to watch him," he muttered. "He said someone named Ethan would be coming for him, and that I just had to be there. I don't know why. I'm sorry. I tried to clean him off a little before Ethan arrived." His shoulders shook, and he looked up at them. "I didn't do anything to your husband, I promise."

Tyra softened a little, but her voice was still firm. "I didn't ask what you did. I want to know what happened to him. What did they do?"

"Tyra." Cameron put a hand on her shoulder, but Tyra shrugged it off.

The boy nodded, straightening a little. Maeve felt a bit of pity for him. Why had he joined up with Anthony?

"I don't know everything, but I know Anthony beat him. He kept asking about Ethan and this Maeve person, wanting to know more about them. I thought it was strange, since Anthony already seemed to know so much about the two of them. After a while he just stopped asking, probably because the man wouldn't say anything in response." The boy shuddered. "They kept this high-pitched sound on the whole time too, I don't know what it was, but I was told I couldn't shut it off. About drove me crazy. And then the chill. He had the doors open, and the man was kept uncovered. The medic said he had hypothermia."

Tyra nodded, her face white. "Thank you." She put her hand on his arm.

The boy nodded, his face showing some terror now. "The man had woken up a couple times. Kept asking me to turn the sound off before he passed out again. But that was the one thing Anthony had been adamant about. I couldn't turn it off. I'm sorry. I didn't want to cause your husband any pain."

Tyra hugged the teen. "How did you get mixed up with this?" Tyra asked.

The boy looked at the officers around him. "I didn't mean to. Anthony just came up to me after I fought with my parents. He offered me a place to live. Then he used me to get to some of my friends and other people, and he wouldn't let me leave." With tears in his eyes, he looked to Mygyer. "I just want to go home, but I'm scared. Anthony might kill me. Or my family."

"Mygyer," a voice behind them sounded. They all turned to see a man running up to them. "Will got shot."

Panic flared into Mygyer's eyes. "How'd that happen? Where are they?"

"Patty and Will were checking up on Ricardii, they—"

The teenager's gasp quickly cut off the rest of the man's explanation.

"You know about Ricardii?" Mygyer asked him quickly.

"Not a lot." The teen tried to take a step back. "I only know that a big deal was supposed to be going on today with them. That's all, I promise."

Mygyer nodded and turned back to the new man. "Okay, Lance, what else?"

"It was Ricardii, Anthony, and a couple of other people. It sounds like as they pulled up, everyone was leaving the house, and they immediately ended up in a firefight. Only Patty had a gun, so they had to pull out, but not before Will was hit. She got far enough away, then called for an ambulance."

"Is he okay?"

"There was a lot of blood, but she thinks he'll be fine."

Mygyer ran a hand down his face, swearing softly. "Alright. Cameron, hand this kid off to someone else to take to the station. We'll stop by Will's home and tell his mom everything that has been going on and get her to the hospital."

Cameron nodded, his face just as pale as Mygyer's, and walked the kid away. Maeve watched them, feeling her eyebrows furrowed in concern. She was worried about Mason, and she had liked Will the moment she met him—the kid was sweet.

Mygyer turned toward Tyra. "I know you're in a hurry to get to the hospital, but it's going to take them a bit to get Mason stable. Are you okay if we take a small detour before we get there?"

Tyra barely hesitated before she nodded. Maeve knew she wanted to be there for her husband, but Mygyer was probably right.

They got back to the car, then drove to Will's house. Maeve got out when they got there with Mygyer. He glanced at her and gave a small smile in gratitude as they walked toward the door.

Mygyer hesitated a minute, taking a breath, then he knocked on the door.

Maeve cocked an eyebrow when she heard someone yelling in Spanish. The voice got closer, until a lady opened the door. Her hair was up in a messy bun, back in a headband. She had a broom in her hand, and she took them in with one glance. "Yes?"

"Are you Mrs. Lopez?" Mygyer asked.

"Yes." Her tone was short. She put the broom to the side and drew them outside as more little feet sounded. "What is it?"

"Is Will your son?"

Various emotions flashed across her face. Fear, anger, worry. "Yes. Did he do something wrong?"

"No." Mygyer shook his head and grabbed out his badge. "On the contrary. He's been a great help to my team. Mrs. Lopez, your son has been working with the FBI for a couple of months now. He didn't want to worry you, so he didn't tell you."

Mrs. Lopez' hand flew to her face as she gasped. "I thought he'd been getting into trouble," she muttered. "I didn't want my younger kids to be influenced. You mean he hasn't been hacking into things?"

Mygyer chuckled. "Actually, he did that too, apparently. Your son is really good at what he does, but he's been doing it for us." His mood quickly sobered.

"Mrs. Lopez, we have some bad news," Maeve said softly, wanting to soften the blow and share the load with Mygyer.

Her look turned to concern. Mygyer lowered his head. "Will was shot on a last mission."

Mrs. Lopez scrambled for a grip on the door handle. "You sent him on this…Mission?" Her voice was angry.

"He volunteered, but yes." Mygyer shook his head. "He's not trained in field work. Typically, I wouldn't even let him out there, but we hadn't thought there'd be any danger. We were just supposed to talk, and he wanted to observe. But they got into a firefight right as they arrived."

"Where is he?"

"They're taking him to the hospital. We're heading over there now, if you want to drive with us."

Mrs. Lopez hesitated a moment, then nodded and opened her door, yelling in Spanish a moment. Maeve heard a reply from inside, then Lopez shut the door and started down the stairs with Maeve and Mygyer.

Mrs. Lopez asked question after question about what they did and how Will was doing as they drove. Luckily it didn't take too long to get to the hospital because Maeve was starting to feel awkward beside Lopez.

Tyra got out of the car and walked inside as soon as the car stopped. Lopez was right behind her. Maeve had to jog to catch up to Tyra.

Ethan was waiting on the seats inside, his head in hands. As they approached, he looked up, then stood.

"Is he okay? Have you heard anything on Mason?" Tyra asked immediately. Ethan pulled her into a hug.

"I haven't heard yet, Tyra. They took him back, but they haven't been out to tell me anything."

"And my son?" Lopez came up behind them.

"Your son?" Ethan looked at Mygyer in question, confused.

"Will was shot. Have they brought him through yet?" Mygyer answered.

Ethan's eyes darkened. "Will? How? I thought they were just there to talk."

"Yeah, that's what we thought." Mygyer's voice was hard.

"Is he okay?" Ethan asked.

"That's what I want to know," Lopez said, voice rising. "I want to know how my son is."

Ethan put a hand in front of him in a calming way. "Mrs. Lopez, I haven't seen your son yet." He stopped as quickly as he started as the front door opened and paramedics came rushing in, a doctor next to them, all pushing a gurney. Lopez ran toward the gurney, sobbing. Even without moving, Maeve caught sight of the blood covering Will, and the oxygen mask on his face.

"Please move away, ma'am." A couple nurses rushed forward to pull her away, back to the waiting room.

Maeve caught a glimpse of Patricia walking toward them, her pace slow. She had blood on her hands.

Mygyer pulled her into a hug. "Are you alright?" he asked her.

Patricia nodded but dug her hands into his jacket and sobbed. "It's all my fault. I should've checked before we got out of the car, they were leaving the house and ran back in. They ran out the back before I even got Will out of there."

Ethan reached out and grabbed Maeve's hand. His was shaking. She squeezed it and stepped closer, wanting to give peace to him if she could.

Maeve pulled Ethan and Tyra both to a couple seats a little bit away from the others.

Tyra was shaking even more than Ethan. Ethan noticed at the same time Maeve did and grabbed his sister-in-law's hands in his right one. "He'll be fine, Tyra. Isn't that what you've been telling me?"

Tyra nodded, but sniffled. "Yeah, I know he will be, but..." She bowed her head. "That kid with Mason...He told me what happened to him. I'm just worried about how he'll be. It was all terrible, and I don't even know the details. And that kid seemed so scared of Anthony. Jeez, Ethan, you guys are all in lot of trouble with this Anthony, aren't you? He's already tried to get you, got Maeve and Isabelle, and now Mason. Is he ever going to leave us alone?"

Ethan pulled her into a half hug. "I...I don't think so. Not until he's in jail or dead. Especially since I'm not going to leave him be like he wants me to." He sighed, sinking further into his chair. "I'm so sorry, Tyra. I shouldn't have let Mason come down here. It's all my fault he got caught."

Tyra pulled away sharply, turning to glare at Ethan. "Take it back," she snapped. "You know how much your family and I love you?" She laid a hand on his arm. "Mason would never regret coming here, and I don't either. His love for his family is one of the biggest reasons I fell in love with him. He always knows what to do to help another. I'm upset he got hurt, but he would be miserable if you refused him to see you. He's always loved you. Nothing will stop him. But you've got to stop acting like it's your fault every time someone gets hurt. It's not your fault. It's Anthony's fault." She hugged him full on. "We love you, Ethan. Get that into your stubborn skull."

Maeve smiled at her, feeling glad that Tyra had the courage to say what Maeve hadn't—at least not yet.

They then sat in silence together for about another hour.

Maeve caught sight of the doctor coming toward them first and stood to meet her as she came toward Ethan.

"Ethan, we got your brother settled in," she said. Maeve wondered how she knew him, but then realized he had probably introduced himself before they got there, or maybe from when Ethan had been in the hospital before.

Ethan and Tyra stood. "Thanks, Dr. Nance," he told her. She nodded and started to lead the way.

Dr. Nance talked as they walked. "Mason has a deep wound on his head. We believe that's one of the earlier injuries, but it kept getting aggravated through his…treatment these last few days. He had a broken rib that had nearly poked through his lung. It's a miracle it hadn't, since that would've almost surely caused his lungs to bleed, and he would've died. A couple other ribs were cracked, but overall safe except some deep bruises. I want to keep a close eye on him because there might be some internal bleeding or something that we haven't detected yet." She looked all of them over quickly, stopping outside a door.

"Along with the bruises are his fingers. I don't know exactly what happened to his hand, but the X-rays look as though his knuckles had been crushed under something heavy. His bones were fractured in a couple places, and the swelling is bad. We want to look into some options, like screws or rods to help stabilize everything. My hope is that they'll be able to heal on their own, with only a splint, but I'm not sure how lucky we'll be. My best bet would be plates and pins." She noticed how pale Tyra was turning and put a sympathetic hand on her shoulder. "Do you want me to stop?"

"No." Tyra waved dismissively. "No, of course not. I need to hear this."

Dr. Nance nodded, giving Tyra a look, kind of like she was proud. "I know it's hard, but it'll be best to know beforehand. With his fingers, we don't want to make any decisions until he's awake to give us details, like how well he can move his fingers, and how much it hurts.

"Anyway, the next injury that's giving us most concern is his feet. They're bruised, and his left one has some open lacerations. They're not bad enough to warrant surgery or stitches. We are still working on warming him up. But the main point of concern with all these things is the chance of infection, of course. So we gave him some antibiotics, and I'm hoping he'll react positively and won't have the infection everyone is worried about."

Dr. Nance finally stepped back. "Good luck, you guys. I believe he'll be okay. Be strong for him, though."

Tyra nodded and pushed her way in, as if she couldn't stand another minute away from her husband. Ethan thanked the doctor again, then grabbed Maeve's hand and followed his sister-in-law inside.

~26~

Ethan felt exhausted. The night had been long between worrying over his brother and trying to gather information about where Anthony went after the shootout at the Ricardii place. Ethan found himself back in the hospital next to his brother after a long night of near to no sleep. He'd asked Patricia, Mygyer, or Mrs. Lopez to come get him when Will woke up. He wanted to show support to his team, but he also needed to be there for Mason.

Tyra had fallen asleep in the chair next to her husband, her hand lightly grasping his good hand. She had asked the nurses if they'd be bothered with her sleeping in there overnight, and to not worry about waking her up or anything. She'd told Ethan that nurses had received a lot of ill feelings from guests who stay overnight with patients. They would complain about the lack of commodities, or often get in the way of the nurses' work. The nurses hadn't cared, however, and seemed glad about her sympathy in their plight. They assured her that most of the time, guests were fine.

Ethan yawned, then looked over his brother. The sheet covered him, hiding most of his bruises. Warming him up had been a long ordeal last night, but he seemed stable now.

Putting his hand gently on Mason's forehead, he checked for fever. Maybe a little hot, but he didn't think there was a fever. Hopefully not. Ethan would hate to see infection set in. Mason groaned and his eyes opened at the touch. Ethan leaned forward in the seat, resisting grabbing onto Mason's mangled fingers.

Mason met his gaze, eyes distant. "Ethan…please turn off the sound. Please…" he closed his eyes tight. Ethan listened for a moment, trying to hear any sound his brother was hearing.

"Mason, there's no sound, bro." Ethan brushed Mason's hair back. "How're you doing?"

Mason weakly licked his lip. "I still hear the sound." His voice seemed sore and pained. Ethan had to do something.

"Do you want me to turn on some other music or something?" Ethan asked him. Mason nodded, looking at him again.

"What happened?" he asked. "I just remember Anthony asking me about you…and I think there was a kid trying to give me water."

Ethan nodded. "Yeah, he hadn't liked seeing you hurting."

"I don't think he turned off the sound either," Mason winced. "Jeez…hurts…"

"Where is the worst?" Ethan brushed back Masons hair, keeping his voice quiet to let Tyra sleep.

"My head, feet, and fingers. And my back, and…I don't know, just everywhere." His voice shook. He looked around, then was surprised when he caught sight of Tyra. "How long was I out? When did she get here?"

"We got you out yesterday evening. It's about ten in the morning now." Ethan rubbed his brother's arm gently. "Are you warm enough?"

"Yeah, I'm okay." Mason bit his lip as Ethan started some music softly. "I missed you guys."

Tyra shifted awake, out of the ball she lay in, then saw Mason was awake and scrambled forward. She shifted her grasp, pushing back his hair. "Hey honey," she murmured, tears clogging her voice.

"Tyra…where're the…" he grimaced, squeezing his eyes shut. Tyra seemed to know exactly what he was going to ask.

"The kids are with your mom. They're fine." Tyra kissed his forehead. "Don't worry about them; how're you doing?"

"I missed you." Mason tried to sit up. "My throat hurts. I really need some water. They barely gave me any."

"Let me get the nurse." Ethan started, but right then the door opened, and Dr. Nance stepped in. "Great timing. Can Mason drink some water?"

Nance smiled at Mason. "Of course. I'm glad you're awake. We have a couple things to test if you're feeling up to it."

Mason hesitated. "What things?"

"We need to see how your fingers are doing to determine if it needs some pins, or just a splint." Her eyes were sympathetic. Mason looked at his hand, eyes downcast. They were already wrapped, probably because they had been split open from whatever had happened.

"It just hurts," Mason said.

Nance nodded. "It's bound to. We could give you some more medication to help the pain, but we need you awake and aware so we can test your fingers. I'm sorry you hurt. Let's get you up for a drink." She pushed a button on the bed, lifting Mason up slowly. "Grab his pillow, make sure it doesn't slip down," Dr. Nance told Ethan. Ethan did so, looking at Tyra.

"Just do a little bit at first," she told Mason, handing the water to his wife. Tyra took it gratefully and helped her husband get a little sip, then more when he asked for it. Dr. Nance stopped Mason halfway through, smiling. "Let's see how you do with that," she told him. Then she pulled the clipboard off the end of the bed.

"Okay, are you ready?" Nance asked him.

"I…I suppose so." Mason took courage from Tyra, looking long at her. Tyra gave him a loving smile, tinged with worry and sadness.

Dr. Nance nodded and slid the breakfast tray stand closer, then put Mason's hand gently on it. Even with her care, Ethan could see the pain in his expression.

Both Mason's wrists and three of his fingers on his right hand were wrapped. Ethan knew the wrist was from the ropes digging into his skin. Ethan tried not to wince at his brother's abuse.

Nance slowly unwrapped Mason's fingers. Mason closed his eyes, muscles in his jaw clenching. Tyra stood, wrapping her arms around Mason as carefully as she could, and Mason laid his head on her pregnant stomach, sighing softly. Ethan forgot sometimes that she was pregnant, since she wasn't terribly big around and she didn't let anything stop her.

"Okay, Mason. I know this is going to hurt. I need you to push past the pain and do the best you can, okay?" Nance sat on the side of the bed. "I don't care what the best is, but I need to see it."

Mason nodded, opening his eyes, but not moving away from his wife. Ethan tried to relax in the chair, but it was hard.

"Mason, do you want to be alone, or do you want your family with you?" Nance asked, giving Ethan and Tyra a look as if to tell them not to say anything.

Mason shook his head. "No, I want them in here," Mason told her, putting his hand on Tyra's stomach. He looked up at her. "Baby is kicking a lot."

Tyra smiled at him. "Yeah, she is." She kissed his head.

Mason smiled, amused. "Still so sure it's a girl?"

Tyra nodded. "Told you, its mother's intuition."

"Are you sure you didn't go have it checked?" Mason kissed her tummy.

"I wouldn't have gone without you, dear." Tyra looked at the two of them. Ethan felt awkward, feeling as though this was a moment between the two of them. But it was over just that fast, as Mason turned back to the doctor, his good hand still enfolded in Tyra's fingers over her stomach.

"Okay, I'm ready," Mason told Nance, somehow looking better than he had a minute ago.

Dr. Nancy nodded, eyes shining at Tyra. Ethan knew one of Tyra's best traits had been the ability to calm his brother. "Okay. If it becomes overwhelming, please don't push past that. Do you understand the difference between pain, and overwhelming pain?"

"I…I think so."

"Great. I need you to try and keep still. I'm going to just touch you on various points on your fingers and I need you to tell me if you feel me at all, or if the pain gets worse, or any change."

She started before he could reply, lightly touching his fingers until she drew reactions. She touched the tip of his fingers first. That drew mild reactions, discomfort, and a little pain when she pushed harder.

Then she went to the middle of his fingers, which drew a way stronger reaction. He had to blink back tears a couple of times, and winced, telling Nance that the pain was severe.

When she did the rest of his hand, he had mild pain that she seemed relieved by.

"Okay, Mason. This one will hurt a lot." Nance wrote some things down on the clipboard before putting it to the side. Mason took a weird breath, as if he couldn't believe that he'd have to do something worse than he already had, and Dr. Nance caught onto it. "I know it's hard. We're nearly done."

Mason bit his lip, but he didn't protest, just let his good hand, still clenched to Tyra's, rest back on the bed.

"Mason, I need you to extend your fingers as much as you can."

Mason stared at her as if she'd grown wings, eyes dismayed or shocked.

"Maybe it's too soon for that," Tyra suggested softly.

Nance shook her head, mouth curling into a concerned frown. "I'm sorry, I wouldn't force you to do this if I could help it. The longer we wait, the worse off your fingers will be and the less chance you'll have to get full range of motion in them. If you don't want to use your hand again, then we don't have to worry about this."

Mason looked like he was going to cry. He chewed on his lip, jaw tight, throat swallowing. He looked at Tyra, shaking his head and mouthing something.

Tyra leaned in front of him, putting her forehead on Mason's. "You've got this, Mason. I know you can do it. It'll be pain for but a moment."

Mason trembled but nodded against her.

Nance smiled. "I can give you more medicine after, Mason. As soon as it is over, I will. We'll need to get you into surgery anyway to get them holding as soon as possible."

Ethan put a hand on Mason's shoulder, trying to support him.

After another long few seconds, Mason's injured hand started trembling violently, and his fingers straightened slowly. He couldn't get them all the way straight; as soon as he reached his endpoint, he gasped. "That's as far as I can go." He quickly let his hand relax again. Ethan couldn't see Mason's face, since he stayed turned toward Tyra, but if the shudder in his shoulder was any indicator, he was either crying, or the pain had been far too intense.

"Thank you, Mason. Now one more thing and we're done." Nance wrote once more on the clipboard. "Just curl your fingers into a fist."

Mason did so, but he could barely move before he shook his head and looked to his doctor. "That's all I can do."

"You did wonderful, Mason. Thank you." She wrote some more, then stood and patted Mason's leg. "I'll go get you some more medication. You just rest."

"Can I have some more water?" Mason pleaded.

Nance hesitated, but only for a moment. Her face softened. "Of course you can. You two help him get the last bit down."

"Can I also get some clothes? After…after being *there*, I want my clothes again." Mason trembled.

"I'll see what I can do. I'll be back in a few minutes."

Tyra grabbed the cup and helped Mason drink. Before they could get him settled after he finished the water, Mason got his arm over Tyra's shoulder, and he pulled her close. Knowing immediately that this needed to be a private moment, Ethan stood.

"I'll give you a moment alone," he muttered. Tyra gave him a grateful look as she pulled her husband close, still mindful of the bruises.

"I'm here now," Tyra comforted quietly.

"I thought I wasn't going to see you again. Or our kids." Mason sobbed out before Ethan could get out of the room. The words almost made Ethan want to stop, but he didn't. "It was so cold; I don't know if I can ever be warm again."

Ethan felt a wave of guilt wash over him. He knew the others had asked him to stop blaming himself, but the words reminded Ethan of his mistakes.

Ethan stepped partway down the hall and leaned against the wall, putting a hand to his eyes.

"Ethan?" Maeve's small voice cut through the quiet. Ethan looked up, surprised because he hadn't heard her approach. She took the softest steps.

"Yeah?" Ethan looked at her as she closed the last few feet, then pulled her close and rested his forehead on hers, brushing back her hair in the same move.

"Have you seen Mason yet?" she asked him.

"Yeah. Just came from there. He woke up. I left him alone with Tyra for a bit." Maeve leaned on him, giving him the peace he craved.

Maeve nodded. "Mygyer found me. Told me to tell you that Will woke up as well."

Ethan lingered while holding Maeve, even with the words. "Okay, I can go see him. Do you want to come?"

Maeve looked him in the eyes, then shook his head. "I think you need to do this yourself," she told him gently, then kissed his cheek. Ethan smiled, knowing she was right and loving her more for it. He pulled her into a tighter hug, resting his head on hers.

"Thanks Maeve. You're a blessing to the whole family."

Maeve snorted, pulling away. "No, your whole family is a blessing to me."

Ethan put his hands on Maeve's belly. "How's the baby doing?"

"Good." Maeve nudged him away. "Go see Will. I'll wait here."

Ethan smiled at her and walked to where he knew Will would be.

When he entered, he saw Mrs. Lopez sitting by her son. She looked up at him as he entered, then back at Will. Will had opened his eyes at the entrance of Ethan, and he looked over.

Mrs. Lopez put a hand on his son. "Baby, I'll be back after I take a refresher," she told him, kissing his head. Will nodded.

Ethan took her vacated spot, smiling in gratitude. "I didn't mean to kick you out."

Mrs. Lopez waved dismissively. "I'm tired of arguing with him. Maybe you can tell him how he should've told me about this job he took up." Despite her sharp words, her eyes were concerned. "But seriously, I need some air."

Ethan nodded and leaned close to Will as she left. "How you doing, kid?"

Will cracked a smile. He looked more exhausted than anything else. Probably have him on a pretty good dosage of pain medication. "You're not too much older than me," he said. "Only like five years."

Ethan grinned, not debating, though he was a year off. "Touché. How're you doing, Will?"

"I'm okay, I guess." Will closed his eyes. "I'm tired. My mom is worried about me. Seems everyone is. I didn't really feel the hit when it happened, and now I think they have me on a million pain relievers."

Ethan gave a small smile. "Trust me, it'll hurt again soon enough."

Will looked at him. "That's right. You were shot a couple months ago. Does it feel back to normal yet?"

"No. Don't think it'll ever be quite the same." Ethan sighed. "Heard you lost a lot of blood."

"I guess so. Think that's why I'm tired." Will shrugged one shoulder.

"Will…" Ethan hesitated. "I was wanting to ask you. Do you like this? Being on this team? This danger? Seeing some of the things we do? I know you hadn't liked to see the pictures of my brother, and these sights aren't pleasant or anything."

Will didn't answer right away, then he took a long breath. "I mean, I never do like to see people hurt, seeing Mason…that was hard. And I don't like seeing the other things either and sometimes I'm worried one of you guys will get hurt." He snorted. "Never thought it would be me." He looked vulnerable.

Ethan put a hand over his. "What is it?"

Will couldn't meet his eyes. "I thought it *should* be me. You guys are always so kind, and you're doing so much good, then I hear about what the people in mafia families have done to you. It should be me hurt, not you guys."

Ethan's eyebrows furrowed. He tightened his grip. "Why would you think that?"

Will shuddered. "My father was—is—a big time mafia boss. The Oracle." He couldn't look at Ethan as he pulled his hand away. Ethan couldn't hide the shock, but luckily Will didn't seem to notice. The Oracle was a boss in the Endoro family. He still had not been picked up, and only his most trusted advisors and street bosses had ever seen him; he hid himself well.

"Will." Ethan forced himself to relax, to hide his shock. "Do you want to explain what you mean? To talk to me about this?"

Surprised, Will looked back up. "Aren't you angry?"

Ethan tilted his head. "Should I be?" Then he smiled. "I can't blame you for who your father is." He grabbed Will's hand again. "I know I've never taken a lot of time to know you, Will, but if you want to talk, I'd love to know."

Will looked at him, then finally nodded and cleared his throat. "My ma…she didn't know my dad was part of the mafia. He was charming. Turns out he was just a psychopath. He was very good at manipulating or acting how he knew he *should* be. He fooled her for years. My youngest sibling, Christina, was two before she found out.

"When she finally found out, she left my dad. Just vanished with us kids. I was twelve. Because my mom needed my help, she told me about my dad, but never told my siblings. They probably wouldn't remember much of my dad now, to be honest." Will hesitated a moment. "My mom has always been scared that one of us may become like my dad. That's why she kicked me out when she thought I was getting into trouble." Will ran his hand over his eyes. "The last couple years, I wanted to know what happened with my dad. I didn't want to see him or anything…Well, not mostly, anyway. I knew he'd done some bad things. But I also had some good memories of him too. I thought maybe he'd be able to change. So, I learned anything I could about him. I hacked into the Ricardii case. But what I saw there…I don't know, I just can't see my father ever changing."

Ethan stayed silent a couple moments, thinking that over. "And why did you decide to be on this team? Why did you stick with it? Why are you helping us out?"

Sighing, Will picked at the blanket, meeting Ethan's eyes now. "I don't agree with the chaos my father is causing. I saw what he did, and what others have done to you guys. If I can, I'd like to help." His voice cracked. "But I'm just so torn."

"Why?"

"Because I want to do right, but I don't think I could ever point out my father. I don't think I could turn him in." Will sagged, looking crestfallen. "How could I be on a team when I might not be able to do the right thing at any one time?"

Ethan stared at Will. He couldn't answer right away, feeling as though he knew exactly where Will came from. "Will." He waited until the teenager looked up. "Everyone on this team knows what you feel. If my family was in the line of danger, I doubt I'd be able to choose between them and the greater good. Jeez, even with Mason taken, I knew what Anthony may have been up to, but all I could think was how I would save my brother. And if you or anyone else on my team was in trouble, I wouldn't hesitate to try and help. We're human, Will. We have our weaknesses and our attachments. And that's not a bad thing. The most we can do is always try to do our best." He patted Will's hand, noticing the weary lines on his face. "You're getting tired, bro. Maybe I should let you be."

Will smiled at him, tears filling his eyes. "Thank you, Ethan."

"No problem. Just remember it when you decide if you want to stick with us or not." Ethan started to stand, but Will grabbed his hand.

"I really don't mind being called 'kid,'" he murmured. "Somehow, it makes me feel a part of the team. Is that weird?"

Ethan grinned. Nicknames always seemed to help the connection between certain members of the team. "Sure, Kid, but only a little. Rest up. You have a lot of healing to do. And I still want to know what happened at Ricardii's when you're feeling up to it."

¤ ¤ ¤

Maeve was allowed to go with Ethan, much to her appreciation, to question Annie. She was worried, of course, wondering what Annie knew about everything that had happened, and if she had hidden anything from Maeve. She couldn't imagine Annie hiding something important, but Maeve couldn't ignore all the coincidences.

Ethan slid his hand in hers, and she looked up to see his gaze still forward. It appeared he had just instinctively given her his hand as he thought. That made Maeve smile.

Ethan caught her look and smiled also, his shy dimples showing.

"It'll be okay," Ethan promised, kissing her forehead. Maeve bit her lip, fighting not to show her giddiness at seeing Ethan's smile. He made her feel all faint.

The thought of what she had to face, stopped the smile as it came, she sighed. "I'm just so worried that she's lied to me all this time. And we need to figure this out, Ethan. Before Anthony does anything else to hurt us." Or anyone else in this mafia business tried to hurt them, for that matter. She'd hated seeing Ethan healing, and though he seemed to be feeling better, physically, she could still see that he got exhausted or pained more easily than he should. Then Isabelle and Maeve having been taken, and now Mason…Man, Maeve was just tired of feeling hunted.

Ethan didn't respond; she knew he didn't need to. He didn't want her stressing, though there was a bit of a reason to. More than that, Ethan couldn't promise her anything—nor would he lie to her. Instead, he just tightened his arms around her. Maeve sighed, both hating and loving his honesty with her, but adoring his arms around her.

After a couple of long minutes, in which she felt herself relaxing against Ethan, they arrived. Her anxiety picked up as Ethan clambered out and ran around the car to get to her door. Maeve stared at the building as Ethan let her out. It had always felt familiar to her, but now it seemed as though secrets were hiding about in every corner.

Maeve rang the bell with shaking hands, gripping Ethan's hand in hers as she did so.

"One minute!" she heard Annie say from inside. Probably about that minute later, the door swung open. Annie looked over them, then seemed to swallow heavily, though she smiled. "Oh, hey, Maeve. How're you doing, my girl?" She gave a hug, but her reserved greeting made Maeve fear that the suspicions were right.

"Annie, I'm sorry to impose on your day, but can we ask a few questions?" Ethan pulled out his badge, somewhat reluctantly.

Annie nodded, pulling the door open and looking resigned. "Can I get you guys some tea?"

"No," Ethan started to reply, but Maeve interrupted.

"Yes, please," Maeve nodded, squeezing Ethan's hand as he looked at her.

Trust me.

He must have, since he didn't say anything else as Annie let them in and went to get some teas.

Ethan looked at her imploringly.

"I know Annie," she said. "When she gets stressed out, she needs to be doing something with her hands."

Ethan shrugged and started to look at the pictures on a wall. Maeve listened to the sounds in the kitchen as she found a seat on the couch, her knees weak. How could she be here, essentially condemning Annie? How could she think this wonderful lady had anything to do with the terrible events of the past?

Annie came back in within moments, carrying a tray in shaking hands. Ethan offered immediately to take the tray and put it on the coffee table.

Annie wrung her hands, looking between the two of them. "Well? What can I do for you this evening?"

"Please, sit," Ethan murmured. "I just want to ask some questions, is all."

Annie hesitated, glancing at the couch beside Maeve. "I'll just stand, if it's all the same to you."

Ethan nodded. "I don't mean to bring up the past, but what can you tell me about your husband?" As soon as Ethan said it, Annie started picking up some piles of magazines with her trembling hands. Ethan looked down to watch the movement, but Maeve was watching Annie's face. If Maeve knew Annie at all, she knew how upset this meeting made her.

Tears had crowded Annie's eyes.

Apparently, Ethan had noticed that as well, despite looking at her hands. He stepped closer and put a hand on Annie's arm. "Annie, I don't mean to upset you. I just need to know, for Maeve's peace of mind, and my own. For all the people who may or may not have been hurt by him."

Annie began to cry, looking at Maeve. Maeve knew she should go up and comfort the lady, but she couldn't bring her legs to move.

Finally, she nodded and sat hard in the chair. Ethan stepped away and sat beside Maeve but leaned closer to Annie.

"You don't know what it was like to live with that man," she finally said. "When I was a girl, I never believed in my self-worth—I married Victor. He was abusive and manipulative, but that's what I believed I deserved at the time, then continued to believe." She shook her head. "I found out about a year before my husband passed away that he had also been a part of a mafia family. Even more than that, he had been there when your parents were killed."

"Why didn't you tell me?" Maeve asked, hurt.

Annie looked at her, her eyes sorrowful. "By the time I knew about it, the case was closed, and you weren't around. Victor warned me not to say anything. Then he died, and I didn't see the point in dredging up the past when I didn't even know the person who had been with Victor."

Maeve clenched her fist. She felt sympathy for this woman, sure, but also frustration. "And what about when I came back? You knew what I was looking for, the answer I'd been searching for."

Annie looked away. "I was scared. I tried so hard to work up the courage. I even finally got the courage, but then I heard fighting, and I panicked. It brought up a lot of memories. Then I thought I'd be arrested because I didn't go in and report what I knew." Annie stood again and paced, her hands shaking out in front of her.

The frustration sank from Maeve's mind as she understood Annie's fears suddenly. Maeve remembered living on the streets. If she had witnessed something back then, she doubted she would have worked up the courage to tell anyone. And Annie had known so much pain from someone who should have loved her. Really multiple people, including herself.

Maeve stood and quickly swept Annie in for a hug. She stopped pacing immediately and hugged Maeve tightly, hands trembling violently. "I'm so sorry, Maeve. For everything."

"I understand, Annie," she murmured, looking at Ethan as he stood, but not pulling away. Ethan put a hand on Annie's shoulder.

"Is that all, Annie?"

Annie nodded as she pulled, but then paused and shook her head, looking at the floor. "There's one more thing. Just let me go get it." She scampered from the room quickly.

Maeve reached for Ethan's hand again, glad that she was there, and he was with her.

Ethan gave her a soft smile, underlined with sadness that told Maeve he didn't like this anymore than she did.

Annie came back, holding a paper. "Don't be mad."

Ethan reassured her. "Of course not."

Nodding, Annie handed the paper over. "When this came the first time, it was addressed to both me and my husband. Victor had finally told me what he'd done. I think the guilt was starting to catch up to him. I hadn't told anyone, and that last year was peaceful with my husband…another reason I didn't want to say anything. A couple weeks before he died, he'd started talking about telling the police. Then he got sick and died after a couple weeks."

Ethan read what was on the paper, and his face hardened. "Was this the only one?" Curious, Maeve looked over his shoulder to read it.

Remember, don't tell anyone. You know what will happen. - T

Annie shook her head, looking scared. "No." She handed over one more paper. "Another one came a couple days ago. Right after you came back, Maeve."

Ethan read it before Maeve could, but the photo that was with the note made the hard lines even deeper.

Don't tell anyone unless you want them hurt. - T

Maeve didn't have to ponder who it was for long. The picture showed Maeve and Ethan right after the attack at Annie's restaurant. They were holding hands, sitting on the ambulance while the paramedics checked Ethan.

Maeve felt panic flare in her gut. She looked up, searching for anything out of the ordinary. The blinds were closed, nobody would see them from out there. She grabbed onto Ethan's biceps of his right arm, trying hard not to let her fear overwhelm her.

Ethan swallowed heavily. "Annie, I need you to come with us. I won't let you go to jail or let whoever this is hurt you. We've got to get you away from here."

Annie nodded almost immediately, relief flowing into her eyes. "Oh, please. I don't want to be here anymore."

Ethan nodded, pulling Maeve close to his side again. "Just take a couple minutes to pack up some things you'll need, Annie. If you don't mind, I'd like to get you somewhere safer."

Annie nodded again, gave them a burst hug, nearly sobbing in relief, then ran to go get some stuff.

Ethan kissed Maeve's cheek, then stepped away and grabbed his phone out of his pocket. "I've got to make a call," he told her. "Will you be okay?"

Maeve nodded, trying to be brave.

Ethan stepped out of the room, and Maeve looked around again nervously. It was stupid; no one was around, no one would be able to see them with the blinds closed. But even still, Maeve felt concerned. The picture had disturbed her. That someone was watching them and knew they were here, that they knew Ethan was involved as well, the fact that Ethan had been heavily bleeding in the picture. They knew he was hurting, and where they were.

And they knew *nothing* about this man. For all they knew, it could be someone close to them.

The idea made Maeve nauseous. She sat down on the couch, burying her face in her hands. Why did she have to bring this up too? It was already hard enough with Anthony, and now Maeve was just adding one more problem to their plate.

Annie came back before Ethan with a small backpack in her hands. Maeve looked at the bag in surprise.

"We ready?" Annie asked, more in control of her emotions now.

"You ready already?" Maeve asked, raising an eyebrow.

Annie looked down and shrugged. "There's not much I really need."

Maeve shrugged as well and looked over as Ethan came in. He glanced at the bag but didn't seem to see anything weird about it. His face was back in a careful mask that told Maeve that he was worried but planning. It was the look he gave whenever he needed to get something done, especially in his work.

"Let's go." Ethan checked out the window, then the front door. He seemed cautious, but Maeve was glad.

Man, how twisted a life she lived. Would she ever get a break?

~27~

Anthony stared silently at the man across from him, waiting for his host to tell him why he'd been invited, especially after being so quickly dismissed before.

And the holdout continues, Anthony thought. Anthony really didn't mind waiting as this man stared him down, trying to intimidate and study him at the same time. It was a good move to try and make someone uncomfortable. Anthony just refused to let himself be pressured in such a way. His ability to stay calm and collected in any circumstances was one he'd possessed even as a child when he'd gotten carted off to the principal's office almost daily. Anthony could—and would—win any standoff because he wasn't worried about waiting in what most would deem awkward or nerve-racking silences. He could find the smallest things to entertain him at any moment.

At this moment, it was how his host's eyes continuously scanned up and down Anthony, as if he found him to be a creature that he loathed and wanted dead, but wasn't sure how to do such, or even if that's what would be most beneficial. He amused himself as he thought about what this host may be thinking about what he found in Anthony.

Anthony tried to display a guarded interest, not worrying about hiding his curiosity—since he was, in fact, curious as to why this man wanted him—but also doing a little of his own scrutiny. A little tilt of his head and barely a smile, just to show he wasn't closed off. His hands rested on the sides of the chair, and he sat back to appear relaxed but kept both feet on the floor and refused to slouch.

Then Anthony saw something he hadn't right away. This host of his was quite still except for his eyes and a little bit with his head. But then, also, his finger. Just one fingertip, barely tapping against the side of his cup of tea or coffee. It barely moved and didn't make any sound Anthony could hear, and from the distance and angle it was barely seen at all.

Anthony figured that this host had a bit of nervous tension in his body. Anthony thought up some possible reasons as to why. Just because he was here? The reason he had been called to meet? A sick grandmother? Anthony didn't know, but he had a feeling he would find out soon. Anthony refused to let people be a secret to him if he could help it. He would research and ask around.

But he'd be patient about it.

After all, if he'd learned anything these last few months, it was that he had to have patience. He'd lost Maeve because of a bit of poor planning on his side. He'd let Ethan chase him away from a fight.

That latter part may have been a good thing. Anthony had not been ready to meet the other man as of then. He needed much more time to prepare.

And prepare, Anthony did, but Anthony had more than just revenge in his mind. He'd wanted his own family, and he'd slowly rebuilt that. He'd had to remove the weak recruits after he had used them to get to the better ones.

And now that Anthony fairly trusted his soldiers and street bosses, he could move onto getting rid of some loose ends.

Capturing Mason had been easy enough, but he was merely a distraction. With the worry for his brother, Ethan would be less focused on the case and more on his brother. He'd be more exhausted with the constant threat over his head. He'd slip up, and Anthony could come in for the kill when the time was right. Then Maeve would be his.

Sitting there, Anthony felt his thoughts stray a little. Knowing Maeve had been Santorini's gal had only deepened his desire to have her as his. Santorini had been too trusting. Too stupid. He'd left his mark on Maeve, sure, but he'd been careless to let the whore go. He'd been careless about Ethan.

Anthony may have let her go last time he'd had her, but he had a different end goal in mind. He'd given Maeve a little leeway on the rope, just enough for her to feel as though she were free. And how much more painful would it be for her when she was jerked right back into his grasp, where she belonged? She would be his forever as soon as he lay his marks on her. He'd done so to many girls before, all on their chests. The only one he'd kept alive was that girl from Maeve's shop, and that was only because he had to leave a message.

Maeve would be a lot more satisfying than the others he'd killed. At the thought, he felt his fingers curl just slightly, on the chair. That outward movement snapped him back into the room, with his host still staring at him.

Great, you called me here just to stare at me. If he knew he merely wanted to do that, Anthony could have just mailed him a picture.

Even with that, Anthony knew the bit of scrutiny was necessary for this man.

The door opened then, and his host's wife stepped in. She was a chubby lady, who had a habit of making food pretty much all the time.

She chided Anthony's host. "Oh dear. I better get you some tea or something while you wait," she told Anthony. "What do you want? A cookie? Coffee? Tea?"

"Sure, coffee and cookie please." Anthony wasn't going to be intimidated. If this man was going to take forever, he might as well eat.

She nodded, chuckling, and walked out. She was only gone for a minute before she was back with the coffee and a large sugar cookie. Halfway through, his host finally snapped. "Mabel, leave."

His wife nodded and scampered out. Expectant, Anthony looked to his host but pulled the coffee to his lips, careful of possible heat. It was the perfect temperature. Tasted good too, though maybe slightly bitter.

As soon as the door shut behind Mabel, his host leaned forward. "The police are searching hard for you." His tone was wary, disapproving.

Anthony finished taking another drink before leaning forward and putting the cup onto the coffee table. "Yes," he said simply.

"You've been doing well rebuilding," he said gruffly, reluctantly acknowledging.

Anthony felt frustrated by the short comments, he didn't know how to reply.

"What did you want me for?" Anthony finally asked. He preferred the quiet to this small talk, never getting to the point.

His host nodded, and Anthony realized he'd let his frustration loose a little. The man seemed almost relieved by such.

"I have some people I want you to take care of for me," his host told him. Anthony had not been allowed to know his host's name—real or street—and he found it annoying.

"Why would I do that?" It wasn't condescending, it was just business. They both knew it, and his host would surely expect it.

"Here's the deal." His host clamped his hands together in front of him. "You want support; I want these people dealt with. I am not about to publicly associate myself with you when you're already walking a thin line being captured, but I can support you from a distance. If you respect the distance I set up and take care of my problem, I will give you the support." Before Anthony could think about the deal, his host continued. "Also, if the police end up getting you, or you fail in any other way of that sort, I get the people you built up."

The last bit was pushing it; Anthony knew even his host could tell. Anthony thought in silence for many moments, maybe close to a minute, then started tapping his fingers on the arm of the chair. Something about the deal, or maybe the man himself, warned Anthony not to trust him entirely, but it was possible to do what needed to be done without having to fully trust the man.

"What can I call you?" Anthony asked, narrowing his eyes. Would there be any extension of partnership?

The man across from Anthony smiled. "Most in the family call me the Host," he said, laughing. "I wasn't kidding when I told you to call me that the first time."

Anthony felt the side of his lip start to crack a smile, and he allowed it, but refused anything further.

"I want that picture." Anthony nodded to the one behind the Host. He turned in surprise. It had been one that Anthony had noticed when he'd walked in, immediately liked, but had forced himself not to look back at.

"Why?"

"I like it. I want to be able to study it. It has a story hidden in there, and I want to find it." Anthony leaned back. "Deal or no deal? Your support and this picture for some anonymous killing."

The Host leaned back into his seat, studying Anthony again as if *he* were as curious as the painting.

"Deal."

Anthony nodded shortly. "Who are these people?" he finally asked.

The Host smiled, telling Anthony that he thought Anthony should be eager for this task.

¤ ¤ ¤

Ethan knew he needed to get some sleep, but there were so many things going on at the same time. Trying to plan all of them, then also push down his stress, resulted in very little sleep. The past week, he'd had less than five hours a night. And now, with Annie added to their watch, and the threat from the note, it seemed as though he may never sleep again.

Mygyer rubbed his face, tiredness showing with how drawn he looked. Maeve and Annie had fallen asleep on a couch, both curled up on opposite ends. Cameron was on the other side of the table, typing away at the computer again. Patty was looking through the files with Mygyer. Ethan had been staring at the information they'd gained on this case and Maeve's for so long, he felt he could quote it word for word. His eyes were too bleary to see the lines anymore. They really needed to go get to sleep. It was nearly one in the morning, and they'd all had some busy last few days.

Earlier that night, as Mygyer and the others were about to leave, they'd received a note on the door that brought them all back to work, except Liz, who had left earlier. Since Maeve and Annie didn't know what to look for, they gave up trying to help, but Ethan couldn't risk them being elsewhere. Ethan didn't even like leaving Mason in the hospital—his stay had been prolonged since he'd had a fever and they wanted to fight any possibility of infection that may come. At least Mason had a guard on him though.

Ethan had told Tyra and his mom to postpone anyone else coming up, just for now. He planned to get Mason back to Kansas soon anyway, but with the threat to Annie, Ethan didn't think it was worth it to have more come there yet.

Tomorrow, Ethan would get Annie, Mason, and Tyra back home.

Ethan pulled the note back toward him with a sigh, rubbing his eyes. He slowly read through it again, his brain struggling catching what it was saying even though he already knew.

It was a tip as to where Anthony would be next week on Monday. Some anonymous person said he wanted Anthony out of the way, and that they, Ethan's team, wanted Anthony in jail. He'd make sure Anthony was vulnerable, and it was a win-win.

What worried Ethan was that this man obviously had his own plans while trying to get Anthony in prison. What plans could that be?

When Ethan looked back up, Cameron had laid his head on his folded arms on the computer. Mygyer was rubbing his face again. When he stopped, he caught sight of Ethan, then looked around the table and sighed.

"We better go get some rest. We won't be able to do anything with no sleep." Mygyer hesitantly stood and stretched, then walked around the table to put his hand on Cameron's shoulder. Cameron raised his head. "Go get back to your hotel and your daughter, Cameron. We're all going to bed for the night."

Cameron was too exhausted to argue. He just stood and nodded, closing his computer as he did so.

Cameron and Patty stood together. They had hotel rooms at the same hotel.

Ethan put a hand on Cameron's shoulder and looked at Patty. "Ride with each other. I don't want either of you to fall asleep behind the wheel."

Patty nodded at him, giving him a look before leaving the room with Cameron.

Ethan went over to Maeve, crouching beside her. She looked peaceful, and Ethan really didn't want to disturb her, but there was no other way to get to the hotel.

Before he did so, he gently ran his fingers through her hair, pushing it back from her face. What Ethan wouldn't give to be able to go home, without the stress of anyone out to hurt them, just to live a normal life with her for a while. They'd seen each other first in terror on a night Santorini tried to break Maeve and teach Ethan. They'd met officially after Ethan had been injured, and she was there for him while he'd healed. And now they were back in the chase.

Right then, Ethan prayed to God for something different this time. Not just to find Anthony, but to be able to go home safe with Maeve and have the real chance to court her. Or marry her.

That idea shot a thrill through him. It just felt *right*.

Mygyer picked his way over to them, and Annie woke, as if sensing a new presence. She blinked at them, uncomprehending, before she sat up. "We heading out?"

"Yes." Mygyer helped steady Annie as she stood. He and Annie moved toward the door but waited for Ethan.

Knowing they needed to go, but still unwilling to wake Maeve, he slid his hands under her instead. She shifted and half woke up, but only moved closer to his chest as he picked her up.

Mygyer held the door open for Ethan, flashing him a look. Ethan knew what that look meant, but he didn't let himself respond to it right now. Mygyer always thought that people should separate their personal and work life, but even more than that, Ethan suspected he had been hoping Ethan would end up with Patty. And while Patty was amazing, Ethan didn't love her. In fact, he thought of her more like a sister than anything else.

Ethan sighed as he walked past, heading to the car. He wished he knew what to do about Anthony and wondered if that note was something they should trust. He wanted Anthony behind bars so badly, but what if by getting Anthony out of the way, they helped someone far worse?

They hadn't been able to match up any handwriting or find any fingertips from the note, so they had no idea who was behind the tip.

Ethan pulled Maeve a bit tighter, kissing her head. The warmth she made him feel had him praying once again that God would keep her safe.

¤ ¤ ¤

Mason could barely bite down his frustration. His right hand was rendered practically useless, which was his dominant hand. It was so strange to realize how impaired he was—how much he really used his right—when he was forced to use his other.

The fork felt uncomfortable in his fingers. As he endeavored to get the chicken in his mouth, the fork slipped sideways in his fingertips, and he nearly cursed as the meat dropped onto his lap.

Sighing, he put the fork back down and cleaned up the chicken from his hospital gown.

Mason had tried to convince the hospital workers to let him change into regular clothes practically every single day, but the doctor had refused. He needed to be able to access Mason's body to check up on the bruises and other wounds. Mason hated being out of his clothes, especially after his humiliation of being half naked while Anthony beat him in whatever way he wanted. He just wanted to wear some real clothes again.

Mason squeezed his good hand and closed his eyes. It was hard. He remembered seeing Ethan's dark gaze when he'd been healing from being shot. Remembered how Mason had only wanted to see the light in them again. Mason tried to keep happy for that reason. He knew his family worried for him. His mom had called him many times since he'd been in the hospital, and Mason got a chance to talk to her and his kids, but it wasn't the same. He wanted to be there with them. He wanted to see his kids. To hug the daylights out of them.

Though he figured that trying to do so would cause him more injury than anything else. His bruises had turned a dark blue and black color—or at least most of them. Some were green, some were purple.

They all hurt.

Mason heard the door open and saw Tyra walk back in. She had stepped out only to use the bathroom. Now, as she came closer, he could see the lump under her shirt from the pregnancy that made him smile all over again.

He loved his family.

Tyra gave him a bright smile. Mason didn't know what he would've done if Tyra hadn't come down to be with him. She was his solace in this world of pain. She had continually supported him, held him. Even more, she kept him thinking straight. Every time they had to do tests or check his injuries, Mason kept flashing back to how Anthony had beaten him. Then the pain would make him think he was still there. Having Tyra with him through everything had made it endurable.

Tyra seemed to notice his frustration. As she approached, she kissed him quickly. "Do you want me to feed you, honey?"

Mason sighed. "No, I wish my hand would just work." He looked at both his hands, frustrated with both the uncoordinated and the injured one. The sight of the pins in his fingers was kind of gruesome. Mason had asked if they could put a cast over it to hide it when he went home—he didn't want his kids to see it, even if he knew Owen would find it interesting.

Tyra smiled in amusement. "Maybe this'll be a good thing. It'll help your left hand catch up to the right."

Mason snorted, smiling a little. She could make every problem feel small.

"Teriyaki chicken, huh?" Tyra sat next to him. Mason scooted a little so she could be more comfortable, but it made him wince. Tyra put a hand on his arm. "Careful there."

"It was the only chicken they had," Mason told her. He grabbed her hand and rubbed his thumb along it.

Tyra used her other hand to stab a piece of chicken and fed it to him. Part of him was embarrassed. The other part just loved how she looked at him too much to care that he couldn't do it himself—at least not while also holding her hand.

"How are you feeling today?" she asked him.

Shrugging one shoulder, he finished chewing before speaking. "I'm okay. Better now that you're back. I'm ready to go see the kids and get out of here."

Tyra nodded in understanding, then smiled. "The kids miss us. They want to see you. Also, your team called. Michael said they're concerned about you, and praying for a speedy recovery." Michael was Mason's work partner. He was the one who found clients and dealt with the financial aspects, and Mason was the one who went out with the team to build the projects.

"That would be nice," Mason agreed. "How're they doing without me?"

"They're managing. They have plenty of work; they're just not able to do all your amazing finishing touches." She kissed him again, then put a hand on his head. "No fever. That's good." She looked worried, but she still smiled.

Mason didn't want to make Tyra worry, but a sigh escaped him before he could stop it. He looked down at his mangled hand. "Don't think I'll be able to do those finishing touches either."

Tyra lifted his good hand and kissed his fingers. The movement brought his gaze back up to hers. "I'm sure your hands will be back to their original work in no time. Until then, I'm just glad you're alive." She put his hand on her cheek. He ran his thumb over her skin, brushed back her hair, then scooted forward to kiss her.

The movement was sore on his back and the rest of his body, but the result was worth it.

"I haven't told you the best news," Tyra said as she finally pulled back. "Dr. Nance said you can head home soon. Also, I told Elisa that we'd be home soon. They're all ready to see you."

Mason grinned, sitting back. "That's great. I'm excited to get home."

Tyra nodded. "I talked to Ethan. He seems to think that you being taken had been a distraction for his team. He doesn't think Anthony is going to kidnap again. It's strange; I think they're finally getting some idea as to what's going on, but they either can't or won't tell me."

Mason smirked at her slightly affronted look. "A bit of both, I'd guess." Then he furrowed his brows as pain started to trickle in again. The medication had blocked his pain receptor sites, but now it was fading, and he knew soon it would be nearly overwhelming until the nurse got him his next dose.

Tyra started to get him another bite, but Mason shook his head. "I think I've had enough," he told her, relaxing on the pillow behind him.

Tyra nodded, then gave a small, shy looking grin. "Scoot. I wanna sit next to you."

Mason did as she said, slowly. It was surprisingly hard to do so, since he couldn't use his right hand at all, or his left foot easily, and his whole body gave him pain anyway. But, again, he figured the result would be worth it.

Tyra got under his sheet and lay facing him. "Does it hurt too much for me to lay against you?" she asked.

Mason shook his head. "I guess we'll see." He held his good arm out for her to lay down on it, and she gently snuggled into his side, laying her head on his shoulder, arm across his chest. There was a little pain from his shoulders. He'd been hung from the ceiling long enough his upper back and shoulders were sensitive. But it was ultimately fine, so he kissed her head and relaxed.

"You don't know how worried I was," she whispered with a deep exhale.

"Well, you left the kids without us, so it must have been pretty bad," Mason joked. Tyra had rarely left kids, always taking them on trips with them.

She chuckled. "But I knew you'd be okay. I asked God to watch over you, and I got confirmation that you'd be safe and make it back to me. That's when I knew I had to come down here to be here for you." She nestled into his neck, her breathing turning deeper. Mason had noticed her exhaustion in the black circles under her eyes, and he knew she was falling asleep.

Mason enjoyed holding her as he fell back to a light doze.

He didn't know how long he was asleep, but he awoke to his doctor entering the room, and his bruises getting a little more tender. Dr. Nance saw him and Tyra snuggling and she gave a smile. She seemed to understand them, somehow. Mason was glad.

She kept her voice quiet. "How're you feeling, Mason?"

Mason assessed his body. Some of his bruises pounded fiercely, probably mostly because Tyra lay on him. He didn't want to tell her that in case she made Tyra move. He liked to hold the love of his life, and Tyra needed the sleep.

"A little better," Mason said, honestly in the way of how his mind felt. He felt more at peace now than he had since he'd been out.

Dr. Nance nodded. "We believe you can go home now," she said. "I'll just do your final checkup, and when Ethan gets here, you can go to the hotel with him, then head home whenever you decide to. Doing that, though, you need to know that the pain is going to be intense. We have your meds and everything, but they'll wear out a lot faster once you[re active. It will be hard to function with the bruises, and it will take a while for your hand to get back to normal. It may never get back to the full capacity you once had."

She must have seen the crest-fallen look on Mason's face at the last words because she smiled. "Mason, this will be a hard journey, but one I have full confidence of you making. Especially with a supportive family that you have. I will get you in contact with a doctor and physical therapist down in Kansas that I believe will be beneficial to you. I can even give you a number to some good therapists, if you feel like you'd want to talk to anybody."

Mason bit his lip. It took him a moment, but he finally nodded. He didn't want to go through this hard process, but he remembered Ethan once again—the pain he'd gone through, the darkness, and how he'd gotten through it. Mason knew that Nancy was right; with the support Mason had, he could make it through. Having a doctor and physical therapist was a must, and a therapist would probably be good as well… just maybe not quite yet.

"Thank you, Dr. Nance. For everything," he said softly.

Dr. Nance nodded but laughed. "I'm not done with you yet." She stepped closer. "We're going to take your stitches out today."

Mason was kind of surprised. He had expected them to be in longer. "Are you sure they're ready?"

She nodded, seeming amused by his concern. "Yes. We don't want to leave them in too long, otherwise they may try and become part of your skin." She cocked an eyebrow. Mason hesitated, unsure if they may really start to do that or if she was just teasing. He decided against asking either way.

"What time is it?" Mason asked instead.

She looked down at her watch. "Nearly noon now. We figured we'd let the two of you sleep for a while. We know how hard a time you both have sleeping at night right now."

Mason nodded, yawning. She was right; they both did have trouble sleeping. Granted he had trouble sleeping in most cases, not just at night. "Has Ethan been back in?" His fingers had gone numb under Tyra.

"Not yet. He called and asked how you were doing. I told him you were still sleeping, and I told him not to worry about coming in until after I finish taking out your stitches and putting a cast over your hand." Dr. Nance checked his clipboard. "How's the pain, Mason?"

"Fine."

She raised an eyebrow. "Don't lie to me."

Mason looked down. "It's manageable. I hurt, but I'm okay."

Dr. Nance nodded. In the moment of silence, Tyra shifted, then slid off Mason carefully. She smiled at her husband. "Hey, honey. You okay? Did I hurt you?"

Mason shook his head. "No. I'm hurting a little, but I'm okay. Promise." He grabbed Tyra's hand as she sat next to him, despite the needle-like pain as his fingers came back to feeling.

She nodded and looked at Nancy. "What's the plan?"

¤ ¤ ¤

Ethan walked the halls of the hospital, Maeve holding onto his arm. She sensed that her presence seemed to calm his worry. She knew he was worried about the flight tomorrow. She was a little worried too. Ethan and Maeve wouldn't go home yet, not until Anthony was caught. She didn't like the idea of letting Mason go home without them though. What if Mason needed help and Ethan wasn't around? Plus, she was worried about Annie; she was a nervous wreck that something might happen now that she'd finally told the truth.

Maeve slid her hand down his arm and into his hand, leaning closer as they walked and looking up at him. "It will be fine, Ethan."

Ethan nodded, putting his arm around Maeve. He didn't look sure, but for now, he was resigned to agree with her. At least outwardly. She put her head on his arm, thankful he still wanted her. Her fear that he would have pushed her away and not want her anymore, was still there, but it was doused. Big time.

Maeve felt her phone vibrate in her pocket. She didn't move to grab it right away, but after a few seconds she pulled it out. Kelly.

Maeve felt herself smile. Her good friend always made her feel happy.

Ethan saw the look and he pulled away. "Go ahead and answer," he said. As if she needed permission.

She did so. "Hey, Kelly!" she said, voice happy. She didn't let go of Ethan's hand even as he tried to extricate himself.

"Hey, Maeve. I haven't heard from you since you left. How are you doing?" Her voice was chipper, with a hint of concern leaking through.

"I'm sorry, Kelly. It's been chaotic. I'm doing good though."

"That's okay, love." Maeve could hear Kelly's grin. "I heard you got back to Chicago with Ethan and Mason. How's Mason doing? I heard he was injured."

Maeve frowned. "Yeah, he's doing okay though. They're one tough family." Maeve looked at Ethan as she spoke, smiling. "It's hard to see him hurt and all, but with Tyra's support, he'll be fine."

"Sure, sure," Kelly said quickly. "Hey, when will you be back, do you know? You and Ethan?"

"Well…" Maeve hesitated. "Mason is coming back tomorrow, but I don't think Ethan and I will be back for another few days at least. Ethan wants to get Anthony." And Maeve wanted to figure out who killed her parents. "Why?"

"No reason. What are you doing?"

Maeve lifted an eyebrow, not believing her friend.

"Just at the hospital about to visit Mason."

Kelly was quiet for a second. "Alright, my friend, I'll let you go. Just call me when you get back."

"Will do." Maeve hung up and put her phone back in her pocket.

"That was fast," Ethan commended, looking down. "Everything okay?"

"Yeah." Maeve grinned at him. "It was Kelly."

"I know," Ethan chuckled. "Most girls I know talk forever on the phone."

Maeve shrugged, enjoying the teasing tone of his voice. "I don't like talking over the phone much. I'd rather be in your company while I have it."

They reached Mason's room. When they pushed in, past the guard at the door, they found Mason's bed in the sitting up position. His eyes were closed, but he opened them heavily as they entered and gave a small smile.

"Hey, Mason." Ethan stepped closer to the opposite side of Tyra. "How're you feeling?"

"Tired," Mason admitted. "They took some of my stitches out, so it's a little more tender now."

Ethan sat on the side of the bed carefully. "I heard that you could get out of here today."

Mason nodded. "Just waiting on a nurse. Doc checked on me not too long ago and said she believed I could go. A nurse was going to just get me some pills I could take when the pain gets bad. But could you two help me get changed?" He looked at Tyra and Ethan. Ethan looked at Maeve, right as she felt a blush rise on her face.

Ridiculous, since she had been willing to help Ethan. Granted, that was because he hadn't had anyone else to help him. Plus, Mason was married to Tyra, so that was a little awkward.

Tyra smiled at Maeve. "Dear, can you go get us some water?"

Relieved, Maeve nodded and escaped the room, feeling a little like an idiot.

It didn't take long to find a vending machine to get a water bottle, but she dawdled there to give as much time as possible for them to finish getting dressed.

As she stood there, she noticed a figure in the reflection of the glass, standing behind her, and her heart skipped a beat.

Anthony.

She turned her head quickly but stopped just as fast.

It was just a man that had some similar physical attributes to him.

She fought back a shudder, taking a deep breath and trying not to clench the water bottle too hard in her hands as the man gave her a weird look and took her place at the vending machine as she moved away. She took a deep breath to make sure she wouldn't pass out, then decided to head back to the room, feeling her feet moving quicker and quicker every step. She was panicking, even as she tried hard not too, and she felt completely stupid for doing so.

She entered the Mason's room without knocking, and quickly shut the door firmly behind her. She didn't even have the composure to be embarrassed as she realized Mason had only halfway dressed.

"Maeve, what's wrong?" Ethan looked surprised and worried. Maeve gasped in some breaths, trying to shake the fear.

Ethan exchanged a look with the other two before helping Mason sit on the bed, coming over to where Maeve still pressed her back against the door.

"Maeve?" She let him draw her into an embrace even though she couldn't hug him back yet. "What happened?"

"N-nothing," she managed to stutter out. It was strange how her logical mind knew it was being an idiot even as her body reacted like it had been a real threat.

"Maeve? Talk to me." He ran a hand through her hair.

"Really, it's nothing." She took another deep breath, calming at the feel of Ethan's arms around her. "I promise."

"I don't care if it feels like nothing, Maeve. You're freaking me out."

"It's just…" she felt herself blushing. "I saw a guy downstairs that looked a little like Anthony. It wasn't him, but it just freaked me out a little, is all."

Ethan stiffened against her, holding her tighter. "You're sure it wasn't him?"

"Yeah, sure. I'm sure." She took one more deep breath, then pulled away from him. "I'm okay now. I'm sorry."

Ethan shook his head. "Maeve, you have no reason to be sorry. He's done a lot to hurt all of us. I think we all will feel like we're on our toes for a while. But it's okay. I've got you. We're safe," he whispered, brushing her hair back. Maeve nodded.

Maeve heard movement from Mason and Tyra, and then Maeve felt Tyra's hand on her back. "You ready to get out of here?"

"Yes please." Both Maeve and Mason answered simultaneously, then smiled at each other. Mason was standing behind Tyra, good hand in his jacket pocket, the other one held in front of his stomach. He looked shaky, which made her feel glad when Tyra stepped back to join her husband, wrapping an arm around his waist.

"Alright, let's go," Ethan said. They helped Mason sit in a wheelchair, though he didn't seem happy about it, he didn't complain. Once they got to the car Mason struggled his way standing, taking a deep breath before he even pulled himself into the car. He noticed their looks and smiled at them though.

"I'm okay," Mason murmured. "Just feel a little drained."

Ethan slipped the wheelchair away and he and Tyra moved to his side to assist him in.

"You're doing fine," Maeve smiled at him. She wanted to hug Ethan's brother as she realized she still had not done so since he'd been back. She would be forever grateful for Mason understanding her need to figure her life out—even before she fully realized it herself. "I'm so glad you're back safe."

Mason looked at her, smiling. She loved the look of acceptance in his eyes, and even the happiness. Sure, he was hurting, and like Maeve and Ethan, there were things that could chase away the light in his eyes if he let them, but Tyra was a constant support, they all loved him, and he had a firm belief in God. "Me too," he told her. "God watched over me. I could feel His love and Tyra's prayers the entire time." He kissed the top of his wife's head as she climbed into the car beside him.

Maeve smiled, and Tyra pressed closer to Mason, laying her head on his chest. "I knew only God could keep an eye on you."

Ethan caught Maeve's eye and forced a smile. Maeve could see the worry in his gaze, as well as the tiredness. But Ethan was trying hard to keep happy, and to stay close to Maeve and his family, and she was glad.

~28~

Ethan pulled his brothers' bag over his shoulder, adjusting it tighter as they walked from the hotel room. Mason had been out of the hospital for two days now, and were going to meet the rest of Ethan's team and Patty at the Chicago FBI headquarters. After a quick debriefing with his team, they would then combine with the Chicago agents so they could get a plan in place.

Mason looked worn out, but he was only holding onto Tyra's hand now, no longer leaning on anyone. The pace was painfully slow—painful for Mason anyhow, and painful to watch. Ethan bit the inside of his lip as he tried not to jump in and help.

Mason saw his look and smiled in his direction. "I'm okay, Ethan."

Ethan forced a smile and nodded. "I'm glad," he said, but still couldn't fight the worry. He'd been wanting to get Mason and Tyra on a flight back to Kansas, but his brother was still in pain and wasn't sure he wanted to do the flight yet. Annie had already gone back and her and Ethan's mom were getting along swell.

Mason moved his injured hand in front of him more and winced. It was in a cast, which relieved Ethan. It would protect the healing skin and keep the pins from getting snagged on anything. Also, the sight was kind of sickening. Mason hadn't wanted to talk about what had happened while he'd been in the shed. He'd told Mygyer a bit to have on file, but had asked that he would keep it private.

They walked over to the station—it was right across the street from the hotel, so it wasn't far, which was nice. When they got in there, they headed straight for the boardroom.

Ethan prayed that this tip would not turn into a trap.

The team went silent as Ethan, Maeve, Mason, and Tyra entered the room. Mygyer looked up at them and gave a small smile. "How're you doing, Mason?"

Mason grinned. "I'm well, Mygyer. Thank you." He looked as though he'd been going to sit on one of the chairs around the table, but Tyra pulled him over to the couch instead. "How are you?"

Mygyer nodded in appreciation. "I'm good." He pulled the file from the table and slid it down to Ethan as he chose a chair a couple seats down from the director.

"Anything new?" Ethan asked, not opening the file because he had already read through it so many times, his head hurt.

"No. Our best bet is to still go through with the tip." Mygyer frowned, worry streaks in his face. "I've talked to Chief Brooken; he's on board with pulling some officers there to support us if it is some sort of ambush." He looked around at everyone technically not on the team, Maeve, Tyra, and Mason. "We'll have to figure out what to do with you guys. I don't want you there, but I also don't trust that this isn't something to try and get one of you guys again. I would have preferred to send you all back to Kansas with Annie, but Maeve, you said you weren't willing to leave."

"Not until I figure out who killed my parents," Maeve confirmed. Ethan looked over at her. She looked so confident. Beautiful. Her back was straight, and the only thing that showed she may be uncomfortable was her hands between her legs.

Ethan caught himself smiling at her, even as worry flooded over. He wanted her safe more than almost anything else.

Almost. But more than that, he wanted her to trust him—he couldn't try and push her away again. Not even to keep her "safe."

Maeve caught him looking and smiled softly. Embarrassed, Ethan looked back to Mygyer. His director didn't seem to notice the look as he swept on. "Exactly, but I don't want you there during this. We'll have to find someone to stay with you or something. And Mason, you sure about not going back?"

"Not quite ready for a long flight, I don't think," Mason admitted. "And I want to be here for Ethan and Maeve." He looked firm despite the obvious pain and weakness. Tyra nodded her support next to her husband. Ethan knew that they missed their family and kids desperately, but they didn't want to leave them alone.

Mygyer stared at him for a couple long seconds before sighing in the face of the Conten stubbornness. He had plenty of that from Ethan and knew how it would go. "Alright. Protection for all of you. Let's figure this out then."

Ethan had to fight his own nervousness and worry as they finalized plans. Not to mention the uncomfortableness between him and Patty still. As they worked, Ethan found that he missed Will. The teenager had always been the bright spot in the room, keeping them laughing, or at least keeping the tension light. Ethan used to be that, but not at the moment.

Mason, Tyra, and Maeve had moved to the couch outside the glass doors while they planned. Mason laid with his head in Tyra's lap, probably asleep again. Maeve and Tyra had a movie playing, but they were quietly chatting throughout.

Mason's injured hand was in front of him, and Ethan couldn't help the slight cringe when he glimpsed it. His brother had an immaculate hand in all the work he did. It was one of the reasons why business had gone so well for him. He had an eye for detail and would add in designs if the client wanted such. But that had always been done with his right hand. Ethan worried he would lose his mobility. And what would he do then? Ethan could only pray that he would be able to get his use back.

Time gradually passed, they met up with the other agents, and it wasn't until they were done with that that Ethan was able to leave the room and get to his family and Maeve. He was glad that they were able to go to the hotel for another night sleep after that long planning session and before the raid tomorrow. He felt confident in their plan, but definitely not entirely sure about the source of the tip. But they had to run with it anyway.

"You done now?" Maeve asked as he approached, standing and quickly grabbing his arm. "Looked like an intense planning session."

"It was." Ethan rubbed his face, but then smiled at the three of them. "How about we get some dinner and head back to the hotel for the night?"

"Sounds good," Tyra agreed, then gently nudged Mason awake. "Love, let's get going."

After he woke with a quiet groan, Ethan gently helped him sit, then stand up, only to have Mason stumble slightly. Ethan stopped his collapse and helped him sit back down.

"Whoa! Mason? You okay?"

"Yeah, just… I think my feet are done with this day."

"We'll get something easy on the way back so you can get off your feet sooner." Ethan promised. "Let me help you out, alright?"

"Just give me a minute and I'll be fine." He lay his head in his hands, slowly rubbing it.

Mason, are you sure you're okay?" Maeve asked softly.

Mason looked up at her, and Ethan felt sure he would brush off her concern, but instead he looked away. "My head is pounding," he admitted. "I feel like everything hurts, and I'm gonna explode or something." He winced and shook out his hand. "Sometimes it gets worse when I first wake up. Just give me a couple minutes."

"Do you need some medicine?" Ethan asked, eyebrows furrowing.

"Just give me a minute," Mason repeated.

Tyra pulled him gently into her hold, adding her fingers to his hair, and his brother relaxed into her, even if his face stayed scrunched in obvious discomfort.

Tyra gestured to the bag on the side, and Ethan grabbed it, digging out the pain medicine he knew would help his brother. As soon as he got some out, Tyra spoke: "Hon, I'm going to give you some of your meds, alright? Drink it down for me."

Mason nodded but pushed his hand hard into his head again, body shaking. Tyra got him some pills and a water bottle, then gently persuaded Mason to drink at least half of it. Mason did so, but he barely opened his eyes. The light probably hurt his head also.

After a couple long minutes, Mason finally forced himself away, still visibly shaking. "Okay, let's go."

"You sure?" Ethan put a hand on his arm, ready to help him up, or keep him still, whatever was needed.

"Yeah, I want to get back to the hotel. I'll be fine." He took a deep breath, eyes barely open, and Ethan gently helped him back up to his feet, slipping under his shoulder as he did so. He knew the move was painful to his brother, who was bruised, but it would be better than fully walking on his tender feet.

"Okay, we got this." Ethan and Tyra both took a side, while Maeve grabbed the bag. Ethan nodded at Mygyer as they passed, noting the worried look in his eyes that definitely followed them until they made it to the end of the hall.

Ethan felt the same worry, but he was grateful his brother was alive and getting better.

Cameron scanned his eyes over the monitors, keeping track of where each of his teammates were, and that all the Chicago agents were also in place. Cameron had been surprised that the Chicago team actually let them have equal say, as most people liked the take control of their own areas. However, they knew how personal this case had gotten for the team, especially Ethan, and so they were working well with the invading Kansas team.

But Cameron wouldn't let anyone sneak up on any of his team or the other agents. His job had been decided early on as surveillance, and he was alone since the Chicago team's usual tech gal was out of town for a family reunion, so he had to make sure to stay extra vigilant.

He was grateful that the job was paying for his hotel here, because money was tight enough with raising his daughter. His mother had come with him here to Chicago so that she could help watch Kammy for him while he worked, and he owed her everything. He'd mentioned the work trip to her, and how he'd have to bring Kammy because he couldn't leave her for that long, and without asking, she had immediately replied that she would come with him. Yesterday she told him how she and dad were planning to move so that they'd be closer to him, and he honestly couldn't hide the relief. He'd hated leaving Kammy with babysitters or daycare while he worked all the time.

Movement on the screen caught his attention, and he saw Anthony, a gun in his hand that was pointed at the back of Ethan's head about ten feet away.

Cameron leaned forward in the seat and spoke quietly. "Ethan, Anthony is behind you with a gun. Ten feet. He hasn't shot yet, so don't do anything to make him."

Ethan paused only slightly before continuing forward with more caution, angling himself so that he was closer to the wall.

Then Anthony spoke; "Drop the gun, Ethan." Ethan hesitated, then slowly bent to do as Anthony asked. "Where is everyone else? How did you find me?"

Ethan started to turn around, but Anthony quickly stepped closer and pushed Ethan away from the gun before stepping out of arm's reach. Ethan stumbled but righted himself against the wall, slightly closer to the man.

Cameron leaned forward, is heart beating as he suddenly wished that he was there to help his teammate.

"He's a good five feet behind you, Ethan," Cameron said softly. "Don't try anything risky. Wait for Mygyer; he's heading toward you."

Anthony looked around, then seemed to spot the camera in the darkness. He turned the gun to it and shot it.

"Did he shoot Ethan?"

"No, he shot the camera," Cameron replied, hating that he was now blind. He watched as Mygyer picked up the pace. Then he heard Anthony's voice still coming in strong from Ethan's mic.

"Let's go. Walk ahead of me. How did you know I'd be here?"

Ethan didn't respond right away. "We got an anonymous tip."

Anthony snorted. "He sold me out? Well, I can't say it surprises me."

"You know who it was?"

"Shut up!" Anthony snapped. Cameron suddenly realized he hadn't breathed since Anthony stepped out and took a slow breath.

A scuffle in the earpiece sounded, then a gunshot and a sharp ringing.

"Mygyer," Cameron said, voice tightly controlled. "Please tell me you got there."

Mygyer didn't respond, but a couple more shots fired before silence. More anxious, Cameron leaned forward. "Mygyer, are you okay? What happened? Do you see Ethan?"

"Affirmative," Mygyer's voice answered. "Anthony is in custody. Ethan is okay. We're getting out of here."

He relaxed in relief. "How's Ethan?" He heard Patty ask.

"His ear is ringing from the shot right by his head, but otherwise he's fine."

Cameron sat back in his seat, still keeping an eye out, but not as tense now that it was over. He watched and listened as everyone wrapped up at the site. As soon as everyone was on their way back, Cameron finally closed things out and sat in silence for a couple long moments before getting up.

He exited the room, finding Mason, Tyra, and Maeve on the couches where they'd been told to wait. Maeve immediately look up, and Mason slowly sat himself up from where he was once again laying on Tyra.

"How'd it go? Did they get him? Is Ethan okay?"

Cameron smiled at her. "Ethan's okay." He answered the most important part first. "We got Anthony, and they're all heading back now."

The relief in all three of their faces was immediate.

¤ ¤ ¤

Ethan rubbed his ear as he walked. He'd noticed his teams concerned looks, but his ears were by far the worst of him. He felt a little bruised along his arm, where he'd collided with the wall, and scraped a hand when they scuffled on the ground for the gun, but those were nothing. His ear was the worst of it, but even that was more annoying as it rang. It hurt a little, but not enough to be a problem.

He looked up as he entered the room behind Mygyer, grunting in surprise as he suddenly had an armful tossing herself at him, but he instinctively wrapped his arms around Maeve, holding her close.

He held her for some long seconds, before she pulled slightly away to kiss him quickly. "Are you okay?" she asked as her eyes scanned him, as though looking for injuries, even though he was sure that Cameron would have told her he was fine.

He grimaced and put a hand to his ear as he nodded. "My ear just feels a little hollow, but I'm fine. The guns were loud near my ear." He watched the horror flood her gaze and realized he could have kept that worry from her. But he also knew she'd wonder why his ear was bothering him later, not like he'd try that hard to hide it.

He was barely aware of the rest of the team continuing on, leaving them alone for a couple of minutes. Ethan smiled and pushed her hair back, changing the subject before she could dwell on it. "Now we can figure out your mystery and get home."

Maeve pulled him tight, and he let himself relax for the first time in what felt like days. "I honestly don't know how much I even care about that anymore. I just want all my loved ones safe," she admitted.

Ethan ran his hand soothingly down her hair a couple minutes before finally pulling away. He didn't know what to say. He knew there would always be something in Maeve that would want answers, but he also wanted his family home and safe.

As they walked toward Mason, his older brother made his way carefully to his feet and pulled Ethan into a hug as carefully as he could with his arm in the sling. His warmth felt as solid as always, despite the fact that he was obviously taking care not to cause himself any extra pain. "I'm glad you're back safe," he whispered, then he smirked slightly. "Think we head can head home now?"

Ethan looked at Maeve, unsure, but kind of hoping. "I know Maeve wants to find the men who killed her parents."

Maeve grabbed his hand and leaned into his side as Tyra hugged him too. "I mean, I do, but I also really want to go back home."

Ethan squeezed her hand. "Do you mind if you stay out here a little longer? I've got to go finish up with the briefing."

"Of course." Maeve stood onto her toes to kiss his cheek, then pulled away and joined the other two back on the couches.

Mason was clearly in pain again, it always got bad about an hour before he could take the next dose.

Ethan followed the rest of his team back into the boardroom so they could all brief. The room was full, and Ethan was one of the last ones in, to the surprise of nobody.

"First off, good job today, everyone." It was the Chicago Director, Landen the started them off. "I was impressed with everyone's ability to get the mission done and keep a level head with the few surprises. We had the opportunity to talk to Anthony, and for those who weren't there during the discussion, we'll go over it quickly." He tapped his fingers quickly on the table, his face grim. He then went on to explain how Anthony believed he'd been set up by a mafia boss named the Host. The only thing to help them identify the man was a painting Anthony had convinced the man to give him.

None of them had any ideas how to find this man, nor any proof that he did anything wrong. Ethan was questioned and talked a lot since he'd been the one undercover in the case for months, him and Patty would be the ones with the most knowledge on the people.

They would go look at the picture and try figure out who bought it; probably having to work backward by finding who painted it, then who was selling it, before they would be able to figure out who owned it.

The briefing was longer than Ethan had expected, which was probably stupid of him, for it being such a big bust with many combined units helping, but as soon as they finished, he was up out of his seat.

The Chicago Director pulled him aside first, however. "Ethan, it was good to work with you." He held out his hand to shake, and Ethan smiled in gratitude as he took it.

"Thanks. You as well."

"And we will keep working on that other case of yours. I'm not sure we'll find anything out, but we'll let you know if we do. It's mostly a cold case at this point, but I'll keep it on the back burner. My suggestion is to let it go for now, and let us work through most of it. Go home, get away from this case, and get back into your old job. You did a great job helping us."

"Thank you for keeping it open." Ethan relaxed his shoulders. "We know it's a long shot, but it would mean a lot if we can find anything out. Let me know if you ever have any questions or need any help."

They shook hands again, then Ethan was finally able to slip out the door and head back to his family and Maeve.

Spotting them, Ethan smiled. The Director was right, he'd have to talk to Maeve about the likelihood of finding anything out. He knew she'd always have the itch to know, but he also knew that she was tired of being here and being in danger.

It was time for them all to go home. He'd finally ask Maeve on that date.

Mason felt tired, which was kind of ridiculous since he'd been sleeping half the day away. But Dr. Nance had been right; it was exhausting to be in pain. Mason didn't want to let himself sleep, however, since they were on their way back to his mother's house now. He was excited to see his kids and other family members.

"How're you feeling?" Ethan asked from behind. Mason felt a hand on his shoulder.

Mason looked back, trying for a small smile. "Tired. But ready." He licked his lips, looking at his hand again. It was sensitive, but not terrible thanks to his medication. His butt was tired of sitting, first in the airplane and now in the car. However, he also knew there would be a lot of sitting to come because it's not like he was in good condition and could just stand all the time. But at least at home he would be on a soft couch or on his bed.

He was mainly relieved that this drama with Anthony was over finally. "And I'm really glad you're all with me too," he added.

Ethan squeezed his shoulder quickly before he withdrew. Mason gave a quick look back to see him grab Maeve's hand distractedly. Maeve shot a look of pure joy at Ethan, then noticed Mason watching and smiled shyly. Mason couldn't help but feel amused as well as relieved that the two of them seemed to be back on friendly terms. He wanted to see Ethan happy—and Maeve as well, honestly. Her life had been a hard one; she deserved a good guy, and Ethan was as good as they come.

At least most of the time, Mason mused as he remembered wanting to punch Ethan just weeks before. He couldn't decide whether to be amused by the memory or ashamed.

Mason reached out in his heart to his God, thanking him that He'd helped Mason through his time captive, and helped his family through everything else since this ordeal began.

From the driver's seat, Tyra smiled at Mason, that same relief in her eyes that they all felt. Mason instinctively held out his good hand, glad for the first time that his left hand was not incapacitated so he could hold her hand from the passenger seat.

He kissed her hand, then relaxed against the seat, letting his head fall so he could sleep.

When he woke, Tyra had stopped the car and was staring at him. When she saw him awake, she ran her thumb along his hand. "You ready?" Mason looked around and saw that they were now sitting in the driveway of his mom's house.

Mason nodded, blinking away tiredness, and reluctantly let go of Tyra so he could get out. He managed to stand, despite the throbbing in his feet, and Tyra joined him in seconds.

They barely made it to the door before it was swung open. Isabelle was there, her hands over her mouth. She sobbed and stepped forward, looking at Mason.

"Hey, sis," Mason said, holding his good arm out. She immediately sank into his embrace and didn't let go for close to a minute. When she finally pulled away, she studied him again.

"You look just as bad as Ethan had," she told him, eyebrows creased. She spoke quietly, as if she wanted a chance to talk before the rest of the family knew they were here.

Too late, he thought as he heard footsteps pounding on the ground as Mason entered the doorway. Seconds later, Owen was rounding the corner. "Dad! Mom!" He pulled them both into a hug at once. Mason crouched to hug him better, feeling stiffness, but not caring because he got to hold his son.

"Hey, bud," Mason whispered.

Owen sniffled in his shirt. "I missed you. I was so worried."

"It's okay, bud. I'm here now, I'm okay." Mason's voice caught. He pulled away and gently wiped Owen's tears. "How are you and your sister?"

"Lila is coloring," Owen chuckled. "Everyone is in the kitchen, except the kids. They're playing in the backyard with Uncle Scott and Aunt Riley watching. Lila just wanted to do a picture in the family room." He hugged Ethan, then held his father's hand as Mason stood again. Mason felt tempted to cry as he started to walk again. More family came barreling their way. Fallon was forefront, grinning despite the obvious worry.

He hugged Mason, but no one could really get a good word in edgewise due to everyone seemingly speaking at once, and they were all swarmed with seemingly a million hugs before they could take another step. Even Annie was there.

Mom took his good hand in his when everyone was finished and squeezed it lightly, tears in her eyes. "I'm so glad you're okay, Mason. Your momma was worried."

Mason smiled a little, despite the exhaustion. He was about ready to collapse, but he knew that if he sat now, he may never get back up so they could go home. "I missed you," he told her, kissing her tear-stained cheek.

She brushed his less bruised cheek. It was soft enough that it didn't really hurt, but it reminded him that he had a long way to heal.

Elisa smiled. "You look tired. I know Riley and Scott will want to see you, so let's get them so you can get home with your family." She looked to Tyra and Owen, reaching her free hand for Tyra. His wife grabbed it and squeezed it.

Mason had always been blessed with such a wonderful mother. She'd always supported Mason, and immediately loved everyone, making all her kids and in-laws feel at home right away.

"Thanks, Mom." Mason blinked back his weariness, reminding himself that he could rest soon.

They walked back into the kitchen slowly, once again due to Mason. His feet were getting more and more tender as he stood. Tyra must have noticed it; she stepped closer to him and put a hand on his arm. "Hon, why don't we just sit down here for a bit?"

Mason wanted to protest, knowing if he sat, he may never get back up, but instead he looked into her worried eyes and found himself nodding.

"Okay."

The back door opened before Mason could even take a step toward the family room with the couch. Riley came in, then let out a half-sob noise and rushed toward Mason, throwing her arms around him. Luckily, she missed his bad arm, but the rush of movement didn't help his bruises. A rush of nausea rushed through him, and he blinked a couple times to fight the shakiness.

Riley stepped back after a moment. "Thank God," she whispered, studying him. "I'm sorry, I didn't mean to–"

Mason smiled a little, interrupting her. Riley had always been a little reckless like that. "It's okay. I'm just glad to see you."

Scott came up behind his wife, put one arm around her, but held his left hand out for Mason. Mason took it, feeling a little amused. Scott had always been the most reluctant to give hugs, given that he was usually nervous. He felt a little sad as he gripped the hand with his left, reminded once again about his right hand injury, and wishing it was better already.

Scott pulled him into a hug, halfway surprising Mason. Mason couldn't hug him back because both his hands were currently preoccupied.

"Good to see you, man," Scott whispered.

"Come on," Tyra told him as they finished. "Let's sit you down."

Mason nodded and went after his wife's encouraging nudge, smiling at the others. Most of them followed, but a few broke off, as if realizing that they didn't all need to be there.

As Owen said, Lila was in the family room, lying on her stomach and feet kicking in the air as she colored. The sight was so familiar, he once again had to stop tears.

Lila looked up as they entered. "Hi Mom, hi Dad," she said casually, as if they'd only been gone five minutes, then went back to her coloring. Mason smiled, laughing a little.

As Mason sat, Owen climbed up beside him and leaned on his good side.

"Careful, bud," Tyra warned, but Mason wrapped his arm around his son, pulling him close and earning a little glare from Tyra. He just smiled, uncaring about his own injuries when he got to hold his family close again. He kissed his son's head.

Tyra turned to her daughter, putting her hand in their daughters' hair. "How are you, darling?"

Lila grinned. "Good." She finished her picture, then grabbed it, hugged her mom, then skipped over to Mason. "I made this for you, Daddy." She handed it to him, holding her hands in front of her. Mason saw the stickmen drawing of their family and felt amused.

"Thanks, love," he told her, holding his hand out from around Owen. Lila climbed onto them and sat half on Mason and half on Owen, leaning her head on Mason's chest.

Tyra looked at him, as if silently asking if he was okay. When he nodded, she sat beside him, on the arm of the couch, and ran her hand through his hair. Mason leaned his head back against her growing stomach, and for the first time since the restaurant, he didn't care about what he'd lost because his family was enough.

He closed his eyes, sighing with relief.

¤ ¤ ¤

Ethan was on the phone when Maeve walked in. He winked at her but kept his attention on Mygyer over the phone. "And did anything show up with it?"

"No prints or anything. I was wondering if you wanted to check the picture out though. You may have been in this man's house without knowing it." Mygyer's voice was exhausted. Ethan knew his director had flown in from Chicago early this morning, and he'd been working since. Ethan was lucky that he'd been able to leave earlier, not having to do near as much paperwork.

"Sure thing, Mygyer. Then go rest. It's your break too."

Mygyer chuckled. "Right. Okay, I'll send it over. Talk to you later."

He hung up before Ethan could respond. Ethan turned to Maeve, and she wrapped her arms over his shoulders right as he did so.

"How's it going?" She asked.

Ethan shrugged. "They didn't find anything that helps much. He's sending over the picture to see if I've seen it before." He wrapped his arms around her waist. "How's Mason?"

She smirked. "He fell asleep in seconds. He's sitting with his family now."

Ethan smiled a little, imagining that, and relieved that he was back safely.

Maeve didn't speak for a moment, then she pulled him close for a quick kiss. "Annie has gotten along well with your mom," she said as they both sat.

Ethan chuckled. "I bet." And knowing his mom, Ethan was sure Annie would have a new appreciation for herself. His mom always seemed to be amazing at showing people their self-worth. Even seeing Annie when they first came in, smiling as she greeted everyone, showed a change in her.

Ethan felt content sitting with Maeve's hand in his forever, but the universe had other ideas. Right as he allowed himself to relax, the back door opened, and a rush of kids stampeded in, all complaining about being thirsty and wanting to make something to eat. He spotted Andrew, Mallory, and Zee in the group, so he figured the rest had to be friends. He'd met Riley's little girl for the first time, having given birth to her while he was in Chicago. It had made him instantly guilty that he'd left his family and hadn't come back for a visit the whole time.

Mallory saw the two adults first, and she grinned and rushed to give a hug to Ethan, then smiled shyly at Maeve before giving her a hug as well. "Guess what?" she asked her uncle as Andrew and Zee came in for a hug. Zee was teeny beside her cousins.

"What?" Ethan felt amused by the bunch of kids as they all fought over what they wanted to eat.

"I'm in Young Women's now," she said proudly, showing Ethan her necklace. "A couple of these girls are from the Ward."

Ethan looked around and Maeve followed his gaze. Before Ethan could formulate much of a response, Mallory flounced back to the other girls. Andrew smirked after her sister.

"She's been weird since she joined," he admitted.

"Girls will just continue to get weirder," Ethan told him in a half whisper. "How's Scouts been going, anyway?"

Andrew scowled, and his hands slipped into his pockets. "Fine."

Ethan raised an eyebrow. "That response was so *not* fine."

Shuffling uncomfortably, Andrew looked at the other kids in the room—most of them happened to be girls. "I hate Scouts," he said, bitterness in his voice. "I hate going to church. The other boys are either jerks to me or practically ignore me. Sunday School is okay—I'm in the same class as Mallory, and some of the girls are nice to me."

Ethan's eyebrows furrowed, and he leaned closer to the boy. "How have they been rude? Why are they jerks?"

"I don't know," Andrew hissed, then his shoulders slumped. "I think it's because I can't read very well."

"What do you mean?" Ethan looked surprised. Andrew's scowl deepened.

"I read really slow. The words hurt to see, and sometimes the light hurts my eyes too. When I try to read, I can't, it's like…my brain understands what I'm reading, but it hurts a lot, and I get a lot of headaches. Then when I try to say what I read aloud it's like my mouth can't form the words. I can read okay if I do so silently, not without pain, but I can. But reading aloud…" He sighed and kicked softly at the ground.

"Have you told your parents?" Ethan asked gently.

Andrew took a quick step back. "No. I don't want to disappoint them. Please don't tell them," he pleaded.

Ethan frowned. "Andrew, you should have it checked out. Your vision could get worse or there could be something wrong. They need to know. Your parents won't be disappointed in you just because you have a hard time reading or something being wrong with your eyesight. They love you."

Andrew shrugged, looking to the other kids, a blush in his cheeks.

Ethan grabbed his arm encouragingly. "Go ahead and play, Andrew. Don't worry."

Andrew nodded, though when he walked back toward the others, he didn't look very enthused, and Maeve noticed that he didn't talk to any of them, just kind of awkwardly stood on the side.

Ethan watched his nephew until they left the building again. He felt the frown on his face, then Maeve's hand grabbed his again. He looked at her.

She smiled. "Andrew'll be okay."

Ethan sighed, worried about the kid. "I hope so." He loved all his nieces and nephews.

Maeve nudged him playfully. "He will. He's got a great uncle and wonderful parents."

Ethan smiled, about to respond, but the door from the family room opened and they were interrupted. Again.

Ethan got the text right as Isabelle and Charles walked in. Isabelle grabbed Maeve's hand and kissed Ethan's forehead.

She sat in the seat beside Maeve. "I can't believe you guys are back now. I'm so glad."

Ethan smiled at his sister. "Glad to see you, sis." He unlocked his phone as he spoke, then frowned when he caught sight of the painting in the picture. He peered at it, bringing the screen closer, and felt his face lose color.

Maeve caught his look and squeezed his hand. "Ethan? What's wrong?" The other two turned their attention to Ethan, and Charles looked over his shoulder.

"Do you know that painting?" Charles asked gently.

Maeve leaned closer and looked at it before Ethan frantically searched to redial to call Mygyer back. He stood, letting go of Maeve, waving for them to give him a minute, and exited the room to talk alone.

"Mygyer," his director answered.

"Mygyer, I know that painting! It was of the mafia boss, the Host."

The Host was so hidden, even local law enforcement didn't know of his crimes or his name. And he entirely separated his two lives so that no one knew he lived a double life. Except Santorini, and now Ethan. Santorini's sister was married to the guy, and after Ethan earned trust, he'd been invited to the house. Ethan told his team about the man, but they had absolutely nothing they could pin on him.

Mygyer was silent, as if racking his brain for memory. "The house you went to about four months into your assignment?"

"Yes."

Mygyer paused again. "Alright, I'm sending over everything we have on the guy. I'm not sure we'll have any more luck with him this time, but…We'll try."

Mygyer hung up before Ethan could say anything, even if he wanted to, so Ethan opened the messages he received and looked through the new pictures of this Alex Hutchings. It had been a long time since he'd been to the man's house, but he recognized him. The door opened behind Ethan. Ethan looked to see Maeve step out and came up to his side, putting a hand on his back.

"All okay?" she asked softly, concern in her voice. Not wanting her to think anything was wrong, he started to turn his attention to her when she suddenly gasped. That caught his attention faster. "Who is that?" Maeve grabbed his phone and looked at the picture closer.

"Alex Hutchings. He's the man who owned the painting Anthony had hinted about." Ethan studied her, confused by her response. "Do you know him?"

Maeve nodded slowly, looking back up at Ethan. "Yeah, he's the guy I saw at my parents' house the night they died."

Epilogue

"Good news," Ethan said as he opened the door, spotting Maeve in the kitchen next to his mom immediately.

Maeve looked over at him. Ethan paused to kiss his mom's forehead, and Maeve's lips. He also put his hand on her stomach. Any day now, she was due.

"What's the good news?" Maeve asked as he sat next to them. Before he could tell them, Ethan saw movement behind and noticed that Annie was also in the room. She had been getting herself some tea, but now watched Ethan as well.

Ethan smiled, leaning forward. "They caught Alex." It had been a long, harrowing time to get the man, since he'd never even been caught speeding. The Chicago team, with the distant help of the Kansas team, and every other law enforcement in the city had nothing whatsoever to go off, other than Ethan being in his home one time with Santorini and Maeve's memory of him.

Maeve gasped. "Really?"

Ethan nodded and grabbed her hand.

"Is everyone okay?" Maeve's eyebrows furrowed in concern.

Ethan nodded. "Sounds like it went off pretty much without a hitch."

"That's a relief." Maeve sighed, covering his hand with her free one.

"Love, your toast is ready," Annie told Maeve. "What would you like on it?"

Maeve started to stand. "I've got it." She struggled into a standing position, her belly making it difficult. Ethan stood to help her as Annie protested.

"I can get it for you," she said. Maeve smiled, then gasped and grabbed Ethan's arm.

"What is it? What's wrong?" Ethan stepped closer, but felt his feet slip, almost tossing him to the floor. He steadied himself and looked down as Maeve laughed, her hands covering her mouth. A puddle of water surrounded the two of them.

"Um…" Maeve giggled again as his mom and Annie both came closer. "I think my water broke."

"You think?" Mom asked sarcastically, laughing too, though Ethan wasn't sure if it was from Maeve's attitude, the fact Ethan had nearly slipped, or that Ethan's eyes suddenly felt as huge as an owl's. "We need to get you to the hospital. Ethan, come on son, help her out of her puddle."

Ethan jerked out of his shock, nearly stumbling again as he started to do as his mom asked a little too fast. "Right, okay, um, Maeve, just…Here…" He helped her over to his mom before following, eyes traveling down her soaked yoga pant legs.

He couldn't believe he almost slipped into stuff that used to be inside her.

The ladies left the room before Ethan gathered himself, then Elisa snapped at him from the other room to grab the keys and hurry up.

He did so, suddenly feeling his heartbeat loud in his ears. Maeve's baby was coming!

"Can you drive, Ethan?" Mom asked as they got close again. Ethan didn't hear her well, he was staring at Maeve as she suddenly cried out, grabbing her abdomen.

Mom stopped momentarily. "Breathe Maeve, breathe."

Mom saw Ethan, then shook her head and turned to Annie. "Grab the keys from him, let's go. Ethan, are you coming or not?"

Ethan didn't have words to reply, but Maeve grabbed Ethan's hand tightly and practically dragged him to the car. As they pulled out, Ethan's brain finally settled back inside his head.

"Mom, I thought you said the sacs don't usually break open like they show in the movies."

Mom shook her head, barely sparing a glance for him as she held Maeve's hand. "I guess Maeve was in the minority on that one." She ran a hand through Maeve's hair as Maeve gripped Ethan's hand again. Ethan forced himself not to hold on as tightly, rubbing the back of her hand.

"You okay?" Ethan asked her, feeling concerned.

Maeve nodded, trying to catch her breath.

When they got to the hospital, Maeve had already had another contraction. Ethan had been going to let his mom go in with Maeve, but Maeve wanted Ethan there with her, which he felt honored by, but also scared and nervous. He felt like he was in the way, but Maeve didn't seem to care or notice if he was. Annie had called the rest of Ethan's siblings to tell them the news, and they had all come in at one point or another to say hi, but most either went home or went into the waiting room.

The next hours were excruciating for Ethan, and clearly more so for Maeve. He stayed beside her the entire three hours until she went back to deliver. She begged him to stay with her even then. He just about passed out a couple times, and they had to pull a chair over for him. But Maeve was amazing, especially considering she had a baby coming out.

Another hour later, Ethan was sitting with Maeve as she slept, his arms wrapped around her baby boy. He slept in his arms, having milked from his mom, cried for a while, and gotten checked and cleaned up by the doctors and nurses. Ethan felt exhausted, but he couldn't fathom sleeping because he was too busy staring at the baby and thinking about how Maeve's eyes had lit up after he'd been born, even with as exhausted as she'd been.

He adjusted the blanket around the baby, then looked up when he heard footsteps. His mom came back in. "Honey, how are you doing?" Her voice was gentle as she sat next to Ethan. Ethan looked back down at the baby and smiled softly as he answered.

"Tired, Mom, but good." He exhaled and leaned into his mom's side as she wrapped an arm around him. "He's beautiful."

"Yes, he is." Elisa had both amusement and awe in her voice. "He is going to be so loved."

Ethan nodded, feeling his own heart jump with agreement. He looked up at Maeve and gently pushed back some of the hair that had fallen into her face. Suddenly, Ethan had to get out of there. He stood quietly and handed the baby boy off to his mom. "I'll be back a little later Mom. I'm going to get some fresh air."

Elisa looked like she had been going to ask where or why, but one look at his face silenced her. Instead, she smiled and gripped his arm momentarily.

He exited the room and headed for the waiting room, where he found Mason and Isabelle still waiting. Isabelle had fallen asleep against her brother's shoulder, but as Ethan came closer, Mason looked up and carefully shifted his sister awake as he stood. He pulled Ethan into a tight hug, which Ethan reciprocated, grateful for the support after the long day.

"You doing okay? You look exhausted," Mason said as he pulled away slightly, letting his hands fall to Ethan's shoulders instead. After the long months of therapy, Ethan was relieved to see his hand doing better, now only scars, shakiness, and a bit of stiffness showing he'd been injured. He was back at work, and though he couldn't keep up with as many as the small details, Ethan had no doubt he was on his way to being able to do so.

Ethan nodded, yawning. "I'm super tired," he admitted as Isabelle swept under Mason's arm to give Ethan a hug also.

Mason nodded in understanding. "How is Maeve and the baby boy?"

Ethan found a smile flitting on his lips. "Both sleeping. I needed to get some air for a minute."

Isabelle chuckled. "Is this the air you were looking for?"

Ethan shrugged, too exhausted to try for a response. "Can you two help me with something?"

¤ ¤ ¤

Maeve woke up to Elisa in the chair beside her, her son in her arms, and Ethan nowhere to be seen. She frowned, immediately feeling a flood of disappointment. She'd been hoping he would stay with her.

Elisa noticed she was awake and reached a hand to Maeve's. "Hey, darling."

"Hi, Mom." Calling her mom had become completely natural; however, seeing her holding her baby made the moment even more surreal. She never thought she'd have someone like Elisa if she had a baby.

"How are you feeling?" Her eyes were compassionate and gentle.

Maeve took a deep breath, thinking about the answer. "I feel good." But as she looked around, she suddenly felt tears prick her eyes and roll down her cheeks before she could stop them.

Elisa didn't seem alarmed by the contradictory words and emotions. She smiled softly. "Wanna talk about it?"

"Where did Ethan go? I thought he was going to be here when I woke up." She brushed her hand across her cheek, frustrated that she was crying over such a stupid little thing.

"He went out for some fresh air a bit ago. He'll be back soon. Is that what's bothering you?"

Maeve gestured to the side. "I don't know, everything seems so sad and glorious at the same time. I just don't know right now."

Elisa nodded, looking down at the baby. "I understand. Just hormones from having the baby."

Maeve followed her gaze, then had the irresistible urge to once again hold her son. "Can I hold him?"

Elisa looked surprised. "Of course, love, he's yours. You don't have to ask." She laughed lightly and stood to position him in Maeve's arms. Maeve held him close, watched him a couple moments, then finally came back to the decision she'd made when she first held him.

"I have a question…something I wanted to talk to you about."

"Okay." She sat down on the bed beside Maeve.

"I wanted to name him…Well…" She stuttered over the words, unable to get over the fear of asking. She didn't want to hurt Elisa in any way.

Elisa put her hand on Maeve's leg, and Maeve's fears washed away. "I thought he looked like an Edward to me, and I really want to name him after your husband and Ethan's father."

Elisa froze a little, then tears rolled down her cheeks. "Are you sure?" she asked, grabbing one of Maeve's hands now.

Maeve nodded, holding her baby Edward a little tighter. "It just feels right."

Elisa leaned forward and peered at the baby's face. She exhaled long. "You're right, he does, doesn't he?" Elisa met her eyes. "Of course you can name him Edward. I'm honored, and I'm sure my husband would be thrilled."

Before either of them could continue the conversation, a soft knock sounded. Maeve looked over in anticipation and saw that it was Ethan. Irrational anger soared through her. "Where have you been? I thought you would be here!"

Ethan turned sheepish as he exchanged a look with Mom. "I'm sorry, I only went out for some air—"

"But I don't get to go out for some air!" Maeve pouted.

Elisa chuckled. "I'll let you guys talk." She patted Maeve's leg, squeezed Ethan's arm, and left the room.

Ethan came forward and sat on the chair slowly, watching her as if she'd snap. That made her realize how pathetic she was acting. "I'm sorry, Ethan. It's just been a really long day. I didn't mean to snap. Hormones and all…"

Ethan smiled. "That's okay, Maeve. You have every reason to snap right now."

Maeve shook her head but didn't argue. "So, what were you doing then?"

Ethan shifted onto the bed beside her, but didn't answer her question. Instead, he asked his own. "What were you and my mom talking about?"

Maeve looked down at Edward. "A name for him."

"Did you decide on something?"

"For his first name, yes, but I haven't decided on his middle yet."

"What is it?"

"I want to name him Edward." Even saying it was confirmation, and Ethan's breath gave a quick inhale as his hand paused where it had been touching the baby's head gently. Ethan slowly looked up at her.

"Really?" He sounded choked up. Maeve nodded, unable to form words because of the tears that came down again. *Golly, stupid release of hormones*, she thought.

Ethan brushed her hair back from her face and wiped her tears. "I think that's perfect."

"And I had an idea for the middle, but I wanted to ask you about it first," Maeve admitted softly, unable to keep his tender gaze.

"What's that?" he asked, bringing her eyes back up to his.

"I liked the idea of Derek."

This time, Ethan froze and withdrew his hand, his eyes turning guarded. "Why?"

Maeve knew he'd had a hard time with his undercover name ever since he'd gotten out. But Maeve wanted to have the name for a different reason than Ethan hated it.

Maeve snatched his hand before he could withdraw all the way. "I know you have problems with that name, Ethan, but there was both good and bad associated with it. I want you to have a new start with it. If it weren't for Derek, we never would have met. My life would be so much different without you, Ethan. I know Derek had done and seen some terrible things, but he made a life, and he saved mine."

Ethan looked at the baby, then very reluctantly looked up, tears in his eyes. "He does look like an Edward Derek," he sighed. He tried for a smile. "Okay, I'm willing to accept that. I can try and change my mindset on the name. I do like what he did for us, after all." Then he grinned. "If you'll do one thing for me."

"What's that?" Maeve asked, wondering what his smile could be about—what could bring him out of his memories so fully?

"Can we make him Edward Derek Conten?" Before Maeve could reply to the absurd question—she wanted to point out that her last name wasn't Conten—Ethan continued, lowering to his knees and pulling out a small box. "Will you marry me, Maeve? I love you, and I want to be in your life, and I know you'll probably say that I need to think this through, and this is too fast after the baby, but I've thought about this since the first time I saw you when I got home, and I know I really, really want you, and I want to raise Edward Derek, and I want to have you guys forever—"

Maeve sat up and swung her legs to the side as she threw her free hand around his neck, while also being careful with Edward between them. She kissed him firmly in order to shut him up. "Yes," she whispered. "Yes, please yes, Ethan. I love you too, and there is no one else I want raising Edward with me."

Ethan grinned, kissing her again, then getting the ring out of the box and slipping it on her finger. She barely glanced at it as she tucked her head against his shoulder, remembering the time she'd first been held by his arms, and thanking God that He had brought them together. The beginning of their story may have been hard, but she knew that as long as they stayed together, and stayed close to God, they'd make it through the rest of their story.

M. C. Topham was raised in various places inside the state of Utah and California. She'd gone on a church mission to Japan for a year and a half, enjoying getting to know a new culture and plenty of people while she taught about Jesus Christ and the English language. She now lives in Utah with her husband of two years, a dog, and a cat.

She graduated from a Massage School and Footzone School, and has been house-cleaning since fifteen. She now enjoys all of those as self-employed, part-time jobs, making all her days diverse so she never feels bored.

However, writing is her real passion and becoming a published author has been her goal since she'd started weaving stories around age thirteen. She published her first book at sixteen and looks forward to continuing her dream.

Follow on Instagram: m.c.topham
Follow on Facebook: M. C. Topham